SAY CHEESE!

SAY CHEESE!

VASSILY AKSYONOV

TRANSLATED FROM THE RUSSIAN BY ANTONINA W. BOUIS

RANDOM HOUSE / NEW YORK

Library of Congress Cataloging-in-Publication Data

Aksyonov, Vassily Pavlovich.
    Say cheese!

    Translation of: *Skazhi izium.*
    I. Title.
PG3478.K7S5713   1989   891.73'44   88-43172
ISBN 0-394-54363-7

Manufactured in the United States of America
24689753
First Edition
Book design by Jo Anne Metsch

CONTENTS

SAY CHEESE!

EPIGRAPH

I

After the movies, photography of all
the arts is the most important for us!
—V. Lenin or J. Stalin

WHEN AND BY which of the two possible authors this quotation
was spoken is not known with accuracy. But in our day, the
famous Soviet "New Wave" photographer Maxim Petrovich "Ogo"
Ogorodnikov, having had a few in a private Paris club, babbled on
about the art of photography. Here is what was gathered of his ideas:

"Photography is the connection between visible reality and the astral.
The mystery of emulsion, the essence of the photo process, is hidden
in the relocation of cosmic and astral powers. All we have to do is take
childlike joy in this minor mystery revealed to us by Higher Benevo-
lence, all we have to do is assume reverently that there are myriad great
meanings behind this small one. But instead, we explain photography
with mechanical nonsense.

"Let's talk about this, gentlemen, like children. I love everything connected with photography, gentlemen—the camera, the bag, the shoulder strap. Strung with all my equipment, I feel like a knight-errant. I

love to wait on foggy mornings for the birds to fly past, to enter bustling airports and get a fix on our modern ethos, to run around stone drunk so that only blurry signals cross the ocean in the direction of Valhalla. And I love to suddenly sober up and see Attica and Hellas, where like a storm cloud smoky Zeus observes the esplanade.

"I love the object's sound and its meaningful resonance, be it as ugly as a spider, be it as lowly as a sheepfold. I love to observe the worldwide tumble, wrapped in my toga, and in that toga, in my Russia red and miserable, I love to have round tables with Party bigwigs, the local thieves, and toss tobacco crumbs into my beet soup. I love to make a scene in Moscow, to set up a ballyhoo with friends. . . . Say cheese, my friends! *Skazhi kishmish!* Attention, watch the birdie!

"I am a sinner, I confess, and sink upon my knees: there are days when I, a drunken goose, seek out girls with fervor unremitting, but through my drunken haze I suddenly see the olden days—two pairs of skis, my wife, the Caucasus, and the early moon arising. . . .

"The lies of mediocrities are painful, but the unseen Viewer sees it all when your unclean finger secretly prods the developer. I go out. The strap of my Hasselblad pulls on my shoulder. Night in the neighborhood. Is heaven to the right? Is hell on the left? Where are we going in the Moscow blizzard? But my automatic shutter clicks. My cosmic girlfriend's face is lit. One thousand watts. Birds come flying from the darkness. A wide-focus shot. Waltz, tango, boogie-woogie—that, basically, is why, kind ladies and gentlemen, I have been in love with photography all my life."

But how did all this begin—no, not this drunken confession of a dissident photographer named Ogo, but rather socialist photorealism itself? How did this mighty branch of art begin, before which even Soviet literature, that indispensable servant of the Party, pales?

2

THERE EXISTS IN the vault of folk wisdom of our day yet another slogan relating to photography: DIFFERENT PEOPLE HAVE DIFFERENT STOMACHS. This slogan is attributed again to Lenin, or Stalin, or to the entire Soviet people. For some reason this wisdom is not placed on posters or banners, yet in the Union of Soviet Photographers, the PhU USSR, it is known to all. Broad theoretical interpretations deal with the phrase's particular "ideological significance," but the quote has a practical use as well—specifically, it is helpful in combatting drunkenness at Rosfoto Restaurant.

At this famous establishment the mathematically average member of the PhU USSR consumes no less than a half kilo of vodka products per sitting. "Watch out," the maitre d' will say. "People have different stomachs, you know."

"I know," the mathematical average barks back. "Pour!"

Strangely enough, Rosfoto Restaurant had the very same name before the Bolshevik revolution, for its building was home to a petty-bourgeois organization of photographers who were trying to plant in Russian photography the mores of dyed-in-the-wool objectivism. The restaurant hadn't been renamed, because the Bolsheviks assumed any abbreviation was one of their own devising, and Russians forgot all the old very quickly, associating everything around them with "the only possible regime." Who, for instance, would ever show any curiosity about the genesis of the glorious Budenny felt helmets with knobs, the long greatcoats with crisscrossing trim, and geometrical shapes for distinguishing marks? The understanding is that Marshal himself worked with other marshals in developing this exquisite uniform design, which simply reeks of *Mir Isskustva** and early *moderne* with Scythian inspiration a mile away. It has been completely forgotten that the uniform had been designed by the artist Vasnetzov in 1916, that the new uniform had been prepared under the old regime, and all the Bolsheviks

---

* *Mir Isskustva* [*World of Art*]: a Russian artistic review founded in 1898 in St. Petersburg by A. Benois and S. Diaghilev. The artists associated with it were known for their inherent refinement, stylization, and ornamentalism. As standing for "pure art" and the "transforming power of art" *M.I.* was criticized by the Soviet ideologues as being "petty-bourgeois decadent." This kind of criticism was habitually followed by a severe proletarian blow on the head, although the Red Horsemen in *M.I.* helmets did transform the Scythian steppes into collective farmlands.

had to do was open the Moscow Arsenal, sew on their stars beneath the knobs, and rush off to attack Warsaw.

Even in our day *Homo sovieticus* is surrounded by signs of the old Russia, which he doesn't even guess at. The majority of objects for petty personal use, in fact, are leftovers from "landholders and merchants." Half-liter bottles, for instance, or matchboxes, by the way, or Mishka candies, Carmen soap, a can of sprats, Chypre cologne—all were developed *before*, while the things that appeared *after*, like electric shavers, simply seeped through from the West. The Sovdep in all its years never came up with anything for the everyday use of its citizens, only things for historical aims—devices like the Katyusha, a jet mortar with a girl's name.

Such random thoughts come to you when you sit in the historical wood-paneled room of Rosfoto Restaurant. For the last fifty years this place has been the "battleground of Soviet photographic art"; exactly one half-century has passed since the day when the famous Russian photographer Arkadii Melancholny came back from emigration, all tears and snot, and turned over his Kodak to the GPU. "Accept my repentance, O builders of the new world! Yes, I did photograph the tsar and ex-Premier Kerensky, yes, I photographed the cruiser *Aurora* at the most inconvenient moment ... I repent.... Look, I'm on my knees! Comrades, let us extend the principles of socialist realism to Soviet photography!"

The GPU grimaced, so the rumors say: Hah, thinks himself a new Maxim Gorky, does he! That cooled the neophyte's ardor a bit. "You're no Gorky for us, Comrade Melancholny, photographers are not writers. We provide writers with socrealism so that they don't get too smart, but with you shutterbugs things will be simpler. You'll reflect our new day without any socrealism, you'll capture our young joy, and you'll go wherever we send you!"

And, according to rumors, the half-dead man rebelled. "I won't," Melancholny declared. "For all my love of the internal glands of the proletarian dictatorship, I won't, comrades! The Party can't overlook photography!"

This whole story, I repeat, is passed on by rumor and whispers, talk and hints. The archives of the ChKGPUNKVDMGBKGB* are closed forever not only to modest scribblers but to wise historians, and therefore to the entire human civilization, and naturally to all extraterrestrial civilizations. So, for lack of access to the holy archives of the proletariat, we'll greedily use hearsay.

After his speech to the GPU, Melancholny worked up wild energy, flashed around Moscow, and suddenly surfaced near the Nikitinsky Gates with a slogan in his teeth: "After the movies, photography of all the arts is the most important for us. Ulyanov [Lenin], Dzhugashvili [Stalin]."

Nearby the gates, in a *Mir Isskustva* house stolen from Maxim Gorky, lived a leader of proletarian art. Supposedly dropping by on the basis of their émigré friendship, with the newly discovered slogan in one hand and his camera in the other, Melancholny quickly set up his tripod, set his production tool on self-release, quickly sat on the arm of the chair, cheek to cheek with the great artist, and whispered hotly, ruffling the legendary walrus moustache, "Je voudrais votre passion, Alexis! I beg you, say cheese! The birdie will fly out right now!"

He had broken through the ice of misinterpretation: a week later the militant organ–newspaper *Word of Truth* printed a picture of two giants of Soviet Russia, sitting in an armchair under the founding slogan of the leading lights of humanity. Here was printed the CC All-Union Communist Party resolution about the dissolution of the old photo-group Focus, wherein, under an innocent-seeming cover, bourgeois objectivism had built itself a nest. A Union of Soviet Photographers was established, true to the ideas of socialist realism.

Big things began happening in the Rosfoto building on Miussy Square: congresses, conferences, clashes, agreements, friendship weeks, cooperation decades, plenums on ideological issues. The Union's bud-

---

*To decipher this beautiful acronym we must learn to take in one gulp the following combination of words: Emergency-Committee-Chief-Political-Management-People's-Commissariat-Internal-Affairs-Ministry-State-Security-Committee-State-Security.

This reflects a gradual change in the Soviet secret-police name and evokes an old Russian saying: "All dresses are becoming to her!"

get grew with every year, and with it grew the authority of its founder, who now signed himself differently—M. Enthusias. His pictures of those years lost their clarity, as if the camera picked up a strange infirmity of the hand. Of course, the critics explained the fuzziness as due to "revolutionary agitation," a necessary component of socrealism, and not at all due to the use of warming spirits.

Critics aside, a comrade-in-arms was hurrying to M. Enthusias' side, a dependable Bolshevik of noble blood, named Bluzhzhaezhzhin, who carried a royal gift from the Kremlin: a case of Stalin's personal wine. According to rumors, the wine was delivered to Miussy Square at the same time as the famous box of chocolates to Maxim Gorky, which caused that man to join the majority for good. According to the same rumors (the archives are as usual silent), dependable Bolshevik Bluz uncorked with reverence a bottle of the amazing wine, which resembled the historic malmsey of the hunchbacked Briton, himself handed the glass to his teacher, and himself made it clear that a refusal to drink immediately would be construed in a negative light. To be more convincing Bluz knocked back a glass himself. After the drink, Enthusias né Melancholny was sent to his eternal rest in the Kremlin wall, while the deliveryman Bluz became General Secretary of the Union of Soviet Photographers. When he learned about the incident, Stalin uttered the slogan that would determine for many years the development of Soviet photography:

DIFFERENT PEOPLE HAVE DIFFERENT STOMACHS!

3

THERE'S NO NEED to give a detailed chronological account of the glorious history of Soviet photography, for it is inseparable from the heroic deeds of our entire nation, Party, and State.* But let us say that the

---

*In the course of the narrative we will have to take an occasional dive into history, into 1956 a bit and into 1968; we'll have to mention 1937 more than once and not always for the reasons you would think, but simply because that is the year several of our heroes were born, including the aforementioned Maxim "Ogo" Ogorodnikov. These plunges, however, are not so important to us, for our main goal, in keeping with the directives of the Party, is the illumination and photographing of the heroics of our days.

testaments of the classic Melancholny-Enthusias, whose huge portrait in seated position with an open jacket of good Belgian cloth, with crossed leg, the foot shod in an Anglo-shoe, a Franco-scarf flung over one shoulder, and East Switzerland glasses glistening humanely, ornaments the vast vestibule of the citadel on Miussy, which . . . where . . . because of which . . . this sentence drags on outlandishly and with only one goal, which is to say that Melancholny's testaments have not been forgotten. The Party bestowed its vigilant attention upon photography. Moreover, by the late thirties the Party had selected a special group of workers, conscripted in the "most secure" way, who eventually grew into the powerful, albeit supposedly nonexistent State Photographic Directorate of Ideological Control.*

If the secret police appear in nature, just wait: opposition will inevitably follow. Life proves the inexorability of this law. After almost forty years of the PhID, an inappropriate mental ferment and an uncontrollable displacement of bodies arose in the creative atmosphere of Soviet photography. Decadent Western catalysts began seeping into the formerly healthy milieu. Even a native mysticism bubbled up meekly.

This is how it began, what was subsequently called a "trench war in Soviet art" by Western journalists, the affair of the *Say Cheese!* album and the New Focus group of photographers: in 1967, to everyone's surprise, the top of the Kremlin hill thawed a bit. The Party, apparently, was restructuring itself: in the rear they were breaking through the Gothic walls of Prague, but the front ranks were performing falsely liberal maneuvers. They permitted stage plays of rather daring form and rather wimpy content, they published some books by writers tortured by Stalin, they invited jazz musicians from abroad, they opened new photo exhibits—in a word, the Party was letting the creative intelligentsia loosen up a bit.

And in that unexpected "small thaw" three young photocelebrities, Ogorodnikov, Drevesny, and German, who then considered their grim

---

*Known among the grateful People under the nickname Internal Glands, a playful joke on the "organs" of state security. The Glands did not have a sign outside its offices, though it did have an enormous staff, and a parking lot which would have been the envy of any ministry had it had the secret data on the number of cars belonging to the PhID, as the Glands was more officially called.

Moscow a scene of unending fiesta, met, hung over, at the Sandunovsky Baths. With the first pint they began discussing the idea of a new "young" photomagazine.

"Just the right time to dare it!"

"And why not!"

"Let's go!"

"Where?"

"To the Central Committee, to Demenny himself! He knows me, he congratulated me on my show in Tbilisi!"

"And I drank with his assistant. Not a bad guy."

"Come on, call your not-bad guy."

"Right from the baths, you mean? Hello, is this the CC? I'm calling from the Sandunovsky Baths...."

Incidentally, at that time our three friends didn't have a thought of acting without the Central Committee. Our ironic frondeurs never doubted the "leading role of the Party," for the August night of sixty-damn was still eighteen months away.

The times were such that in less than a week Politburo member Phal Demenny—whose very name evoked the nation's pride and glory, the Ural blast furnaces—received the trio in his huge office with a view of the Spassky Tower of the Kremlin, where, according to rumors, the life secret of Russian Marxism* was kept.

Comrade Demenny was given the idea, not without bathos, for a new "young" photomagazine, an experimental platform for the immature talents who, precisely because of their immaturity and lack of outlet for their talent, might find themselves "on the other side of the barricades." It can be said to the visitors' honor that they had an idea of whom they were dealing with and therefore did not avoid demagoguery.

The meeting was rather strange: two of the four participants wore sunglasses. Comrade Demenny himself was of course husbanding his

---

*Any "populist" movement, like Soviet Marxism, must be interwoven with folk-lore, fairy tales, and horror stories. Not without reason a kernel of Soviet Marxism has been "situated" within the walls of the ancient fortress.

vision, which he had ruined by working at a blast furnace in the first five-year plan. And the famous photographer Slava German, naturally, was hiding a black eye which he got the night before at the coatroom at the Rosfoto Restaurant.

"An interesting idea," Comrade Demenny said, supporting his guests. "A fruitful and promising idea. Thank you, comrades, for your initiative. Please put your proposal on two pages and I'll take it to the Secretariat. I'm sure that it will be well received. We all remember Lenin's words on photography. It is hard to overestimate the significance of your art in our scientific-technological age. . . ."

Not believing their own ears, the young men listened.

"Such complex times," sighed Demenny. "You can't avoid dialectics, not even in the resolution of comparatively simple issues." He moved a piece of paper on his desk. "And there are so many *contradictions*. . . . Now you, comrades, recognized masters of Soviet photography, why did you go to that provocative demonstration against the resurrection of Stalinism?"

"Comrade Demenny!" gasped the talents, who hadn't expected this repercussion from last year's events. "We were just worried that the co—" Oops, they almost said the "cockroach," "—that Comrade Stalin might be returned to the Mausoleum with Vladimir Ilyich . . . to be resurrected. . . ."

"It was frivolous, friends," Comrade Demenny reproached them gently. "You must trust the Party. In everything. You see, there is no resurrection of Stalinism in the offing. Trust, that's what we need now, like air. In the future, comrades, bring any problems to me. Perhaps you're having problems with travel abroad?"

The farsighted one had guessed right: Ogorodnikov was not allowed to go to Italy, nor Drevesny to Canada, nor could Slava German even get the green light for fraternal Poland.

"Oh, the bureaucracy!" Comrade Demenny made a note near his elbow. "There won't be any problems with that anymore. Our Soviet photographers should travel and bring back artistic and ideological values from the other side."

The notable meeting harmonically reached the final note. Comrade

Demenny rose. "Let's say it Komsomol style. The magazine will be! And periodically!"

Our three astonished geniuses left the CC neighborhood and headed down Marx Prospect, toward a restaurant, without even discussing where they were going. On the way they sputtered and chattered on as if they weren't thirty-year-old men, discussing which artistic schools would flourish under the roof of their new magazine, which conceptual framework, and so on, revealing honest-to-goodness, shameless innocence.

At Rosfoto the shifts were changing, and thus something like its legendary "former" atmosphere reigned: cleanliness, quiet, peace. Wood panels were reflected in the mirrors, which in turn were reflected in the aquarium, in which swam mirrored carp, reflecting everything. In the corner a respected customer was feasting, an old man in a tuxedo, carnation in his lapel, none other than the General Secretary of the Photographers' Union of the SSR, Comrade Bluzhzhaezhzhin. Champagne in a silver bucket, caviar in a crystal dish, carp in the skillet. "Bah, why, it's three of our daring youth! Please join me!"

They sat down and began guzzling champagne, all Nouveau Monde at that, which goes very well with hot bagels, especially when smeared with caviar. With that accompaniment they decided to let the powerful old man in on things: if Comrade Demenny himself approved, Comrade Bluz wouldn't spoil things. The leader of Soviet photography did not react very actively, however—either he was as drunk as a skunk or he was hallucinating. At any rate he was sure that he was either in Paris or at the railroad station restaurant in Rostov-on-Don during a battle between different-colored armies.

And then he surfaced. "Yes, we've earned our workers' happiness!" He pointed to the bread and caviar. "With sword in hand, comrades! How many lives were laid down under our strong and kind regime for the sake of the radiant future! Come to my house, my boys...." Another plunge into time: "There isn't a whiff of your soviets in my house...." A desperate surge to the surface: "Ever since I came to believe in the triumph of socialism! ..."

Slava German innocently asked, "When did you come to believe in the triumph of socialism, Your Excellency?"

The suddenly glazed eye, the gaping jaw, the icy whisper of a ventriloquist. "I believed in socialism right after the kidnapping of General Kutepov."*

This soirée with the coryphaeus of socialist realism ended with an instructive scene at the coatroom, where, as he got into the raccoon coat held for him by the porter and pulled out a snuffbox, Comrade Bluz at last spoke out about the daring magazine project, though it was unclear how it had ever sunk into his muddled brain. "As for your magazine, comrades, we won't support you because you are setting up a Trojan horse beyond the bastions of socialist realism. What fashion plates you are—wanting to see a Politburo member! People dream of audiences like that for years! No-o-o! What was it our predecessors used to say? Fuck you, forget the rest!"

"And an Ossetian's broad chest," one of the young men added, recalling Mandelstam's poem on Stalin.

Time, however, showed that the senile Comrade Bluz had other arguments in his favor. First it (that is, Time) simply kept quiet for several months, then it called and—in the voice of the "not-bad guy" with whom German had gone drinking—said that the magazine proposal had not been accepted and that Comrade Demenny wished comrades Drevesny, Ogorodnikov, and German luck in their creative future.

And then came "fraternal help" to Czechoslovakian socialism with a human face; the whole face was overgrown with shaggy-browed Brezhnevism. Things grew more or less clear.

And so, my dear reader, here is the very place for a deep historical sigh. O Russian revolution, how geriatric you seemed from the very start! Pathetic but lustful, a cruel auntie with bile in every cell . . . born middle-aged, you just got dumpier every year, didn't get richer but

---

*The kidnapping of the White Russians' leader, General Kutepov, was one of the most successful KGB operations in Paris in the thirties. Thus, Mr. Bluzhzhaezhzhin, who at the time was an émigré himself, had a weighty reason to start believing in the triumph of socialism.

saved up useless crap. How many more ages will you grow older, so far from God and so removed from Man?

4

HAVING SIGHED A bit on this strange topic, let us move by express excursion to those more recent times when the vocabulary of the Soviet intelligentsia was dominated by the two metaphysical words "already" and "still"—that is, let us slide forward into the cast-iron seventies.

People still wagged Aesopian tongues, still managed to travel abroad and back, still "dragged" a shot or two onto the pages of some journals, still "pushed" into a show or two, still smiled as they saw comrades off into transoceanic and biblical vistas, still cheered themselves with the idea of stubborn existence in their homeland, still drank vodka as of old; but already climactic depression was spreading throughout Moscow, already almost a third of one's friends were "over the hill," already photographers and artists and writers were being replaced with lively oinking by a new litter of snappers, daubers, and scribblers, already the bottom of the barrel had been scraped, already the creative unions were turning into annexes of Ideological Control. Nevertheless, on one hungover Monday the idea was squeezed out, as if from a wan lemon and defizzed Borzhomi water, for publication of an uncensored underground photo album—let's give it one more shot!

And so, a few years before the events that begin in the next chapter, there came together a group of photographic rebels. Nothing better can be said of them than the words of the author of our epigraph: "The circle of their actions is narrow, they are very far from the People. . . ."

COOP FRATERNITY

I

SUDDENLY, IN OUR DAY, honored General Valeryan Kuzmich Planshchin was called on the carpet and told in a strict but comradely manner: "Now you, General Planshchin, have been fussing with the photographers of the Polish People's Republic, while right under your nose, in a model communist city, a secret section called New Focus has appeared with ideas of rabid objectivism and unscientific idealism, and these boys are putting together a clever album under the title *Say Cheese!* Immediately form an operative group, even a sector. Here's your budget—three million. Will that be enough for a start?"

And General Planshchin mused . . . Enough or not enough?

But no, it doesn't do to begin our story this way: what the hell for, really, are all these generals, all these police cases, can't we manage without them to start a Russian tale, can't we at least keep to a minimum the KGB "soldiers of the invisible front" . . . ?

Autumn, the microregion, the meek sad thoughts, our dreary lyricism, the aging new construction, the once proudly planned fifth building of the Soviet Cadre Coop, which in six years had yet to become living space . . . Soviet Moscow always had these unlucky new constructions. Years would pass, but the walls never reached the planned heights and the roofs were never laid, or the panes were never put in, and there was no end to the mud. Sometimes a forgotten rusty crane would start turning, two or three lazy figures would appear on the beams; the "dirt demon," otherwise called a dump truck, would roll onto the site with a hooliganish U-turn, dumping a new mound of bricks, 48 percent rejects, and once again for many months everything would come to a standstill and the construction would grow old and naturally bring on sad thoughts.

Past the construction site and over the mud, on planks that seemed to have been laid for the ages, thousands went their way from the Aerodynamic metro station to Cosmic Boulevard, along which stood the luckier sisters of the sad construction, turned into real housing and giving decent shelter to these thousands moving through the twilight. The side street, disfigured since construction began six years earlier, lived its bustling, disfigured life. The shady-looking driver from the Dieta store unloaded his under-the-counter orders. A four-door Volga was pulled up to the back entrance of the coop store. Private owners, the "kulaks," dragged lead batteries from one Zhiguli (Russian Fiat) to another, but the weight of the objects did not correspond to their size, or to the strained curve of the kulaks' backs. A line quickly formed in the back of the grocery store—they had got in a shipment of bananas!

Probably no one even noticed the young red-haired man come out of entrance 3 of building 4 of the Soviet Cadre Coop. But something flashed inside a first-aid van parked by the fence of the construction site.

The young redhead with the thick beard was none other than thirty-year-old member of the Soviet Photographers' Union Alexei Okhotnikov.* The fourth building of the coop was, to tell the truth, the place of Alexei's illegal domicile. For over a year he had lived in the small two-room apartment of a photographer who had gone on a month's

---

*Let's agree right now not to confuse Alexei with the already-mentioned forty-year-old member of the same union, Maxim "Ogo" *Ogorod*nikov. The ancestors of the former were obviously hunters *(okhotniki)*, furnishing their tribe with game, while the ancestors of the latter, most likely, brought the first turnip into Slavic tents from their garden *(ogorod)*. When you pronounce Okhotnikov's name, don't stint on the *o*'s; as for the native Muscovite product, Ogorodnikov, give the *a*'s all you have and you won't go wrong pronouncing it Agarodnikov, gulping the last syllables quickly.

visit to his wife, a West German citizen, and for some reason had not yet returned.

And so Alexei came out on porch 3 and flung a long scarf over his shoulder. With his long leather jacket, scarf, and fiery beard, the northern son did not look too much like a Soviet subject. Yet when he had first appeared in Rosfoto Restaurant, the Slavophiles were delighted—"One of us, he's ours! An addition to our regiment, the yids will have to make room for a profoundly Russian genius." What the curs didn't know was that Alexei considered himself part of the European division of the Russian nation, which even before the construction of Petersburg had brought lumber to the West. The evil men did not know that Alexei had spent his youth in the shadow of the statue of Peter the Great, in contact of sorts with international seamen, whence he had got, incidentally, the above-mentioned leather raglan in trade for a couple of bottles of vodka.

Actually, the so-called Slavophiles had begun to notice rather quickly that their favorite hero was sitting with "the wrong element" at the restaurant, saying "not quite the thing," and most importantly publishing photos in which the soul of the People did not breathe, and when in his cups going on about the Shroud of Turin being the mother of universal cosmic photography. That is to say, Alexei was totally at odds with root materialism. It had suddenly turned out that the fellow wasn't "one of us," either because he had been deceived by Zion or wasn't pure in the first place, what with that suspiciously biblical curliness. . . .

"Do-onkeys!" Alexei would say to himself, rolling his Arkhangelic *o*'s, as if he were rolling them down the ice of the Northern Dvina River. "Do-onkeys! They think I am a silly stump from the taiga, but I had already been dragged in to the GPU when I was sixteen for our school magazine, which we called *Prague Angle*. They think I idolize their classics, but in Arkhangelsk we grew up on the world's avant-garde, so to speak. . . . How can those *donkeys* understand our northern city, where European envoys arrived as early as the fifteenth century? I was just a kid when my aunt pointed out two men in pea coats—two wonderful Russian writers, the conscience of our generation, she said. I secretly photographed the conscience of our generation from behind the knee of Peter the Great. I'm proud of that work to this day, men! Our city is the city of archangels, related to the California city of angels, but older and more mysterious. . . ."

So anyway, the lummox Alexei came out on the porch and saw the first-aid van by the new building's fence. Now's just the time to slip away, he thought. Now there's my Zaporozhets* parked behind the porch of the magazine *Soviet Exposure.* I'll just go over to it and if I can get it started, then back out onto the drive. The drive is full of dump trucks. Everything's covered with mud. *They* will pull out after me. At that moment an oncoming truck's left rear wheel will hit a puddle and its whole windshield will be covered with yellow mud and— smooth sailing! While they're turning on their wipers, I'll make a quick left turn and vanish in the twilight. In the meanwhile Probkin will come to the apartment and receive the Danish journalists, while I have time to go over to Tsuker's to pick up the film. Two good deeds done.

That was Alexei's plan as he stood on the porch of the cooperative apartment house where for the last two months, in the illegally occupied apartment, a "bomb" had been under preparation—the publication of the uncensored photo album *Say Cheese!*

A group of photographers determined to break out of the ideological zone met here almost every evening. Jokingly they called themselves New Focus. The joke had a bad smell about it, for the old Focus was the "petty-bourgeois organization of wingless objectivists" smashed by Comrade Melancholny-Enthusias. The "cheese-ins," the meetings of this New Focus group, always transpired not quite seriously against a background of bohemian disarray. Sometimes it was five or six people, including the female sex, singing and drinking, and sometimes it was suddenly almost fifty crowding in and laughing so hard it rattled the undependable elevator in the stairwell.

Recently at a coop board meeting some retired activist had demanded the immediate eviction of the suspicious Alexei Okhotnikov. In a clearly understandable tone the retired activist expressed himself to the effect that they couldn't look through their fingers at the fact that an apartment in a housing community for Soviet photographers had

---

*A Soviet-made compact car, nightmare of my younger years. The most dependable part of it is a towrope.

been "turned into a haven for gatherings of a certain element, with a dubious air." That had a good ring to it, and the board members, assuming that the old man was "empowered," had begun waxing with civic wrath—but the chairman of the board, in his usual glum manner, eyes on the floor, had moved that the issue be taken off the day's agenda, since it "is not within our competence." Board members had to move out of the old activist's group, feeling as if they knew their asses had been whipped, knowing what the formulation implied—that is, to whose omniscient competence the issue must now be entrusted.

And so—I'm afraid we'll have to use this almost Homeric expression often, since any digression in prose is like a zigzag on the way home to Ithaca—and so the young red-haired man stood on the porch and planned his escape route from the first-aid van, which for the last three days had been parked in the same place near the fence of the construction site, across the way from his door.

I'll call Ogo from a phone booth and tell him not to come, Alexei thought. That's how we'll fuck them over in the finest tradition of the underground. . . .

But this fellow Alexei was only an amateur conspirator; the ensuing few minutes demonstrated that he had gotten everything mixed up, the time either too late or too early. In any case, he was quite surprised to see his friend Probkin approaching.*

Probkin, like Alexei, was pushing thirty, which he considered a youthful age that allowed him to "be naughty," even though he was the paterfamilias of two boys, aged seven and three, and a baby girl. He drove a diesel Mercedes Benz-300, a heavy German limousine. How Probkin managed this luxurious MT (mode of transportation)—in view of the bleakness of the general economy and his perpetual personal

---

*The philogenesis of Probkin's last name cannot be traced at all; it does not correspond to the healthy root *prob*. I admit that his name reveals a certain element of authorial wiliness, a clear avoidance of the path of direct association, which would have had a character called Debauchersky appearing in the twilight. Really, his external looks seemed to illustrate Moscow's walking sin: red, always parted lips, transparent eyes fixed in a lingering glance on today's leading idea. Venya Probkin was a very typical Muscovite; seeking a high, and always being ready for sexual escapades, are what characterize today's male Muscovites to a degree which completely eludes Western strategic observers.

poverty—remained a deep, impenetrable secret. He usually answered direct questions by sighing, "That car is my cross," meaning apparently that the car had caused him to be the general envy of the Soviet Cadre Coop. "How can they envy us?" Probkin would say in amazement. "Masha and I eat almost nothing but noodles." He wasn't lying about that, either: Masha, a general's daughter and former beauty, was beginning to look like noodles herself from their pasta diet—pasty white and gaunt, with signs of unpassing weariness. Of course, the envious neighbors said that Masha was worn out not by the pasta or even by the children, but by the boundless debauchery of unfaithful Probkin. Yet that could be believed only partially, since nothing was more important in the young man's life than "providing for his family."

It was "only for the sake of his family" that Probkin made the rounds of Moscow—bases, warehouses, telephones, institutes, deals to do hack work. Sometimes after a particularly wild night his pals, for a joke, would remind him of Masha and the kids. Probkin would turn white and whisper with his eternally red-wet lips, "Don't touch my family, you vipers, they're the last thing I have left. . . ." A typical scenario was Probkin in a tizzy: "Guys, it's terrible, I'm knocking myself out, my Masha needs shoes." He would dash around Moscow in a state of anxiety but finally put his exhausted wife's feet in priceless Italian boots from Monte Napoleone in Milan.

Public opinion, naturally, was annoyed by all these doings. Just imagine the starving family on a Sunday outing: exhausted "saintly" Masha in boots from Monte Napoleone and red fox jacket, the children little lumps of the space age in bright-colored moon boots and down jackets, the head of the family pale and hung over, tormented by a Sunday conscience, dressed in a suede coat and leading an enormous Newfoundland named Longfellow with a black coat and glistening white teeth and sparkling whites in his sly eyes; it didn't look as if that monster lived on pasta alone. . . . These weren't oppressed Muscovite slum dwellers, this was international speculation incarnate!

"We have to get to the bottom of this," the members of Soviet Cadre would say after a Probkin Sunday stroll. "We must determine without delay the sources of his income, we must let the corruption squad know, and whoever else should know, for maybe that Probkin is in the pay of the West?"

But on Monday morning, Probkin would go from door to door in the coop asking for a loan. "Just a ruble, just some loose change, we have nothing but noodles to eat." What about the dog? the neighbors would ask. "That dog, comrades, is on a list with the Defense Ministry, and gets meat rations, but we can't take the dog's food, how can we, comrades?" Why don't you sell your Mercedes? the neighbors would rail. "I'll have to," Probkin would sigh. "That car is my cross." He would stand in the hallway, licking his lips and peering inside the neighbor's apartment with a pathetic greed, his long hair pushed to one side, revealing his enormous forehead, and the neighbors would suddenly feel a strange sympathy for him. And so would arise the special relationship that had saved Probkin so far. A neighbor who gave three rubles or even one would feel like a patron of the arts, entitled to a corollary condescension toward the parasite.

Nevertheless, in Moscow's semiunderground art world, Probkin was known as a talented photographer. Officially, he was on staff at the monthly *Soviet Ball,* and his published pictures were in no way distinguishable from mass productions, but at the same time his "other" pictures and slides circulated in attics and cellars, and there were people who found that his shots "had something." Some aesthetes even numbered him along the New Photographers. "Here, gentlemen," the aesthetes said to one another, "we all theorize, while stars are born in the New Photography even from crooks."

There was, however, a crying *need* for theory, since no one had yet been able to delineate the limits of New Photography. Its fundamental principle seemed to be that in one dimension of a photo some things stood out with superrealistic clarity while other details, which apparently did not interest the artist, seemed "out of focus." It was hard to say why New Photography incurred the greatest wrath of the Party ideologues, why it was this blurry movement that their strike regiments attacked, putting aside for the time being the usual hassling of "retro," "classic," "poetirhythmic," and other "immature and harmful" tendencies. It was obvious that this strange focusing led to distortions of the "real" socialist reality, but *how* did it do that? Alas, it couldn't be explained by the old secret of sticking a thumb into the developer and smearing the emulsion. In the work of the great comrades who pioneered that Soviet method, all the "whirlwinds" in the photos, all the surges and misty distances, were of course "innovative"; they expanded the creative vistas (not to be confused with whiskeys) of the socrealistic technique. The pernicious New Photographers were undoubtedly involved in the decadent "Western process," and their attempts to explain the peculiarities of their pictures through a combination of optical and *spiritual* reasons were, of course, the machinations of "home-grown metaphysicians," upon whom the Party had declared uncompromising war.

Once a militant unit made up of three Party regional committee activists had come to the editorial offices of *Soviet Ball*. In response to numerous complaints from laborers, the regional committee had decided to investigate the activities of Veniamin Probkin, to see if he corresponded to the position he held, or whether he was in fact compromising that progressiveness-that-we-serve.

Alas, just as the complainers—or stoolies, in other words—had supposed, the investigation turned out to be a simple matter. Like bubbles from a submarine blown up in Swedish waters, various suspicious things began to surface: Probkin's financial reports, faked business trips, vague prize money in the satirical photo contest run by *Click,* bills for "business banquets" at Rosfoto Restaurant, receipts in Japanese. Even the biography of the Mercedes was outlined briefly in the fog.

In a word, V. Probkin was hit like a Swede horseman at the battle of Poltava, or rather, drowning like a Russian submarine near Göteborg, two and a half centuries later. Then the Party dreadnought tossed him a lifesaver.

"Recant New Photography in the *Photogazette,* Comrade Probkin, expose its treacherous twist, and then your economic naughtiness will be forgotten. If you don't help the Party, all this will be passed on to the corruption and embezzlement squad, and you'll face trial before public opinion on morals charges. Think of all the young maidens you've despoiled in Moscow, Comrade Probkin, damn your eyes!"

There were not many who thought that the semicrooked Probkin would send the Party people to hell, but he did. Moreover, at a closed Party session he announced that for the sake of his art, that is, the sake of this stupid New Photography, he was prepared to accept an *auto-da-fé*.

The chief committee man chuckled at that *"auto-da-fé,"* thinking that Probkin meant an auto supply store—but then, when they explained to the committee chief that a "sacrifice" was meant, he grew furious and demanded that Probkin immediately be expelled from the Party. Everyone gasped: even though this was a Party meeting, and not just an ordinary one but a closed session, for some reason it had not occurred to anyone that such a dubious character as Probkin could be a member of "our" own Party.

In that particular situation—as, incidentally, it does everywhere—there had triumphed the law of dialectics known as the Two-ended Stick: on one end, membership in the Party seemed to be good protection from the OBKHSS* embezzlement squad, but on the other end appeared an unattractive situation—a non-Party man could manage to avoid the squad somehow, while a man discharged from the Party would be thrown right into the monster's jaws.

It didn't take a lot of torment for *Soviet Ball* to fire Probkin. They used the traditional Moscow line: "When you get back," meaning back from the camps, "drop by. We'll set you up with hack work."

So, out of his job, out of the Party, and under investigation, the New Photographer had prepared for the worst. Then there had been a sudden switch, and he had brightened.

Right at the crossroads he had met Alexei Okhotnikov, with whom several years ago while on a business trip in Arkhangelsk he widened the window to Europe: with a wide-angle lens, gentlemen, between the legs of Peter the Great. Come with me, Alexei had said, and so Probkin found himself in a circle of people with whom he had not been on very

---

*I wouldn't have offered this incomprehensible abbreviation to American readers without being induced phonetically. Pronounced as "Ou-Ba-Khaes," doesn't it sound like a dragon's name? Perhaps it helps to be in one's cups, but . . .

good terms before because of his Party and magazine affiliations. In a word, he found himself in the photographic underground of Moscow, in the incipient New Focus group, where, to his enormous surprise, he found his former idols, the "dinosaurs of the sixties."

Probkin had spent his life—my little life, as he put it—feeling like a lone partisan in a hostile national (even though he was a pure Russian) and ideological (even though he was a Proletarian) environment, but then he had abruptly discovered a whole group of renegades that met and daringly went out to hunt for its success in Soviet labyrinths.

What a new life Probkin began, what flights! A spiritual, that was it, *spiritual* life, one he had never known. Taking mixed drinks at Alexei's illegal domicile, Probkin daringly threw himself into conversations about art as a means of "secret esoteric communication." What a wonderful period of his little life! "Gentlemen!" he would shout, trying to be heard above the general hubbub. "Did you know that I first felt like a human being with you people?"

Strangely enough, thanks to New Focus, the OBKHSS embezzlement squad turned its foul face away from Probkin. One of the New Focusers turned out to have friends in the central apparatus of Internal Affairs; it can't be said that the investigation ceased automatically, but summonses for chats came less frequently, and the case was clearly drying up.

It's really amazing, Probkin had thought more than once, that it is so hard to coordinate various things here. Really, it's not bad at all, that it is impossible to coordinate the Soviet system, as a whole. Take, for example, the fact that the PhIDs were on our tails, the old photogs from the Union incited them, making political changes, brewing up a major, horrible ideological scandal, while the colonels from the highway patrol still adore guys like Andrei Drevesny from the olden days, and they know nothing yet at the Ministry of Internal Affairs, nothing at the Moscow city hall, they haven't had time to coordinate with them, and that's what makes it possible to still live in our country. The country is technologically backward, and that's terrific. If the cruel powers had working computers, life would be impossible.

In a word, V. Probkin was really enjoying the recent turn of events in his life, while at the same time truly, sincerely ready to deal with strife, with prison, with that infamous *auto-da-fé,* the loss of everything in the world, even his diesel Mercedes. He was even prepared to sacrifice his "sex network" chicks for the sake of art, even though the last was not required, fortunately or unfortunately.

Things were getting worse in that area, with women, that is: the sight of any female made his jaw drop, his lips moisten, his eyes glaze over, and an unbearable gravitation grow in his groin. He had to take the lady by the hand immediately.

It rarely happened that the female person would remain deaf to such a powerful call. More often, she gave in, to be rid faster of that "strange young man." With every month of his little life, the young talent's collection of female friends increased.

The rare evenings in the family sanctum sanctorum had turned to torture for Probkin. Masha bristled at every ring and Probkin, sweating, his traitor's eye askance, would run to the phone, pretending to have business relations, drily checking the address where he had to "pick up materials," and as he put on his jacket, would plead with his noodle, "Masha, trust me!"

2

WHEN HE CAME over to Alexei Okhotnikov, Probkin naturally said, "Please call Masha and say that you've sent me to Lionel's, and that I'll be getting back sometime around midnight, anyway no later than two. . . ."

"Oh, at it again," Alexei chided his friend. "You don't think enough about art, I'm afraid. Just look around. Notice anything?"

Probkin immediately saw the "ambulance" by the dirty fence.

"Again?"

"Precisely. And we're expecting the Danes in an hour, and then Ogo will show up, and somebody else will call. . . . So we'll get a good head count tonight. We really have to fuck them in the ass by the laws of the underground."

"Any proposals?" Probkin asked readily.

"We'll pull out a sack of anti-Soviet stuff each and drive off in opposite directions," Alexei proposed. "Whoever loses his tail comes back and receives the Danes. Okay?"

Of course, Alexei had got it all wrong again: the Danes were already turning into the side street in the full shimmer of Scandinavian glory—a turbo Volvo and a blonde at the wheel, representatives of the newspaper *Gulfstream*.

"Do we scatter?" Alexei asked uncertainly. "It's just the time for it. Blatant interference by world imperialism. The comrades are confused. We split. The Danes find nobody home and leave. We call them later. Everything is mixed up."

"Are you crazy?" muttered Probkin, unable to take his eyes off the straw-haired woman at the wheel. "Remember what Ogo always says—never run away, ever. Don't hide anything. According to the constitution we have the right to do everything we're doing. Who's forbidden me to meet with foreign girls?"

"One-track mind," grumbled Alexei.

A white mane swished in the twilight—and then a flash: the thin woman in a jacket with padded shoulders had barely gotten out of the car before she took several photos. Her camera, naturally, was interested in the joyless life of a totalitarian society, in the retarded girl who was always playing quietly by the garbage bins, just beneath the slogan RAISE THE BANNER OF SOCIALIST COMPETITION! on the ruins of the new construction.

The girl was escorted by Per Ruberhardt, chief and only reporter at the Moscow office of *Gulfstream*. Our fellows were horribly worried: no matter how hard they tried to be cool, meeting foreign correspondents under the watchful eye of PhID was not a cozy-comfy pastime. Nevertheless, Probkin hurried over.

"May I help you, miss?" he asked in English.

The woman photographer even slipped in surprise, seeing two civilized men in the midst of Soviet "parochial life." Then another flash, from her this time, not a photograph, but a smile: what fantastically white teeth they grow in Scandinavia!

Alexei, of course, began "burning with embarrassment" in the proximity of the woman, didn't know what to do with his hands, how to handle his long beard. In his embarrassment, he paid "zero attention" to the girl, and pretended to continue a folksy argument with Probkin.

"I'm surprised at you, old fellow. . . ."

Damned Probkin, in the meantime, went gabbing along beautifully in European, as if to taunt: Here's a lesson for you, silly Alexei, you seaside intellectual from the city of Arkhangelsk, just watch this slick Moscow operator overcome the language barrier without the aid of alcohol.

Finally finished shutting up the Volvo with all its locks and alarms, Ruberhardt came over and began chattering in Russian, sprinkling case endings and pronouns wherever they fell, spinning deformed nouns with mutilated verbs, lisping in a Baltic way, but with a Gallic ease and absolute comprehensibility.

The woman, whose name was Nellie, had just flown in from Copenhagen; Ruberhardt was writing an article on underground Soviet art and had asked *Gulfstream* to send her as soon as possible. "I haven't seen her in a long time."

Glad we didn't slip away, thought Probkin. Here's a good chance to get to know my Scandinavian colleague better. That gave him the old gravity, and elbowing away his friend, he led the woman toward the house while quickly ironizing about Soviet reality, especially about that first-aid van, which, "just imagine, miss, hasn't budged from its spot in three days, and inside are four slobs with listening equipment, they must be recording everything that goes on at the headquarters of New Focus, just imagine, madame, and incidentally, my friend Alexei lives here, yes, this one, imagine, *le mouzhik,* and now you can imagine the sound tape of those Alexeiic noises, just picture the experts trying to analyze all of those sounds, really, you have to feel sorry for them. . . ."

Hearing his name in the ugly Anglo-Franco-German babble, Alexei grew even shyer, rolled one eye wildly at the woman, pushed his chest at the man, blurted something abour Russian artistic potentials, spiritual renaissance, and encouraging winds from the city of archangels.

It took the Danes no less than a quarter hour to get from the car to the apartment. The woman photographer was already laughing nervously, sensing what Probkin had in mind. A Danish woman like that, of course, could excite a whole Moscow neighborhood, which is what now happened in building 4 of the Soviet Cadre housing coop. Some residents shied away from the colorful group of dangerous people with the laughing blonde in the middle; others came intentionally close, staring severely at the relaxed international youth that paid no attention to their vigilance. Why did they let people like that into "our capital," anyway?

Waving arms, speaking all at once, and not listening to one another, the four finally entered the apartment, where, on the desk in the corner, lay a huge dummy—the size of a gravestone—of the uncensored photo album *Say Cheese!*

After examining the photographs on the walls and sticking her finger between the pages of the semimythical album, the Danish woman realized that she was in the company of masters, titans of photography, and that *she,* a modest newspaper photographer, should thank her lucky stars and sleep with the first person who asked.

The phone never stopped ringing in the controversial apartment and the doors, as usual, slammed constantly—the New Focusers were gathering for their evening cheesing. Someone brought a bottle of Stoly; everyone brought something, and everyone, as usual, carried on with the most seditious crap and foul language, and kept pointing at the ceiling—*that's where the bug is.* They wanted the Danes to know the conditions under which the Soviet intelligentsia had to live and how daringly they disdained those conditions. The foreigners, of course, nodded in understanding—that's one thing they didn't doubt, that there was a bug, and let us add, it was there, otherwise what was General Planshchin's subdepartment for?

"But where's Ogo?" asked Ruberhardt. It was with Ogo, known to the readers of *Gulfstream* as Max Ogorodnikov, that he wanted to do the main interview. "I hope he'll be here?"

"He will, he will," Probkin promised readily, caressing frightened Scandinavian knees under the table.

The windows in the small apartment steamed over from the hot pelmeni. Alexei cooked them in a frying pan the size of a hubcap. His technique was his own—he poured raw pelmeni in the frying pan and dumped a half kilo of margarine on top. When smoke started to rise from the pan, the pelmeni were ready. "Oh! Real Russian dumplings!" the Danes said.

A mind-boggling array of drinks stood on the table—cheap Soviet port wines like SunGift and Smile next to a bottle of twelve-year-old Chivas Regal.

"The guys from *The New York Ways* brought us that yesterday," the Cheeser named Shuz Zherebyatnikov explained to Ruberhardt. "They apologized that they hadn't had time to drop by the hard-currency store to get some Danish beer, that is, your beer, Ruber, some Tuborg. Sorry, all we have is one bottle of Chivas. But we're happy to have even that. Understand, Ruber? We're happy with anything of good quality, because we usually have to drink rotgut, by-products of the decay of the socialist system. . . ."

"But where is Mr. Ogo?" the Dane kept asking.

"He's coming, he's coming," they assured him. "You have enough time to make a quick trip to the currency store and back. . . ."

OGO

HE ONE EVERYONE was asking about—the one who flashed by at the beginning of our narrative with nonsense on his lips—was just now strolling quite close by, in the dark alley between buildings 1 and 2 of Soviet Cadre.

Maxim Petrovich Ogorodnikov was a bit over forty, and in the moments when his lanky figure fell beneath the only streetlamp in the alley, you could make out his large nose and, below it, his fuzzy, piebald moustache. A longer exhibition would undoubtedly reveal a marked brazenness in all his features and distinguishing marks—characteristic, incidentally, of many of fortune's darlings and stars of modern art. A strange thing would become apparent, too: his entire elongated-bony artistic type was amazingly malleable—in the course of five minutes you could see an old man, a disciplined athlete, or a shabby aesthete.*

This alley was a favorite haunt of closet liberals for joint, apparently accidental walks, with whispers over the shoulder. "Have you heard, Br'er Rabbit?" One of these supposed liberals was accompanying Ogo, actually seemed to be walking him, holding him firmly by the elbow

---

*However, we don't have five minutes right now and can only see the largish nose and fuzzy moustache, peeping out from the raised collar of a London raincoat, appearing periodically under the streetlamp.

and breathing hot, concentrated whispers up onto his left cheek. He picked up Ogo "by accident": "Bah! Whom do I see! Have a minute?" and led him to the alley, recounting with a hot whisper and mocking— "Swine, I tell you, real swine!"—the recent meeting of the coop board, at which the retired activist had proposed evicting Alexei Okhotnikov and sealing off the apartment, which had become "a den for meetings of a suspicious odor. The most amazing part is that our grim chairman immediately tabled the issue, because it is not within our, note, not our competence. You realize, of course, old man, whose competence it *is* in . . . ?"

To the liberal's amazement, his companion simply guffawed in response to this important announcement; Ogo never doubted for a minute that the apartment was bugged and surrounded. The strange part was why PhID was watching for so long and doing nothing—they must be planning something disgusting beyond all expectations. Well, fuck them.

"Beg pardon?" the liberal asked.

"Fuck them!" Ogo repeated with a certain pleasure. "I'm tired of thinking about them all the time. They simply do not exist for us. In general fuck them!"

"Drop it, old man, drop it," the liberal whispered even more hotly, holding Ogo's arm more tightly, leading him deeper into shadier corners, into the unsightly mists of Moscow's photographic world. "We love you here, old man, we appreciate you here, don't be hasty. . . ."

"You call that love?" Ogo said, his moustache bristling. "They've killed all my albums, one after the other, the magazines won't take my pictures. . . . You think I don't recognize the signature? Now they've postponed my show indefinitely, all my trips have gone down the tube, I'm not allowed out of the country anymore, my foreign mail is blocked, my phone is tapped. . . . They really *appreciate* me here? Who needs that kind of appreciation!"

The liberal goggled at him. In the dark along the alley crammed with prefab parts, such walks had a second meaning and even a third; and Ogorodnikov knew that the liberal could quite easily stroll with secret policemen and the liberal sensed that Ogo knew it, and therefore such walks were a link between the disfavored photographer and the powerful and invisible figures from the ideological (criminal) investigation department.

"Nevertheless, you're not planning to ... ?" the liberal asked barely audibly or inaudibly, just by moving his lips, just by rounding his already round eye, with a turn of that rounded-to-the-limit organ.

"Yes, I am!" Ogo announced loudly. "Those bastards will drive me to it, and then I'll get lathered up for the plunge!"

"Well, I must be going," the liberal suggested immediately, first peeking out, sucking air through the corners of his mouth in the cleft of the alley, then slipping under the streetlamp, under the arch, past the drugstore, into the entryway, and into his bachelor apartment.

There, in his lair (as he liked to call it), the stoolie liberal flopped on the bed, wrapped his legs in a Hungarian plaid, asked his maid (he had this maid, Mme. Plotsky) for a glass of Yugoslav punch, pulled the Czech phone closer, dialed the number of his friend—a trusted man, a smart cookie, a professor of photographic studies—and, in passing, among other things, told him about Max Ogorodnikov's intention "to toss his cap over the hill."*

Meanwhile Ogo walked between the buildings, but in the other direction, then came out at the crossroads and raised his walking stick to hail a cab. This was why he got himself a walking stick: so that like some foreign devil, he could come out at the crossroads on a misty autumn eve and "raise his walking stick to hail a cab."

As he stood with his upraised stick he imagined his just-uttered idea of "lathering up" skipping from phone to phone and wondered how upset the interested parties would be tonight.

Behind his back was entrance 4 and the Danish journalists' parked Volvo, as well as the sagging fence of the new construction and the first-aid van, with three cigarettes glowing inside. Ogo stood right under the streetlamp, revealing himself on purpose, because he rejected surveillance outright. Let the bastards violate our Soviet constitution, but *we* won't. We're not doing anything secret. All the gang gab about New

---

*The cursed subject of crossing the "sacred Soviet borders" has tormented people for decades and thereby given birth to innumerable slang expressions, like "lather up," "toss a cap over the hill," "exit man," "nonexit man," etc.

Focus and *Say Cheese!* on every street corner; only the lazy know nothing about it. The PhIDs, by tailing us, are forcing a conspiracy. It's a good trick: just start watching someone secretly, and he'll become a conspirator willy-nilly.

Ogo made a point of hanging out under the light, shouting "Taxi! Taxi!" He even began juggling his unique walking stick to make sure today's crew noticed him. His thoughts at the moment were in strange contradiction with his own personal rules.

Let the bastards get confused, if they've found the Danes. Everyone must think that I should be at Alexei's, and here I am going off in a taxi. After him, gentlemen of the Cardinal's guards!

When he got in the taxi he realized that he had accepted the game, that they had "gotten" him, tuned him to their wavelength. If you're aware of them behind you—whether you hide from them or not—it's all the same: you're playing their game. Until tonight he pretended that he didn't see them, but from this moment something changed.

He grew angry with himself and turned his head to see his tail, but neither the van nor anything like it was visible behind the taxi—just the number 70 bus lumbering along, and behind it, of course, the most frequent Moscow vehicle, the dump truck. So, the game was shameful and his first move in that game was stupid and incongruous.

Practically howling with fury that resembled a sharp toothache, Ogo leaned back in the seat and tried to recall something peaceful—say, for instance, the Place de l'Opéra in Paris. That's a good one, Ogo thought: on a transparent autumn *après-midi* I'm walking along, partly on business and partly just for the hell of it, along the Avenue de l'Opéra and I drop by the Café de la Paix to see if there are any letters for me there. That café maintains a marvelous nineteenth-century tradition: the habitués can find letters addressed to them on a board by the door, covered with green baize and equipped with metal clips to hold the mail. . . .

Yes, Ogo was tormented by longing for Europe in the fall. To set up his tripod at the entrance to the Tuileries and take lazy photographs of the passing moment in Parisian eternity. . . . That's a strange thing, he realized—Lenin's tomb, just like the pyramid of Cheops, stinks of decrepitude and decay, while the gates to the Tuileries bring a certain sense into civilization, hinting at something yet to come. . . .

Or Berlin: Unter den Linden, run, run, run, crawl under the barbed wire, belly over the round part of the Wall and sigh with enormous relief and childish glee—got away again!

Well, then, Ogo asked himself, why didn't I get away to my beloved autumn areas when I had so many opportunities? Because besides autumn with its European nostalgia there are other seasons, too. . . . Oh, yes. . . . Why is it, why is Europe so much like home to me? Then again, it could be hereditary: who were my father Peter O. and his buddy Vladimir L. if not the émigré scum roaming about Europe at prime time of their lives?

Now I'll never see Europe. *Black wings blocked the road,* went the poem learned in school. Now they won't let me out, except to follow in my father's footsteps, into emigration. "We believe you have children there in the bourgeois vistas, don't you? Bon voyage and try to forget your homeland, for a few other things were born here besides you. Socialism, for instance. Appreciate the humanity of today's Leninists— you're not imprisoned or shot, simply kicked in the ass at your own request. . . ." Owwww, the toothache was starting again, just made worse by dreams of Paris. Spend my whole life in the power of the sons of bitches? My whole life with an unnaturally turned neck and head, a semipermanent handicap from this damned regime? Fuck you, you won't see me in emigration. . . .

"Fuck you all!" Ogo said out loud.

"You said it!" mumbled the driver.

2

WHILE OGO WAS suffering from a toothache, General V. K. Planshchin's operative group was working operatively for the good of the people, specifically by maintaining contact with the first-aid vehicle which remained parked near the falling-apart construction.

Captain Vladimir Skanshchin, who was directly assigned to the case of M. P. Ogorodnikov, one of the leaders of New Focus, warily squinted at his chief and softly swore over the radio at another captain, Captain Slyazgin, who was on his eighth hour in the van.

"Damn it, Slyazgin, you can stuff your Danes! Fukko-mokko! How could you let Ogorodnikov slip away? Now he'll be on his own all evening, you really are an asshole, you know."

"You're letting yourself go here," Slyazgin roared in reply, his teeth crunching at the general's damned pet.

Captain Slyazgin was very upset. All this time the bastard Skanshchin was in a nice warm office studying the art of photography or doing field work at the restaurants at Rosfoto, the Actors' Union, the Writers' Union, the Journalists' Union, while he, Slyazgin, an experienced worker, had to spend twelve hours at a time in that shitty van, wasting expensive Japanese tape to record the chatter of the "Cheesers," "New Focusers," or whatever they called that crowd, all of whom should have been wiped out a long time ago instead of having all this time and effort wasted on them. This isn't creative work, I'll just quit and go out to the Far East project, I'd rather pull down those fucking railroads than . . .

"You're a bum," Skanshchin said into his mike. "A bum and a louse."

Meanwhile, pretending not to hear his favorite assistant's foul language, General Planshchin made marks on papers, handed pieces of paper to his fellows and girls, and at the same time spoke on the telephone, that is, he harrumphed, sometimes interrogatively, sometimes affirmatively, and distractedly uh-huhmed.

Suddenly the general stood up, went over to Skanshchin, and by pressing a button put an end to the squabble between two talented operatives.

"There's news," he said. "Ogorodnikov has decided to emigrate."

"What!" exclaimed Skanshchin, profoundly astonished and upset. "How can that be? We've just started working with the man!" He was sincerely saddened, his hands began to tremble. He could have used "a good tumbler of cognac" then, as the general liked to call it. It really hurt to lose a specialist in photography. They had just begun working with the man, and the work was interesting. Creative. Working a man like Maxim Petrovich Ogorodnikov was like reading a foreign book in a good translation, a *Catcher in the Rye*, you might say. Of course, it was a shame that a man like that put his talent in the service of world reactionaries, but if he hadn't there wouldn't be any work then, right? And if you dug around in the art, incidentally, you could find a healthy grain. In Ogorodnikov's Siberia cycle, for instance, those dump trucks were so fucking fantastic—your basic poetry of labor, in principle, a historic optimism....

"Hm," General Planshchin mused. "This emigration seems too simple somehow...."

"Precisely!" Captain Skanshchin responded with enthusiasm. "Too simple! It's an unlikely possibility. Why, just compare Ogo's physiognomy with that of the basic masses. There has to be something more complex than that."

The extremely agitated General Planshchin went over to the window. It's silly to mention, and it seems like hitting the reader over the head, but the ruby stars of the Kremlin were visible from the windows. The general made a face as he recalled the "basic masses" of the Photographers' Union, which took such delight in denouncing each other and had such ugly mugs that it was better not to see them first thing in the morning.

"Hm," General Planshchin said even more thoughtfully. "Too simple...."

3

ONCE SOMEONE SAID to Ogo, "You are one leg up on many of your colleagues—you have such wonderful, truly *Soviet* roots!"

There was no topic more repulsive, more scorned for a man who had cursed the very year of his birth than his famous roots, even though they really did exist, albeit not deep but strong, going down under the skin of the Party, and therefore into the people, for we know that "The People and the Party are One." Ogo's father had come straight out of Lenin's guards, and had more than one picnic with The Founder at the sawmill near Paris. His father turned out to be a man of sturdy bones, so to speak—he had passed unharmed through collectivization and reconstruction, from Ilich (Lenin) to Ilyich (Brezhnev), in the department of "the sharpest weapon of the Party"—i.e., in press—and died decades earlier in the highest ranks. But some time back, precisely in early 1937, a new personal car had come to Ogorodnikov senior from the Special Garage, the latest model Packard, and at the wheel was a cadre of the new generation, a young blonde with the innocent curls which so delighted the aging warriors of the *nomenklatura*.* And so, just at the end of that "Packard" 1937 year, which our hero in his cups now called "damned" and "Bartholomean," a child appeared in this world and was immediately called Maxim; most likely, named for the adored Maxim Gorky, father of socialist realism, who had recently passed away with a chocolate bar in his hand, as we mentioned in our epigraph.

Mme. Ogorodnikova, even though the leather seats of the Packard were long forgotten now, still woke up curly-headed, full of energy, still a cutie and a major author on questions of morality, and it was not ruled out that she held a high rank in the security organs. She often appeared on the TV, medals jangling, usually on some anniversary or other, most often a war one, for she was an adjutant of Ogo's father, who was a member of the Main Political Directorate, and she would still lift her eyes upward and with emotional intonations talk about her frontline youth, never once blushing.

Alas, as far as Ogo was concerned, his mother had turned into a "TV bimbo," and his second closest relative, October, his older half brother on his father's side, he saw primarily on the tube, too.

October Ogorodnikov was a figure of some mystery, an international commentator who had spent years in Brazil, then the USA, then was ensconced with all due appurtenances in Paris. He emanated a certain aura of power, a real battery of Party energy. He usually appeared on the home screen in periods of dramatic confrontations between the powers of peace and socialism and the powers of war and reaction, describing the situation in weighty tones right from the frontline positions, that is, either next to the Arc de Triomphe or in front of the Capitol. October's lies did not vary in any way from, say, the usual newspaper and television lies, but viewers considered him someone special, a source of special information.

Ogo never considered his mother seriously, but as a teenager, he worshiped his older brother. It was actually October who infected him with

---

* *Nomenklatura:* a Party "honor register," the top layer of the Soviet cake Napoleon, i.e., a list of the "most equal" of equals. Unlike the *NY Times* "Best Sellers" list, once you've been added to the *nomenklatura*, you're never dropped from it. But if the unthinkable happens and you do drop, you've no chances for coming back, whereas our authors can, at least theoretically, climb up again.

a passion for all sorts of machinery, which later turned into a passion for photography.

In general, what wonderful times they were, the naïve Soviet early fifties! Two brothers from high society, one a lanky teenager, the other a handsome young man, took turns driving an enormous ZIS-110 limousine, puttering for hours over the engine, which resembled the Dneproges power station, rapturously operated all kinds of "war trophies" and "reparations" mirrors, all kinds of Kodaks and Praktikamats; theory and practice, a real man's life, which included all kinds of motor sports, and sailing, and iceboats. They spoke very little in those happy hours, and words were not necessary—movements replaced words, and a diagram of an engine or radio was a blueprint "for everything."

For example, a scene from the summer of 1952 on the road to Barvikha: down a new smooth highway (naturally top secret, strategic, built by German prisoners of war to connect state dachas with the capital), the two brothers drove in a convertible limousine. On the back seat, which was covered with Morocco leather, sat an object that Hollywood would envy, a stylish girl nicknamed Eskimo. Legs that never stopped! No one was chatting foolishly. October was busy at the wheel, blending into the turns, whistling through his teeth—a melody commensurate with the thin line of his neat moustache, the slow fox-trot "Gulf Stream." Fifteen-year-old Maxim Ogo managed to get a picture with his Leica, in the side mirror, of Eskimo (the name came from the finger-licking good ice cream pie, not from the people of the North) and was already picturing the fantastic shot in which the mindbending knee would be in the forefront and the round face with its large, scornful mouth in the background. The girl was silent, first of all because there was no one to talk to and secondly because she wasn't the talkative type.

The militiamen at the intersections saluted. Pine trees swayed. Off in the distance, a young Leninist's trumpet sounded. A screeching turn around the *Girl with Oar* sculpture. October shook his head unhappily: the tires shouldn't screech. He went around the *Girl with Oar* once more, this time smoothly and strongly. They drove into the dacha gates. Hey! Two friends in the yard, boys from diplomatic families. They towed a boat on a trailer with a new American engine, a Mercury. "Have to look into it. Fine. The three of us are off to the lake, and you, Eskimo, teach the kid about the art of tender passion." *Octo-ber,* the girl whined, but all she heard in response was the receding hum of "Gulf Stream." Fine, she said. Let's go, Ogo. And here we trip over ellipses. . . .

Toward evening love-struck Ogo drove Eskimo back to town on his motorcycle, and upon his return saw the weary but happy friends on the veranda with new girls. One was teaching the group how to do the boogie-woogie. What rhythm, what movement, O United States of America!

October lifted an eyebrow inquiringly upon seeing his brother.

"October, she's amazing," yesterday's boy whispered with a shudder.

"I've noticed you mooning over Eskimo a long time," October said with a smile. "Congratulations. And now take a look at the machine our friends brought."

Maxim Ogo got weak at the knees—on the table stood a new American tape recorder not bigger than the average radio!

In the fall of that blessed year the evening rag ran a lampoon on Moscow's *stilyagi* under the title "Weeds." The main targets were the sons of academicians, but the son of "Ogorodnikov himself" was mentioned, though in passing.

"A horrible hassle," as October called it, took place in the family. The father banged his fist on the mahogany and shouted about "betrayal of ideals." Soon after that lampoon October disappeared without a word to Maxim. The mother shrugged, as if to say, I don't want to know about it—he's either off to Kamchatka to make big bucks, or he's in some military school. The father merely grumbled—"We'll see, we'll see, maybe he'll turn into a real man yet, that miserable weed."

A few years later, October returned. Everything seemed to be the same—the cars, the cameras, the girls, the jazz—but something was added: for instance, excellent English. October became an international journalist and quickly, year after year, became one of the best, joining all sorts of editorial boards and learned councils, even working his way up to deputy in the Supreme Soviet of the USSR. Of course, he spent most of his time abroad and once, in his cups, admitted to Maxim Ogo that "I really can't take more than a month at a time in the homeland of socialism, and to tell the truth, can't imagine how people live here."

Maxim looked at his brother through his viewfinder and it seemed to him that the renowned international commentator was the same old *stilyaga* of the fifties: he combed his hair, still rather thick, into a semblance of a "Canadian bob" and smoked unfiltered Camels, the crystal dream of his weedy youth.

As for October Ogorodnikov's articles, they were remarkable for their falsehood even amid the usual professional sellouts, even though they glistened with so-called details that were aimed at the elite readership.

October at first treated his younger brother's "lefty" stuff mockingly, as if the photos were childish pranks. With every year, however, as Maxim got more "beastily anti-Soviet" (another of October's bons mots), they drifted farther apart.

Sometimes Ogo learned thirdhand that October had been back on vacation and had even seen his mother, that is, October's stepmother, and that he had even visited Max's first wife and brought presents, but didn't manage to call on his brother. . . . That's the way things are sometimes—busy, busy. . . .

4

BUT HOW DID it happen that such a famous Soviet photographer as Maxim Ogorodnikov could become a dissident, so to speak? This question was discussed often in Moscow's liberal-artistic circles as the story developed. After all, he had been on the board of the Union, even received, they thought, the prize of the Lenin Komsomol. . . .

"And who was on the prize committee then? All leftists" was the opinion of the perspicacious observer. "Really, comrades, Max Ogo followed a totally natural path of development. It's a direct path from frivolous liberalism to dissidence, you must agree. What's odd is that the authorities have been dillydallying with him so long, that's what's so strange."

All this was spoken in the new fashion, in a tone that did not make clear on whose side the speaker was.

"Really, he and his friends have been on the edge for so many years . . . sometimes, you know, all that creativity looked like nothing but an attempt to run down the authorities; nevertheless until just recently they considered Ogo one of their own ... er, of our own. .... It's strange that the group had official trust for so long."

Finally during such discussions a barely perceptible division would take place: one side would cast doubts on the former official positions of "that group," while the other doubted its nonconformist qualities.

"Just a minute, just a minute, what's so strange about that? Just recall Ogorodnikov's early albums, all those reportages from the great construction sites of communism."

Having just ingested cognac—for these discussions invariably took place in various Houses of Creativity where strong spirits had recently been allowed to be sold once again—someone would chime in:

"Incidentally, those early albums were interesting, fresh, and sincere! Quite different from the usual official stuff. Remember, it was Ogo who photographed that fight in the line to buy champagne! What modeling of faces and characters!"

"Are you trying to say that he didn't also take all those pictures of dams, dump trucks, and bulldozers?"

"Well, weren't all those things *there?* And didn't those albums give you a feeling of a strange absurdity?"

"Attention, br'er rabbits, here comes our editor. He's not a bad fellow but let's talk of women, instead."

5

A HALF YEAR before that foggy evening,* on a May morning, the phone had rung. Ogo felt right away that it was something shitty. A person and his telephone develop a certain intimate relationship. It's no trouble for a communications machine to warn its owner of something shitty. There are different kinds of rings. You can tell right away if it's a friend

---

*What foggy evening? my reader will ask. You've lost track of the mud-splattered Volga taxi in the wings of the novel, but it's still driving through the foggy October evening, crossing Sokol Square, going past the airport station, Dynamo Stadium, and Ogo, with his head pulled into his shoulders, sits next to the driver, and with baleful eye looks into the not-so-distant past: a half year ago.

calling or if it's just something shitty. Actually, it wasn't anything too terrible, just a certain Captain Skanshchin from GPU; it was like, "Guten morgen, this is the Gestapo calling." The voice reminded Ogo of the hockey player who lived in the next building, a glib Muscovite. "In principle, you should know me, Ogorodnikov."

"Haven't had the honor," Ogo replied, following literary tradition (the gendarme and the liberal lawyer). He had managed to find the right put-down tone of voice, despite the fleeting clutching sensation in his guts.

"Haven't they pointed me out to you at Rosfoto?"

Ogo, even as he chuckled haughtily, did remember the captain. He recalled the vague blondish face at the tea table—with a meat pie in his mouth. A consultant of the secretariat, eternally gamine with her bangs, stood on tippy-toe and pressed her eternally firm knobs against Ogo's arm, whispering in his ear with her eternally perfumed breath:

"Want me to show you your kurator?"

Ogo had already heard that lately a whole subdepartment of PhIDs, young men in suede jackets, with wedding rings on their paws, were hanging around all day long in the bar, buffets, and restaurant of the famous club in Moscow. They sipped cognac, smoked American cigarettes, and not only did not hide the way they used to but, on the contrary, struck up intellectual conversations and introduced themselves openly as so-and-so from the PhID. What marvelous steps in socialist progress—you no longer had to guess who your *kurator* was, now he would be pointed out to you, your personal specialist, nothing more and nothing less than your political physician, for how else is one to understand the word *kurator?*

"We should have a little chat," said Captain Skanshchin in a voice well developed in courses for operatives. At that moment he was standing by the phone in the general's office, and his senior comrade was directly observing the start of the operation.

Usually, according to the book, people would get terribly frightened by such invitations, you could sense it over the phone line. The first call from the Glands was half the job, as Captain Skanshchin's senior comrade, General V. K. Planshchin, taught him. In this particular case, however, the phone call wasn't having its desired effect. Usually the captain just made his voice a bit tougher and the client was his, he could set a date in a hotel room just as if dealing with a whore. In this particular case, however, the client expressed the opinion that while they really didn't have anything to talk about, he was willing ro *receive*—"receive, Comrade General!"—Captain Skanshchin and a comrade at his house. "You heard him, Comrade General, you heard his tone, as if I weren't calling from the Glands but were some shutterbug hoping he would take a look at my work. Just think, Comrade General, he even managed to cast doubts on my 'comrade': What comrade is that, he asked. And he didn't even make the appointment for today, he set it for the day after tomorrow, and I didn't even dare bring up the hotel, Comrade General, when he put it that way. Now you say that at moments like that their adrenaline gets flowing, Comrade General, but I didn't notice it with him. . . ."

Young specialist Skanshchin was wrong in doubting the erudition of his senior; just between us, the adrenaline *was* flowing, but Ogo was sneaky enough to get hold of a tranquilizer and take three tablets and doze off before the officers came.

At the appointed hour the officers appeared in well-cut suits and ties, "to be received." The photographer opened the door, standing in jeans and suspenders and slippers, and covered his mouth, not disguising his yawn. Later Ogo was amazed at how well that had come off. Strangely, *they* were the ones who looked off-balance at the meeting. Of course, that might have been their tactic, to appear bewildered—"Forgive our incursion into your creative laboratory. . . . Believe us, we wouldn't have disturbed you here, if not . . ."

"This is just my study, not a laboratory," Ogo replied, still seeming to be struggling with a yawn, fooling himself with that simpleminded sleepiness. "The lab is in a completely different place."

"Khlebny Alley, number seven, apartment twenty, right?" burst out Captain Skanshchin.

All General Planshchin could do was wince and give his junior partner a dirty look: what a jerk, wasting a perfectly sound trick, developed over decades. Would this sneaky-eyed beast be surprised by this information? He'd just laugh at youth.

"Have you been there?"

"The captain was joking. We were speaking figuratively about your creative laboratory. Just in the sense that we wouldn't have come if it weren't for extreme circumstances."

"Please, come in, take these armchairs, please," Ogo said, and plunged himself down in his favorite. An awareness of the wild incongruity of all his personal property, surrounding him at this moment, ran suddenly up Ogo's spine.

There should have been bare walls and not a Macedonian rug, bought fifteen years ago in Skoplje. At best (or worst) a portrait of the Knight of the Revolution, but certainly not photographs of dissidents; Solzhenitsyn and his children; fog and in the fog the contours of the Church of the Transfiguration; Sakharov on the shore at the Black Sea, bare feet on the pebbles. And there was photography's greatest dissident, Alik Konsky, photographed in his place of exile, Soho, in New York, masked faces behind him, the haughty grin that so irritated the Glands in Moscow, and at least five or seven pictures of persons well known to the Glands, and here was one of his favorite works—the crowd in front of the courthouse during the trial of Ginzburg and Galanskov,* just at the moment when brakes squealed at the crossroads and everyone, dissidents and "glanders," turned their heads in the same direction.

Unlike the walls of his real creative laboratory on Khlebny, those of his study held no naked women, but there was something embarrassing, albeit dressed, floating out of the photographic fog: a shot of Tallinn, the smell of coal smoke, the pathetic neon CAFÉ sign, he's twenty-four, she's thirty, white vest and white beret, pathetic talk of national independence. . . . For some reason it seemed disgustingly shameful under the unsmiling gaze of the senior PhID.

"I see you've been there," Ogo said.

"Several times," the general replied. "It's the Latin Quarter, right?"

"Right. Rue Mazarini," Ogo said with some relief, and even though Paris was shamed, the unrecognized Estonian capital was honored.

---

*The infamous trial in 1968 of four young people who dared to publish the *White Book* about previous infamous trials of other young people. The young people who protested the Ginzburg-Galanskov trial got their own trials in due course.

The general, close to sixty, with a messily balding head, took off his jacket and questioningly set it on the back of the chair. "May I? It's rather stuffy today." The young specialist immediately followed suit, revealing dark circles under his arms, and there was a whiff of the locker room. The general showed Max Ogo his open hands.

"As you can see, Maxim Petrovich, we have nothing."

"What kind of nothing?"

"No technical equipment," the senior man explained. "As you see we've come to you without ... technology. We hope that you'll be honest with us, too. . . ."

Ogo felt a bit dizzy from still vague but vile sensations, and in order to hide the dizziness reached for his cigarettes on the table. Captain Skanshchin did it again—he pulled out from his pocket a choice— French Gitanes or Soviet Marlboros. "Help yourself."

So, they were fully informed: Ogo preferred Gitanes—got parcels from his third wife, who lived in Paris—but whenever he ran out, he switched to the local product of détente. Something was wrong, thought Skanshchin desperately, feeling the general's dissatisfied glare. I must be gaffing it again. . . .

"I never considered myself a crook. What do you have in mind?" Ogo asked.

General Planshchin waved a hand—as if to mean "A piffle, not even worth talking about"—but his wolverine eyes stared straight ahead at Ogo's forehead.

"I'm just trying to say, Maxim Petrovich, that we're not recording our conversation. I hope you aren't either." Jackets were off, hands were outstretched, faces clear. . . .*

A chilling thought went through Ogo's belly: These creeps are taking me *completely* seriously, they seem to consider me an enemy and an equal. Disaster! Several bubbles burst in his stomach, and a light grumbling rose to the surface. Luckily, he saw himself in the mirror in the far corner and thought that the angle was right, that the whole *mise-*

---

*The author must once again complain about the lot of the Russian novelist who cannot avoid the ubiquitous Glands in describing contemporary Russian life, who cannot even give the representatives of the Glands any human traits, for at that very moment Planshchin and Skanshchin were lying—they were recording.

en-scène—two detectives sitting upright in the stiff armchairs, an artist lazily lolling on the couch—was working in his favor.

Vanity had a bracing effect, as well: they must consider him the leader of the Cheesers, otherwise they wouldn't have come. And basically they were correct—he was the leader—though the *idea* had arisen in the dental center of Timiriazev Region, in a conversation between Alexei Okhotnikov and Venechka Probkin, who were in neighboring chairs; both had been left by their dentists to wait for the novocaine to take effect. But I am the founder, Ogo thought, if only because the idea wouldn't have lasted a week without me. And, really, I'm the only one in the group that they have to take seriously—my name and my international ties. . . .

He smiled in the spirit of this latest thought and said, "I'm not recording you either."*

The officers quickly exchanged a glance—not even a glance, but a certain muscle of the face twitched at the same time: they had figured it correctly, this was a serious case—that cool calm tone instead of the fright and holy terror every Soviet citizen must feel at the thought of such sacrilege as recording our Soviet Glands.

Ogo called on the help of the Olympic gods and prepared for battle. I'll wipe them out with my first question: Have you gentlemen, or, rather, comrades, ever taken a photograph? Do you even know what it *is?* If you keep an eye on us, we must assume that you're on top of things? You ought to know how people eat and drink photography? Maybe we have just been underestimating you catastrophically? Nevertheless, let me doubt that your inquisitiveness goes back to Papa Schultze and his glowing substance or even further back to the true wise men—the alchemists, the great wizard Kristof Adolf Baldwin, and his smoky nights in search of *Weltgeist,* for your ideology hadn't been born then, wasn't even suspected, but the chalk as it dissolved in aqua regia absorbed moisture from the atmosphere and left a precipitate in the bottom of the retort that glowed in the dark. You're not going to

---

*Does it need pointing out that Ogorodnikov was not lying?

maintain that you inherited the archives of the Inquisition, are you? And
if not, then what the hell are you doing poking into other people's
business?

"Well," the general said. "Why don't you start, Captain?"

Planshchin dramatically turned grim. It was beginning to look like a
TV show based on a thriller by Yulyan Semyonov.

"I won't hide things, Maxim Petrovich, we have it."

"It?" Ogo was taken aback by the stress on "it," the artistic disdain
and the ancestral alchemists were forgotten, and thus what he had
planned as a struggle began for him with an affront. "It? *It?*" he mumbled. "You have it? Sorry, I don't understand. . . ."

The general was beginning to enjoy their meeting.

"Come on, Captain, explain what we have in mind, or Maxim Petrovich may be thinking about the wrong thing entirely."

Ogo felt that the wolverine eyes were contouring him somehow, as
if the slightest change in angle and volume was immediately contoured
on some invisible background. What was this ridiculous bluff? How
could they have "it," if "it" didn't even exist yet?

"We're talking about your work, about your album *Splinters.*"

General Planshchin smiled as the ill-starred artist jumped up from
the couch in astonishment. Jump around, Comrade, it's good for you,
you've been playing the genius too long.

Skanshchin thought, What great jeans Ogo is wearing.

"*Splinters?* You said *Splinters?*"

"Exactly *Splinters,* Maxim Petrovich, your own little *Splinters.* . . .
What else did you think? Maybe you've photographed something else
. . . em . . . contradictory?"

Ogo flopped back down into his favorite couch indentation. Fantastic! Bizarre! They were interested in *Splinters,* the album he had all but
forgotten. He had finished the album three years ago, it began with an
epigraph from a popular song: ". . . and the chips flew in all directions!"
He had put it together over the course of years, starting with those early
days when New Wave Moscow photographers traveled in motley crews
to the Far East in search of the "young hero within themselves." It had
been so much fun in those days, that whole gang, the generation of

Ticket to the Stars, your membership in the avant-garde determined by your age.

But even back then, against the background of fiestas and festivals, strange gloomy shadows had begun to appear in the negatives. The carnival cavalcade of shots would be interrupted by a blank—either a memory lapse or, on the contrary, a moment of awakening. Year after year everything gathered—from Moscow to the lands of Gulag—and finally came the photo idea, historically-and-utterly naïve. The logging machine of Stalin's spirit rumbled across an enormous expanse of the earth, and there was nothing but land covered with chips. Would life break through?

Understanding at last what he wanted, Max Ogo had then dropped his drinking and all his women, dropped out of attic exhibitions and official shows, and spent two years doing nothing but wander around with his "primitive one" (as he called his favorite camera), clicking, and doing magic in the lab. The final album held just over a hundred shots, all so easy somehow, fragments in the strangest combination. . . .

Two faces dominated the whole collection, all the splinters: a Stalinist bastard, ageless and sexless; and a post-Stalin retard, mouth parted because of adenoids, a jerk-off "eternal youth." The first with the gravity of a Politburo member was watching pensioners playing chess on Tversky Boulevard. The latter, desperate and drunk, was explaining something to two volunteer police and a militiaman on the corner of Liteiny and Nevsky Prospect. Max didn't know either one and never met them after taking their pictures; however, those faces were present everywhere in a one-on-one struggle, that is, they were in places where they weren't, including the purely nonpolitical subjects, landscapes, and still lifes. "The Runaway," for instance, could be guessed at in the sharp turn of an urban river with a deserted embankment and a small stone lion in the back. "Guard," for instance, floated up like a gaseous cloud from the barely perceptible pattern on the unglued wallpaper above a still life of a completely abstract character—a plate of good cabbage soup, a bottle of French cognac, an embroidered towel on the back of the Viennese chair, and a fellow-traveler corkscrew.

When he completed the album, Ogo naturally spent some time being hailed as a genius. First of all, the friends who saw *Splinters*—and there were only a dozen or so who had—said, "Ogo, you're a giant!" and secondly, he began respecting himself quite a bit—a person like that, moustache, glasses, droopy nose and yet—a genius! Actually, it was like that with every new collection, after all the previous "dubious" ones, and that's the way it was after this first truly "dangerous" one. Of course, he celebrated more this time—danger, it seemed, added to the genius.

"We are primarily interested, of course, in how your work got abroad, Maxim Petrovich." The eyes were still photocopying Ogo, showing that they would not believe a single word, but still allowing for the possibility of an unexpected crack-up with urine and saliva drips.

"Abroad? That's news to me." Ogo answered questions like that almost automatically, because in the last three years quite a few of his pictures appeared accidentally in albums and shows "over the hill," and the old goats in the apparatus of the Photographers' Union asked from time to time: abroad? how? He could hear genuine surprise in those questions, as if postal service did not exist. "Comrades, I am interested in something else," Ogo continued. He noticed a quick look and wink between the PhIDs, there was something positive in it this time, it was possible that his use of the dear word "comrades" had elicited it, he was using the dear "comrades" and not "gentlemen," maybe he wasn't a total loss. "*Splinters* is a private thing, done for my friends, but how did it get into your hands, comrades?"

The captain coughed in the style of a Soviet spy movie, that is, with a certain degree of machismo, showing that whatever else their failings might be, the knights of the revolution knew the rules of male friendship. "There are a lot of stoolies in your group, Maxim." Disgust blew a bubble on the young face. "If you only knew how many!"

My Volodya's doing fine now, thought the general, and smiled.

"If you have no idea how your work got abroad, then we can only join you in your bewilderment...."

He's right, though Ogorodnikov, let's be confused together, comrades. How could you have missed that bright-orange VW? An endless stream of dirt demons, empty Moscow trucks, had passed by, the crummy Moscow spring had been in full bloom, he had handed his

case through the VW window, and it had taken off, leaving him truly
bewildered—was that the way *Splinters* really reached the New York
art agent at last and came to rest in his safe?

But first Ogo should ask them, or better yet himself, what this hassle
was all about. Why bring the general along just to deal with *Splinters?*
Ogo really hadn't planned on publishing it, he didn't dare, despite the
substantial sums offered from overseas, while both Slava German and
Shuz and really almost everyone had much scarier photos in their draw-
ers nowadays. Maybe the dear comrades were just bluffing? Maybe they
were creeping up on New Focus? It was hard to imagine that they
found his album scarier than the collective *Cheese!* All the ages of Soviet
power considered the collective the greatest threat and danger. But why
try to guess? And there's no point in trying to outfox them. I have
nothing to hide, they're the ones with something to hide, they're the
secret gang, not us.

"So what of it?" Ogo asked haughtily, like a Polish princeling. "Does
that mean you consider my album anti-Soviet?"

The young captain winced with dismay, as if to say, Once again our
noble intentions are misunderstood. The old general also grimaced, but
not without a reminder of "the good old days."

"You're oversimplifying here. Who couldn't see in *Splinters* the
tragic fracture of the times, reflected in the creative work of a contradictory artist?"

"Oho," said Ogorodnikov. "Congratulations! It sounds just like a
review in *Foreign Photography.*"

The general flinched: He doesn't know my rank, the bastard, what a
bastard. I have to let him know who he's talking to.

"In general, to keep it short, my dear Maxim Petrovich, we will not
permit the publication of your album in the West, in the sense that you
will not be able to be a Western genius here in your homeland."

"Could you clarify that?"

"Yes. If *Splinters* appears in the West, you will have only two
alternatives."

"What does that mean?" muttered Ogo.

"Publicly renounce the work."

"Which, of course, you will not do," Volodya Shanshchin said.

Why not? thought Ogo.

"Or slam the door," the general concluded.

"That is?"

"That is say good-bye. Go where you are being published, join Chet-verkind, Konsky, and all those who felt alien in their homeland. To tell you the truth, we would not like for Soviet art to lose such a professional. . . ."

Captain Skanshchin interrupted with a whiny voice.

"Even *our* people love you, Maxim! All strata of society appreciate you. You are our symbol of everything progressive."

"What do you mean?" This time Ogo was truly confused.

"But still," the young captain moaned, "you're an optimist, I mean, you couldn't say, I mean, that you're a pessimist, could you?"

"As for me," the old general said drily, obviously working in contrast with the young captain, "personally what plays a significant meaning for me—"

Meaning isn't played, Ogorodnikov thought drearily.

"—what plays a significant role," the general amended, "is your roots. The glorious revolutionary name of your father, the real Russian pro-letarian traditions."

Being reminded of his roots always angered Ogorodnikov, as we have already seen, and now it infuriated him. Ogo rushed in an unknown direction, his long arms and legs seeming to form a large wheel under the attentive gaze of the Chekists. Bubbles of indignation flew from his mouth, sounding something like the cackles of an eagle, which created a fortunate unintelligibility, obscuring the anti-Sovietism and White Guardism he proceeded to spew.

"Roots? Growing in the thirty-seven-times damned field of 'thirty-seven? I'm breaking the chain of brutish growth! Take me away, I have nothing to do with the underground rot! A hydroponic product! I con-nect with civilization by the pipelines of photography! Hands off! You keep foisting tacky ideas on me, all bullshit of struggle! For me *Splinters* is metaphysics, metaphotography, while for you, at best, it's some tragic creak of the times, but really it's a movable pawn in your shitty ideo-

logical struggle. What are you trying to scare me for? I'd long forgotten
about my *Splinters,* and you're trying to bluff me, rubbing my nose in
my Bolshevik roots...."

That was the approximate gist of Maxim Ogorodnikov's cackle or
rumble, if you took out all the interjections, which included, alas, the
uncomfortable-sounding fukko-mokko as well as various ungrammati-
cal sounds. When he finished, he thought, Uh-oh, I've said too much,
looked in the mirror at the officers, and suddenly saw on the faces of
his uninvited guests a kind of enlightenment, a removal of waste
products.

"Are we to understand, Maxim Petrovich, that you are not planning
to publish *Splinters* in the West?" Planshchin asked.

"I never did," Ogo barked. Am I lying or not? he wondered. He
didn't know.

Is he lying or not? calculated Planshchin. He didn't know.

What was that stuff about hydroponics? mused Skanshchin. He
didn't know, but it was cool. He'd have to look for it in dictionaries
later.

At that moment of the conversation strange sounds emanated from
the foyer—a key turning in the lock, the click of heels. Viktoria Guryevna, Ogorodnikov's second ex-wife, who "helped him with the house-
keeping," came in.

"Viktoria, let me introduce you," he said wearily. "These are comrades from the PhID."

Both cavaliers immediately stood up and made her acquaintance via
handshakes. The captain's body language made it clear that he was
impressed. The general gave his host a reproachful look—why reveal
state secrets like that in vain? On the other hand, he was relieved. At
last "Ogorod" showed a normal human reaction to their complex
profession—he introduced them to his second ex-wife, Viktoria Kazachnekova, born 1937, resident of ...

She handled the situation beautifully.

"I'll make you some coffee, boys," she said in a deeply feminine
voice, and went off to the kitchen, her cavalry boots clicking.

Boys! That simplicity made even the experienced Chekist smile pleasantly, while the younger specialist expressed his good feelings with a strong slap on the knee—oh boy!

Motherfucker, thought Ogorodnikov, falling into deep depression.*

"You're making a very important decision now," Planshchin was saying. "Refusal to publish *Splinters* will definitely mean that you are remaining in the ranks of Sov—" The general hesitated, as if he suddenly did not wish to say his favorite word. ". . . In the ranks of our art."

"I didn't make any decision, I simply never intended to do it."

"I understand. In a word, if we conclude our conversation like gentlemen, if everything will be okay, then in general you won't have any problems from our organization. All your publications will be in order and your travel abroad will continue. So, we're fine?"

"Well, if it suits you, we're fine!"

Well, thought Ogo, at least he has the tact not to force a handshake on me. You can find something manly in their manners—they talk as if they would never lie. . . .

I think there's something human appearing in this creature, thought Planshchin. Will we really come to terms with him?

"Here's the coffee, boys!"

Viktoria rolled the coffee table into a study where the weather shifted

---

*That last remark seems an appropriate place to remind the reader that in the basic stream of narration, Max Ogorodnikov is still in a taxi headed for the center of Moscow, and at the present moment the car is waiting for a green turn signal from Leningrad Prospect onto the square of the Belorussian railroad station.

Gentlemen, the narrative genre is undergoing metamorphoses left and right that are not subject to the silly literary theories of our day. While a fragmented, disordered flow of memory and consciousness would be "much closer to reality," we, however, are using the more conventional horse, even if footnotes are unconventional stirrups, giving up rodeo delights for the sake of the rider's interests, for in this narrative the plot is no less important than the verbal flow.

And so for whatever reason exactly, while waiting for the turn signal around the momument to Gorky, Max Ogo remembered how his second ex, her cavalry boots clicking, went off to the kitchen to make coffee for *them*.

"Motherfuckers," Max sighed then.

He's right, thought the cabbie.

The arrow flashed. They drove on.

and encouraged smiles, and men's smiles always warmed this influential
lady of the Moscow theater.

Skanshchin turned to Planshchin with a mute question, and the general nodded. From Volodya's briefcase came a bottle of British ice—
Beefeater's gin in its original plastic. It was the right move—Ogo
responded in kind, taking out a bottle of Armenian cognac. A fine end
for the match.

"To our meeting," Volodya Skanshchin said with total sincerity. He
gulped down a shot and smiled at this client to whom, if the truth be
told, he had grown accustomed. "Don't be upset, Maxim."

"I'm not," the client said with a shrug.

"However, an artiste always wanna ..."

"Artist wants," corrected Viktoria.

"Thanks," the captain said. "He always wants to show his child to
the intelligentsia. Aren't I right?"

"Comrade Ogorodnikov overestimates the intelligentsia somehow,"
the general said. "You call those people with university badges the intelligentsia? Do you think they'll applaud you for *Splinters?* No, my dear
man, the intelligentsia won't understand you, they'll tear you to bits. Of
course, your album is an outstanding work of art—"

Shall I attribute that opinion to the gin and cognac? wondered Ogo.

"—and so, comrades, let's not bury your album conclusively. Let's
wait!"

"For what?" Ogorodnikov shuddered.

"What do you mean for what?" General Planshchin shuddered. "For
our intelligentsia to mature."

"What are we talking about?" Viktoria asked.

"The art of photography," Volodya Skanshchin explained in a low
voice.

"Ah," she said, and leaned back.

"Speaking of photography," the general said, and as if brushing off
a mote of dust, lightly touched the dissident's knee. "How do you see
its position in our country, Maxim Petrovich?"

Max suddenly felt the triteness of the situation like a wave of nausea.
I'm drinking with Chekists in my own home, being clever (?) or cow-

ardly (?) or bluffing brazenly. Aren't we ever going to get out from under them? Never? Be under them forever? Under these mobsters?

"What art," Ogo said crudely, "what art can you be talking about? What art can there be if the secret police is involved in it?"

Ogo got up and went to the window, letting them know that their time was up. Had he overdone it? he asked himself. Well, they were taught by their godfather* early on to treat talent carefully, like a naïve and beautiful whore.

Planshchin signaled Skanshchin—time to split. They had achieved a great success today, the dialogue was begun, no point in developing it now, the burbot might get off the hook.

"What a way you have with you, Maxim Petrovich—the police! Where do you see the secret police? Well, all right, thanks for the hospitality, as they say, in this house, we're off to another. . . ."

"Maxie, so long!" Viktoria said, taking off a yawn with a neat hand movement.

"Oh, Viktoria, you must know all the famous theater people!" the panting Volodya said as he accompanied her to the elevator.

Viktoria began humming something in a deep voice. The lady had spent her whole life in the theater, and for the last five or six years held a high-level position in the Central Box Office. Naturally, she had slept with many celebrities, and the mention of a name would usually start her singing in a good humor.

"What can I say? Not all of them."

"Tovstonogov, how about Mikhail Shatrov?" The young man peered into her face.

"The birdies sing tra-la-la. . . ."

The general left Max's apartment with the "young people" and by the time he reached the elevator, he thought that it had been too easy, not at the right level, something was missing from the day's picture. . . .

---

*Allegedly Chairman Lenin once said, "We should treat talent carefully: this is the People's property!" If one combines this premise with the Soviet slogan "The Party and the People are One," a logical but never-proffered conclusion may be easily deduced.

The elevator went down without him, he went back to Ogorodnikov's door. It wasn't locked yet. The general went inside and saw a long back with stuck-out elbows. Both hands in his dangling disheveled hair, Ogorodnikov stood by the wall in the foyer and seemed to be wailing what sounded like "ba-as-taa-rds."

The general leaned against the opposite wall, took out his cigarette case, and tapped a cigarette against the lid. He saw his reflection in the mirror deep in the apartment and realized that Ogorodnikov had noticed his return, even though he hadn't turned around.

"I couldn't leave without telling you a rather unpleasant thing, Maxim Petrovich ... our colleagues ... well, beyond the ocean ... are watching you closely ... working on you.... After the dissidents were crushed, they decided to develop a new stratum of opposition within our society ... made up of writers and photographers working on the edge of loyalty...."

"Madness," Ogorodnikov moaned as if pulling away from a dentist's drill. "Who needs me over there?"

General Planshchin observed him with fatherly concern. He had seen a number of suspects in his time, but this was one of the best.

"How you underestimate yourself. A great artist like you is worth fighting for. Tell me, have you ever come across a certain Clifford Zussi in your travels?"

"I have," Ogorodnikov said, even though, of course, he had never met the man with the feline name Zussi.

"What about Veronica Frondike?" Planshchin asked, narrowing his eyes.

"Yes," Ogorodnikov said, even though he had never heard anything that sounded like it.

"What about Mikhail Markovich Gribovich?"

"Certainly met him." Ogo had pulled away from the wall at last, turned, and seemed to hang over the general. "Am I to take this as an interrogation?"

"No, no, Maxim Petrovich!" The general spread his arms widely, as if playing an accordion. "We're concerned about your safety, or rather your reputation. Try to stay away from these people, no matter what they promise you. . . . That's just my *personal* advice. . . . Well, that's it, Maxim Petrovich, I think that's everything, oh, no, excuse me, one more thing. . . . There's a very familiar face in your *Splinters*. A Stalinist personage. By the way, that man is alive and still working for . . . for us. . . ."

"Not you?" Ogorodnikov thought that his face had turned to stone with the tension.

"No, it's not I," the general said grimly, filled with cast iron, readily displaying his real feelings for the photographer.

And with that they parted. Both felt a strange satisfaction, for grimness and controlled growling seemed more natural weather conditions for the end of the match. The general went off to analyze the illegal tapes, and Ogorodnikov with a bottle in his pocket hurried over to his pal Shuz Zherebyatnikov, and told him the whole story over drinks, with details and quotations.

"Shit," said the mighty and hip Shuz, proud that he, as opposed to the rest of the intellectual Focusers, had spent time in the camps—he did five after Stalin for trying to undermine elections to the Supreme Soviet of the Moldavian SSR. "Shit, Ogo, once it stinks of PhID, you can open all the windows and it won't go away. It's not their overseas colleagues, but the PhIDs themselves who are trying to work you over, it's bluffing and scaring you, saying we can get you on spying charges if we want. I'll bet they won't take their eyes off you for a minute and they'll keep screwing you everywhere, their manners aren't worth dried crab lice."

In Shuz's cellar, where the conversation was taking place, Ogo's brakes failed: his hands shook and his skin was covered with adrenaline slime. What am I being dragged into? Where's my photography, where are my women, didn't my life used to be pure and laconic?

Shuz seemed to be aware of what was happening to him, even though he paid little attention to the people around him, and he slapped him hard on the back and used his favorite word on him.

"Remember Solzhenitsyn's classic triad, motherfucker: 'Don't believe, don't fear, don't ask.' That holds for all the KGBs, including our PhIDs."

Ah, Shuz! An incredibly broad man with gray shoulder-length locks, a tangle of gold chains around his neck, a couple of massive rings with seals on his right fist, you could break somebody's jaw with rings like that—what a man who doesn't believe, doesn't fear, doesn't ask his whole life long. . . . Ogorodnikov cheered up—I'll be like that, too.

"There's just one thing I don't get," Shuz said. "Why didn't they ask anything about *Say Cheese!?* It can't be that they haven't gotten a whiff of it by now. All right, we'll get it, Ogo!"

They set off for Rosfoto, drank hard all evening, and left with some girls, of course. He wanted everything to be as usual, but everything was different now, and he didn't sleep well with the girls, either, that night— he was bothered by a bad thought: what if the girls were stoolies?

What lice, what rats they are, thought Ogorodnikov, how they quash the whole society, how they corrupt all and sundry . . . seventy years . . . destruction on such a scale. . . .*

6

SIX MONTHS HAD passed since the spring visit of Planshchin and Skansh- chin and in that time everything had become clear. Shuz had been right—the PhIDs' honor was worth just the price he had named. First of all, they blocked all of Ogorodnikov's trips abroad. One after the other, trips to New York (arranged by the Photographers' Union), to Berlin (arranged by Goskino, the film department), and to Paris (arranged by OVIR, the passport agency, a purely personal visit to see his children by his third ex, Nadine) fell through. The explanations were always ridiculous, no explanation at all: "Considered unsuitable," noth- ing more. The PhID was not hiding, it was making a point of its sig- nature, occasionally sticking out its little face, wrinkled in vicious craftiness.

---

*Beyond the dirty taxi windows, Moscow floated by in a murky mass. A gath- ering of faces appeared near the Cinematographers' House. He's right, thought the driver. I'm driving a good one, that's a fact. . . .

Once Ogo went to see his current legal spouse, the glaciologist Anastasia, in the university town near Mount Elbrus. They soared the whole night, yodeling with delight, and in the morning he looked out the window and saw two ridiculous idiots in matching hats. They were moving casually along the wooden sidewalk and staring up at Anastasia's windows with salacious grins.

Another time Ogo was at Sheremetyev Airport to meet the famous Alexander Spender and his wife and daughter. And, bam, what a surprise, there in the waiting room sat the modest knight of the revolution, Captain Skanshchin, having a cup of coffee. Sit down, Maxim. "What a small world, you have a cup of coffee and run into a good man. Flying abroad, are you?" The sour milk in his eyes was replaced by a cold hooliganism. "You're meeting Alexander Spender? A fine thing. This Mister Spender isn't one of your colleagues from Langley, is he, Maxim?"

Ogorodnikov's jaw quivered in disgust. "How can you work in photography, Vladimir, and not know Alexander Spender?"

To Captain Skanshchin's honor, he never took offense at criticism of his ignorance. He blushed, of course, but he drew the right conclusions. "Thank you, Maxim, for the criticism, I'll keep it in mind."

It was clear that Skanshchin had driven out to the airport only for the sake of asking Ogo about the colleagues. Shuz was right—they were working on him. Feeling, probing, pushing. . . .

Once, around Orthodox Trinity Day, while wandering around with his camera, he met a sweet, pensive, dreamy girl in the rain, she was right out of a French movie. In bed she was marvelous: no sooner would you think of something than she would be doing it. If I weren't married, I'd marry her, thought Ogo customarily, as he fell asleep. When he awoke, the girl was not next to him, vanished like Cinderella, how marvelous, what tact, as if she had known he always woke up in a shitty mood. Suddenly, under his duplex balcony, he heard whispering and rustling. He came to the edge and looked down through the railing to the lower part of the room. The girl, coat open, was leafing through his secret albums and whispering into the telephone. Ah! Seeing the moustache and dangling shaggy hair, the pince-nez dangling on a string through the railing, she gasped theatrically. Her heels clattered on the stairs. A gray Volga was waiting for her, a young man in a blazer at the wheel—if not Skanshchin, then his twin. The little spy ran over, looked up at the window, laughed brazenly, and ducked into the back seat. Another move by the knight. Bravo, Comrade General!

One time he found in his mailbox a crumpled envelope with an Artillery Day design—a soldier with a cobblestone face and a rocket like a bushy-tailed bitch. Inside was a typed text:

Kike toady Ogorodnikov! How can you call yourself a Russian photographer when you do your dirty deals with Fisher, Puker, Zlatovsky, Serebrovsky, and German? Stop your shameless dealing with kikes, or else the Homeland will punish you, you cur!

Russian Patriots

First Ogorodnikov merely choked on rage and couldn't even think. Then he dialed his phone and read the letter from his new poison-pen pals to everyone in Moscow, shouting that he was going to give it to *The New York Times* and Reuters, to let the world see how they were blackmailing him, let them write down every word, he had nothing to hide, he hated the stinking monsters, his Russia was different, it wasn't Soviet!

Hey, Ogo, they soothed him, "Don't freak out like this, there are letters like that all over the place, just flush it down the toilet. . . ."

Suddenly there came a characteristic ringing of the phone. General Planshchin's voice.

"You can be assured that the authors of this provocation will be found and punished."

On the extension, Skanshchin's voice, like a hurt calf's, added, "I'll dig out those bums from beneath the ground, Maxim, trust me! Those pieces of shit are defaming our international ideals. . . ."

Ogorodnikov asked in hostile tones, "And what did the authors of the provocation have in mind, could you tell me? Maybe New Focus? Maybe our collective album, *Say Cheese!*? How am I to interpret 'kike dealing'?"

An indefinite pause. Then Skanshchin muttered, "I don't quite . . .

what are you. . . ." A new pause. Planshchin: "It's hard to talk to you in this mode, Comrade Ogorodnikov." Dial tone. The unmentionable had been mentioned.

The unmentionable, so to speak, rather that which had been mentioned in the telephone conversation, the ill-starred little album, had moved forward a lot in the last six months and had turned into a bulky venture. Twelve copies the size of a good gravestone were made, designed in accordance with the "aesthetics of poverty" cultivated by Alexei: tied up with shoelaces and covered with matting, and looking good.

"Twelve and no more, gentlemen," explained their most experienced friend, Chavchavadze. "The Soviet Constitution lightheartedly permits freedom of the press on our territory, but just imagine the swinishness that would occur if the citizens followed their lighthearted constitution. The citizens, however, know that preparing texts or photo albums in more than a dozen copies is punishable by law as an illegal action comparable to brewing moonshine. The Procurator's Office of the USSR has an internal memo to that effect."

The gathered members applauded. The first uncensored publication of Soviet photographs, with a printing of twelve copies. And we don't *need* more than twelve! Willy-nilly, it will be a milestone in history. And that's what we'll say, all blue-eyed and cute: Here's our first edition, if you like it, publish it, if you don't we'll survive.

Shuz was "showing the fuck off," to use one of his own expressions. "It's not to be ruled out, boys, that the goats will take our *Cheese!* for publication. What else can they do, but take it and try to mess it up? Why are the PhIDs just following us around? Why haven't they worked us over from the start and blown up our whole book? They're in a real shitty situation with us. Of course, it would be a snap for them to get rid of me, but they could get burned with Ogorod, and what could they possibly do to Chavchavadze, forgive me, signore, with his iconostasis of war medals? That would be an unbearable stink."

Naturally, the entire company was abusing alcoholic drinks and with each bottle moved further away from tactical considerations and closer to what Alexei termed "instinctual boorishness."

"Are we supposed to do battle with the PhIDs?" they asked one another. "A base idea, isn't it? Let the writers battle their agents, because they make everything up, distorting our wonderful reality, and what is wanted from them is either more or less invention. But *we*, gentlemen, we don't make up anything, right? Our job is to click, right? You see something worthy of being seen, you see it in a certain light with corresponding shadows, you tell it, 'Hold it, watch the birdie, skazhi kishmish, say cheese,' and—click! If PhID wants photography to change its direction, all they have to do is to change reality, right? And as for our intimate relationship with emulsions—that, really, is no one's business.... Better they should keep their eyes on their classic photographers, who are always jerking their thumbs in the developer to combine realism with impressionism, that is, shitting up nature...."

All the ideas in Okhotnikov's illegally inhabited apartment in the coop Soviet Cadre were expressed loudly, with a marked disdain for the eavesdroppers of PhID, except for one—their scheme for getting *Cheese!* over the hill. While indulging faint hopes in the common sense of the "goats," they all had the basic alternative in mind—publishing the album in Paris, Milan, or New York. It wasn't said, but it was assumed, that Ogo would take care of it all. Who else but Ogo with his connections beyond the curtain, with his languages? And really, Max could make himself understood in all the basic European languages. Ogo's father, who had been Lenin's comrade-in-arms in the pastry shops of Zurich, taught his heirs languages in order to promote world revolution. The father's plans worked out in October's case, but as for Max, alas, the advance of history was halted, and a better use could be found for his knowledge. With this consideration in his mind and with touching anxiety for his Czech comrades, Ogorodnikov senior went off to another world, not having lived to see another glorious page in the history of his party or the shameful page in the life of his younger son.

The shameful page was unfolding fully. With customary depression, Ogo looked out of his window almost every morning at the gray Volga and the two creeps in it, who were always pretending to read newspapers. Now, as he approached Arbat Square and the Prague Restaurant, he thought that, basically, this was the first time in a long while that he was rid of his tail. He was suddenly overwhelmed by an inadequate and wild joy, as if in Moscow the absence of a tail presented a man with great possibilities for adventure.

"Stop by the Prague, pal?" he asked the driver, and as he got out of the taxi he winked at the gloomy fellow. "That's how things are, pal."

"I agree one hundred percent," the driver said. "The whole rotten mob."*

---

*And so our hero's taxi ride, which began near the River station and was necessary in order to inform the reader of background events and also to get Ogo away from the surveillance, ends on the Arbat, near the restaurant Prague, for it is no longer necessary for either aim.

Of course, we could have ended the whole photography story here and as an existential experiment subordinated only to one logic—the logic of chaos—followed the taxi driver to his garage, spiteful with the authorities.... But alas, our professionalism will not let us, reminding us of the necessity to continue spinning the plot, having as our primary goal in writing adventure novels to begin and to end.

I admit that in my émigré separation from my native tongue it would be nifty to recall a key phrase from my former life—"All work is beginning and ending!"

FRIENDSHIP

I

GORODNIKOV FOUND HIMSELF in the bustling crowd near the Prague Restaurant. Steam poured out of all the doors of the model establishment of the Department of People's Nourishment and people ran in; it was a generous evening and something good was being offered inside. Max Ogo at his marvelous age of forty-two stood on a street corner and relished his unnoticeability. No one paid any attention to him—what bliss! Behind his back in a niche stood an enormous cast-iron vase of the late Stalin period. Its presence in Arbat Square had warmed his heart back in his youth, too—he had always felt that in case of anything (what? what?), he would be able to catch his breath in that vase, have a smoke—and even now at his marvelous forty-two there was pleasure in the sensation of having that cast-iron refuge against his back.

Streetlamps hung over the square here and there, drizzle visible beneath them, and once his eyes had adjusted, he could make out on the far side of the square the crenellated towers of the former palace of the art patron Mamontov, now the House of Friendship with the people of foreign lands, inside of which was located the corresponding institution regulating friendship between inside people and outer peoples, the Committee of Friendship Societies. Ogo looked at the towers for a while, he couldn't take his eye from them. The meaningless landscape suddenly gave rise to the stirrings of a vague idea.

Berlin! Without another thought he plunged into the underground passage, shoving aside his weary fellow citizens, ran under the square, surfaced, pulled on the carved doors, and burst into the palace. As he removed his raincoat in the coat room, he caught his breath. *Berlin,* whispered Chekhov's ghost all over Moscow, *Berlin, Berlin, West Berlin....*

A year or so ago Ogorodnikov had run into an old billiards buddy, Nikita Burenin, a consultant on friendship with the populace of both Germanies and of West Berlin. "Lissen, Ogo, want me ttto ppput you in nnnext year's pppplan? Ssssome shitty ccconference of somme ffffucking Ernst Thälmann assssociation of pppproletarian art with young Ssssocial Christians for a Europe without bbborders.... In other words, want to drop by West Berlin?" Wan and lean, corduroyishly brown, Nikita was relaxed to a disgusting degree that evening and hiccuped beyond his usual measure, which meant that he'd had over a half-liter. Ogorodnikov, naturally, was in a rush, agreed, and forgot all about it, and only today—like a trumpet's blare—remembered, and wondered: What if?

The angels of patronage had long flown the coop of Mamontov's palace, and here reigned the vaguely grinning demon of friendship with pretensions to eternal occupancy. From the doors along the corridor came now the rattle of typewriters and the mumble of telephone voices.

The passport clerk of the foreign travel department, Ludmila, sat with her back to the door and, as usual, was wheeling an important personal deal on the phone.

"Wait, yesterday you said lilac and now you're saying beige?... Well, well ... what do you think? Powder blue?... The FRG?... What about Yugoslavia?... Japan?... No problem.... What about the beige?"

Since last year, Ludmila's rear end had grown even rounder. In the corner, drying by the radiator, was a pair of black "stocking" boots, which, when pulled on, turned Ludmila's legs into those of a grand piano. At the present moment the lady was wearing fuzzy slippers, also imported. Even in this establishment, where flies died of boredom in midflight, Ludmila was renowned for her laziness and sluggishness. In the past, Ogo had accelerated her movements and, consequently, the receipt of his foreign-travel passport, with the aid of imported cosmetics, or imported purses, and once even brought her a pair of imported shoes, which had not fit his fourth wife, Comrade M. Vasilyeva. Ludmila took a childish delight in such "souvenirs" and in fact did give accelerating commands to her rear, enmired in Moscow's mercantile morass.

In general, this lady exuded fragrance like a merchant wife painted by some *Mir Isskustva* artist and was espoused to a respectable KGB orphan.

Ogo interrupted the knitwear discussion with a kiss to the fresh lobe of her right ear. The erotic charge jumped straight to her blossoming bowels, and the passport clerk quivered.

"Ah! My dear, I'll call you back. Ah! Maxim, how could you? A respectable comrade, and how do you behave yourself?"

Beneath mohair heaved the hills of Valdai, heights in the heart of Russian Federation. Plucked eyebrows arched and piggy eyes glowed. The visitor held in the palm of his hand a heavy, alligator-skin butane lighter.

"Ronson!"

"The very same. A belated present for your husband for Constitution Day!"

Two fingers lifted the lighter from his palm as if it were a rare insect.

"Now, that's a brand! Now they know their stuff! Now won't my Uri be pleased!"

Ogo sat down next to her.

"You know, Ludmila, I spent so much time traveling abroad this year, I almost forgot about our Berlin, Ludmila. . . ."

The passport clerk gasped. "Didn't Nikita call you? That's so slipshod. But what else can you expect from that Burenin?"

She dug into a file, rustled about, then another, rustled, then—ye gods of Olympus!—tore herself away from her seat, and opened a drawer in a secret cabinet. What do we have here on that conference?

"But is the passport ready?" Ogo asked casually, his guts frozen in fear.

"The passport?" Ludmila fixed her heavy gaze on Ogo, then turned to another cabinet marked alphabetically, and cried out joyously upon discovering her quarry in the O-P-R section.

"Here's your little passportie! It's been ready since April."

Here she grew a bit flustered for giving away a state secret, compressed her lips, as if to say she hadn't told him because she wasn't supposed to, but then, in apparent recollection of the Ronson, gave him a friendly wink.

"You know how we like to drive people crazy. Here, sign the receipt."

The astonished Ogo was holding his foreign-travel passport, received under the auspices of the House of Friendship. The Cinema Committee and the Photographers' Union also had separate passports for him. Before every trip, the appropriate institution gave him his passport, to take it back later and pass it on to the corresponding depths of the secret giant of the USSR.

"What date do you want the ticket for?"

The tension had taken its toll, and he muttered something inane—ticket? Just go ahead and order it, just like that ... ?

Ludmila did not notice anything suspicious. As if he were one of their own, she said, "In general, that conference in West Berlin is a shambles. Burenin is letting the whole thing run itself. You know, the Komsomol sent two hicks from Siberia, I don't know what they use for brains over there.... You know, Maxim, I'll get you an individual ticket. You'll fly alone. So, what date do you want?"

"Tomorrow," Ogo said, but stopped and forced himself to relax. "I guess the day after tomorrow...."

"Day after tomorrow then," sang Ludmila, opened a ledger, then thought a bit and reached for the phone. Ogo wiped his brow.

"Oh, dearie me, we don't have an Aeroflot flight the day after tomorrow. Shall we go on Thursday then?"

"Okay. I'll drop by tomorrow to pick it up."

"Oh, you're rushing me, you're rushing me...."

"I'll drop by tomorrow and bring you an early present for March eighth. Will Madame Rochas suit you?"

Ludmila glowed. "Wonderful then! I'll go for your ticket first thing in the morning!" And then, in the best tradition, she lowered her eyes. "Your moustache tickles, Maxim dear, really, what a moustache...."

"A dangerous woman," Ogo muttered languidly, apparently leaving the subject open.

Still stunned, so hyped his ears were ringing, he dashed out onto Kalinin Prospect. A fine, scummy rain drizzled on his head, there was nothing around but the usual November (that is, the Great October) general scumminess, but beyond the distant spire of the Ukraine Hotel, Mother Europe loosed a setting sunray. Could the comrades have made such a gross error? Could they have shut off all exits and forgotten the House of Friendship? Would he really slip out?

First of all, not a word to anyone. He must appear in public immediately, so that his tails wouldn't worry or look for him. He rushed over to Rosfoto, the Photographers' Club, and spent the rest of the evening table-hopping, hanging around the bar, telling Brezhnev jokes to inveterate stoolies, and then picked up a girl—everyone's fingerprints all over her, the well-known plant Violetta. That night in his creative lab on Khlebny Alley, he swore his love to Violetta, promised to divorce his wife, Anastasia, who was beautiful but as cold as a glacier and was living amid glaciers and could go look for the Yeti there.

Violetta kept giving him astonished looks—didn't he know who she was?—but nevertheless struck dreamy poses when he illuminated her with his lamps and clicked from various angles. A seditious thought passed over her hair and face from time to time, like the wind—maybe she should break off with the Glands?

In the morning he drove her to the Central Market and bought an enormous bouquet of roses at three-fifty apiece. The jerk could have bought me a pair of boots for that amount, thought cynical Violetta, but she was impressed nevertheless—what a fragrance of the Caucasus!

He had not noticed any surveillance that day, but still, after bidding the stoolie good-bye, he hurried to the House of Friendship by means of a few distracting maneuvers: he left his car in the TASS parking lot, went to the box office of the revival movie house, then to the House of Culture for Medical Workers, then to the Mayakovsky Theater, then to the secondhand store, then to the dormitory of the Institute of Theater Arts, and from there via the service entrance out into the empty alley.

Amazingly, everything at Friendship was ready: his ticket to Berlin, the paperwork for his business, the pathetic hard-currency allowance—everything that a Soviet "cultural worker" needs for a trip.

Nikita Burenin was waiting for him in his tiny room next to the office of the voluptuous passport clerk. His long legs in corduroy and soft moccasins stretched from wall to wall.

The bachelor Nika, eternally boyish, resembled Ogorodnikov in that they both belonged to the rare type of tall, thin, and long-faced Russians. He spoke all the German dialects and in principle could have had pretensions to a good career, say in the diplomatic corps, but year by year, and even decade by decade, he sat in his cubbyhole as consultant to the Committee of Friendship Societies on friendship with German-speaking peoples, at 180 rubles a month.

Getting drunk sometimes (though no more than once a month) in some creative club, Nikita would tell his drinking buddies, "In my past there is something shameful, something so vile, that it makes me sick to look in the mirror." Bleary-eyed, with a crooked smile, he said this with such a strange tone that one might think he was bragging. His companions never exhibited any curiosity about Nikita Burenin's shameful secret, come on, all right, as if the whole concept of "the past" was incompatible with the corduroy man.

While the only person close to him, his intelligent mother, was still alive, Nikita was allowed abroad—to the GDR and to Berlin, and once or twice to his beloved Federal Republic—but after her demise all the trips stopped. "They explained to me that they cccouldn't let me out without an anchor. I really don't have any ancccccchors."

Ogorodnikov sympathized and liked Burenin and it was certainly mutual. And now they were liking each other, sitting in the small room, long legs extended. Burenin explained the manner of traveling to West Berlin. You arrive at GDR's Schönefeld Airport and there you will be met by the luminous persons from our consulate in West Berlin. . . .

"Can't I manage without them?" Ogorodnikov asked lazily.

"Easy, Max. You won't be let through the Wall by the Eastern guards

without them. That's the rule, old man, for our delegations. I've called
the consulate, everything's okay, Max. You'll be met by this Zafalontsev, incidentally, not a total jerk, he knows your pictures. He'll take
you through Checkpoint Charlie, and turn you over to the idiotic West
Berlin proletarians, who will take you to some lousy hotel in Charlot-
tenburg. . . ." Burenin's smile seemed pathetic to Ogorodnikov, and suddenly in the pose of the relaxed, ever-young man there appeared a sense
of doom. Burenin's eyes slid helplessly from Max's face to the corduroy
corridors of his own trousers.

I hope he doesn't think I'm going to defect in West Berlin?

I hope he doesn't think I think he's going to defect in West Berlin,
thought the consultant with understandable despair and understood
shame. Has he figured out that I've figured out that his trip is just a
mistake made by the corresponding organs? Does he know that I know
what a fucking situation he's in?

"How is your 'just fine' doing, Nikita?" Ogorodnikov asked.
"Obtained any anchors?"

"What for, Max? What do I need with anchors now? I'll be half a
century soon. I'm a good five years older than you. . . . What do I need
with anchors? So I can go to Germany? To Austria? Want to know
the truth? I'm as sick of Germany and Austria as I am . . ." He snorted
and without looking in his eyes, slapped Ogorodnikov on the knee.
"Quatsch und scheisse. See you, Max."

They said good-bye.

The next day Ogo spent all his time with his new "bride," the pretty
stoolie Violetta. Where did this passion come from? wondered the ret-
icent and modest young woman. He explained it to her in the classic
words: "That day I went through you from comb to feet, like a provincial tragedian with a Shakespeare drama. . . . Understand?"

"I think I do," she whispered, turning away.

At the end of the day he even brought her to the Cheesers, that is,
to Alexei's apartment. Fortunately, not that many people had piled in
that night—Fisher, Vasya Shturmin, Andrei Drevesny, pale and aloof in
another fit of grandeur, and Probkin. . . . The last-named stared in astonishment at the love-engrossed Ogo and Violetta, and whispered to his

friends; "What's the matter with our chief, why'd he bring her here? Everyone in Moscow knows that worker like a peeled egg, I've chipped at her shell myself. . . ."

Ogo, to the accompaniment of vodka and horrible pelmeni with onions, told the girl without any embarrassment about *Say Cheese!* Then he told his friends that they had a very important thing to discuss and no later than tomorrow. Violetta leaned back on the couch, shutting her eyes, making it clear that these important matters did not interest her in the least, while Ogo asked Alexei to get as many people together at a time when he was planning to be in the Western sector.

Then the lovebirds left the Cheesers and went off to visit their old friend, the closet liberal with a round eye. The short way turned out to be long, because they stopped at least a dozen times for prolonged kisses, and then from the deep pocket of his British raincoat Ogo pulled out a bottle of champagne, noisily uncorked and emptied by the "play trumpeter" method along with loud declarations of love. Captain Slyazgin gnashed his teeth in the van.

They burst in on the liberal. "We're high! Open up your iconostasis!" The liberal was stunned—open his iconostasis, colorful collection of imported liquors?

"Please, this is simply an exposition, nothing other than pop art!"

"Open it up, you son of a bitch, are you my friend or a jockstrap, I'll make it up to you, let's drink to love!"

While the liberal, grunting, selected the cheapest bottle in there, some Yugoslavian vermouth, Ogo and Violetta spun in a dance on the Bulgarian carpet, shoes flung aside, past the desk where an article on the work of Alexander Spender had been interrupted at the phrase "The tragic fracture of the times affected the creativity of this contradictory master." Turning with the bottle, the liberal did not find anyone in the room. But he heard the noisy, delighted panting of the two so overly familiar bodies in the bathroom.

Parting from Violetta at one in the morning, Ogo went to the Central Post Office. Shuz was waiting on the steps. A strange figure. The gray artistic mane fell on the shoulders of a heavyweight boxer, and a thief's eight-pointed cap was pulled over his eyes. They went into the calls room, which despite the late hour was filled with Georgians and Armenians.

"Shuz, don't faint. Tomorrow I may be over the hill."

Shuz, whose name was created in the thirties by his enthusiastic parents from the acronym for the inscrutable School-University-Zenith, did not faint.

"For good?" Upon learning that it wasn't for good, he simply nodded, but it was clear that he was pleased.

"Shuz, I'm off on official business, in principle I should go through customs without a problem. Should I risk bringing out *Cheese!?*" He gave his friend a brief account of how everything had happened and was happening. "It looks as if I'm on a lucky streak and the PhIDs are looking the other way. Of course, walking through the cordon with the album under my arm may be a risky game, but on the other hand, I may not have another chance."

The expensive leather coat added to Shuz's monumentality. He stood in silence for a moment, reminiscent of some classic Soviet art work, and then asked a question that had nothing to do with the case. "Pal, did you let Anastasia know you're splitting?"

Ogo gasped—he'd forgotten his legal wife!

She spent months on her mountain expeditions, and naturally her spouse forgot about her. What can you do, people of the mountains and the plains are far apart, alas. When you look down from Mount Elbrus on a clear day you're horrified by the pollution even in the nearest valleys, and you can forget about the vileness of cities. Anastasia had been in the academic settlement in Azau Valley for two months now, and our hero had forgotten about the existence of his sixth legal wife, no, wait, his seventh if you counted Viktoria. He was ashamed, but maybe at the moment for the sake of the conspiracy, it was better not to bring her up. Shuz, however, had a different approach. He had friends all over Moscow and the post office was no exception. Bypassing the Georgian-Armenian line, he whispered to an operator and five minutes later called to Ogo.

"Go to booth eleven!"

"Anastasia," said Ogo, "this is the gypsy calling. We're leaving for

the western slope of the Pamir Range tomorrow, and I wanted to dou-
ble-check the date of the symposium."

She has to get it, he thought. First of all, I'm calling her Anastasia
and not Nastya, and then she has to remember "gypsy."

"Now you're calling it a symposium?" she said with that familiar
voice that always made him horny. He pictured her in the dark hallway
by the telephone, a window behind her with every crevasse of Elbrus
visible in the moonlight. Why didn't he drop this crazy game with the
PhIDs and fly there?

"As if you didn't know the dates of the symposium yourself, you
treacherous gypsy." Anastasia laughed. "I hope you'll call from Pamir?"

He gasped with delight—she figured it out immediately, what a
woman! I thank the Almighty for a gift like her and repent, repent,
repent my filthy, profligate life.

As he hung up, he saw that Shuz was aiming his camera at him from
five or six meters away. They went outside. The night air had grown
colder and more dry, and held the scent of coming snow.

"Well, how did she react?"

"Listen, I thought we'd agreed more than once not to take each other's pictures," Ogo said with evident annoyance.

"I wasn't taking pictures, I was just looking. You had a wild face
and pose, like, like. . . . Okay, Ogo, let's talk business. It's too risky to
take the album. When you figure things out, give us a sign from over
the hill and we'll try to do something from this end. Okay?"

In the morning, as soon as he opened his eyes, Ogo called Violetta
at her job in the service bureau of the Architects' Union of the USSR.
He made a lunch date with her at Dom Kino, the filmmakers' club.

At about that time General Planshchin came into the office where
the operatives were working. His favorite worker, the gifted Captain
Skanshchin, as always, was very emotional in his work. At the moment
he was looking through the latest reports on his case, the case of M. P.
Ogorodnikov, shaking his head, and giggling.

"What an optimist that Ogorod is . . . a real optimist, Comrade General. . . . Violetta called in, too, to finalize details. . . . Say what you will, he's a real optimist. . . ."

General Planshchin, his face heavy once again, held the pile of reports in his hands. Didn't that Ogorod realize where all this was leading?

2

EVERYTHING WAS AS smooth as grease. Ogo drove up to the Architects' Union fifteen minutes before schedule and saw his *kurator* Captain Skanshchin pulling away in a Zhiguli from the driveway and down to the end of the alley under the NO THOROUGHFARE sign.

It was a sunny day with a nip in the air. The ice crust on the puddles cracked under Violetta's approaching steps. The face of the thick-haired, buxom worker revealed miscellaneous human emotions, welcome and hope.

At Dom Kino, naturally, there were tons of friends. Casual Kichko-kov swept past their table and whispered, "Max, don't you know who she is?"

"Sit down, Kichkokov," Ogo invited the man, whose reputation also left something to be desired. "Violetta and I would be happy if you'd lunch with us."

Kichkokov didn't make them beg. Not believing his fortune, he watched them set the table with caviar and smoked fish, champagne, cognac, and shish kebab at three times the price. He didn't understand why the haughty Ogo had suddenly invited him, but then, as he watched the magical caresses of hands and legs under the table, he guessed—love needs a witness.

At the appropriate moment Ogo hurried off to take a leak, and from the bathroom ran out the back way to the street, dove into his Volga, drove off, left his car near the Tishinsky Market, and hailed a "lefty" cab. A half-hour later he was at Sheremetyev International Airport.

The customs agent he got had a law school pin in his lapel.

"We haven't seen any of your work in print lately," he said.

"Well, you understand the times we're in, zastoj,"* Ogo said, as if

---

* *Zastoj* (stagnation) is a word frequently used today, in the era of *glasnost*. Max Ogo, one of the earliest birds of the new times, tossed this word around when it wasn't so popular.

talking to one of his own people, and apparently this flattered the customs man, who did not touch the attaché case or the camera bags. With a customs man like this, Ogo could have brought out several copies of *Say Cheese!* But who could plan on an intelligent, human being?

The airport was almost empty: after the Afghanistan events détente was beginning to stink, and tourists, that is, contemporary humanity, began to see the ferocious jaws of the silly matryoshka doll. Ogo strode briskly through the empty room to the border control—then suddenly felt someone looking at him, and tripped.

So, it didn't work. Turned out, miracles didn't happen. The important thing now was not to lose face. I won't let them mock me, he told himself. He took out a cigarette and slowly, without lighting it, turned around, and saw beyond the glass wall a solitary woman, whom he recognized easily as his legal wife, Anastasia.

She didn't move. He didn't come closer. No doubt about it—last night she called Shuz and found out when and where I was flying. Apparently she decided that I won't come back from Western Pamir, hurried to catch a flight at Mineralnye Vody to see me at least from afar one last time. Ah, the incorrigible romanticism of Russian coeds!

This formulation helped him overcome the sentimental desire to rush back to his beloved at the last moment, like in the movies, and be trapped by the wolfhounds chasing him. With this formulation he approached the sacred border of the socialist homeland, and while the round-faced dolt with a Komsomol button examined his passport, he glanced at the lone figure and repeated, "Incorrigible romanticism of Russian coeds." He met the attentive gaze of the Komsomol blockhead border guard without tension and almost distractedly.

The guard pushed a pedal in his booth, the turnstile opened, and Ogo was outside the borders of his homeland, even though that didn't at all mean that he was free. Those animals could get him back even from the international zone or lock him into the toilet on board a plane, he knew, as they recently did with the delicate ballerina V., and they could grab him in a snap in a "fraternal republic." Still, his heart fluttered when he crossed the turnstile, his soul felt an upheaval in crossing as the grim bolshevism of the soul was overbalanced by its airy liberalism. Despite his international experience and his anti-Party feelings, Ogorodnikov remained a Soviet man, albeit an ideologically handicapped one.

Where were the Russian coeds with this incorrigible romanticism? The glass partitions led him farther away. Anastasia could have ruined the whole thing.... "People come back sometimes from prisons, from beyond the border never...." Enough of Anastasia.

He went into the bar for a glass of cognac. Then he went to the pay phone, called the cinematographers' restaurant and asked for the waitress. "Rita," he said, "it's Ogo. Shuz will be there in an hour to pay my bill. Got it? Kisses." He went back to the bar and got another cognac, using a foreign accent when he asked for a hundred and fifty grams. His mood was swiftly improving. In the mirror he saw an international art photographer. If they came over and asked him *to come with them,* he would raise a stink. Let the secret be made known! We demand the immediate separation of art from state! Glory be to the nonobsolete romanticism of Russian coeds! *Bitteschön,* another hundred and fifty!

At that moment a hand came down on his shoulder.

So, it had happened. Courage, I call on you! First, finish the cognac. They don't serve it in prison. Then—shake off the vile paw.

"What's the matter, old man?"

"Oh, it's you! I thought it was someone else!"

"Are you hung over or something?"

"You got it."

"Where are you off to?"

"Ethiopia."

"Good for you, Max! Now's just the time to be in Ethiopia."

"And where are you bound?"

"Brussels. To cover the NATO Council session. I think October's going to be there, too."

"Give him my best. Tell him his little brother is off to Ethiopia."

"Good for you, Max. It's very important to be in Ethiopia now."

"I know, sweetie. That's why I'm going."

"See you."

Ogorodnikov thoughtfully watched the fat-assed political commentator walk away. What an amazing phenomenon of our times: a man appears on TV with his thin European face and no one in the audience suspects that he has this opulent Central-Asiatic ass.

A half hour later they called his flight, and Ogo, pretty well stewed by then, collapsed in his seat, only to awaken in the soft dusk of occupied Central Europe: Schönefeld Airport, German Democratic Republic, bastion of progressive humanity.

BERLIN

I

IRST THOUGHT: *even here* it's better than at home. Second thought: here it's even worse than at home.

The border guards had Nazi mugs, Marx's portrait implied a field day for fleas, the coat-of-arms insignia of the compass and T-square looked like instruments of torture.

"Ihre Papiere, ihre Papiere . . ."

Three mouse-gray guys were searching the huge backpacks of English boys and girls on their way from China. The Soviet photographer got only cold respect, a two-finger salute.

Behind the control line Ogorodnikov saw a familiar scarecrow in Peruvian poncho with a pipe between his teeth: Oh yeah, my Berlin colleague Wolf Slippenbach. They had studied together a long time ago at the cinematography department at the Gorky Institute.

Usually Wolf stayed in his studio on Chausseestrasse, photographing flowers. His endless series of flowers "had something," as they say. He called them *Wolfenblumen,* "Wolf Flowers." The Party men had once asked him what the ideological meaning was of Wolf Flowers. "They are simply Blumen, and I am simply Wolf," he said.

Where was old Slipp off to? "To Yugoslavia, to a resort."

"Congratulations," said Ogo. "You'll finally be able to slip off to the West from there."

"I've changed my mind, Max," Slippenbach said. "I'll never slip off to the West. There are too many communists there."

Ogo saw himself and Slipp reflected in a glass wall. We look ugly together, he realized. Tolerable taken singly, but together we're real anti-socialist elements.

"Look at those two gorillas, Max," said Slippenbach. "I think they're waiting for you. When I walked past I heard your name."

Two bruisers in their late thirties with matching umbrellas were staring in confusion at the passengers from the Moscow flight. Their uptight demeanor was evidence of their Sovietness. Here was something strange: you'd think that having enslaved half of Europe, they'd look at all those peoples with a conqueror's gaze—but no. A Soviet in a social-ist camp is the most benighted, most contorted-looking person, as if squeezing a hernia between his legs.

Ogo looked at the two of them. Probably one was that Zafalontsev from the consulate, the one he'd heard about from Burenin in the pass-port office. What if the PhIDs have caught on and sent their gorillas after me? he wondered. Why haven't they approached me? My appear-ance doesn't coincide with what they imagined? The PhIDs must know what a criminal looks like. Why don't these two confused souls go to Information and have the cultural figure paged? They were whispering—"He probably didn't come ... he isn't here ..."—but they didn't go to get help. Were they too shy? Didn't speak the language?

Strange diplomats nowadays. But there was no other way through the Wall. Ogo tipped his hat. "Pardon, comrades, are you waiting for me? Maxim Ogorodnikov, at your service."

Just as he had thought: Comrades Zafalontsev and Lyankin, from the consulate. "We certainly hadn't imagined, dear Maxim Petrovich, that we would identify you, a member of the Board of the PhU USSR, born 1937, laureate of the State Prize, in this guise. We thought you were part of the crowd. We were confused by your moustache. All's well that ends well. In short, welcome to Berlin! Is this comrade with you? He's not. All the better. All right. The car is outside."

2

ON THE WEST side you could go up to the Wall and piss on it, you could smear it with any political slogan or dirty words you wanted, but in front of the East side of the Berlin Wall were empty houses, antitank obstacles sticking out of the cobblestones, huts for the communist guards, barriers. Beyond was Checkpoint Charlie. A GDR border guard, with an inscrutable mien that could be taken as mechanical subordination or hidden hostility, saluted the Soviet flag on the diplomatic Mercedes. The British soldiers on the other side seemed to be playing cards and paid no attention to the car passing from the East.

Inside the Mercedes, officially Soviet "territory," Comrade Zafalontsev changed radically. The shyness and awkwardness were gone. Sprawled on the front seat, turned back toward his guest, he spoke with professional semiweariness, with the mockery and semicynicism characteristic of Soviet Talleyrands toward the land of their accreditation.

Maxim Ogorodnikov looked at the Western billboards flashing past and listened to Zafalontsev's instructions, struggling against disgust. He tried to keep his expression inscrutable, but his cheek twitched, and he hiccuped, and Counselor Lyankin raised his thin Chinese eyebrows and sniffed the cognac on Ogo's breath.

" . . . The people from the United Front of Socialists in the Arts along with the Baptist Academy reserved a room for you in the Regatta Hotel, incidentally quite a nice one. Tomorrow one Tom Gretzke will come to see you. Be careful with Gretzke, he works with us, but his philosophy is anarchic, he's a slippery comrade. We'll get in touch with you at ten A.M. Okay? Your stay is for three days but I think we'll be able to throw in an extra day or two. And we might be able to let you load up at the embassy store. I'll arrange these things higher up. Okay? Well, here's West Berlin before you, Maxim Petrovich. Your first time here? Hm, the city's changed, it's drab compared to the days of the cold war. The economy's drying up, the cultural life is dwindling. . . . Well, in general, let them dry up and die, it's not for us to feel sorry for them."

And he winked like a thief. "Right? The decline of this city is in our own interests, right?"

Zafalontsev waited with interest for the guest's response to this test, watching his face closely.

I'm not going to grovel with this character, thought Ogo. I have to let him know he's got my rank wrong. Don't they realize who's in their car? Go to the stable and order a whip for yourselves, boys.

"I don't understand you," Ogo said.

"What do you mean, you don't understand?" Zafalontsev puffed his lips, as if speaking to a child. "What do we in the socialist camp need with West Berlin? That's the whole idea, what could be simpler ..."

"But I don't understand you," Ogorodnikov said very clearly, and there was distant thunder in his voice, and his Gorkian moustache, that trademark of socialist realism, was bristling.

The astonished Zafalontsev twisted his neck, leaning over the front seat with his pouting lips and bulging eyes. This test was his personal invention, and he had always used it successfully on visiting comrades, but he had never had such a mysterious reaction. It was like being hit over the head with a bag of chalk, and in the presence of Lyankin and the ever-alert driver. Zafalontsev muttered distractedly. "I was just following the logic of my thoughts, Maxim Petrovich ... what's bad for the capitalists is good for us communists ... right? ... What's healthy for the Russian is death for the German ... you know?"

Ogorodnikov spoke with open menace now, as if banging a leather shoe on each word: "I ... DO ... NOT ... UNDERSTAND ... YOU."

Frozen amazement on the Chinese face of Counselor Lyankin. The chauffeur made an approving roll of his shoulders in Ogorodnikov's direction.

Zafalontsev finally got it. I must be addressing him improperly by rank. The visiting laureate clearly indicates subordination. A complex case.

Having come to this conclusion, Comrade Zafalontsev immediately changed his manner. "Here's your hotel, Maxim Petrovich. Room with a bath, we checked. You know, don't bother too much with this revolutionary mob, Maxim Petrovich, or they'll wear you out with all their discussions...."

"Thanks for the lift," Ogo said drily, shook hands all around, and left the car.

He went into his room, tossed his hat in one corner, his bag in the other, jumped up, and grabbed for the ceiling—the West! His raincoat flew to the floor, amd Maxim, like a diver, made for the bed—to the telephone. The telephone! The iron curtain parted with a light creak, like a bamboo curtain in a bordello, and the yellow phone book invited him into the open world—Paris, Milan, New York, London, Tokyo.... Autumn, island of freedom....

That night a sensational rumor spread through the photophilic circles of the above-mentioned world capitals, as well as through the communities of Russian émigrés—Maxim Ogorodnikov had somehow arrived in the West.

WEEKEND

I

NOISEY FISHER CAME to Alexei's apartment-headquarters and brought with him an unfamiliar young man.

"What do you want, motherfucker?" That was Alexei's greeting.

"I just came by to talk about art," said the skinny Jew to the broad-chested northerner. "Isn't that allowed? Do you have a woman here, Alexei? Is that it?"

"Come in," said Alexei, and went off to the kitchen.

In one of the illegally held apartment's two rooms a huge table stood under a bright lamp and on it, like a coffin, lay the dummy of the photo album *Say Cheese!* The rest was plunged in darkness, or so it seemed to the guests. A few minutes later, however, they saw that around the table and in the corners reigned incredible disorder: mounds of files and packages, magnifiers, a paper cutter, metal boxes, vials, bottles, jugs. . . .

With an appropriate gesture Fisher made it clear to his companion that now he was in the inner sanctum, in what might be termed the refuge of the free spirit, where the uncensored album *Say Cheese!* was being produced, and which might become . . .

"Become what, excuse me?" asked Fisher's companion, a quiet blond man of twenty-five or so.

"A landmark in the history of Soviet photography," Moisey Fisher said.

"How interesting," said the young man in an awed whisper appropriate to the occasion.

Alexei appeared with a pot of boiled potatoes, a piece of butter, and a started bottle of a disgusting Soviet "cognac-type" drink. "I don't have anything else."

For some reason Alexei felt that all guests had to be given something to chew on or to wet their whistles with. Sometimes his apartment held Parisian snobs chewing sauerkraut and swallowing incredible Soviet alcoholic garbage. "Oh, that Alexei Okhotnikov," they later said about him in Paris.

"If you'll allow me, I'll add a bit," the young blond man said with astonishing tact. "Quite by accident . . . totally unexpectedly . . . but perhaps timely. . . ." From his briefcase he extracted several packages of marvelous waxed paper, unwrapped them, and offered society about two hundred grams of smoked salmon, approximately the same amount of broad thin slices of the dying breed, Stolichnaya sausage, and a certain quantity of Swiss cheese, well known to Muscovites from fiction. To which he added a jar of Greek olives and a bottle of the Georgian wine Tsinandali, long gone from the scene.

"This is living, folks!" exclaimed Alexei.

"You said it!" Moisey Fisher said, rubbing his hands.

"Where do you get rations like this?" Alexei asked, squinting at the young man.

"You see, I have access to the buffet on the third floor of MGK CPSU,"* the guest explained calmly and modestly. "No, no, don't worry, I'm not from there, just chance relations . . . well, and sometimes I drop by and get limited amounts of this and that." He made a com-

---

*During the late seventies and early eighties, when socialism entered its officially announced "phase of maturity," all delicious items of the once-famous Russian cuisine rapidly vanished. Only places like the buffet of the MGK CPSU (Moscow Party Committee) appeared to remain adherent to gastronomic tradition.

mensurate gesture with his elongated hand, showing the gently etched destiny lines on the palm.

Alexei liked the young man's looks, with his European-Russian face and thick longish but not-too-long hair, as was fashionable then. His suit wasn't bad, fit him well, and looked like Finnish tweed. And no formality about him, either—the collar buttons undone, the ascot awry. Alexei liked, too, the young man's speech and movements; he really liked the above-mentioned hand gesture, as he did the hand itself, to tell the truth. He caught himself feeling homosexual stirrings and therefore asked with put-on gruffness, "And who might you be, young man?"

"Oh, forgive me, I haven't introduced you," Moisey Fisher said with social ease. "Olekha, this is Vadim Raskladushkin."

Alexei grunted with pleasure—he even liked the name. "May I guess you're a photographer, too? You've brought your pictures for *Cheese!?*" he asked without any gruffness now.

"You know, Alexei," Vadim replied, "of course, I'm a photographer, but you know, I wouldn't dare offer my attempts, so to speak, to be alongside such masters as you or Moisey, not to mention such giants as Slava German, Drevesny, Ogorodnikov. . . ."

Alexei liked that speech, too. They raised their glasses. Astonishingly, the lousy "cognac-type" drink seemed good brandy to all three. There arose a moment of spiritual communion.

"You see, Vadim and I were out for a walk, philosophizing," Moisey Fisher explained. "And I thought that it wouldn't hurt to introduce you folks."

"What interests me, sir, is photography per se in its relationship with the environment," Vadim said. "Now could you, on the basis of your own experience, enlighten me?"

"Oh, come on, guys!" Alexei had already scrambled up to the first level of intoxication, the one which he later, when hung over, would always call "primitive communication." "I'm like the soldier in the joke, always thinking about the bitch but to little avail. Take the national delusions of our photography. They say this nationalism doesn't exist at all, that there's a real internationale, world standards. But an American photographer asks his subject to say 'cheese,' so that the mouth opens to reveal a keyboard of teeth, thus demonstrating optimism. The Russian cameraman politely asks people to say 'raisin,' to make cupid lips, thus hiding the rot and vile tendencies in the mouth. A profound difference, folk and gentlemen!"

They had the second glass of the strong and aromatic brandy, and Alexei flew up all at once, beard and mane, to the level he called "primitive pathos."

"There is only one social commission for me—catch the fleeting moment! Wander the earth like God's nomad and click away with your own camera.... The photographic process joins us with the astral world. The photograph is the print of prana. From that point of view"—a gradual move to the step of "primitive challenge,"— "from that point of view, well, what the fuck do they keep hassling us for?"

Here Alexei took a little rest, and in the pause—once again with extreme tactfulness, indicating that if not for the pause he would never have dared interrupt—Vadim posed a question.

"Excuse me, sir, who are 'they'?"

"The PhIDs," the master of photography explained immediately, and squinted his left eye. "You wouldn't be one of them, would you?"

"God forbid," Vadim said with a smile.

"The writers have their LIDs, and that's sort of understandable," Alexei continued. "The writer is a viper who deforms reality with his vile imagination. The LIDs demand that the writers deform reality the way the Party wants, they want *soc*- rather than *sur*realism, they pressure and denounce the writers and that's completely normal, a very natural thing in our society. But what did the poor photographers ever do to the Party? After all, we merely click at reality and nothing more. Why pick on us and not on reality? If you shitheads"—here Vadim smiled gently at the unexpected crudity—"don't like your own faces, then change your own faces, not the photographers. Here, just imagine this, two years ago the Union sent me to be 'reshod,' to illustrate the work of the Komsomol conference. I brought back a series of portraits of lowlifes from the conference, and they said to me, That's anti-Soviet. I shouted, How can this be anti-Soviet if those faces are your own? Right, right, they said, and I could sense the PhIDs tuning in on me.

"Or, here's another example, Moishe went to the Far East to work at that fucking BAM railroad under construction.... He has to live, he has to feed his family, right? Remember, Moishe, how they blocked your BAM series?"

"And how!" said Fisher, and clicked his tongue.

"A Zionist perspective on the Soviet people, they said. Now, where, where can you find Zionism in there, Vadim, except for the signature on the photos? And even then Fish is fish in every language, and Moishe uses Japanese optics." Alexei took Vadim by both knees with both hands, bent over the suitcase that served as table for the feast, and stared right into the eye of his young guest. "What's more important for a picture, the optics or the eye?"

Vadim smiled. "In your discussions, as in your last question, there is a certain sneakiness," he said.

"Some!" Alexei laughed.

The phone rang, and releasing his new friend's knees, Alexei went into the corner, to one of the mountains of garbage, that is, to the site of useful things.

Well, what do you think? asked Moisey Fisher with his eyes.

A genius, replied Vadim in the same way, a sign of the times....

Alexei's caller was Ogorodnikov. "Hello, Ogo. No, they're not here yet, just Moisey Fisher with a friend. They'll start dropping by in about two hours. What time should I expect you? I shouldn't? That's not businesslike, man. The people will be disappointed, especially the foreigners, and especially, of course, women of foreign background. A joke. Come on by, maestro. You can't? Are you far? In Berlin? Big deal, take a taxi and come over. You want me to send Probkin for you? You're not at the restaurant Berlin? What are you trying to say? In the *city* of Berlin? In West Berlin? What? What? Cut!" he shouted, and dropped the phone. His bulging eyes and bristling hair created the impression of a starting fire. Of course, this unbecoming astonishment did not last more than a few seconds, after which Alexei picked up the phone and laughed joyfully, shouting incomplete sentences like "Fantastic," "End of the world," "Totally go," asking about the West Berlin "party cadres," that is, about girls. He even sang a line from Vysotsky,* "How are things in your free world?"

After he hung up, he wiped his hands on his shirtfront, leaving streaks of damp.

"Moisey, do you understand what's happened? Ogo got away to the West right under the noses of the PhIDs! He said that Shuz will explain at our general meeting. You see, Vadim, and people say that miracles are impossible in our world. Life shows us otherwise, and how could it be any other way, if humankind only lives through hope for a miracle!"

Vadim got up, thanked the host for his hospitality, and said that he did not feel right staying inside the Cheese Coop at the time of such an extraordinary sensation, which would naturally demand intensive discussion among the initiates.

Alexei liked this reaction. Seeing him off, he gave Vadim a packet of his private "Pacific Ocean" pictures, mauled his delicate shoulder and frail hand, invited him to come by often, whenever the mood to philosophize or whatever else struck him. . . . Here our northern genius grew embarrassed like a girl and grumbled in order to cover up. "But get the hell out of here, go on, you see we've no time for you now. . . ."

Vadim came out onto the steps of the Soviet Cadre Cooperative and naturally saw that there was madness akin to panic in the ambulance parked across the way.

"There's no end to these games," sighed the young man, "no end to these very strange, very strange, strange and chaotic games. . . ."

2

A FIFTY-YEAR-OLD MAN, heavyset and governmentally grim, stood by the window in his apartment, on the eighth floor of a high-quality state building known to all in the Atheist Alley of the capital. It was none

---

*Vladimir Vysotsky (1938–1980), poet, bard, balladeer, and actor, was an idol of Soviet youth. Although none of his songs had ever been recorded or printed officially, his popularity in the USSR was higher than that of Elvis Presley and Bob Dylan combined. Posthumously V. is loved and worshiped by all strata of the Soviet populace.

other than Fotii Feklovich Klezmetsov, first secretary of the Union of
Soviet Photographers of the Russian Federation. Actually, the first secretary stopped only for an instant by the window, as if creating a pause
in conversation with his important guest, but once he stopped he
seemed to stick to the window: he saw something strange beyond the
window, in his own Atheist Alley, and he couldn't figure out at first
what that strangeness was.

Atheist Alley (which got its name in the third decade of evil memory
of our century) was gloomy on that evening. A comparable crowd along
it was moving in two directions, from and to the metro station at the
Prospect of the Dove of Peace (which got its name in the fifth decade
of our century, when the sanctities of the third decade fell into question). With the crowd from the Dove of Peace came a bicyclist. This
was the strangeness—a bicyclist in the middle of winter.

None other than Vadim Raskladushkin was merrily sending his
energy through the pedals to the wheels, as if he had but one goal—to
enliven the urban landscape. The Muscovite citizen's first reaction to
any eccentric was, naturally, a bad one: "Look at them. Driving around
all over the place—can't get away from them even in winter." But with
Vadim's approach, the thoughts of the Muscovite citizen changed. Why
shouldn't a young man ride a bicycle if he feels like it, why not pedal
if the pedals work?

Such was the anti-Soviet sight of the slim cyclist with a mane of
golden hair beneath his warm cap, riding upright on a bike with high
handlebars, maneuvering among puddles and clumps of dirty snow in
the gloomy alley with the stupid name. He wore a light wool coat, a
camera on his chest; attached to the bike frame was a briefcase, inside
which one could easily picture tasty things in decently limited quantities.
A pleasant sight, really, smiling and nodding to passersby.

Even the first secretary, Fotii Feklovich Klezmetsov, allowed himself
to soften his governmental gaze and to think: Here we have a young
Russian man riding in the middle of winter on a bicycle of our Soviet
make; where else is that possible?

With this kindly Russian thought, Fotii turned to his important guest
and felt discomfited: he realized that the important guest had not taken
his attentive gaze from him throughout the pause. But the pause passed;

the guest defocused his heavy analytical gaze, smiled, and patted the armrests of the leather armchair. "So comfy! Finnish?"

The important guest, of course, had already noted how capitally everything was organized in this not fully habitable apartment: the Finnish furniture, Japanese sound system, "fraternal" (viz., Czech) crystal, and in the kitchen—well, forgive me—France reigned. No objections, in general—why not live in plenty when you've lived half a century? The host had done a lot of good, even though, it must be added, he'd had his share of mistakes.

It's silly to hide it, thought Fotii in response, there were mistakes. The Party knows that no one is insured against mistakes, even Itself.*

And so, a frozen frame: the important guest, sinking in the armchair; the host, frozen in an awkward position by the window; between them a low table with a bottle of French cognac.

---

*At this moment, my respected readers, we must employ the freeze-frame technique once more, not at all in order to show off the "cinematographic method," which, to tell the truth, has gotten rather trite in modern prose, but out of strict necessity to travel into Fotii Feklovich's past, for without that our main concern— the plot—will creak. Bring Fotii onto the page without his past, and the plot won't collapse, of course, but there will be a contortion to it, with periodic squeaks and screeches. Pseudomodernist chaos will begin spreading throughout. Who needs it? The reader wearied by ubiquitous modernism will sigh, and set aside the book to creak and screech on its own.

MISTAKES

M, YES—THE first secretary's mistakes happened not in his stormy youth, as one might have imagined, but in the prime of his young masculinity. He screwed up; there were things he failed to figure out.

It was in Fotii's youth—back at school, when the pale-haired, gawky kid from the sticks was called Fotik by everyone—it was then that he developed correctly, even though the times were complicated and "contradictory." On the one hand, the Party had put an end to the excesses of the cult of personality; that is, you didn't have to worry about unexpected firing squads. On the other hand the foundations hadn't been shaken; after sober thinking young Fotik decided that an "inoculation from execution" wouldn't hurt for the future.

This "inoculation" must be understood allegorically, of course, in an "expanded historical meaning," of course, just as a denunciatory note to the Party committee could be seen as "snitching" only by very "primitive" logic. So, if we were to follow this primitive logic, we would find that Fotik had "squealed" on the department's demonically handsome Slava German, but if we approach the question in an expanded way, we will easily see that in that small signal, not dangerous for German, there was less of a squeal than of "theoretical confusion."

It was a simple question that Fotik put to the leading theoreticians: whether S. German's juvenile musings on the competency of a one-party system were "compatible with the position of the modern Komsomol."

Everyone in the department believed that Slava had been kicked out not for his talk on the one-party system but for his *Poetry of Flesh,* that is, a series of photographs made with his classmate Polina Shtein. How the students agitated! Fotik Klezmetsov was of course among those who demanded the "immediate reinstatement" of Slava German. It was during this "struggle for justice" that Fotik was noticed by the students and the academic leaders; after he successfully defended his diploma he went out into the world with a reputation for being "not indifferent," as they used to put it then. In that quality he joined the Party in response to their call of the Twentieth Congress—if we don't join, then the "indifferent" ones will!

It was a good, amazing, fertile time, and Fotik's reputation immediately got him a job at the central *Photogazette,* a militant organ always ready to embody the "principles of advancing humanism." At staff meetings Fotik directed sharp questions at certain "musty"* members of the editorial board whose stubbornness still awaited "a better application, everyone understand what I mean, comrades."

And so—such were those amazing times—the daring Fotik was included in a delegation for strengthening photographic ties with fraternal Poland. Fotik was warned, of course, that the situation with Poland now was complex and contradictory, and that if in the process of meeting with comrades there arose any theoretical difficulties, then, without hesitation, he should report such difficulties to the highest authorities.

Fotik returned from Poland on wings: "What a battle they're having there with mustiness, boys!"

---

*"Mustiness" was a quality ascribed to the old-guard Stalinists. Euphemism is the most favorable mode to convey messages in the socialist Byzantium. Instead of calling a spade a spade, people prefer to make vague gestures or give a strong wink.

"Were there any difficulties?" asked those who had sent him.

"Some," he admitted.

"What difficulties is People's Poland encountering on the path of its development?" they asked.

Fotik recalled in written form all those basically inevitable theoretical doubts—*who* had doubts, when, where, at which clubs and editorial houses the young Poles whipped themselves into heated arguments. "The boys get carried away sometimes, switch one concept for another...."

Only a drunken bastard like Slava German would call Fotik's theoretical note a "denunciation"; only a bum like Slava would get into Fotik's desk in Fotik's absence, allegedly to put his crummy pictures, his wino mirages, into it; only an obnoxious, aggressive, and ungrateful (yeah, ungrateful!) louse could pull out from the desk a "theoretical" note and cry "Stoolie!" with the desire to punch Fotik in the name of the ideals of youth.

But nobody at *Photogazette* believed Slava German; everybody knew that he and Fotik were rivals for a girl, for Polina Shtein. And Slava German, as soon as he sobered up a few months later, reinstated a "working relationship," though not friendship, and printed his pictures in *PhG* through Fotik and got a small fee.

In a short while Fotii Feklovich had become the youngest department head at the newspaper and had acquired new friends, progressive-thinking consultants of the country's main house; in a word, he had developed "in the right direction" until one autumn evening in 1962 he wandered into the Club of Humanities Faculties to an exhibit of the young group called Photoanalysis. And here in the corridors filled with stormy youth Fotik came face to face with the above-mentioned Polina Shtein, who since graduation had managed to travel to Kamchatka and to have two children by the talented Leningrader Andrei Drevesny. Here in the crowd was Drevesny himself with a new girlfriend and the new Muscovite geniuses like Ogorodnikov and Slava German, naturally; everyone was saying that Slava had gone down the tubes, but the smokestack was still alive with an English pipe between his teeth, puffy but as handsome as ever. Also here were Moisey Fisher and some new boys with girls they had picked up—and all of them, it turned out, made up the young group Photoanalysis, daring the heights of Soviet photography, as proclaimed their gray-haired mentor Zbiga Merkis, recent cosmopolite and bourgeois formalist, now a declared Soviet classic. Outrageous masterpieces hung on display, a delighted crowd buzzed all around, and "Song About a Black Cat" came from the main room—famous bard Okudjava awakening the youth.

And here Fotik sensed that something new was coming, and that the "Komsomol cafés" with their discussions on how to "Fight mustiness!" were getting old hat. He had to make sure he wasn't left behind. Overwhelmed by an unfamiliar sensation—theoretically termed "inspiration"—Fotii Feklovich joined the new movement then and there, illuminated by Polina Shtein's eyes, which, hm, let's be direct, had not in the least been damaged by Kamchatka or by her having had Andrei Drevesny's children.

In hindsight he would say that he had chosen the wrong door and that the radicals' Olympus had not affected him in any way. Well, he slept with the beautiful Polina a few times, but she had been under the influence every time, didn't even remember in the morning what she had done or with whom, responded to his marriage proposals with scornful laughter.

And yet ... and yet ... The whirl of those days added to his "moral experience," as Fotik mused after becoming a leading Soviet theoretician on questions of the morality of photography.

At first there was nothing but affronts; his own work, alas, did not elicit delight in his comrades. Fotik never could figure it out: his arsenal of technical tricks was no worse than other people's, he had plenty of erudition, his inner world was rich, but his pictures never pleased viewers. Ashamed of himself, he nevertheless learned a secret trick—smearing the emulsion with his finger, creating inspired swirls ... but all in vain. All those comrades-in-arms, those Slava Germans and Ogorodnikovs, never took him seriously, never even criticized him, and if he ever turned to them for friendly advice, say, "Which track should I follow now?" they would stare at him in amazement—"Track, did you say, how did you put it, Fotik, *track?*"

It was hard to ride the crest of the "New Wave," but suddenly fate gave Fotik a good break. Looking through the usual garbage in back issues of *Soviet Culture* magazine, he came across a forgotten essay by rehabilitated formalist Zbiga Merkis, which contained lines like this: "We, the photographers of the Revolution, look with anxiety and excitement at the still not perfectly clear but certainly inimitable features of the young masters of the fourth generation of Soviet photography...."

That line, set in tiny print, was overlooked by the authorities, yet it had quite an explosive charge in it: a hand extending from the twenties to the sixties, reaching over the generations of Stalin's shit eaters. Earlier a line like that would have interested Fotik primarily from the theoretical point of view—shouldn't he ask the Party to explain it?—but now, spending a half hour over it scratching behind his ear (he had a favorite unhealed scab there), he saw a new meaning.

In a week's time a bomb went off in *Photogazette,* a two-column article, "The Fourth Generation of Soviet Photography!" Moscow gasped: that Fotik! He traced all the traditions, counted and named everyone by decade, leaving no one out, and came up to the present young masters, heirs of glorious traditions, the Fourth Generation! Why hadn't anyone seen it before, why had no one been able to count? Count for yourselves, if you have enough fingers on your hand!

The first generation: revolutionary avant-gardists, suprematists, constructivists—even though they worked with German technology, they brought glory to our country....

Second: the first Soviet camera was made from spare tractor parts ... the stormy development of socialist realism with certain regrettable side effects of the cult of personality ... let's not talk about the people airbrushed from prints and lit out of negatives, why dig around in wounds, the Party has condemned the guilty and the achievements were enormous, comrades....

Third: the ones who went "with Leica and notebook" and some "with machine gun," the frontline photographers of WWII ... we remember it all ... no one is forgotten, nothing is forgotten ... forward, comrades, for the homeland, for ... Stalin ... um ... just for the homeland, comrades! ...

And here's the fourth: the generation of the 1956 Twentieth Congress ... young, enriched by tradition and erudition ... space age, scientific and technical revolution ... absorbing the best, rejecting the worst. ...

Thus in one fell swoop the unsuccessful photographer and desk jockey Fotik became theoretical leader of the Fourth Generation, the most important critic and historian of photography in the late thaw period which he himself "discovered" (no one remembered Zbiga Merkis's line, not even Zbiga). Whenever any clumsy Stalinist attacked the Fourth Generation, Fotik would let loose a barrage of citations from the founders of Soviet photography, and the audience would applaud— another victory for the Fourth Generation! Even those "obnoxious vipers" whom Fotik was defending came to appreciate his efforts and accepted him as one of their own, no longer expressing surprise whenever he led the drunken Polina away from the table.

Fotik came to love his protégés, listened closely to their chatter, pored over their new works, and disapproved of only one thing—the "religious" fad. It was in those years that talk about God began, so weird in the era of scientific and technological revolution. The new geniuses were going too far from the tenets of Marxist philosophy, going on about God, spouting lofty nonsense, crying sometimes when mentioning the Face—He gave us His Face in Jesus. ... Atheism was on the wane, and had arisen "not out of education, but from an inferiority complex," you see. Photography, you see, was "God's work, and not the triumph of Progress. ..."

Polina Shtein, of course, on the crest of these ideas, was baptized and had her illegitimate children baptized, too.

Fotik preferred not to speak out on this topic, but deep in his heart he was incensed by the new fashion. He was upset by his comrades who in their "extremism" were casting a shadow of doubt on the position of the entire Fourth Generation, on the goodwill of the sector of the culture department of the CC CPSU.*

---

*Central Committee of the Communist Party of the Soviet Union. Isn't it beautiful? Isn't it almost V.S.O.P.?

Fotik was careful not to alienate the Fourth Generation, but sometimes he did pose tactful questions to Ogorodnikov and Drevesny, asking them to "define positions," so to speak.

Suddenly Fotik began noticing a dangerous eccentricity in himself. Sometimes at the table, after three or four shots of Stoly under Polina's gaze, he would bang his large fist and start "performing." Who better to talk about God than he, Fotik, whose grandfather and great-grandfather were clergymen? And who better to talk about the betrayal of the people than the nephew of a de-kulated sower? And who better to talk about the mockery of the intelligentsia than the grandson of a graduate of the Bestuzhev Courses for Women on his mother's side?

The miserable morning after a performance like that, Fotik would call all his pals: Did I overdo it last night? His insides trembled not from the lies, dear comrades, but in sensitivity to danger; his body, hung over, was a good receptor for the aura that always hung over the meetings of the Fourth Generation.

Well, as for those shitty geniuses—any one of them could shout enough blasphemy to fill a hundred strict-regime camps. Fotik was amazed by the patience of the Party and grew convinced that there was something "to it," that "someone powerful" was backing the "religious" trend, that "we're headed in the right direction, comrades."

He guessed wrong, he blew it. In 1968 Fotik let down his vigilance, didn't catch the expression on the face of a deputy in charge of the photosector of the CC CPSU. The high-ranking comrade's cheekbones were a good guage of the class struggle. During tactical maneuvers of the ruling class the cheekbones receded, and his face turned into something resembling his mother-in-law's yeast dough, with candied fruits for eyes. But when the subordinate classes grew bolder the cheekbones came aggressively forward again: We won't give up our Kremlin rations, we'll destroy humanity first! Well, in 1968, when the battle for Kremlin rations was being fought with tanks in fraternal Czechoslovakia, the deputy for the sector and his cheekbones were especially formidable. No fatherly forgiving chats with mischievous geniuses! When Fotik telephoned he was severely chided and warned not to call over trifles all the time, "these are serious times, you'd better think about defining your position. . . ."

After 1968 the Fourth Generation was stricken with a more acute marasmus, from which only drunken guffaws could be heard. Fotik ran around, sniffing the air, and finally caught the scent of folk dialect. He began joining people at the club who drawled their *o*'s, squeezed hard when shaking hands, looked you straight in the eye, and used a folksy "howdy"; suddenly roosters began crowing in Fotik's articles. What more could a Russian want than to be in his native Vologodchina, and all the more so a Russian photographer—set your tripod on a hill, eyeball it, like our forefathers taught us, in the native sun, and click away with our own Rus camera, at everything "authentic" that pleases the soul: the groves, the valleys, the hills, the kolkhozes that have stepped through a lean year to today's bounty, the delicate pale-green silky shimmer of the plowland. . . .

His eternal enemy Slava German did not miss the opportunity, of course, to embarrass Fotik at a meeting of the landscape section: "You asshole, don't you know that plowland can't shimmer? It's just dug-up dirt! You ignoramus!"

Fotik looked around for support but saw nothing but mysterious smiles on the broad faces. The guardians of domestic photographic paper had a perfectly understandable suspicion of him: yesterday's *stilyaga*, hanging out with foreigners, with aliens. . . .

An incomprehensible indifference was evinced in theoretical circles. After all, they knew (they wouldn't have forgotten) about Fotik's former intellectual curiosity, they knew about his invaluable (albeit few) questions. Of course, as an honorary member of the Fourth Generation, Fotik had been avoiding the comrades from the "theoretical circles," but for understandable reasons, for the good of the cause. Now, running into such comrades, he gave them meaningful looks and greeted them with portent, but alas, got nothing but indifference in return. They must have had a surplus of offers of theoretical services.

2

AND YET, LITTLE by little, Fotii—he had dropped the too young "ik," pushing forty now, after all—Fotii was clambering out of the "historically determined quagmire," as he called it to himself. Some article would slip through "on morality" or he'd be asked to lecture at the section on native landscape, or be invited to the zonal conferences on "Photographer—the Lens of the Party," or to be part of some ten-day delegation. . . . One such delegation became the turning point in Klez-metsov's fate.

It was beyond the Caucasus Range in humpbacked Tbilisi, a capital of ever-blessed Georgia, in the city where it sometimes seems that socialism has been softened by light breezes of eternal fertility. It was a ten-day "friendship seminar"; the huge Moscow delegation stayed at the Iveria Hotel and was headed by the outstanding photographer of social-ist realism, Matvey Grabochey.*

During the festivities Fotii watched from afar Grabochey's bald head, which for some reason turned greenish at moments of emotional excit-ment, and wondered how this comrade had managed to hold on through all the leaders from Stalin to Andropov. It wasn't just his rep-utation as a "loyal soldier" and "fiery tribunal"; no, there was more to it, a kind of . . . masonry. That was it—he was a Party Mason!

All night from all the rooms of the Iveria came the noise of toasts. Eros floated in the corridors of the fraternal arts celebration, and where Eros flies, sedition hovers. Once in the hallway Fotii bumped into some-thing almost forgotten: blue beret, blue jacket, dark shirt, girlish waist, his brief romance—Polina! Not a woman but a miracle! The Semitic and the Slavic blended into a wonder of nature: all she had to do was turn to you and you lost your class consciousness.

It turned out that Polina was in Tbilisi on a business trip, covering the conference for *Decorative Arts* magazine. She unburdened herself to him with the latest Moscow horrors: Slava German took a dive, but they brought him back to life; Andrei Drevesny and Alik Konsky had

---

*Seven-time laureate of the Stalin Prize, thrice of the State Prize, once (alas, that's the limit) of the Lenin Prize, deputy of the Supreme Soviet, member of the CC CPSU, Hero of the Soviet Union, deputy chairman of the World Council of Peace, editor in chief of the propaganda monthly *Socialism* . . . in a word, if you list all his titles, you won't even notice them running to the edge of the page.

a fight at the club, brawling like mortal enemies, and broke a lot of chairs—"What do you expect, Fotik, everyone's on edge. Andrei's doing hackwork at *Hunting and Fishing,* Ogo's stooped to designing displays at houses of culture. The KGB's really getting vicious, striking at the very best . . . what do you want, Fotik, that's the way it is. . . ."

What more did he want? She was all he wanted, even though she wouldn't acknowledge him as the father of her last two children. He stood in the hallway, amid the footsteps of the conferees and the loud toasts; he was a man growing heavier now, thick glasses on his nose, greasy folksy hair—yesterday's Fotik, tomorrow's Fotii Feklovich—and his head spun either from the endless Georgian toasts, or from the wet cloud of nostalgia that was as tormenting as *coitus interruptus.* I want her as much as before, he thought—no, *more* . . . even though so many years have passed, even though she's passed through so many hands. . . .

That evening, in the Funicular Restaurant, at a meeting with the heads of the fraternal republic, Fotii watched his Polina in the company of two Georgian Komsomol leaders and quietly grew enraged. Having put away a sufficient amount of the high-quality brandy, he began shouting something horrible about Stalin's crimes—the lies of today, the stifled socialism, stoolies everywhere—"I hate communism, I hate it . . . !"

Under the narrowed gazes of the republic's leaders and of Pop Grabochey, the Komsomol leaders hauled Fotii out of the enormous room. In principle, they could have finished him off quietly in the nearby boxwood bushes but Polina ran behind, tearfully begging mercy on the fool. It's not hard for a pretty woman to strike a deal with two lowlifes; Fotii Feklovich woke up in his hotel room on a vomit-covered rug.

He didn't remember a thing, but something horrible and irreversible sucked at him and swept him up and then in a flash, as if on a screen: the enormous room at the Funicular Restaurant with hundreds of people eating a buffet, Polina with the Komsomol playboys; the bas-relief high on the wall and its sneakily preserved profile of the Father of the Peoples; the "soldier of the Party" Grabochey with a wineglass in his right hand, extended as if to shoot. . . . He heard someone's voice screaming something monstrous—"I hate communists!"

And then it came to him: That's *my* voice, my *own* voice! I'm finished....*

<h2 style="text-align:center">3</h2>

IT'S AMAZING HOW everything changed after that historic night. The long years of struggle with Polina ended; she capitulated and acknowledged Fotii's paternity of her second set of children. Just try to deny it, those kids had Fotik ears. Moreover, she married him and bore another future guards officer, the first one indisputably his. Polina began inculcating respect for their new father in her older two daughters, who were registered as Andrei Drevesny's, and she herself showed her husband an almost slavish devotion, creating a home-and-hearth that was exemplary and contemporary in the best sense of the words. Who would have thought that this bohemian broad of the Fourth Generation, brazen Polina Shtein, could have turned into such a hausfrau?

Of course, it wasn't too great with Polina's patronymic. "Lvovna" gave away her leonine background, but a stain's a stain and we don't

---

*The rest is shrouded in fog and with every year recedes; if you desperately want to forget everything, you will; or at least, everything will be blurred. With high-intensity fog headlights we can see the blurred outline of Fotii Feklovich at the door of Grabochey's superdeluxe suite at the Iveria Hotel, but we're unlikely to get past the door; to tell the truth, we don't really want to—it's evil.

Fotii knocked; (ten years ago in the smoke of oblivion) the door opened. On the doorstep stood the Stalinist soldier in a robe manufactured in heroic Vietnam, looking like nothing so much as a sheet-and-towel man from some steam bath. Through the parting waves of time Fotii fell to his knees. According to one source, having fallen, he cried "Spare me, Boss!" According to another source, he was silent, lifting his suffering face to the leader. All sources agree that after a minute's silence Grabochey said, "Come in," and that the theoretician of the Fourth Generation of Soviet Photographers went into the superdeluxe suite without getting off his knees.

No one knows what happened during the hour and a half behind those closed doors. The author, of course, can easily penetrate this mystery and in principle we could even get into the heart of Grabochey's "Masonic lodge," but let us refrain from further expeditions for reasons of cleanliness.

The night was coming to an end when Fotii Feklovich came out of the room, followed by the strict paternal gaze of Grabochey. When he came out he went where his feet took him, that is, to the reporter of *Decorative Arts*, Polina Shtein, and raped the tired woman with great gusto. That evening they flew off together to the North.

try to hide it, on the contrary, we give a living example of our Party's internationalism. In the long run, Fotii Feklovich became convinced that internationalism in the Party and even in its "armed division" was alive. Judge for yourselves—his wife half-Jewish, and he's moving ahead so quickly.

Not two years had passed since his bowing and scraping in Grabochey's room, and Fotii Feklovich had already become the secretary of the board of the Photographers' Union of the USSR and a deputy of the Moscow City Council, had received an excellent apartment in Atheist Alley, had traveled on creative and ideological business to two hard-currency countries, the FRG and Norway, and had published a solid tome of ideas, *On Morality in Soviet Photography*. It was as a specialist in morality that Klezmetsov found his niche in the head echelon of the creative cadres, and if there occurred the slightest or greatest need up high on questions of morality, they knew to call in Fotii Feklovich.

He wasn't one of those who fooled around and hid in the bushes from sensitive problems, pulling the wool over people's eyes, saying "We're no worse than the rest." "No, we're better than the rest," Fotii Feklovich declared boldly at any conference at all, even abroad, bringing every issue to a head even if it produced "difficulties"; the temporary presence of a limited contingent, the hooliganism of dissidents, slanders of "psychiatry," the fall of Solidarity's explosive plans; the errors of Western photography and its viewpoint, limited by religious indoctrination. . . . No one other than Fotii Feklovich was credited with authorship of the term "mature socialism," even though it first appeared in a speech in the Politburo.*

Ten years passed: from the Moscow City Council Fotii reached the Supreme Khural; from membership in the bureau, the Auditing Commission of the Central Committee; from secretaryship in the Photographers' Union, first secretaryship in the mighty Photographers' Union of the Russian Federation. He was a member of the editorial boards of a

---

*Well, you can't take away Fotii's powers of observation: Soviet socialism has clearly matured, it's even overripe, but we keep quiet about that to avoid stomach upsets.

dozen magazines, headed innumerable exhibition committees, and on television daily enlightened the masses within the framework of Lenin's University for the Millions—"After the movies the most important art for us is photography!"

Physically Fotii became a heavyset comrade, but not a traditional Party-type; he somehow had retained the right to sublety. The long hair and graying spade of beard hinted inheritance from the Russian revolutionary democrats, the powerful smoked eyeglasses hid mean eyes, and in general foreigners had no trouble taking him for a throwback to a more traditional Russian politician, journalist, and liberal. Not even the most reactionary foreigners would rush to call Fotii Feklovich a "Cheka bastard." Not every foreigner noticed the lips of the mighty comrade nor was every foreigner a physiognomist who could pay attention to those lips, but those lips gave him away. Showing through the graying vegetation of beard they evinced extraordinary venom, and even though this figure of "mature socialism" had not had to sign execution orders yet, it was clear from his lips that if he had to, he would sign and ask for more.

WEEKEND 2

AND SO, WE jump out of the "waves of time" onto the small island of the present moment, into Fotii's study, where we left his important guest sinking in the armchair with a bottle of Rémy Martin, the host himself having just expressed a nationally positive thought about the eccentric bicyclist who passed under his windows.

Polina supplied everything necessary for the meeting and disappeared. She had orders not to call him to the telephone. This would be an important conversation.

The general, sipping cognac, considered his host. That Fotii must have more money than me, the general thought. Probably a lot more, he's an ideological general even though in our firm his rank is a joke compared to mine. Plus he gets all those unlimited honoraria, he sets them himself, he's got all the pictures publishers in his fist. Plus according to his *nomenklatura* rank he gets the Kremlin rations, which we Cheka men can't even dream about, plus he's got the Photographers'

Fund two-story dacha in Developkino, neighboring with our real Soviet classics, even though the artistic achievements of this creep are close to zero, and at the dacha, according to latest information, he's got two Volgas salted away—why? investment? uncertainty in his own position? Plus, not to be forgotten, his business trips abroad to soc- and cap-countries, so he's hauling in deficit goods and currency certificates, while I can't even get them to give me a trip to Bulgaria for a new sheepskin coat. Plus, no, really, comrades, this is too much, he annexes to his five-room apartment the two-room apartment of his neighbor "who has moved to the state of Israel," breaking through the wall and creating aristocratic digs. Shit, this Fotii's hauling it in, he is, taking advantage of the Party's weakness for "creative cadres," when really, who is he but a support agent with the code name Poker.

"It's so nice here," the general said. "Looks like you've expanded recently?"

"Well, the apartment next door came free," Fotii said with a certain rigidity. "Well, the City Council decided to add it to mine . . . sometimes I receive electors, and the photographers come, and the TV, and this and that . . . foreign guests as well. . . ."

"A very proper and timely decision on the part of the council," the general said with a nod. "A creative man needs space." He stopped for a second and thought, Should I impress him or not? He decided to impress, and quoted Pasternak. " 'I want to go home, to the enormity of my apartment, which makes me sad. . . .' " The general caught sight of himself in a distant mirror and grew angrier, upset by the reflected almost-old man with messy tufts of gray hair and eyebrows. "I believe you added your neighbor's apartment to your own? I wonder if he knows about it?"

"Forgive me, I don't understand." Fotii's fingers, crossed over his belly in a new positive-national habit, spread in an interrogatory gesture.

"I just wondered whether he knows that you've taken his apartment," General Planshchin said.

"He probably doesn't care anymore," Fotii chuckled, not without some concern.

"Why would that be?" The general's surprise seemed incommensurately passionate. "The man isn't dead!"

"I didn't say he was, that's not what I said...."

Fotii was thrown for a loop, he didn't understand the sympathy for someone who'd left the Soviet Union. A rare example of an unpleasant KGB man, this General Planshchin. Always a hidden agenda, always suspecting everyone of something bad—what a strange, uncontemporary professionalism.

"I didn't say he had died," Fotii repeated. "It's just that he must have forgotten all about his apartment now that he's living in Tel Aviv."

"New York," the general corrected.

Fotii raised his glass. "We're talking strangely somehow today. We used to be more casual, we drank to our Brüderschaft in the GDR, remember?"

General Planshchin smacked himself in the forehead. "Forgive me, Fotii buddy, it skipped my mind. You know how tough things are now, buddy, you understand, don't you?" But the general was thinking, Let him see that *Brüderschaften* don't obligate me to anything. "Anyway, tell me, now, Fotii, what's your relationship with Ogorodnikov?"

"I thought that you would know the gradations of relationships between people in my Photographers' Union," Fotii said drily, to show that the general's psychological games wouldn't work with him and that if he preferred *probing* all the time he shouldn't have invited himself over for cognac. Committee workers of a higher rank than Planshchin had been here and had at least behaved like people, some even got soused, some even tried to embrace Polina below the waist.

"So what about Ogorodnikov?" the general asked, eyes narrowing. "A lot is unclear with him, yes? What do you think, buddy?"

"You sound as if you're planning to arrest him," Fotii said with a laugh.

General Planshchin grew furious, but didn't show it.

"Why such extremes?" He expressed surprise, as if he were being pushed into something. "Arrest a famous Soviet photographer whose work is studied in every Soviet high school? A world name? What were you thinking when you elected him to the board of Rosfoto? You were behind him yourself last year, and now you want him arrested? You shouldn't be such a maximalist, especially toward your comrade, even if he's a former comrade! Ilyich did not teach us that...."

He was slyly wagging his finger at Fotii. What a cynical bastard, Fotii thought, he's mocking Lenin, he can get away with anything. Fotii broke out in red splotches and his blood pressure was clearly going up. The room darkened.

"Now, now, now—" The observant general giggled. "Come on, let's not do that, let's raise our glasses and expand our arteries."

"What are you leading up to?" Fotii asked.

"To the fact, dear comrade, that right next to you, and partly within the bowels of your Photographers' Union, illegality is flourishing." The general said it grimly.

"Is that supposed to be black humor or poetic license?" Fotii Feklovich's arteries had widened, and now he offered Planshchin a lippy face that only a self-controlled person would not slap.

"Fotii, haven't you heard anything about New Focus or the album *Say Cheese!?* Nothing? Not even with the corner of one little ear? Marvelous! All of Moscow has been talking about it for a year, an anticensorship bomb is ready to detonate, and eighteen members of the Union are participating in this provocation, while the chairman of the Union, one of our experienced workers"—here General Planshchin made an eloquent pause and stared at Fotii—"knows nothing! Marvelous!"

The general nobly allowed the first secretary to gather his wits and turned to the "family snacks," taking a bumpy cucumber, biting into a marinated tomato with a groan of pleasure, and delighting in a broiled sparerib, sucking the bone. When he looked up once again at his host, there was nothing left of the "equal position"—before him sat something jellylike. Eighteen members of the Union in a conspiracy! If he wanted to, the general could cover the "theoretician of morality" with so much shit he'd never dig his way out. Well, now the serious discussion could begin. Fotii had been sitting there, puffed up with his own importance, as if he were a classic, as if he hadn't signed anything, as if he weren't working for us, as if he weren't our agent Poker.

The meek and slightly trembling Fotii Feklovich was simply waiting. Experience had taught him to recognize the moments that control fate.

Smug Planshchin was now talking to him as if he were his own man, giving Agent Poker necessary information. "Many years ago, we used one of our men to stick the Drevesny-German-Ogorodnikov group with the idea of an 'uncensored' album. Alas, for some reason, the idea died back then, it didn't come to pass, they couldn't unite the people, all of them turned out to be wildly self-centered, as if they had been brought up in a different society. They were at each other's throats, they were trying to divide up the crown of Soviet photography. We had to shelve the idea, and really, it wasn't even needed, the information flowed freely from our informants. Then suddenly, last year, *without us,* the idea resurfaced, the group New Focus appeared, and they began creating an uncensored, as they call it, photo album called *Say Cheese!* with a clear, anti-Party aroma, or, to be more precise, a real anti-Soviet stink. And now you can expect a news flash at any moment—rebellion in the Union of Soviet Photographers!"

The general strolled along the Turkoman rug, as if deep in thought. He stood by the window, fingers clasped on his chest, waiting for Fotii to speak.

"How did things get this far?" Fotii muttered. "Well, all right, we blew it day to day, but ... how did the Glands let it happen? Is it strategy or something?"

The general sat close to Fotii Feklovich, knee to knee, and put his hand, well developed during the cult of personality, on the mush that was the secretary's leg.

"That's not for you to think about for the moment, Fotii. Forgive the humor, but we'll ask the questions."

O unforgettable Generalissimo! The mush quivered even more under the Chekist's hand. "My dear general, I can't manage without questions when we're talking about the Union that was entrusted to me, and it was the Party that entrusted it to me, and the Party's the one who will want my explanations...."

The little fishie, thought the general, he's still floundering, still trying to get off our hook, those Party boys are getting very cheeky....

"*We'll* be doing the asking now. A very important operation is beginning. Don't bother questioning it; it's been decided high up. At the signal *from me* you will start organizing public opinion within the Photographers' Union. For now, in the most careful manner, prepare information on every person on this list."

Fotii Feklovich held the list in his hands. I could have managed without it, he thought, the composition is obvious. Well, here they are: the father of my children, Andrei Drevesny, my wife's lover; that damned Slava German, of course; the young ones everyone's talking about nowadays, Alexei Okhotnikov, Probkin, and, of course, you can't start up a mess without Fisher, or Tsuker ... hah, here's something unexpected—Georgii! What's the prince got to do with this? ... and here are unknown names—Shturmin, Zherebyatnikov.... You can't call it a Zionist plot, Russian names predominate.... Talented heads will roll, such sensitive lenses, promoted by none other than myself. They have no idea how much I've done for them, how I took care of them all those years, protecting them. And now comes retribution for my good deeds, the hour to sign myself in history.

"Still, General, I can't refrain from asking a question. I don't see Ogorodnikov on your list. Is that an accident?"

"That's a good point," the general said with demonic gloom, as if he hadn't been tormenting Fotii just now. "There are some indications ... I'm afraid to make this statement yet ... we're waiting for confirmation ... some, which we have on hand ... hold on to your chair, Fotii ... it looks like the CIA is acting through Maxim Petrovich Ogorodnikov as its direct agent. So he's being worked on separately and is not on the list of politically immature people, whom he dragged into his excellently planned conspiracy. Is that clear?"

"Bastard," Fotii whispered. His heart joyfully filled with hatred for that obnoxious egoist Ogo, that lowlife seeker of *la dolce vita*, that little aristocrat who finally got down to state treason. No, now it wasn't a pogrom against his talents, but his talent's salvation! The most talented lenses had to be saved for their own good and for ... well ... in general, just for Russia, for the homeland, for the future. They would get a good lesson in political maturity, but they would be saved, and they would be saved once again by Fotii Feklovich, a major social figure of mature socialism.

"And in case everything is confirmed?" He looked into the sharp eyes. It wasn't hard to read an answer in them.

At that highly charged moment sweet Polina, formerly Shtein, came into the room noiselessly, with her heavy bun of hair and her small face, getting dry around her enormous eyes.

"Excuse me, General, but your colleague insists on calling you to the telephone. I didn't want to call you, but he's shouting as if . . . as if . . ." She stopped, smiled strangely, and handed the general the phone. "Well, he's shouting!"

General Planshchin understood that something major had gone wrong. Captain Slyazgin's voice was panicked.

"Emergency! . . . I can't tell you on the phone! . . . Emergency!"

"Where are you now?" The general was buttoning his coat and straightening his tie.

"On my way to Atheist Alley!"

"I'll be downstairs!"

Fotii accompanied him to the elevator. He didn't ask any more questions. They shook hands firmly. Should I insult him now or not? wondered the general. He decided to be insulting, and said, narrowing his eyes, "Think about this properly, Poker!"

2

CAPTAIN SKANSHCHIN NEVER regretted going to work for the Glands. First of all, it was good for the homeland; secondly, it was better financially than his last job, in the organizational sector of the Moscow Komsomol Committee. Judge for yourself: pay was 52 rubles more a month plus 60 rubles for his epaulets, excellent food, a weekly packet with huge amounts of meat, butter, and always a hunk of Finnish cervelat. . . . "Plus! I almost forgot, darling . . . five rubles fifty kopeks 'expenses' per evening . . . well, in case—understand, darling?—if I have to spend time in a restaurant, and I have to do that almost every evening because of the nature of my work. Of course, you can't have a spree with five fifty, but that's only to git—I mean, get, sorry, darling— started, to come in and order a bottle of Cabernet, and then you can't get away from all the treats, people treat the Glands with respect nowadays, not like under Stalin. And the third aspect, darling. . . ."

Skanshchin propped himself up on an elbow, took a pack of Marlboros from the shelf, plumped his pillow, and lit up with pleasure. That was nice use of "aspect," just in the right place and the right time. "The aspect is good, darling, because you keep growing, you can't otherwise, that's the nature of the work; if you don't rise above yourself, you'll be left at the tail.

"Take me, for instance. Who am I? Just like my father, warehouse supervisor, a real proletarian. The Komsomol gave me lots, of course, but zero for my spiritual life. And it's only thanks to the Glands, who help the creative unions keep their ideological weapons clean, that I came in contact with the treasure-house of the arts, and felt human. Here, take a gander—why look and not gander, darling?—well, all right, take a look, think how many complete collections I got in just one year, not every hereditary intellectual would have so many. And here are albums, gifts from the masters of Soviet photography. Very impressive for history, though secret in part: not all masters want it known . . . well . . . that's another story. Maybe you think I just salt these books away, darling? I read them, darling, delve, even take notes. You have to keep growing, life tells you that. Here, for instance, once in Sheremetyevo Ogo mocked me, said that I didn't know the masters of the art. Anyone else would have gotten mad, but I got reference works, and now just ask me, I know all the periods. Go ahead, ask me. Well, come on, ask me, ask me, darling!"

But Darling, instead of asking Skanshchin the desired question, behaved rather differently. A sharp movement of the leg to the left, a powerful turn, blanket and pillows tossed aside, and her largish white body resembled a big fish for a moment, after which Darling, aka Viktoria Guryevna Kazachnekova—Ogorodnikov's second wife, the one who still helped Ogo keep house—took the appropriate position in trembling anticipation.

Captain Skanshchin had to accommodate once again, which he always did with pleasure, and not only physical pleasure but artistic as well. That was another benefit of his present role—access to intelligent and experienced women of an advanced age. At the organization sector of the MGK Komsomol he had never dreamed of brunettes of comparable build. Take her ass, round and solid; take her waist, slender but soft; take her mammary glands, heavyish but within bounds; take and combine the beneficial with the pleasant, the physiological with the aesthetic, service and friendship. . . .

Resting after the procedure, Viktoria pursed her lips and trumpeted "Ooh-ooh-ooh" several times, to smooth the wrinkles around her mouth, and then quite casually and even condescendingly said to the young officer, "All your service benefits, Vova, are mere trifles. Is that how a man should live in our times?"

"I don't get it, darling," Skanshchin said, worriedly. Viktoria's statement cut to the quick.

She grimaced. "It's all so petty, so petty.... A modern young man counting fifty-two rubles for some epaulets, stars, or whatever, agog with delight over some sausage or whatever. No, you don't know how to live!"

She got up abruptly from the bed, hopped like a gymnast, and froze in a yoga position: her left hand around the ankle of her left leg, extended behind her, and her right hand, like that of the leader of the revolution, reaching into the radiant future.

Skanshchin took offense at his darling. It's easy to laugh at my language, why don't you teach me the right way to speak? If I don't know how to live, then teach me, please! I'm ready to learn everything, as long as it's not harmful to the homeland.

He didn't have time to let loose this tirade, however, before the phone rang. He practically fell out of bed—a call from the general.

"Well, Captain Skanshchin, rowing as usual?"

Skanshchin broke out in a sweat, and then darling Viktoria exhaled loudly, confirming her presence for the general's sensitive ears.

"Get here immediately!" Planshchin dropped the phone.

Skanshchin rushed trembling to the bathroom. Just as he thought— a hickey on his neck, the greedy big lips of an experienced woman. He stank. His chin was a mess. No time to shave, no time to wash, if he could only shape up!

"What are you scurrying about for?" Viktoria said disdainfully. "If you look at the big picture, you're living without style."

"No time for style, darling," he muttered, flying into his trousers. "It's government service, after all, darling."

"Ho, ho, ho," laughed the Moscow lady without moving her facial muscles. "Fine government work!"

"Do you think it's better to speculate on theater tickets?" Skanshchin was angry and surprised himself—he had never replied so harshly to his darling, an influential worker in the capital's theater box offices.

"Yes," she said.

"Easy, easy, darling. We're talking about the Glands here, after all. I see that your husband had an influence on you after all."

"Lay off!" Viktoria commanded. "Don't touch the genius!"

Racing in the Zhiguli to the secret apartments of his order, the young Soviet Mason muttered in an injured tone, "Don't touch the genius she says, don't touch him, then who am I supposed to touch, if I'm assigned to that genius?"

At the PhID quarters Father Commander Planshchin was unrecognizable, not a man but a steel gut. His short question—"Where is he?"—froze all Skanshchin's members, including his tongue. "What's the matter, are you deaf, Captain?"

"Here he is," Captain Skanshchin said, pointing to himself.

A gruff laugh came from the corner of the roomy office. Yep, it was Captain Slyazgin in full uniform, all belts tightened, a real cossack, Skanshchin thought.

"Drop the laughter!" the general barked into the corner, and raising himself from the chair, unleashed upon Skanshchin something akin to multistaged thunder. "Captain Skanshchin, I would like to know what you do instead of your duties. Scratch your balls, screw around, drink?"

"It's the weekend, Comrade General," Skanshchin mumbled, like a chastened schoolboy.

Slyazgin laughed even more crudely, with undisguised obnoxiousness. "Weekend ... so he's British now ... what a laugh ... what a laugh ... weekend ..."

General Planshchin, as an experienced psychologist, decided to end the deterioration of intramural relations before anything else. With one glance he shut Slyazgin's laughing mouth, and with another he encouraged—very slightly—his erring favorite, Skanshchin.

"Pull yourself together, Captain."

Skanshchin dashed to the mirror. What was wrong? . . . Well, a piece of his underpants was sticking out from his fly. Easily remedied, no problem. . . .

"The problem, Vladimir Gavrilovich, is that your assigned photographer M. P. Ogorodnikov"—out of his old investigator's habit he interrupted the sentence and showed his subordinate to the chair opposite him—"at the present moment is strolling around Berlin. . . ." It was hard not to draw out this wicked pause. "West Berlin, my dear Captain."

If not for his physical training, and he could thank the Komsomol for that, Captain Skanshchin would have been off the chair. But remembering at that critical moment everything he had been taught as well as examples from patriotic literature, Skanshchin stayed on the chair and even tightened his jaw and narrowed his eyes, knowing that the general liked him best that way.

"Should that be understood literally or figuratively, Comrade General?"

Planshchin tossed several pages of so-called radio interception across the desk. A correspondent of Radio Liberty reported from West Berlin that the famous Soviet photographer Maxim Ogorodnikov had arrived two days ago. "Appearing at a discussion at the Baptist Academy, he incensed German leftists with his amazingly un-Marxist statements. Here, somewhat shortened, is Ogorodnikov's speech, printed in *Die Zeit*. The text has been translated back into Russian. . . ."

Volodya sighed deeply, as if surfacing from a deep dive, and shook his well-trained head. "I can't fully take it in yet, Comrade General. First of all, how did he get there? How can a person get there if we don't let him go? Secondly, Agent Magpie was with him, drinking, sleeping, we didn't have to worry. . . ."

His rival Slyazgin wasn't laughing anymore, but paced back and forth along the office's western wall, cruelly creaking the prerevolutionary parquet floor.

"Captain Slyazgin, call in the boys," the general said.

Skanshchin dove again. All the workers of their sector were coming in and sitting around the conference table. I'm going to burn with a bright-blue flame, thought Volodya. Farewell, life in the capital! They'll send me off to work on the railroads.

"Comrades," the general said to his men, "you're informed of the crisis. The administration of the Friendship Union assures me that the workers whose criminal negligence Ogorodnikov used will be subject to the severest disciplinary measures. Our comrade Captain Skanshchin, let's face it, was also not at his best. This is a lesson for us all. We have to make the appropriate conclusions and remember that the Glands are founded not only on discipline but on inviolable comradely cohesion. We face important operative tasks. I ask you all to speak out. First of all, I would like to hear from Captain Skanshchin, on how he evaluates Ogorodnikov's action."

So they weren't planning to exile him to BAM. Skanshchin's heart filled with gratitude for the general and warmth for his comrades— cohesion, real male bonding. . . . He lifted his head and looked into the general's eyes, enlarged by Swiss lenses.

"A powerful foe, Comrade General," he said musingly. "We face a very powerful and, I would say, experienced foe."

The general beamed: his favorite had guessed, he had guessed the right direction to take!

"Right, Captain! A powerful, clever, dangerous foe!"

GLACIOLOGY

I

THE GLACIOLOGIST ANASTASIA, the present (or if it can be put that way, current) wife of Maxim Ogorodnikov, belonged to that amazing part of humanity whose birthday is February 29, that is, which comes once every four years. It was on that day three years ago that she had the fortune to meet her future spouse. The joke was increased by the fact that it was a double day: that morning she had turned twenty-nine.

Anastasia was standing, surrounded by shopping bags, on the corner of Kuznetsky Bridge and Neglinnaya Street. The snow was turning from wet to stinging, heralding a drop in temperature and icing of roads. Fake furs turn into real crap in weather like that and Nastya's was no exception. Passing taxis were stuffed, she couldn't even share. An old cloud hung over Neglinka, as immobile as the Politburo. Passersby and people standing near her stared grimly. Across the street a group of theatrical young people in line for ten-kopek pirozhki were roaring with laughter, and their inappropriate hilarity annoyed everyone.

And then, luck for Anastasia—a gypsy cab! a mud-splattered Volga stopped right at her knees. "To Lomonosvosky?" she asked. The gypsy nodded. She threw the packages on the back seat and plumped herself down next to the driver. It was warm inside. Marvelous music was playing: Haydn's first violin concerto, no more, no less.

"Do you know the date?" the gypsy driver asked.

"I happen to know," Anastasia said. "The twenty-ninth."

"Bah!" said the gypsy. "Leap year! Lousy weather! But a magical day!"

The gypsy had a longish nose over a fuzzy moustache, and the scarf around his neck was a knockout! He's trying to pick me up, thought Anastasia, and was not mistaken as it turned out.

"How much will it cost?" she wanted to know. The gypsy smiled.

"We'll come to terms, madame."

I think he's a famous actor, Anastasia thought. What an idiotic situation—how can I offer someone playing Haydn a three-ruble note? And what if he's just a fartsa?* If I don't give him three, he'll curse me out.

"Don't worry," he said, coming to her rescue. "Three, just like in a taxi, and if you add a ruble, I'll bring your packages up."

Her mother and Aunt Marisha, as usual, grew a bit stony at the sight of an "interesting man" dressed in foreign things.

He brought in the parcels, took four rubles, thanked her, but instead of leaving right away he began photographing the family of females, backing up, clicking at least twenty times, until Anastasia pushed him out the door. Then Mother and Aunt Marisha gasped, Who was that? Some kind of spy?

In the evening, at the height of the festivities, a messenger, literally a messenger down to his ridiculous uniform, arrived with an enormous bouquet of roses, at least two hundred rubles' worth, and a pack of very strange photographs. The photographed women were in poses that they swore they hadn't struck: Mama and Aunt Marisha were depicted as chaperones, duennas, trying to stop the romantic beauty, that is, Anastasia, from a loving surge toward the photographer.

Despite her approaching big thirty, Anastasia had had a very meager, if not negative, amorous education before now. At a very tender age, she was traumatized by her classmates, who dragged her into the geog-

* *Fartsa:* black marketeer

raphy lab with the aim of a collective loss of virginity. She didn't even remember how many guys there were, three or four; all the jerks swore, twisted her arms and legs clumsily, spilled their vileness all over her, and left disgusting bruises and scratches—but no one got it, even though they were on the gymnastics team. For many years she cringed automatically whenever any man came near her.

It can't be said that she didn't have "romances" in college and later, in the "ice age." She was attractive and the romances arose with all the appurtenances and June moons. Alas, everything dried up in bed, Anastasia couldn't do anything about it, she cringed, grew wooden, and after the first penetration, which always resembled the storming of the Swedish fortress Shlisselburg by Peter the Great's cohorts, began secretly to hate her lover. By her twenty-ninth birthday she had come to terms with her frigidity. What can you do, not everyone has it, I'll live with Mama and Aunt Marisha, they both hate men and they both manage. And then the gypsy cabdriver appeared.

By then Maxim Petrovich Ogorodnikov had successfully ended his fifth or sixth marriage. "The coed," as Ogorodnikov called her, appeared at the perfect moment. He took Shlisselburg with an irresistible attack, and having taken it, stayed. The infamous frigidity disappeared the very first night under the erotic and alcoholically romantic insistence of the sexual revolutionary of the seventies. Let's get married, he said every morning. She adored him, but wouldn't marry him, feeling sorry for Mama and Aunt Marisha.

But one hung-over morning after, they registered their marriage. A half year or more later, they had a church wedding in the Novgorod region parish of Father Gleb, whom Ogo had met at a dissident "kitchen discussion."

Anastasia, however, did not take the marriage too seriously, and even laughed at the word "husband." Mama and Aunt Marisha were not informed of it, and even the meetings of the spouses still were invested by Anastasia with a certain mystery, which sometimes pleased Ogo, as it added a spark, and sometimes angered him, and most often amused him. In general, he accepted the game, and a while later realized that it was convenient.

Three years passed. Half that time Anastasia spent in the above-cloud regions. Returning, she would hold her nose as she entered Ogo's apartment or his studio on Khlebny. "I can't breathe in here! It stinks like sin!" In response Max would shout that there was no proof that the chastity of glaciologettes corresponded to the whiteness of eternal snow. They would laugh, and Anastasia would think: That's how you should live with a man, that's the independence you have to retain, even though she knew very well that their positions were unequal—the whiteness of eternal snows, alas, did correspond to her chastity (she couldn't even imagine anyone other than Max), while every square meter of the studio, alas, really did stink of whores, sometimes presenting physical evidence—panties, bras, contraceptives—left behind. Here she would blow up. "Pig! I'm tired of your sexual swinishness!" Comrade Ogorodnikov in such cases followed his old habit of disappearing into "deep unconsciousness."

In brief, they loved each other, albeit with different intensity.*

2

HE WON'T COME BACK, she thought, sitting on the boulevard near her house on Vorobyovsky Chaussee. He escaped miraculously and now he won't come back. I'll never see him again. They don't let wives join the "nonreturnees." And he doesn't need me anyway. We're strangers, and it's my own fault: I didn't know how to make him love me, I couldn't get over my idiotic man-hating. She had never cried, and now she was weeping into her lap for the umpteenth time in the two days since he left. The corniest plaints shook her, and the melodramatic wails she had always suppressed were let loose. My beloved, my only, cruel life has separated us forever, but believe me, nothing will dim your radiant image in my heart—that's what she was crying, and she wasn't ashamed.

*Hm, writing or reading that phrase, you think: How lousy! "Love with different intensity" sounds about as romantic as the list of chemical ingredients on a loaf of bread. Alas, there was something unbalanced and lopsided in the marriage; in principle they were from different planets. Ogo's every step illustrated some social concept, too many concepts, illustrations, representations for the not very happy woman, who, if she illustrated anything at all, illustrated the incorrigible romanticism of Russian coeds.

The boulevard was empty at this hour, no pickup artists, no one to offer condolences. A motorized wheelchair was moving slowly along the fence. The invalid's large white face was turned toward her. I think my father has a wheelchair like that, she suddenly thought. She hadn't seen her father since before meeting Ogo over three years ago. Why are Mama and Aunt Marisha so hostile to him? Why am I so indifferent? Who is my father? A veteran of the Great Patriotic War, an eccentric craftsman, Mother said once that he worked on contract for some artel, carving little boxes. A frivolous man, Mama said, even though he paid alimony on time. He showed up occasionally when she was a child, a strange visitor on prostheses, moving like a robot. In general, he "didn't count" somehow. She never told Maxim anything about him, and he never asked.

"Nastya!" the invalid called from beyond the cast-iron fence. It was her father at that. "I'm here for you," he said, and aimed his rattletrap toward the gate in the fence. He kept looking back, as if afraid she would disappear.

"I want to explain my appearance to you," her father began, moving closer and turning off his motor. His flabby cheeks trembled, sagging over his shirt collar. The naval fabric was weighed down by an iconostasis of battle awards. Galaxies of dandruff swirled on his shoulders. He was all white, either from nerves or from chronic illness.

"Wait, Papa." She suddenly took his hand and pressed it to her cheek. Immediately she thought this inappropriate, embarrassing, and she started talking to cover her feelings. "Why do you always wear this suit with your medals? Where do you live? Are you lonely? Why are we such strangers? What can't you share with Mother?"

But he was much more shocked by the unexpected touch of her cheek on his hand. He was bewildered. "You see ... you see ..." he muttered, wiping his brow with the back of the caressed hand. "Actually, I'm ... on important business ... something ... something ... I'm afraid you'll be surprised, Daughter." The word came with difficulty, but after that things went more smoothly. "I'm afraid you'll be surprised, Nastya, but I'm here on account of your husband, that Ogorodnikov...."

"How did you know that I ..." She was astonished. "Did I ever tell you ..."

He smiled, calm now. "Do you think it's such a big secret? He told me himself that you were man and wife, when he learned who I was."

"You know each other?" Her gypsy and this invalid didn't go together at all.

"Yes," her father replied, not without pride. "We've met several times at certain ... hm ... certain readings."

"Dissident readings, I'll bet? Papa, don't tell me you're a dissident, too?"

"A member of the Council of Invalids. We fight for the rights of the handicapped, which are more trampled than the rights of the healthy. If you like I'll tell you more about these things another time. But now, we're looking for Ogorodnikov. He's in danger."

"What's wrong?" She grabbed her father's hand again, but this was a different movement.

"The Glands," he said. "Please, don't tell anyone but Ogo. I have a friend who has a friend retired from the KGB. He plays chess with a general from the PhID. He told us that they have an operative plan, developed and approved, to isolate your husband. We don't know exactly how. In any case, you must warn him. . . ."

"Too late, Papa." She sighed. "The day before yesterday he flew to West Berlin. How it happened, I don't know. I was stuck on Mount Elbrus, idiot that I am. . . ."

BERLIN 2

I

THE DISCUSSION ON "The Artist and Power" was held in the old-fashioned building of the Baptist Academy, on the shores of the Vogelsee reservoir. Participating were West Berlin photographers, the Soviet delegation, and also a group of Turkish masters of the lens, for there were over a half million permanent Turkish residents in Berlin. Everyone sat around a large round table or along the walls. The hall was cozy: oak panels, a fireplace and chandelier.

The cultural counselor of the Soviet General Consulate, Zafalontsev, sat down next to Ogorodnikov, as if to hand him a letter (actually, an empty envelope), and whispered, "The topic of the discussion has not been approved by us. All hope is on you."

"Who are these people, Zafalontsev?"

"Basically, undependable liberal elements . . . don't look it, you say? No, they don't look like liberals. Who do they look like to you?"

"Just ballast."

"Aha, that's what we call liberals, anarchists. . . ."

Ogorodnikov feigned majestic surprise. "Where were you educated, Comrade Counselor? Liberals and anarchists wouldn't sit at the same table!"

People around them listened respectfully to the unintelligible conversation between two Soviet comrades, of whom one boomed and the other whispered not so much to his interlocutor as to himself.

"They wouldn't shit next to each other," Ogo elucidated. "You're missing the terminology. A liberal, pal, is the bearer of liberal ideas, that is, humane and gentle ones, while an anarchist by nature is a dumb destroyer, even though he calls on liberty. Get it, see who they resemble?"

"Did you drink this morning?" Zafalontsev whispered with narrowed eyes. "Don't you understand the importance of this event?" The vigilant diplomat was not aware that three Slavist girls from the university were sitting behind him and that the coeds understood some of what was being said. The Turkish participants, lounging as if to smoke a hookah, regarded the young women gravely. Two Soviet representatives from western Siberia were frozen in horror. The Germans were checking their notes. Ogo noticed that one of them was casting glances at him with special daring.

"And who's that?" Ogo asked Zafalontsev.

"He's all right. We work well with him. Joachim von Deretzki, West German, revolutionary photographer from the Rote Fahne group. Well, Maxim, good luck, I'm off!" The counselor's voice suddenly grew stronger, his lips stretched in a kindly smile, and from out of nowhere came fully grammatical German. "Creative discussions are no place for us government employees."

The walking refutation of cheap anti-Soviet propaganda headed for the exit. The director of the Baptist Academy, Pastor Brandt, saw the counselor out with friendly semi-embrace. The chairman of the meeting, a factory boy named Tom Gretzke, who was simple and sly as if from a Soviet movie, winked at Ogorodnikov: Hee-hee, we'll talk without the nanny. The discussion was on.

In the garden outside, a woodpecker appeared on a birch trunk next to the window. He pecked with his beak several times. Ogo watched

with sympathy the most tolerable of the knockers.* The brazenness with
which he still wore the clothes of the nineteenth century! Suddenly,
discovering a generous donation from nature, the woodpecker banged
like a jackhammer, chips flying. *Splinters!* A distant vista unfolded
beyond the window—the lakeshore, the woods. A false distance, which
broke off at the wall hidden in the woods. A false discussion, and
actually the whole academy of baptizers was dubious. Why wasn't
God's name ever spoken here? Just scattered isms. . . .

The other window, near the fireplace, showed the front entrance of
the townhouse, and beyond it the irenic street, paved in small round
cobblestones tucked into each other like eggs; cast-iron rosettes on garden fences, cars parked along the curbs, and among them one bright-
red hundred-thousand-dollar Ferrari. The housekeeper, Frau Kempfe,
stood chatting with the postman on the academy porch, and their two
figures seemed to embody the reasonable Germany, which had invented
a tap for the Russian samovar. A false calm. . . . Ogo took several shots
of that window and another . . . the woodpecker . . . the postmaster's
Tyrolean jacket. . . .

". . . the austere logic of the class struggle dictates simple truths to
us. The artist's duty in a capitalist society is to counterpose his creativity
to reaction, that is, to speak out against government. The artist in a
socialist country does not have the right to act against his government,
even if he sees its flaws, because he might thus damage the most
advanced social system. . . ."

Ogo finally realized that it was that Rote Fahne man speaking,
Joachim von Deretzki, who had even switched to English to make it
easier to understand . . . for whom? For him, for Ogo—it was to him
that Von Deretzki's burning gaze was now turned. With a sharp gesture
the West German pushed back his thin curtain of long hair, like a lady
with her veil.

"I want to put the question directly to our Soviet comrade—do you
agree with my opinion? You, Soviet comrade, would you kindly answer
the question?"

*Among the innumerable Russian synonyms for "stoolie," one of the most com-
mon is *stukach*, literally "a man who knocks," or "a knocker." Such interplay
between linguistics and bird-watching has enabled me to make this footnote.

They sat opposite each other on the perimeter of the enormous table. Can't even punch you in the mouth, thought Ogo. What the fuck kind of "Soviet comrade" am I to you? There are my works in the corner: it seems obvious that you shouldn't ask me questions about socialist government.

The discussion stopped. Everyone was looking at the Soviet comrade. The proletarian Gretzke gulped. Pastor Brandt wiped his glasses in embarrassment. Von Deretzki, supporting his pale face in his hands, hypnotized Ogo with a frozen smile. Incidentally, the Soviet comrade himself pretended that the question wasn't intended for him and stared dreamily at the woodpecker, took out Dutch cigarillos, offered one to his neighbor, lit one, waved the match. . . .

"Mister Ogorodnikov," Brandt called.

"Jawohl," the comedian said with a start.

Von Deretzki banged his fist on the table.

Tom Gretzke gently patted his shoulder and winked at the Soviet comrade. "Ogorodnikov, you vill to Comrade Joachim answering be?" The future quisling had learned Russian already.

Ogo expressed surprise quite naturally. "I'm supposed to answer? Forgive me, Genosse Gretzke, I was a bit distracted. Do you need a reference?" With faked bewilderment Ogo rummaged in his briefcase, pulling out papers, changing his glasses. A very inappropriate copy of the Russian émigré magazine *Kontinent* jumped out. Finally, he said to Von Deretzki, "I'm very sorry, sir, but I didn't hear your question. Would you mind repeating it?"

The revolutionary repeated it, jaw clenched. That must be how NKVD investigators talked in the damned year of my birth, Ogo thought.

"Are you sure the question is for me?" Ogo courteously asked. How I'd like to throw the *Kont* right in your fat mug!

"For you, for you, Soviet comrade!"

Ogorodnikov turned to the Siberians sitting against the wall. "Yuri Yurievich, Petro, maybe you'd like to answer the man?"*

---

*On the day before this discussion Ogorodnikov had taken the Siberians to the Kurfürstendamm and bought them each a leather jacket on his secret American Express card. The guys had never dreamed of such luck. For "leather goods" like

Yuri, who worked in the culture department of the Kemerovo City Committee, bugged out his eyes and sailed off for the land of prostration. Petro, a photographer at the magazine *Siberian Lights,* turned red to a critical degree but did start gabbing about the Marxist formula of art, about who it belonged to, about what *joy* he felt as an ancestral Siberian finding such shared views here in the West, in capitalist surroundings, and how much of an *honor* it was to give the democratic community of West Berlin greetings from the workers of the Sayano-Shushen Hydroelectric Station, "and here is a gift for Comrade Von Deretzki, a souvenir," carved in wood—the place of exile of Vladimir Ilyich Lenin.

"Ho, that was terrific!" Ogo praised the Siberian.

"Are you mocking me?!" shouted the apostle of proletarian art. "The question is for you, Mr. Ogorodnikov! Are you trying to squirm out of it?"

Linda Slippenbach, reporter for a major Hamburg journal and the sister of Wolf, Ogo's East Berlin pal, entered the room and stopped in the doorway. She raised her hand somewhere in the region of her cute ear and waved her fingers at Ogo. He knew that his French visa was in her purse. It was hard to find a more useful person than Linda in Berlin. She knew the whole city, right up to the secretaries of the GDR regional committees on the other side of the wall. She was a woman journalist of the new international breed who were always on the right spot at the right time, who flew across oceans as easily as they drove their VWs and Morrises in heavy traffic, chattered glibly in the basic European languages, almost always including Russian, wore tweed jackets, and still managed to remain feminine and ever ready to get to know an interesting man more intimately.

Ogo smiled amiably at Von Deretzki. "So, my colleague is interested in my opinion on the relations between the modern photographer and the government? With a socialist government, you said? Sir, do you mean Helmut Schmidt or Bruno Kreisky? The government of the

---

that you could forget your Marxist-Leninist homeland. They probably wouldn't turn him in. Of course, they may not have understood a thing anyway. The tongue-tied translator got unglued completely once the dialogue switched into internationally broken English.

USSR, sir? You mean, communist government? So, you are interested in my relations with the government of the USSR? Yes, yes, let's clarify things. Not my relations, but my correlations, and not details, but the question in general.... Well then, that sounds more polite, otherwise, one could have thought heaven knows what. In my opinion, my dear Western colleague, correlations with the government are not particularly essential for an artist."

Linda Slippenbach was timely here, too. She slipped over to the main table and slid her tape recorder along the smooth surface. The machine stopped just where it should have: in the center of the table, between Ogorodnikov and Von Deretzki. When the former began speaking, the latter straightened up and put on wire-rim glasses, like a regular theoretician from Phnom Penh.

The guy must be as poor as a church mouse, Ogo thought. The leather jacket is flimsy, the shirt shitty. He's pissed at the rich and that's why he became a revolutionary. And of course, he's got no talent. They're always talentless, these Stalinist sharpshooters.

"It's stupid to fight the State and it's even more stupid to lick its ass," Ogo wisely intoned, and offered his hand to his opponent, who could not have reached it no matter how much he wanted to across the table. "As one photographer to another you must understand me, Hans, I mean, forgive me, Joachim," Ogo continued, casually waving the unused hand. "We must attempt the realization of many correlations in our lifetime. For instance, with fire and water, with nature ... in particular, with trees ... in principle, the most important is with God—no need to shudder, friend Leonard, oh, yes, I'm sorry, Joachim—man and temple, what do you think of that? ... your own body and the external body, the intertwining of bodies? ... phases, civilization? ... morality and the combination of the colors of the spectrum?—somewhere in there, on its periphery lies the correlation with the State.... Notice, colleague—and you, ladies and gentlemen—what surrounds us at this very moment, what mysterious sprays of time and eternity! The woodpecker in the branches, the reddish cloud scudding by beneath the main grayish mass, and in this window, colleagues, look at the accidental harmony— the postman's green jacket and the red of that Ferrari against all that gray and purple...."

"Stop the slyness!" barked Von Deretzki like a master sergeant. "Evading the question? Hiding under pure art? I see who you are! You are a disguised dissident!" Now he was standing and pointing an exposing finger. "These Russian renegades are all over the place, blackening our Idea! And look, now they're even in Soviet delegations!"

"Take it easy," Ogo said.

Tom Gretzke and Pastor Brandt exchanged worried looks. Gretzke intervened.

"Comrade Von Deretzki is too heated. Our community knows him as an overly temperamental man. Don't be insulted, Ogorodnikov, that in the heat of the moment he called you a dissident."

. "I'm not insulted," Ogo said with a shrug. "I am a dissident, but not a disguised one, as Johann just said. Any real photographer is a dissident. My colleague, in trying to expose me, gave me a compliment."

Ogo rose abruptly. The German rose abruptly on the other side of the table. Almost simultaneously they picked up their cameras and shot each other.

A minute of stunned silence passed; then Linda Slippenbach slapped her thigh and burst out laughing. The three Slavists giggled. Watching them, the Turks smiled gravely. The Berlin photographers turned to each other like basketball players at time out. Tom Gretzke temporized with both hands. Pastor Brandt made oval pacifying gestures with one hand. Yuri sat as if bopped by a beanbag. Petro, encouraged by his successful speech, regarded the proceedings with the superciliousness of superpowers regarding the strife of little nations.

In another minute the "hot fellow" Joachim von Deretzki, standing firm like a monument of fire and steel, began shouting that he approved the activities of the Soviet government and of the KGB, who were cleansing their country from the dissident contagion. General embarrassment ensued once more.

"Well, really, Joachim, you're a bit too much," muttered Pastor Brandt.

"M-m-m," said Chairman Gretzke. Von Deretzki tossed aside his chair with his left hand, seemed to palpate the air in front of him with his right, and then dashed outside. There was a sense of something historic having happened, comparable to the incident at the Susanna Konditorei in Zurich, when the comrades laughed at Vladimir Ilyich's proposal for democratic centralism. Everyone watched him flee. The man's poor hair was flying back rather nicely, reminiscent of yet another hero, the legendary Che on board the yacht *Granma* after five daiquiris. Von Deretzki out on the porch. A splash of something white—Frau Kempfe: Where are you going, sir, it's almost time for the *Frühstück!* Von Deretzki fell into the red Ferrari. The sports car pulled out of the row with a crooked smile, lifted its stylish rear end, and instantly carried the driver into a distance that the participants in the Artist and Power discussion could no longer see.

"Did he get in the wrong car?" Ogo innocently asked. Now everyone else laughed, including the Turks, who hadn't understood very much, and the Russians, who had understood nothing. "Yes, he's a millionaire, that Von Deretzki," Linda Slippenbach explained. "Rather, he's the son-in-law of a billionaire, that's all. . . ."

Over *Frühstück* they uncorked many bottles of Rhine wine. Ogo hoped to relax, and had three glasses of wine in short order, but instead he got a surge of energy and began expounding on the German tendency toward totalitarianism, and on the fact that it was shameful to live beyond the Wall and call it a "border," and also shameful to discuss human rights violations in Turkey in the presence of Russians, for comparing Turkey to the USSR was like comparing the Athens of Pericles to the Persia of Darius. At that, one of the girl Slavists burst out in tears, saying that Comrade Ogorodnikov had shattered all her ideals. Linda was laughing. "He's joking, don't you get his humor?" Pastor Brandt said that he had serious disagreements with Herr Ogorodnikov's concepts, even though he understood the disillusionment of the Russian intelligentsia under the Soviet model of Marxism. Ogo was about to get wound up again, but just then the priest took out the tickets to the jazz festival, disarming the member of the Photographers' Union USSR.

Lunch was ending when Soviet diplomats Zafalontsev and Lyankin appeared and marched across the room straight for Ogorodnikov, looking as if their suitcase had been swiped. They had to have a talk immediately! A hot whisper right in Ogo's ear: Tell Brandt that several technical, purely technical questions have to be discussed. Zafalontsev had completely lost the languid air that he so considered a sign of international style, and wild fear was now in his eyes. Lyankin looked at Ogo as if deciding which hip to throw him over. The three of them left the refectory and went out on the porch.

At the end of the street was a car with a Soviet flag. No, there was no escape.

"Comrade Ogorodnikov," Zafalontsev began rather hurriedly. "Circumstances have changed sharply, and we need to have your program in complete detail. What you are planning to do, where you are headed today, tomorrow, and the day after."

"Friend Zafalontsev, you shouldn't drink before sunset," Ogo suggested, and sat down on a stone lion that guarded the building.

Zafalontsev nervously laughed. "I'm serious, Comrade Ogorodnikov. Much has changed, we'll tell you later. Better yet, why don't we go to the embassy?"

"You mean the consulate, don't you?" Ogo tried to address Lyankin, too, taking his measure as if planning a response to an attack.

"No, I meant the embassy," Zafalontsev said, almost singing the words.

"Beyond the Wall, you mean?" Ogo was truly surprised, as if he hadn't just come from there.

"Well, to Unter den Linden." Zafalontsev got cute.

Lyankin's criminal face moved. "To the capital of the German Democratic Republic."

"I can't today." Ogo rose from the stone lion.

"They're waiting for you." Zafalontsev looked up at him in a way that made everything clear. They missed him in Moscow. The PhIDs were furious. Sending coded cables. They might have come themselves. They must have. They were waiting. Zafalontsev must have realized he had said too much, and rapidly added, "The administration is waiting. I think our ambassador Abrakadin himself. Why don't we go, hm? We'll settle everything quickly...."

"Today is out of the question." Ogo lifted his leg to walk to the Baptists' door.

"Come along!" Lyankin reached over for Ogo's shoulder with his left hand and waved with his right down the street. The consulate car moved toward the academy.

"Wait, Lyankin," Zafalontsev said. "Our friend mustn't have understood. This is serious, Maxim—or do you have something more serious in West Berlin?"

Lyankin stepped over and began turning the bold unruly photographer with his elbow. The driver opened the front door from inside.

"Fuck off, you prick!" Ogo rasped with unexpected fury into Lyankin's face. "Get away, stop pushing. These aren't the old days!" Lyankin had obviously not dealt with such disobedience in a long time; he recoiled. Ogo took the decisive step and put his hand on the academy doorknob.

"I'm tired of you, Ogorodnikov," said the cultural counselor, and sighed. "Let's go, Lyankin, we'll report the independence being shown here."

Before getting into the Audi they looked back, two mean guys in sturdy, middle-class suits, ties up to their Adam's apples. Weren't the ones who brought the kicking physicist out of England last year just like them? A jab of a needle right through the trousers, so that the man turned into a drooling idiot for a couple of hours and awakened in Lubyanka's vaults.

Ogo couldn't take his eyes off them. These aren't the old days, not the old days. . . .

The car drove down the peaceful Mitte Vogelsee. The landscape was born again.

2

"HOW DO YOU LIKE BERLIN?"

"It's unique."

"Unique?"

"Unique, like Venice. Say thanks to Khrushchev and Ulbricht for making your city unique."*

---

*In referring to Soviet leader Khrushchev and East German Communist chief Ulbricht as the creators of Berlin's uniqueness, Ogo has in mind the Wall. Judge for

Ogorodnikov and the director of the Baptist Academy, Pastor Willie Brandt (nothing to do with the former chancellor), were walking across a square to the Karajansary, as they called the Philharmonic here. Tonight it was housing a jazz festival. At first Ogo hadn't understood where he was being invited. "Jazz? You're a jazz lover, Willie? Oh, I am, too, but I'm surprised that you are. . . . Bah, why, this is that famous Berlin Jazz Festival, or as you Germans say it, Berliner Yats Tage, of course, yes, the horns of freedom! . . . No, no, Willie, I'm not exaggerating, for people of my generation in the USSR, they were the horns of freedom."

The Wall was nearby, beyond the translucent linden allées, peacefully turning pink under the setting rays of sun. You could even see the black and blue graffiti and with a little effort make out the word SCHWEIN.

"Excuse me, but what do you have in mind?" Pastor Brandt furrowed his brow. He had a bouncy stride, pink cheeks, and he looked at least fifteen years younger than his sixty. The worn tweed jacket and corduroy trousers were the uniform of Berlin's avant-garde intelligentsia. It was hard to see a man of the cloth in him except for the expression on his face, but who paid attention to such trifles anymore? Of course, Pastor Brandt was carrying a real pastoral umbrella, which had been passed down from the eighteenth century.

"Aren't there any secrets in your city?" Ogo asked.

"Secrets? You're confusing me."

Around the Philharmonic there were quite a lot of people, but not really a lot; at least tickets were being sold quite calmly at all the box offices. Ogo could imagine the crowds this concert would draw in Moscow, with Chick Corea, Freddie Hubbard, Herbie Hancock, and most importantly, Woody Herman's big band with Gerry Mulligan the Great! Of course, it wouldn't be just in Moscow, but in any European capital the gig would be sold out a week in advance. West Berlin was dying out. There used to be so much electricity here! It was here in 1957 that Armstrong played and Ella sang, and young Soviet officers secretly crept into the concerts. That's when the line "Jazz is America's secret weapon"

---

yourself, dear reader, how much of its romantic image Berlin would have without the Wall!

gained currency. Ulbricht shat in his pants, Khrushchev got all excited about "noise music." Why didn't that gang like jazz? Neither Nazis nor Commies could stand it. Because of the improvisations?

He photographed a panorama from the steps of the Philharmonic: sort of a tunnel through the festival crowd and the linden trees to the splotches of sunset on a distant strip of concrete and the word SCHWEIN.

Pastor Brandt stopped in the Philharmonic doorway. "Ogo, I'd like to talk more specifically with you about that problem."

"What problem?"

"The secret, as you called it."

"Well, let's talk about it."

"Are you joking? This isn't the place for a serious talk. Perhaps tomorrow at the academy?"

"All right."

"Eleven-thirty?"

"Okay, Willie, eleven-thirty."

"So, I'm expecting you tomorrow at eleven-thirty for a discussion in my office." He held Ogo's elbow and winked right at his eye. "I'm sure Frau Kempfe will spoil us with something delicious."

Onstage was Mulligan, a fifty-year-old Viking with a gold weapon. The sound of the saxophone seemed to be crowding the air out of the enormous auditorium. The trick was that instead of the saxophonist improvising to the band, he kept a mighty pulsing rhythm against which the whole group improvised.

Enraptured by Mulligan's swing, Ogo felt himself free, young, and full of humor and love. So they still play jazz in the world?

He felt the same calming effect during the intermission of the jazz festival, especially when he ran into Linda Slippenbach with her Berlin bohemian crowd, all slightly in the twenties style. First they smoked on the stairs, discussing the merits of the jazz "fusion," then they headed for the bar to drink champagne, and it was here, on the way to the bar, that the evil pair appeared once more—Zafalontsev and Lyankin.

They walked like a patrol, shoulder to shoulder, through the festival crowds, checking the crowd efficiently, quadrant by quadrant, segment by segment. He couldn't run! They came closer. Either the comrades had poor vision or they had calculated badly, but they noticed their object only when they were practically on top of him. Zafalontsev smiled falsely and treacherously.

"Maxim Petrovich! I was sure that I'd run into you here! It's just what I told the comrades who waited for you in vain—'I'm sure to see Ogorodnikov at the festival, because jazz is "America's secret weapon."' Just as a joke, of course; these aren't the olden days, as you so rightly put it. Just feeling in the mood to joke and fool around. The jazz is so wonderful, unforgettable, Maxim Petrovich, the real thing! Those foolish things, that was just unforgettable, wasn't it? Our generation grew up on that, right? Right?"

Next to him trembled Lyankin's white face, sealed forever with the unsmoothable Soviet leprosy.

3

THAT NIGHT, IN bed alone, he was miserable. Now I can't even sleep, I've got a lousy chill. Maybe I shouldn't go to Paris? General Planshchin will cook up an "international conspiracy" with that for sure. It's not hard to imagine the headlines in *Photogazette* and *Word of Honor*: "The Moral Fall of the Photographer Ogorodnikov," "Ogorodnikov's Secret Lenses," "Whose Film Stock Are You Using, Mr. Ogorodnikov?"

Anyone who hinders them in the least is a serious political enemy. To them my album *Splinters* is a bundle of dynamite, so *Say Cheese!* must be an atom bomb. . . . "Ogorodnikov sold out for dollars." "You sold the revolutionary traditions of your family cheaply, Mr. Ogorodnikov." "The Solzhenitsyn of Photography " . . .

Did he have the stomach to put up with this?

Maybe I should say the hell with Paris, go back to Moscow, drop everything, pick up my equipment, and go to Anastasia in the mountains, stay there a long time, a year, five years, until everyone forgets about me. Photograph everything in those sharp mountain contrasts, cleanse myself of Soviet and anti-Soviet stuff, like those guys who never come down from the mountains, take up meditation, concentration. . . . How do they put it? Gather up all the black fluff into a green frame, and narrow that frame. . . . Surface from an imaginary ocean. . . . Become one with the rainbow. . . .

Tired of lousing around in bed, Ogorodnikov dressed, put on his raincoat, and went into the hall. The dull lights in the Regatta's hallway barely illuminated the few pairs of shoes left out by the guests for cleaning. Downstairs in the lobby, the night porter sat in an armchair, magazine in his left hand, cigar in his right, watching television, which was filled with disgusting splotches of kung fu. A fellow like that night porter could easily be an Eastern spy. A special car could easily be waiting outside the hotel. . . .

The porter, leaning sideways, was getting up from the chair. "What would you like, sir?"

"No, no, everything's fine, don't worry. . . ."

Ogo went out on the street, which was empty. The cars parked along the sidewalk were also empty. The foliage, still half green, drooped under the cloudy streetlamps. It was said that you could live here for years in the Kreuzberg area and no one would ever know.

He left the illuminated canopy of the Regatta Hotel and turned the corner, where it was dark except for slight reflections on the car roofs. After walking several blocks he sat down on a concrete stump, leaned against a building, and lit a cigarette.

No need to exaggerate, the neighborhood slept; the VWs, Porsches, and Mercedeses slept. Only the window of one antique store was awake; in it he could see a green nephrite dog. Of course, there was another wide-awake reveler—the Coke dispenser on the corner.

Suddenly everything floated before his eyes. I'm slipping, he thought. Speed increasing, no way to brake. The nephrite dog grew in size. Collision inevitable. Will I crash or not? Hold on tight to "real things." A sense of humor will save me. The border city of Berlin. A wall between life and despair, it can't be overcome. . . .

Finally he surfaced. That's what I get for smoking and not sleeping. . . .

He was dying to take a leak. He got up from the concrete stump and headed for the nearest archway. A great Russian photographer had spent his young years in this city, trying to live and love in a Berlin not divided by a wall, but he had lived and loved until he began taking pictures like an American. . . .

Suddenly two paces away Ogo heard clear Russian speech.

"Comrade Lieutenant, the street is empty. May I relieve myself?"

"Do it, Matkin, hurry!"

Like an invasion, a Soviet jeep with three soldiers and an officer came around the corner and stopped. Ogorodnikov pressed himself against the wall. Were they sent for me?

Matkin jumped down from the jeep, ran past him, disappeared beyond the arch, and a grateful element tinkled onto the pavement.

"Comrade Lieutenant, there's a Fritz standing there," said one of the soldiers in the jeep, pointing at Ogo. "Is he drunk?"

"None of our business," the patrol commander replied sternly. A relieved Matkin was running back to the jeep. A Russian doesn't need much—he pissed without problems and was happy and even slightly romantic.

"Hey, guys, there's Coca-Cola on the corner!" Matkin exclaimed romantically. "Let's have a drink!"

"First he pisses, and then he wants to drink. Really, Matkin," a soldier said.

"What are you going to drink with? Your cock?" another one asked.

"Cut it out!" the lieutenant ordered. The car set off.

Ogorodnikov felt his kidneys cracking open. He began pissing near the wall. The patrol slowly receded in the fog, round backs in the unseasonably warm pea jackets, the butts of their Kalashnikovs sticking up. Our oafish, clumsy, impoverished Matkins, "guardians of peace and progress. . . ."

The urine gushed out of him and then suddenly stopped, his whole body shuddering; then the stream poured out again. Where was this enormous, incomprehensibly enormous amount of moisture coming from? A bladder can't hold more than three liters, but I've pissed all over the street, my urine has been gurgling down the gutter for over fifteen minutes. I can't stop it, shuddered Maxim Petrovich Ogorodnikov in despair, I'll flow out till I'm empty. . . .

4

THE CRUMMY REMAINDER of the night at the Regatta was interrupted by the telephone.

"Good morning," a mechanical voice said. "I'm calling about the program for the day."

"Who is this?" Ogorodnikov rasped.

"From the consulate. Lyankin."

"Are you nuts? What time is it?"

"Drop the nasty tone. It's going on nine."

"It's seven minutes to eight!" howled the awakened man.

"We'll be over there in about twenty minutes," Lyankin said, and quickly hung up.

Ogorodnikov jumped out of bed, filled with a strange liveliness and anger. Got me! Lousy creeps. They'll drive me to ask for political asylum if they keep it up! I'll show you, you fucking protocol bitches, I'll cut off your noses! You won't find shit in here! I'll be gone in ten minutes!

Eight minutes later there was a knock. Who the hell would that be? He flung open the door. The opening was filled by counselors Zafalontsev and Lyankin, in fresh shirts and ties.

"Have you heard the news? Grandmaster Korchnoi, the defector, was in a car accident, they say!"

Ogorodnikov moved abruptly, shoving his right shoulder forward and down, the way kids scare each other. "Oh, sorry, my shoelace is untied. . . ."

"Let us into the room," Lyankin said. "There are Germans walking around here."

"Come in, please, my countrymen!" Ogo was playing the fool and danced inside with arms fixed in a broad embrace, then turned sharply. "Is his head all right?"

"Whose?" Zafalontsev asked.

Ogorodnikov laughed meanly. "Have you forgotten why you're here, Zafalontsev? Is Korchnoi's head all right, I hope? He has chess to play, he needs to think. Now your favorite Karpov has to protect something else. What something else, exactly? Right, Lyankin, his tongue—to lick your asses!"

The counselor for physical culture choked slightly and looked at the counselor for culture, as if to ask, May I finish the bastard off? "Who permitted you to use such threats against me?"

Ogorodnikov asked, "Such idiotic hints? I can report this to the press, you know."

"*What?*" Zafalontsev asked quickly.

This may be the turning point, Ogo thought. I say "To the press!" and they'll attack with the needle. Maybe they've already been instructed to do that! A shot through my pants?

"I'll take this to the Central Committee!" Ogo roared.

Zafalontsev giggled nervously. "Oh, I'm afraid they won't understand you at the Central Committee."

The three of them sat down on the three chairs of the hotel room, forming an isosceles triangle. Ogorodnikov suddenly realized that the grim scene could turn into a farce at any moment.

"I'm kidding," Ogo said with a smile. "You guys joke, so why can't I? I've been thinking, you know, that sometimes"—and with mock severity he raised a finger—"and I stress the 'sometimes,' it's good to have a drink first thing in the morning. We're Russians,* aren't we?"

"What, do you happen to have some herring with you?" Lyankin inquired sourly.

"I have my Russian soul with me, old man. Look, there's a bar across the street. It's open. What do you say we go, boys? My treat."

Of course, after a certain amount of exchanging looks, coughing into fists, and turning of heads, the proposal was accepted. The troika left the hotel in the direction of the Salonika Bar, in front of which the owner and son and daughter-in-law were trying to mop away yesterday's puddles.

"What's this? Did it rain here last night? All these puddles?"

"They're piddles. An elephant peed here last night," Ogorodnikov explained readily. "Hear the Greeks laughing? *Elephantos, elephantos!*"

---

*And what Russian would refuse a free drink nowadays? In the leading institutes of the homeland a rather strange materialistic fatalism had developed in regard to foreign drinks and certain souvenirs; the important thing was to "take," while to "reciprocate" was another matter. Actually, one could buy a pretty good state secret for a decent souvenir. Western intelligence services hadn't figured that out yet. Either that, or they couldn't budget for bribes.

In the empty bar, which smelled of something unappetizing, they began the shameless rounds of White Horse chased by Schmitz beer. Soon all three men were trashed.

"Do you think you've bought us with this whiskey?" Lyankin asked, poking him with his index finger. "You know how much of this stuff I've had in my career?" He made a sign above his ear. "Don't worry, we're just feeling you out, cocksucker!"

"What's the matter, boys, don't you trust Soviet photographers? What are your instructions for me?" Ogorodnikov asked.

"Oh, Maxim," Zafalontsev replied. "Do you think we're so out of it here in Berlin? I know all your friends in art. Mikhanin-Kuchkovsky had his teeth done here, and we got on capitally. We'd sit and sit, talk and talk.... Don't get riled up, Maxim, we're not the Glands.... Well, our impromptu try about Korchnoi was tactless, okay, but the idea was noble, we're worried about you. We're all post-Stalinists, even Lyankin."

Ogorodnikov scratched Lyankin behind the ear. "I'm glad we've become friends, boys. Now I won't complain about you to the Central Committee or to the Voice of America, and tomorrow, so be it, I'll free the border city of my presence."

The diplomats were seized by mixed feelings, in connection with which another bottle of White Horse was bought.

"You misunderstood me," said the absentminded artist, batting his eyelashes. "Didn't I tell you I wasn't going on to Moscow? I didn't? I must have, yes, I did, I did! I told you three times yesterday that I wasn't going to Moscow. I mean, *am* going to Moscow, but with a side trip first. No, not to Warsaw. Why to Prague? Why are you bringing up Prague, when I told you yesterday three times that I'm going to Moscow with a stop in Paris? ... Right, *Paris* ... no, friend Lyankin, you're pointing in the wrong direction. That's Warsaw. Paris is that way, toward the toilet."

The diplomats were already running for the exit, if, of course, you can call a series of stumbles on barstools running.

Ogorodnikov, sweaty but not drunk, with a traveling itch that flittered from his cheeks to his armpits to his crotch, took a taxi to Mitte

Vogelsee for his 11:30 appointment with Pastor Brandt. The pastor greeted him with open arms.

"My dear Maxim! I'm anticipating with great pleasure, dear Maxim, our discussion!" Clearly anxious, the pastor rubbed his hands, and then pressed his elbows to his sides and did several boxing feints. "So, my dear Maxim, please, repeat your attack of yesterday. I dare to assert that I'll have what it takes to parry it!". . . .

"Ah, Willie, I beg you, don't take too seriously the nonsense that Russian photographers babble." Ogorodnikov rubbed his forehead, but no further spark came. What had we been talking about yesterday? "Ah, Willie, dear Wilhelm, everything around us is so nonobligatory, shaky, and random. . . ."

"Aha-a." Pastor Brandt cleverly wagged his finger. "Not a bad opening, not bad artillery preparation. A treacherous flank maneuver, dear Maxim. Well, why not, now you'll receive an answering blow." Ogo stared at the perfectly trimmed sideburns, the firm cheeks, the button nose, crowned with gold-rimmed glasses; the pastor's fine figure was reflected in the glass door of the bookcase, clearer than the actual person, who was partially in the dusty beam of the autumn sun. "You speak of the friability and nonobligatoriness of modern ideas, dear Maxim, but I dare to assure you that to this day all civilization depends on the fundamental ideas of the Renaissance. . . ."

Here Frau Kempfe appeared. Solemn, curtsying, she rolled in a table with a Meissen coffee service and a cut-glass decanter with liqueur. She smiled encouragingly at Ogorodnikov, as if to say, I understand your position is terrible, Pastor Brandt is an unbeatable debater, but you must still resist, sir!

The Turkish chef and the Spanish maid peeked through the half-open door. Apparently, the whole academy was prepared for this philosophical duel.

"The ideals of man-worship are alive today, dear Maxim. Moreover, the process is not yet completed, and that community of people we call civilized. . . . Excuse me, you don't mind if we tape our conversation, do you? I give you my word, it will be used only within these walls."

O Lord, sighed Ogorodnikov. I'll have to pay for the hospitality, play the tournament debater, assume the opposing view, blast the true ideas of the Renaissance from the false position of medieval fucking obscurantism so popular in Moscow circles nowadays. . . .

Everything suddenly began to dissolve: Frau Kempfe and the little Turk in the chef's hat, and Pastor Brandt, his thumbs hooked à la Lenin into his vest. The parquet floor swayed heavily under the imperial Soviet tread, and open jackets flapping, the much-too-prematurely forgotten comrades Zafalontsev and Lyankin approached.

"This time, Ogorodnikov, quit jerking us around. The ambassador himself sent his Mercedes for you. *Abrakadin,* understand?" According to rumors, the extreme and plenipotentiary Comrade Abrakadin, a gray Stalinist coat-checker with a haughtily lowered lip, considered himself to be the number-one man in Germany, since he sat over that part of it that contained the imperial troops.

Still feeling the flow of surrounding objects, Ogorodnikov rose and asked Frau Kempfe for a cup of coffee. "Alas, it's impossible for me to go—I'm having a discussion with Mr. Brandt. A lot of our future relations depend on . . ." In the mirror he saw a yellowish, long-nosed, and poorly washed fellow with a steaming cup of coffee in his hand.

Then the phone rang and, apparently, it was not a simple call. Pastor Brandt spoke with the most serious respect: "Guten Morgen, Excellenz, Jawohl, Excellenz. . . ." Covering the receiver with his hand, with the most serious respect: "Mr. Ogorodnikov, His Excellency is asking for you—Soviet Consul General Bulkin."

Ogorodnikov heard a voice that seemed to assume immediate and total capitulation just from its sound. "What's the matter with you, have you forgotten? Soviet power must be obeyed always and everywhere!"*

---

*We know that nowadays the authorities with their lascivious smirks sometimes try to refer to the Bible—that is, "all regimes come from God." However, you're not referring to just any regime, you're referring to the Soviet regime, aren't you, Comrade Consul General? That's what an innocent soul would ask. After all, yours

"Who's arguing with that?" Ogo replied quickly. The consul general harrumphed vaguely; apparently the answer had caught him unawares. Then came energetic "lightning-fast" fencing:

"You're behaving extremely ambiguously, Comrade Ogorod—"

"Your colleagues are forcing me to—"

"How do you explain your refusal to come to the embassy—"

"Why am I being subjected to surveil—"

"You're applying for a French visa behind our backs?"

"You're pushing me—"

"You're playing with fire, Maxim Petrovich!"

"You're pushing me to an extreme step!"

With that scream one of the fencers lunged into an attack, and from the pause that followed he understood that it was a hit.

Bulkin sang in a honey voice after the pause, like a matchmaker. How could Maxim Petrovich have misunderstood? We're *concerned* about you. We're all family, after all, not strangers. We just worry that such a fine fellow not ... slip. Want to fly down to Paris for the girls? Big deal! These aren't the old days! You should have just told us ahead of time and we'd have taken care of it. Who should go to Paris if not a photographer? So why not drop by and have some vodka with the ambassador? Abrakadin's a little hurt, that's all, you can understand that. He's a lover of photography himself, so he was hurt. Well, what are you doing this evening? Busy? Well, I thought so. And tomorrow you're off to Paris, right? Well, all right, but, Maxim Petrovich, why those extreme measures, really now? You couldn't put it off to the day after tomorrow? You can't, just as I thought. But would you at least write a

---

doesn't come from God, does it, Messrs. KGB Men? It's not a regime anyway if it violates its own laws a hundred times a day, is it? After all, comrades, a regime is what makes sure the laws are obeyed, right? How can you be called a regime if you do everything secretly, if you decide everything in your dens? Maybe it would be better to call yourselves a power rather than a regime? Just an evil Soviet power, how about that, comrades? So that there's no confusion with the Bible, okay?

That's what an innocent soul would have asked in this brief break we invented. Ogorodnikov's soul was not innocent, if only because it was put into mortal action in the famous Russian year of 1937.

note of explanation to Abrakadin? Well, thanks for that at least. Let me speak to one of our comrades.

A pair of Cupids on the ceiling called on them to keep a sense of humor. Such a ridiculous scene: two men with switches had come for the hooky-playing schoolboy, the street outside was still in the middle of the eighteenth century, the pastor was a bankrupt Voltairean, Frau Kempfe was holding the trembling Turk's hand, the coffee was cold, and the yellow hooky-head handed the phone to the man named Zafalontsev.

Ogorodnikov bowed to him and went to the exit. Behind him came Zafalontsev's "Wait," but Ogo merely muttered something like "Ver-wam" and flung open the door to the porch.

Near the porch stood a Mercedes with a red metal flag, and next to the flag, resting his rear on the car's fender, was the driver. It wasn't the indifferent and quiet man who had driven Ogo from the airport. This was someone else, as if from a different order of troops, a worker from a different department, completely different. He peered greedily into Ogorodnikov's face. For some reason this other man seemed familiar for a second, something not unfamiliar flashed in the dull lupine face. For a second they locked eyes. Then the driver gave a quick just-in-case look over his shoulder and simmered down, relaxed, shaking his indifferent thigh. Following his stealthy glance, Ogorodnikov saw another patrol of the anti-Hitler coalition at the end of Mitte Vogelsee, this time an American one. The jeep was driving slowly toward the Academy. When it came even with the porch, Ogorodnikov walked along next to it. The soldiers, sprawled in their seats, paid no attention either to the Soviet flag on the Mercedes or to the tall German striding swiftly next to them on the brick sidewalk.

Ogorodnikov's newly aware organ of fear was working. Out of the corner of his eye he watched the four soldiers, one of whom was black. In the translucent gray of the autumn day the snow-white triangles of their T-shirts shone brightly in their open shirts. The soldiers were talking about something, and he heard snatches of their conversation. "Yeah.... I liked that chick.... Yeah ... kidding ... you gotta guess...."

Something shameful is happening, thought Ogorodnikov. I am running from Russians under cover of an American car. A shameful sigh of relief escaped my lips when I saw the Americans. However, what do I do next? They're going to speed up and I'll be left alone with our boys. I have to get to the corner with them, there's cross traffic there, I even saw a taxi flash by. I should remember this moment. I should get a photo of the Bird Lake street with the three black figures staring after me, and the reflecting windows of the town houses, and the shedding trees.

Counselors Zafalontsev and Lyankin, as well as PhID Captain Nikolai Slyazgin, acting the part of chauffeur, watched him go most attentively. Everything had happened in one second. The light turned green at the corner. The defenders of freedom drove off. Ogorodnikov took a taxi. The knights of the revolution dove into their black limousine.

5

THERE WAS A new doorman at the Regatta, a round-faced Fritz mama's boy. You had to be blind not to see that he was an Eastern spy, bought, of course, up to his gills, or else terrorized. Give me the *Schlüssel*, motherfucker, and no back talk!

"You had a call from New York," the man said in Russian with a smile.

Ogo laughed. "Terrific! You speak Russian! No more masks!"

"I studied in the zone, sir," the doorman explained in hotel language, his smile a sign of thanks for interest in his modest person. "Subsequently I left the zone."

"Ran off?" Ogo watched the lad's face like a detective. "I'm planning to run off, too. Interested?"

"You don't need to run from West Berlin, sir. People simply move from here."

"Interesting—then I'm just moving, is that it?" Ogo said with a silly smile, took his *Schlüssel*, and went to his *Zimmer*, reproaching himself along the way for his stupid suspiciousness. On the one hand, every well-trained doorman looked like a KGB spy; on the other hand, he asked himself with a slight lift of the eyebrows, where else should the KGB be if not in West Berlin hotels?

No sooner had he entered the *Zimmer* than the phone rang: New York again, agents of a different type, world business in the person of the pimp of the arts, Bruce Pollack.

"Hello, Bruce, still spruce? Don't understand? You should get Russian by now, we've known each other for years. Okay, okay, I'm-also-very-happy-to-hear-your-voice-sir. . . ."

Ogo suddenly realized with a jolt that Bruce was using the formal you, *vy,* in Russian with him. From those hurried notes over the last few years, carried by reporters and diplomats, Ogo had assumed that he and Bruce were on closer terms, and in Ogo's broken English it was always buddy-buddy-you anyway, but now Mr. Pollack's intonations cleared a substantial and rather chilly distance.

"Your arrival in Berlin has excited many people here. They're talking about the album in New York, Paris, and Milan. There hasn't been such a powerful message from Russia before. Thirty-five names under one cover! What has reached us sounds impressive. Congratulations! Can we expect you in New York? Or would you like me to come to Berlin?"

Ogo pictured Pollack swiveling in the armchair in his office on Fifty-seventh Street. Early morning. Steaming coffee on the desk.

"Forgive me, Bruce, but do you realize what it would mean for me to come to New York or to have you come to Berlin? Do you have any idea of my situation?"

"Of course, Ogo, of course!" The swiveling across the ocean must have stopped. "I understand how complicated things are for you, but we've gotten used to the fact that our Ogorodnikov performs miracles. You're so different from other Russians. . . ."

"Don't think that's a compliment. Besides, you must be expecting slides. There aren't any. Only one copy of the finished Moscow edition will reach the West."

"Forgive me, I don't understand."

"In a word, I don't have slides and the album is still in Moscow."

After a certain pause Pollack asked with extraordinary sincerity, "So, what can I do for you?"

"Can you plug a tape recorder to the phone? I want to make an announcement. Okay, here's the text. Ogorodnikov from West Berlin, November fifteenth. I am in danger. Soviet diplomats are trying to take me to the Eastern sector. If something happens to me, please inform the press that this is the work of the State Photo Directorate of the USSR. The photographer Ogorodnikov. Did you get that?"

"Damn it," whispered Pollack.

Ogo giggled. "That's just in case, Bruce. I hope that happens to me before I leave for Paris."

"Do you need a French visa?" Pollack asked quickly.

"Don't worry, I have one."

"Bravo!" The red- and curly-haired New Yorker had clearly abandoned his custom chair to pace the springy carpet with the cordless phone at his ear. Below him, the smoking miasmas of New York. "No, really, they're right, you're the most Western of all the Russians." For another minute or two Ogo listened to Pollack's strangely empty banter. For some reason he didn't mention at all Ogo's own albums, not even the infamous *Splinters,* for which Ogo had just recently been expecting a major advance. For all his reputation as a thriving Westerner, Ogorodnikov could not overcome the unique Soviet shyness in discussing material questions and never initiated conversations on contracts and advances. They said good-bye.

Under the windows of the Regatta walked citizens of the "frontline city." One citizen stood by a poster column with a pipe in his mouth. Well, naturally, you take your pipe on assignment, what else. I'm surrounded, that's for sure. Should I call the police? Ask for political asylum? . . . But that's shameful, capitulation, the failure of *Cheese!* . . . give it all up to them to devour . . . yes, by the way, that would mean the end of my marriage . . . in that sense, forever . . . right, to the grave. . . . He dialed Linda Slippenbach's number and—O miracle!—she was home.

"Hurry, Ogo, I'm off, I'm late for a meeting of the European parliament. Drop by your hotel? You pervert, we're just friends! Oh, that's not what you meant? Oops, what a shame. You want me to be prepared for anything? The possibility of a press conference? You're not planning to stay in the West, are you, dear? Not ruled out? What a sensation,

what a disgusting sensation, what joy for our right-wing press! I'll call
you right after the meeting of the European parliament, okay?"

He hung up. Nothing but left-wing totalitarian bastards all over the
place, don't expect help from them. He tore a piece of paper from his
notebook and wrote with a marker: "Dear Comrade Ambassador" ...
fuck it, I don't know his name and patronymic, and I shouldn't be
writing with a marker ... and in general, it's silly to be writing at all ...
I could send him a poem in praise of Stalin and he wouldn't believe it
now. . . .

Ogo looked out in the corridor and froze with the incredible sensation of emptiness spreading along his backbone—this could be
that "extreme situation," someone was coming and it was too late to
run. . . .

The elevator signal *ping*ed, and a sturdy substance stepped into the
corridor. Pastor Brandt. Coming closer, the German miracle! He must
want to continue the interrupted discussion? "Willie, could you stop for
a second right where you are? I'll get my camera. There, thanks a lot.
Against the background of the bordello like a damask of the Regatta
you stand like the incarnation of European reason!"

"You must not spend the night here," Brandt said, and went into the
room. "Pack your things, I'll take you to the academy. You'll have nothing to worry about there, I've taken measures."

Ogorodnikov, shaken, looked at the priest. Was he really a real,
unfake human being? What could be more brazen for a "progressive
activist" than saving an almost-defector?

While he packed he looked over a few times at Brandt. The clergy-
man was extremely agitated, even though he tried to remain coura-
geously laconic. He paced with his hands behind his back, taking quick
looks at himself in the mirror, frowning sometimes, sometimes insouciantly whistling, and once even flexed his facial muscles, as if trying on
an expression.

When they left the Regatta, twilight was enveloping the street. Two
men stood by the poster column, one of them in Tyrolean lederhosen.
The pastor's white BMW was parked nearby.

"Your car, Willie, is the most beautiful of all," Ogo said as they
climbed inside it.

"I don't understand how you can joke at a time like this," the pastor muttered.

"And you, Willie, in that soft hat and in your old expensive coat, are the most elegant man of all I met in Berlin."

"Is that serious, or just another joke?" Pastor Brandt flushed slightly. On the ride he kept looking in the rearview mirror and even turned around at red lights.

"I even think, Reverend, that you believe in God," Ogo said softly. The BMW lurched, but stayed on course.

6

BOATS BOBBED AT the dock outside the window of the "safe house" on Mitte Vogelsee. Masts bumped into one another. Along the far shore, above the trees, another transoceanic jet was landing.

... How can my lens transmit the wild danger of this night? The presence of the invisible wall, the truncated space ...

Ogo turned on the light and saw himself in the mirror: an elderly, hounded beanpole. For some reason something Jewish had appeared in his face. That's all that's missing from the pleasure of my Chekist comrades. How could I have aged so much in five days in Berlin? ...

I'm going to forget all this vileness, and so I have! And I'll remember something good, I'll remember all the women I've ever slept with, and so I have! I'll remember the Azau Valley, how Nastya and I skied in the night—I never forgot that! Ogo looked in the mirror again and saw that he had clearly grown younger, that he was even younger-looking than his marvelous forty-two. In only a few seconds a change like that! I'll capture this curious physiological phenomenon on film.

Ogo put the camera on automatic and set it on a tripod. He sat down and remembered the lousy stuff. *Click click click.* Now he forgot the garbage and remembered the lovely things. *Click click click.* And once again and again ...

Someone was outside the window, of course, someone was so carelessly scratching at the window. . . . A sharp turn—no one! A desiccated frog of a plantain leaf was scratching at the window. . . .

But Ogo heard voices downstairs. His heart thudded through his body. You won't take me that easily, comrades! I'll fight tooth and nail. He went into the hallway and looked down.

Frau Kempfe sat in an armchair, knitting. The postman reclined like Pushkin on a chaise longue. The young Turk was on the rug, also in a classic pose, checking the catch on a hunting rifle. A theme for a photograph called "European Guard."

In the morning Max was awakened by Frau Kempfe, bearing a full Continental breakfast. "Herr Ogorodnikov, the reverend asked me to tell you that he will come for you at exactly ten and take you to Tegel Airport. Fraulein Slippenbach is very worried, she says that she lost you yesterday and was looking for you. She will be here in an hour. I think that's all. Ah, yes, some Swiss journalist called, *ach mein Gott*, what a crude dialect!"

"My dear Frau Kempfe, your presence always encourages me both as an artist and as a man." Blushing furiously—no no, don't think that way about a poor widow, Herr Ogo—skirts rustling and cheeks blazing, Frau Kempfe quit the boudoir of the half-dressed foreigner. I'll have to trick her, he realized, slip away without saying good-bye. Perhaps I'm walking into a trap, but perhaps this naïve cleverness will get me to Paris. . . .

In the taxi to Tegel airport he fought the fear that was burning his innards. Really, these aren't the old days, they're not going to inject haloperidol into such a famous man; after all, we appear with cloak and dagger only in national liberation deals now, we don't do that to our own people, well, with a few exceptions, like that physicist in London, and that ballerina they shoved into the water closet, but that's not so many incidents, after all. . . .

But the fear kept on and he wasn't sure his legs could carry him to the plane. Well, it was nonsense: his lower extremities worked well. In fact the airport was wonderful—spacious, air-conditioned, perfumed, humidified, imbued with the smells of a comfortable trip; his depression vanished. At the Air France counter he asked to change to an earlier flight. With incredible politeness his request was honored. He lit up a cigarette with great pleasure and looked around. There was the source of his unexpected comfort—loads of military around, Allied officers, most of them American. And beyond the glass wall amid the

Mercedeses and VWs several soldiers were unloading crates from an army truck. White triangles of T-shirts showed under their shirts. Was that a regulation or were they naturally so clean? In principle it was rather shameful to see as defenders those who were against his country. He should have felt ashamed, but didn't. I don't know what they stand for, but it's not Russians they're against. Basically, they are *our* soldiers ... they're defending me.... Nonsense, I have just one defense writ—and that's my camera. I'm independent ... hm ... especially in the presence of these dark-green uniforms with the white triangles....

At the border control sat a German fellow of the American border style, a real sheriff. "Ihre Papiere, sir?" A very friendly Gerenglish question. "Mein Gott! You have a sowjetischer passport!"

The officer thumbed through the red-skinned passport, looked at the French visa, then raised a highly interested gaze at Ogorodnikov. "You don't seem to have an Eastern stamp, sir?" A corner of his mouth went up under the moustache. "That means you got your French visa in Berlin and not in Moscow, right?"

"Jawohl," said Ogo.

The officer shook his head in a way that revealed nothing and picked up the phone. Am I going to get stuck here? The officer was saying something fast in German into the phone, but it still sounded like something from the American movies. The West Germans had lost the Prussian spirit. It flourished only in the "state of the German proletariat." Spelling Ogorodnikov's name, the officer apologized for the delay and waited. A few minutes later, he said *Jawohl* and started taking instructions. Hm, they must have checked with a computer and got an answer right away. Hm, we underestimate these Westerners. Maybe they have no intention of surrendering.

The officer extended the passport to him and said, with a friendly wink, "Everything's all right! Have a safe voyage!"

Ogo passed the cordon and looked back. The officer was watching him with a smile. Yes, thought Ogo, we underestimate them quite a bit.

Now everything was behind him. Going through the hall to the gate, Ogorodnikov celebrated, sending good-byes to all the PhIDs and to Soviet ambassador Abrakadin, none of whom were anywhere to be seen, when he suddenly felt a look of hatred fixed on him. It was coming from a man in a raincoat at the coffee bar.

Why such strong emotions? our refugee wondered. Well, all right, you're a Soviet spy, you're watching me, but why hate me so witheringly? Why can't you be professional about it? Have you been so ideologically offended? I haven't done anything terrible to you, or your bosses, or your shitty Idea, I merely shat on you from a tall tree. Why such passion? You should take care of your batteries....

He met the burning ray of hatred and realized that it was not meant for him, it was burning everything in its way—at the moment, the wall with an advertisement for a trip to the Canary Islands.

No sooner had the DC-10 taken off than the passengers lined the windows to see the white ribbon of the Wall, cutting through the residential areas and parks and disappearing in the horizon. "Grenze! Grenze!" babbled two young men behind Ogorodnikov in agitation.

Without comprehending the meaning or the form of his action, Ogo turned around and hissed, burbled, and furiously crackled. "What the fuck kind of border is that? It's a prison wall, you assholes! It's a camp zone, you Marxist proletarian cretins.... You see me? I'm a zek, I'm an escaped zek from behind your so-called Grenze...."*

*Semantics rules the world nowadays. Renaming "the Berlin Wall" the GDR *Grenze* or "border" gives the whole thing a totally different meaning: it takes on a notion of defense, rather than captivity. Escaped *zek* (prisoner) Ogo flares up at that sly euphemism.

PARIS

I

VERY TIME OGORODNIKOV happened to be in Paris, his former mother-in-law, Mme. Cheremetieff, née Le Boutillier, said, "Don't forget, my dear, this is your home."

Funny, but in her enormous old apartment on Avenue Foch he really did find a bedroom and private bath waiting for him, a change of linens, a dozen Cardin shirts, slippers—ye gods!—a nightcap, and all the books, boots, films that he forgot last time, all the paper and celluloid mess gathered and put away neatly in the velvet-covered secretaire, inscribed MADAGASCAR 1939 in gold.

"It can be no other way, my friend," his former mother-in-law would say. "You are the father of my dear grandchildren."

The Madagascar souvenir, the Tibetan and Indian statuettes, samurai swords, Afghan carpets, Chinese gongs, Polynesian gods, colonial peacock chairs—all were reminders of Captain Jules-Louis Cheremetieff, a brilliant representative of the thirties and forties, writer, pilot, French spy, whose life was interrupted, quite logically, by a bomb placed in his plane.

"Oh, I remember how Jean-Louis left," the former mother-in-law had told him so many times. "I was seeing him off at the aerodrome for Katmandu. He never announced his route, but I suspected that he was off to Lhasa, there was fighting there. He was laughing, the way he is in this picture. His small plane rose sharply into the bright-blue sky and then suddenly exploded. A bright flash and that was all. That's how our Nadine became an orphan."

Why can't I comprehend that this is "my house"? thought Ogorodnikov. Such a loving former mother-in-law. Such wonderful children. My only real children, at that.

Of all of Ogorodnikov's wives, only Parisienne Nadine turned out to be fecund. She gave him a boy, Misha, and a girl, Masha. *Ça va, papa!* they said to him, and every time, he was astonished at how much they changed.

Only Nadine never changed. After their break in 1973 she turned quite hippie, bought herself a pair of camouflage-print shorts and still wore them. Once Ogorodnikov cautiously probed—was this another pair, a copy of a beloved design? ... Alas, they were the same, amazingly sturdy and just imagine, Ogo, never needing cleaning.

After her bohemian Moscow schooling, Nadine developed lasting lumpenpreferences, befitting international intellectual trash—the ability to live happily in cellars, on the stairs, to eat and drink all sorts of garbage, to fuck anyplace at all. It was, say, cute up to the age of thirty, but now, ladies and comrades, she was a bit beyond that, still leaping exaltedly into flights from one country to another in search of new horizons, a new spiritual life, or mythical business propositions. A commune in the Pyrénées, thirty monks of the new formation, who actually turned out to be ordinary Marxist bastards, stealing ducks and chickens from the villagers. Once producers from a new, powerful company went to Moscow to film something epochal; naturally Nadine was with them, indispensable for her knowledge of Russian swearwords. That episode ended, alas, by an assault in the elevator, not for the purposes of rape, but the same old Soviet deal—black marketeering mixed with snitching. Then, dropping off to Japan—Japan!—where there was a millionaire suitor who dreamt of a Frenchwoman of noble Russian lineage, urging her to hurry, and she flew there in those camouflage shorts, hello and then, of course, good-bye. ... Afterward, in the depths of the apartment on Avenue Foch, the children would hear Maman's nicotine cough, throat clearings, and hoarse *merde, merde, merde* and the Russian *foque, beetch, sheet.* Luckily, the kids had no Russian.

This time Nadine, naturally, was away again—"Swedish lessons in Göteborg"—and after his Berlin hassles, Ogo was overwhelmed by a sensation of blissful comfort: his charming little Misha and Masha, the noble widow of the noble spy for France, the slender finger near her dimpled cheek: Remember, my dear, this is your home!

2

OGO CHANGED HIS shirt and was off to the Champs-Élysées. It was almost December in Europe, but the tables were still out on the sidewalks— and look, familiar faces. . . . By the wall of the Café Fouquet a group of bearded-and-hairy types was smiling and applauding, resembling a Moscow group photo in the style of the almanac *Metropol.* He raised his camera and shot: tables, chairs, trees in the wind, the Arc in the distance, the applauding group. . . . Then he realized that these weren't simply familiar typical faces, but émigré friends, artists and photographers, and that they were applauding him.

"Congratulations! Congratulations!"

"On what, guys? To what do I owe this?"

"Why, Ogo, tout Paris is saying that you've defected."

It seemed that last night rumors had spread across Parizhsky: Ogo made it out to the West, it had happened somewhere in Brazil. And there was an article in the French rag *Libération* with a photo—a grim person with a drooping moustache à la Maxim Gorky, the concentration of all sins and diseases: the vile shot had been taken two years ago, when he was seeing a dentist here, an expensive hack on Rue de Sèvres; M. Kogan, the dropout, injected Novocain right into a nerve bundle so that half Ogo's lower jaw was numb for six months. There was a headline, too: ANOTHER SCANDAL OF SOVIET MARXISM. Implying that if Marxism weren't Soviet, it would avoid scandals.

"Alas, gentlemen, I must disillusion you. I haven't left, I'm simply in Paris to see my kids."

The company did droop a bit, but rallied in quest of the latest Moscow jokes. The strange anguish of emigration! In Moscow you suffocate, it feels as if real life is passing you by, you escape, and then, once again, you're surrounded by the sticks, for you're deprived of Moscow now. . . .

For the time being, Ogorodnikov was enjoying himself, forgetting the stress of Berlin, even New Focus and the insidious PhIDs—such are the miracles of Paris. "Gentlemen, somewhere someone is still fucking," they said upon meeting, and then would begin endless discourse on the past, on mutual friends and their eccentricities, and then the distinction between émigré and Soviet would vanish, and here the word "ours" took on its former meaning.

"I wonder if Andrei Drevesny will get a visa?"

"Is it true that Polina still sees him?"

"In New York, in Soho, there was a big brawl outside the Kitchen Gallery, Alik Konsky threw a case of beer at Chetverkind."

"Are you really planning to go back, Ogo?"

They told a funny story. The famous Georgian filmmaker Tamaz Defloridze was on the Place de la Concorde, staring at a new Jaguar. They had come up behind him and asked, "Tamaz, would you sell your motherland for a car like that?" And without turning a hair, he said, "Without a thought!"

But then depression gnawed at Ogo. Either a reaction to Berlin, or it was simply time for it, or he needed a woman. Other times in Paris he had felt a need for a prostitute, a woman for hire, whom he'd rake for money and commit a sin with, without shame, and to whom he'd say all kinds of dirty things. Of course, all this was in his imagination, and he never did go to a prostitute, but all the women he was ever with in Paris seemed cheap to him, sluts, army mattresses.

Sadness ate him now: prostitution was filth, and attraction to prostitutes was even worse. Those bordellos in the Algerian quarter beyond Montmartre were disgusting, and even more disgusting the lines of men at the doors. For fifty francs you stick your end into a magical human creature, empty, and go out. Next! This city wasn't built for vile sensations, or for prostitution. It was built for universal life, for sliding through time on a golden boat.

Ogo went to one of his old mistresses and astonished her with his flawless gallantry. "Have you really come here for good?" she asked. "They say that a traveling 'glandist' gave a lecture at the Soviet embassy the other day and among other things announced that M. P. Ogorodnikov betrayed the homeland."

"They'll have to take their words back," he said, infuriated, not without some faking, and went straight from his mistress first thing in the morning to the so-called culture group, *ambassade sovietique.*

Young mugs sat in the office, unknown to him from other times, specialists in French culture and with French manners, without a hint of Cheka foot wrapping, as if they weren't the ones who had burned avantgarde paintings at the infamous Bulldozer Exhibition. Why don't I ask them about it!

"Tell me, Comrade Myasnichenko, you wouldn't happen to remember the Bulldozer Exhibition of 1974?"

Myasnichenko's glasses had a special quality; they grew darker depending on his smile. The brighter the smile, the darker the glasses.

"Of course I would. How could I not!"

"You scattered the artists then?"

"Correctaroony. It's rather embarrassing to recall now. Sophomoric. We were young and hotheaded."

"You were flamed up, you mean, Comrade Myasnichenko?"

"Exactly, a flame traveled through our class. The boys from Krasnopresnensky committee came flying down . . ."

"Who came flying down, excuse me?"

"From the regional committee."

"But who from the committee? How did you put it, 'from the regional committee'?"

"I see." The smile grew brighter, the glasses grew darker. "The boys galloped in from the regional committee, the Komsomol boys. . . ."

"You mean like in the civil war. Revolutionary inspiration? To beat up artists?"

"That's just what the mood was like, Comrade. The ideological kulaks raised heads. Well, we were young and hotheaded. . . ."

"May I take your picture, Comrade Myasnichenko?"

"I'd be honored. Shall I take off my glasses?"

The sly Rebeshko, head of the culture group, came in softly. Him Ogo knew from previous trips.

"Comrade Ogorodnikov! Welcome!" He sat down, his buttocks hanging over the sides of the modern stool.

"There are rumors circulating," Ogorodnikov said.

"We've heard, we've heard...."

Rebeshko had so much sneakiness and treachery that he couldn't hide it, and so he had to fool people twice or three times as hard.

"There were numerous misunderstandings in Berlin," Ogo said.

"We've heard, we've heard." Rebeshko, melting in smiles, regarded his visitor as a kindly granny does her mischievous grandson. It was a disarming look; even experienced Ogorodnikov found himself sounding like a spoiled brat.

"Our diplomats treated me horribly there. They bossed me around as if I were a corporal from The Group of Troops and not a famous photographer. Who could believe it, they had me followed...."

"Yes, it happens, it happens." Rebeshko turned pink with a new slimy idea. "What if you wrote down your complaints, Comrade Ogorodnikov?"

"Why not? Give me some paper!"

Total silence reigned in the office while Ogo scrawled blame on the whole Berlin network, including the beyond-the-wall monster Abrakadin. Rebeshko's eyebrows called his young staff to even greater quiet, so as not to scare Ogo off.

"To whom should I address my complaint?"

"Address it to our ambassador," Rebeshko rustled, like a vernal cherry tree. "Our ambassador is a very, very enlightened man."

Taking the desired paper, Rebeshko started reading, occasionally poking his finger at a line and reproachfully shaking his head, "Oh, those Berliners, those Berliners," indicating, therefore, that such behavior was impossible in Paris. "Oh, Abrakadin, Abrakadin," he sighed, and the powerful wink turned his eye into a sort of Siberian pelmeni for an instant. "Then how can you be surprised by the daughter?" the counselor on Soviet culture said, opening his hands.

"Daughter? What daughter? Whose daughter?" Ogorodnikov's ears perked up. He must have run across her in Pitsunda, at the writers' resort—a pleasant sight for sore eyes.

"You mean you really haven't heard, Maxim Petrovich? Abrakadin's daughter—what a story, what shame!—ran off to London with a Yugoslav the day before yesterday!"

Ogorodnikov laughed as he walked through the courtyard filled with Peugeot 504s, which looked like KGB Volgas, and out on Rue de Grenelle he roared until it hurt. That's how your own daughters teach you, you Bolshevik hammerheads....

3

MEANWHILE, GALÉRIE ZUSSMAN & Froid got an exhibition of Ogo's photos ready in record time. Of course, the duration of the exhibit was a record, too—one day.

On the morning of the opening whiteflies flew from the St.-Germain skies. The wind picked them up and tossed them around with the plane leaves along the houses imbued with peace and wealth, and suddenly the whole city, which Ogo sometimes considered his home, shifted a bit and revealed a crack in the drapes of a railway car, and in it flashed by his real home in endless snows, a spot of Russian freezing, misery and pity in the midst of the USSR's contemporary ferocity, a flickering flame which he never held in his hands but whose presence he nonetheless felt.

Le tout Paris russe circulated through the three small gallery rooms, and naturally, they all asked, Are you staying for good? You're planning to go back after a show like this? What's so special about this small show? You know, Ogo, don't play the virgin with us. You exhibit a head *like that* of Lenin and then play the virgin.

"Wait a minute, what's so special in that head of Lenin? The People's Artist Vuchetich was sculpting it and didn't finish it and it's just standing there by the fence of his house."

"Voilà, he's trying to convince us that Lenin's head is just standing there, its back to the street and with its ears sticking out like that."

"Please, gentlemen, I didn't drag it there, I'm just a photographer, gentlemen, and nothing more...."

An extraordinary visitor appeared next to the hero. Extraordinary homeliness, puffy though ratlike features, in an extraordinary outfit— fringes, appliqués, "Latin motifs," maybe, something like Aragonesque communism. . . .

In wonderful Franglais the lady asked the usual idiotic question: Is it true that Russian photography is thirty years behind the West?

Readily agreeing and trying to slip away, Ogorodnikov suddenly saw that it wasn't so simple. The Latin motifs expanded and somehow drove him into the corner. A familiar emptiness spread from the small of his back to his solar plexus.

"It seems to me, dear Mr. Ogorodnikov, that in this exposition there are a few things from your album *Splinters* . . . these ears, for instance . . . this moustache? . . . You shudder, monsieur? Perhaps my knowledgeability surprises you? Ah, it doesn't? Then permit a purely journalistic question—are you really planning to publish your *Splinters?* Do you expect consequences?"

He found her elbow in the wide leather sleeve.

"Permit a question in return? Can't the KGB find anybody without a Slavic accent? I hope you understand what I'm trying to say?"

He tried to squeeze her elbow significantly, but squeezing cast-iron rail would have had the same effect. A crocodilian gaze searched his face. After that the ugly fashion plate left.

The animated Rebeshko, Myasnichenko, and other boys from the culture group rushed up to him. "Success, success! The press is out in force! Congratulations, you've won a big battle and put an end to the slander!"

The day dragged on; the people in the gallery kept changing; occasionally cheap champagne was brought around. One of the boys was always in the crowd, even though a good look at the exhibit and an exchange of opinions needed no more than a half hour. Finally, not long before the end of the show, all the boys left, and Bruce Pollack appeared.

With a carry-on bag over his shoulder, distractedly running his fingers through his red curls and pushing his slipping glasses up with his thumb, Pollack approached the hero of the day. A brief moment of awkwardness ensued. Ogorodnikov thought that they were on an informal basis

once again and should be giving each other bear hugs but Bruce prof-
fered a certain restraint and explained that he had come straight from
the airport—he had come to discuss important things.

After the show closed, a crowd of twenty or so went off to La Coupole. Russian émigrés predominated, but there were also Frenchmen,
Americans, a couple of Scandinavians, and one Senegalese. They sat in
the corner of the large room, and very quickly under the influence of
champagne and chateaubriand Ogo's favorite atmosphere of easy-flow-
ing café life took hold. In order to keep his guests from feeling
"pressed," he announced it was all his treat and flashed a pack of rustling francs, his advance from Zussman & Froid.

Bruce sat next to Ogo, hurriedly devoured his steak, and began on
the "important" things. "Forgive me, I want to talk before you get too
loaded, we're in a rather touchy moment here." They began talking
about *Say Cheese!* right away, which rather irritated Ogo. Why did Pollack seem determined not to mention *Splinters,* as if he himself hadn't
just recently prophesied "a smashing success" for the album? It looks
as if he sees me now as only the leader of the new group. . . .

It turned out that New Focus was being viewed by authoritative circles (Which ones? Where did they circle?—Okay, I'll explain later) as a
worldwide sensation. Both Fountain and Pharaoh were prepared to sign
a major contract! Without seeing the album? "Yes, without seeing it,
but only in the event that you, Max, come to New York, and tell them
all about it."

"Wait—New York? If I go off to New York after Berlin and Paris,
our comrades will— "

"They won't find out about it. You'll go to New York for three days
on the Concorde, no one will ever know. We'll get you a separate visa,
no traces on your passport, when you get back to Paris you throw
it away, and that's that. By the way, what luck, look who just
walked in, my young influential friend Philippe, who'll help you with
your visa tomorrow and after tomorrow he incidentally flies to Moscow, he has enormous contracts in the Soviet Union, so that if you
need anything brought out of Moscow, you'll never have a better
opportunity. . . ."

A well-built and excellently coiffed Philippe shrugged wonderfully—nothing is impossible.

"A fine fellow," said Ogorodnikov. "A dependable, terrific guy."

"I have the feeling that Monsieur Philippe speaks Russian rather well," offered Bruce.

"I could have guessed," Ogo said.

"A marvelous meeting," said Philippe in Russian. "In general," he said, "you, Comrade Ogorodnikov, in the long run, please come tomorrow for the American visa. Here with satisfaction is my card."

He extended his card, which already had the time of the appointment written on it. Then, tugging at his flawless flannels, he said good-bye, since he had dropped by La Coupole unexpectedly, and still had a landmark date ahead. His handshake betrayed good tennis and not-bad karate.

"An amazing evening," Ogo said, "so many fortunate coincidences . . . if I had never been to La Coupole, I would have thought it was a setup."

The lawyer's ruddy face, with its "Jewish mama" expression, was turned to his client.

"You know," Ogo went on, "I was warned again today . . . by . . . colleagues of Monsieur Philippe from that . . . hm, from our side?" Ogorodnikov asked. He sat, relaxed, enveloped in a feeling of unexpected coziness, as if he were loafing through reading a thriller in a Paris café.

Bruce nodded. Yes, he knew, of course. Philippe told him about it, of course.

This very same Philippe?

Yes.

"Well, that's terrific," Ogo said, and laughed. "And do you know the gist of the conversation?"

"More or less," said the Jewish mama and put a hand on the bony knee of her protégé, as if to say, Don't pay attention to all these trifles, it's not really your headache, dear boy. Hm, thought Ogo, looking at the freckle face, hm, hm, hm, why is the silence continuing?

Beyond the outline of Bruce's head in the glass wall of the terrace, nocturnal Montparnasse flowed by. Suddenly two snow-white animals stopped in the crowd and stared into the café—a nanny goat and a llama. The pink beads of the mid-France goat and the agate orbs of the Peruvian wonder.

"And what's this!?" cried Ogorodnikov.

"A goat and a llama, if you please," a passing man said in Russian; he was middle-aged and pleasant-looking, with a charred pipe and an ironic acorn-colored bald spot in a rumpled ten-year-old tweed jacket. One worn suede shoe was already pulling a chair over to Ogorodnikov's table. "Allow me to introduce myself. Ambroise Zhigalevich. Don't worry, I'm not an émigré louse. As opposed to my parents, I'm simply a Frenchman. I represent the magazine *Photo Odyssey*, but don't worry, no interviews. . . ."

"Sit down, sit down," Ogo said, and suddenly, seeing that another event had taken place in La Coupole, cried out louder than before, "and what's that!"

In the doorway stood a creature of female gender, tall and wrapped in precious wool; everything was multicolored and flowed. On the head was the golden halo of heavy braids. It was a creature not totally of this earth, and agitating waves spread from it (the creature) throughout the enormous restaurant, and the eaters and drinkers had a feeling of being *present* at something, a *communion* with something. . . .

"I don't believe my eyes," Ogorodnikov said.

"Nevertheless, it is she," said Ambroise, wiping his sweaty brow with a blue handkerchief. "Brigitte Bardot."

She distractedly panned the room and suddenly the ray of her gaze tripped on the photographer's table and directly—incredibly!—focused on the haggard physiognomy of M. Ogo with drooping clumps of moustache.

He looked around—was she looking at someone behind him? Behind him was the wall and two pheasants on the wallpaper. Joy swelled within him like music of Rossini. Of course, let's meet today! Of course, let's talk about the seventh decade of this century! About the salvation of the animal world, of course! Without any doubt, we'll talk of many things!

Suddenly he vomited. What was that? He didn't have time to be aware of it before a brown vileness passed through his whole body, as if pumped from below, he shuddered, and it flowed noisily onto the starched tablecloth, he could make out pieces of food he had just eaten, untouched by the digestive process, including an entire section of tangerine, swallowed quickly, a brown mush with a piercing stink of stomach. And it flowed, and flowed....

Stunned, he regarded the vomit, the disfigured table. Without looking up he knew that everyone's eyes were upon him because his "opera barfo" (the old term from college came back to him) had been accompanied by deafening sounds like cannon booms and groans and had to have attracted attention. Damned French, he thought dully, why don't they have bands in their taverns? He could have barfed all he wanted with loud music and no one would have noticed. Damned bastard frogs ...

Scurrying. "Should we call an ambulance?" "Fuck you, I won't give in to a provocation!" He wiped his face and chest with a napkin and sat in silence, demonstrating total self-control. Mr. Cyanosis, that's what you are, he thought to himself with a mischievous laugh. The supernatural actress took a step toward Mr. Cyanosis, then another step, and then surged forward. That could not be! Contact between peoples usually takes place on fields, beneath the tents of the commanders in chief, and not over a vomit-covered table. He ran and a second later was in the refreshing cold of Montparnasse. The llama was pulling on the clapper of the bell. The goat, beard waggling, rolled a wheel with a parrot.

4

WHAT'S HAPPENING TO ME, Ogo wondered, pacing and cutting corners. I wasn't drunk. I barfed just the way I pissed in Berlin. Where can I ru ... damned age with excess and inadequac ... enoug ... the hel ... the camera's full of vomi ... I'm thinking so fast, I'm losing letters ...

One cabdriver refused to take him because of the smell, another just drove off, wary of his appearance, so he stuck a hundred francs in the face of the third driver: Take me, cocksucker! *Bout* Montmartre! They went. Unforgettable Paris swayed on either side of his thrown-back head.

"We're here. Get out, you stinking ass," said the driver.

"You think I don't understand French?" Ogo giggled. "Here's another fifty for your witticism. You're an asshole," he said to the driver in farewell and got back, naturally, "It takes one to know one."

On top of Montmartre it was empty and therefore foggy; or rather, just the reverse. A dull Schwabian song roared from the Gascognard Restaurant. Ogorodnikov walked where his legs took him, if you could refer to his rubbery extremities that way. Soon he found himself in the north African district, which had once astonished his wild Soviet imagination.

As they say in novels, "there came the sound of guttural Arab voices." The odor emanating from M. Ogo was lost amid their own fragrance. In the night and fog a stump grew up, on which our artist stumbled. It wasn't a stump, but a dark-skinned bumpkin selling leather goods spread on the sidewalk. How many nights has he waited for customers to come out of the dark and buy stupid suspenders with jingle bells? An idyllic scene in a window: the family of an Honest Worker of the East watching TV and eating couscous. And there was the line—just as it had been three years ago. Next to it another, and another, and another: the establishments were situated side by side, but there was no competition—the demand was higher than supply.

Which house to pick? I remember I saw the fair hair of one of the workers in this window that time. Where does the line end, comrades?

"Here," said the man on the end, shivering, wrapped in a blanket.

"Fatigué?" asked M. Ogo.

The owner of the blanket nodded and showed through gestures that he had worked all day with a jackhammer and was still shaking. "But you still feel like fucking?" asked M. Ogo. The blanket nodded again, the body shaking as if still connected to the perforating machine. All the members, so to speak, had gone limp and were trembling, except for one that stood straight like a spear, it had to be calmed, it wouldn't let him sleep, lowering his productivity index. . . .

"Are you mute, or something?" He was mute, but he explained well, everything was clear, all the nuances.

"Dernier?" came a voice from behind.

Two Moroccans had joined them. The whole line was grim, serious, the real proletariat of the world united. And they said that Marxism was dead! Maybe this was just the line to the toilet, worried M. Ogo. Then it moved. Two came out, wrapped in scarves, lighting cigarettes. Two went into the narrow door, and now he could see the "fair curls" in the murky second-floor window. . . .

She must have been taking a break, too, and was cheerfully chatting with someone inside. Some woman!—she handled fifty screws a shift. Let's do a little division and multiplication here. Let's say she pockets a fifth of the income—five hundred francs a day, three thousand a week, that's twelve grand a month—a high-paid specialist! Where else could she haul in dough like that? However, there's the fifty guys she has to handle! Isn't that a bit much? That's a soup bowl of secretions alone! What about the physical strain, comrades? But then again, you don't get money like that for nothing. . . . The girl in the window dropped her cigarette, laughed at someone inside, and went off to work.

On the doorstep a huge guy in a jersey shirt appeared and silently, with his thumb, drew the line's attention to the "Rules of Clients' Behavior." The girls could not be: beaten, bitten, pinched, or kissed (!). The clients were not allowed to: swear, spit, sing (!), use strong liquor, smoke, eat, or approach the girls without first performing the "sanitary procedure." It was recommended that the clients clean up their organs "après" as well, but the management did not insist.

Two girls were working. On the left was a door with a photograph of the "fair curls," who smiled in welcome, spreading her net-stockinged legs. The brunette on the right, displaying the globes of her breasts and the sack of her belly, seemed a little severe, slightly frowning. The male flow was thereby very cleanly separated into two basic streams—those who wanted a "baby" and those who needed a "mommy."

M. Ogo, to tell the truth, was rather nonplussed by the choice: he passionately wanted both. But he headed for the blonde, for she had been the symbol of Montmartre for this whole long period of pretense. In the hallway he bumped into his predecessor. He was dragging his jacket in his left hand and adjusting his fly with his right. The messiness of his face was notable. Don't worry, monsieur, he's a steady customer, said the mighty cashier. Come this way, please, press that button for the sanitary precautions.

He pressed the button. A bluish condom fell into his hand. That was rather disappointing; he had anticipated slurping, moisture, slime.

One more step and he was at the goal. On a blue mattress lay a businesslike and even rather graceful creature. *Alors, alors,* it commanded, examined him, moved its fingers along him, a light pressure and, once convinced of his readiness, offered itself. Ogo accepted the position. The clock started ticking, the hands leaping springily. Four minutes left. You move the organ of your body in the organ of another. . . .

What pleasure and so cheap—big deal, sixty francs plus tax for such bright, colorful, human fun!

Suddenly M. Ogo noticed that through it all Mlle. Annette was looking at him in a side mirror. "You're clearly not an Arab," she said. "Swedish? Drooped by drink?"

"Uh-huh," he replied, trying to get in deeper. "Where are you from, Annette? Schwarzwald? Germany? Want to go to a movie? Tell me, your vagina is artificial, right? It's impossible to take fifty a day. . . ."

"You're getting a bit frisky, friend," she said hoarsely. He even thought he was getting to her, but that was unlikely. "Look, dear, there's less than a minute left, you're not alone, there's a line. Let me help you, you old thing. . . ." So she spoke with her village Schwarzwald accent and used her experienced hand to help him reach the crown of adventure, a rather violent one, refreshing and somehow purging. "Here, throw it over there. Take a paper towel. Vaseline. I don't go to movies. Time is money. I'm studying to be a nurse." The next guy with a blue package in his paw was pushing through the door. "À bientôt! Don't be a stranger, Swede."

In the hallway M. Ogo offered the cashier a Reitmaster cigarette. They smoked. "Did you receive pleasure, monsieur?" Ogo assured him that the pleasure had been immense. "Annette is a fine girl." The cashier nodded. From Mama Silva's bedroom came the squeals of an Arab. From Annette's there was only the rhythmic creak of bedsprings.

"I can understand those poor things," the cashier said.

"Money," M. Ogo said profoundly.

"Exactly!" The cashier grew a bit excited. "Elementary political economics, monsieur. These poor men are exploited on road construction, conveyor belts, they save money to bring it back to their own countries, robbed by neocolonialists, their families are there, but you can't control nature, once a week the worker brings his francs here."

"Then my premonitions were right," Ogorodnikov said. "This is Marxism."

"Marxism is everywhere, it's a science," the cashier said in farewell. "Come again, monsieur."

For some reason Ogo's crotch felt tingly, but his feet were light and his head clear. An enormous moon watched the man headed down into Paris. Farewell, high-altitude ozone of Montmartre! A head with an acorn-colored bald spot peeked out of a dark-green Jaguar. The reporter from *Photo Odyssey* he'd met at La Coupole—Ambroise Zhigalevich, of course.

5

"WHAT A COINCIDENCE! I just happened to see you! You look like you're coming from a brothel, Ogo. I'm headed for a little spot where our fellow Parisian photographers get together. Like to join me? Bravo, just flop into this old auto, into the leather seat of sturdy British work. In those days capitalism was dependable. . . . What did you say? Capitalism is the whorehouse of socialism? You know, that's good! I see that it just burst out, but it's fresh! So, let's talk like pals, all right? I hope you don't consider me a spy? Thanks for that. Oh, Max, I'm pushing fifty, and what has my camera, my pen given me? Believe me, it's not the worst in *Photo Odyssey*. Not a thing except this old beast that's giving us a ride. Yes, I'm drinking! No, never while driving! You might have noticed that I take a gulp only at red lights. Why aren't I sharing? Go ahead, help yourself! I thought you'd be more careful after . . . after what? You call your behavior at La Coupole a monologue? I like that! A confession? Well, well . . . I guess in part it is—a call for compassion, revealing everything. This vile stuff is called grappa, it's just the thing . . . compatible with . . . hm, the confession stinks. . . . Hey, give it to me, don't you see it's a red light? Tell me, why does one man become famous while another, no worse, has to beg for interviews from every visiting louse? We're here, sir, this is our club, I unlock it with my own key, that's the rule. Do you like this bar in the old American style? I see you do. These walls have seen everyone! This is a historic moment—do you have any objections if I turn on my tape recorder? I'm not supposed to write your stinky aphorisms down, am I? And we'll ask the bartender to take a few pictures with this old camera. Keep the negatives, old man! Someday you'll make a lot of money on them! Now let's talk, let's talk like professionals, at last. Tell me, what is photography, that is, how do you Soviet masters of the New Wave understand it?"*

---

*At this point in our narrative we call on the reader to shut the book, then look at the beginning and find Ogorodnikov's revelations, then shut the book again and try to imagine the finale of this disgraceful scene.

SNOWS

I

WHILE FOGS DEPRESSED the peoples of Paris and Berlin, the good Russian winter set upon the capital of Peace and Progress. Russian snow is good in every way, except that there's a surplus of it and, in particular, it complicates transportation. Once, after returning from a business trip abroad to find the city cut in half, Captain Skanshchin of the ideological services had gone skating at Izmailov Park of Culture and—you won't believe this—got stuck in a snowdrift. You could have wet your pants laughing, no other way to put it! At first he'd raced smoothly on the blades, imbued with childhood memories: Boy, we really used to let loose with hockey sticks and metal switches. We lacked culture, of course, but what could you do. We made those four-eyes scatter! And the girls, what we did to the girls! A speeding wall of guys whipping around, encircling a crying upper-class coed. Fun!

And now something brought Vladimir back to the Izmailov skating rink. As he slid down the romantic *allées* all alone, he barely recognized himself; his soul was getting all watery and blurry and stirring with pity for what he used to be: a skinny hooligan with a runny nose.

The snow kept falling. The park servicemen had stopped cleaning

the *allées*, probably off boozing it up somewhere while still pulling shift
pay. Captain Skanshchin experienced an atypical and prickly entropy-
misanthropy. How imperfect was the world! People concerned themselves with nonsense nowadays. Now I, perhaps, was born to become a
pretty good doctor or a promising photographer, alas.... We are surrounded by petty passions, instigated abroad, and I have to perform
unseemly acts—read denunciations, sniff out other people's smells, in
order to protect this society of imperfect and ungrateful people from
even more imperfect ones, that is, not ours, well....

Stumbling on this point, he almost fell into a snowbank under some
pines, but his sports training saved him and he merely rode by on the
"fifth point of support," as the mountain climbers call your ass. When
he got up, however, he received an unexpected gift from fate—a lone,
slender girl was skating up ahead. Of course he hurried after her.

Why not hurry, what's wrong with that, comrades? It's a sin not to
get acquainted in an empty park, not to show the awkward female ska-
ter a dashing sight, not to flirt in the casual manner of the Rosfoto
Restaurant....

The girl was assiduously skating on the narrow strip of ice beneath
snowbanks. Black velour jeans worn tight, a bright sweater, golden hair
showing beneath the hat. Tall, slender, quite acceptable from the rear.

Skanshchin hadn't put on the speed yet, he pulled even and looked
at her face, and that was when he landed in the snowbank out of shock:
the girl turned out to be a—!

How many comparable mistakes happen nowadays, thought the captain sadly as he floundered in the snow. Everything dubious is coming
to us from the West, it's true. How the hell am I supposed to get out
of this shit? This is turning out to be one fucking lousy situation—I'm
getting in deeper!

"Give me your hand, pal!" cried the man Skanshchin had been planning to marry. A fine, open, and sweet face regarded the captain's
confusion. You won't find such a pleasant appearance in most girls
nowadays. And the hand extended to help wasn't so bad, either. It
pulled, and Captain Skanshchin flew out of his snowy prison, and for a
second he imagined himself a snowy ball, what a miracle! None other
than a world-class athlete!

"Forgive me, friend," Skanshchin said, shaking himself off, "I mistook you for someone else. What sport do you do?"

"Many," the young man said with a smile. And what a fine smile he had! We keep grumbling about the Komsomol, but look at what fine young people it brings up! "Why don't we get acquainted?"

Skanshchin smiled in return and offered one of his aliases. "Valery Timofeyev."

"Vadim Raskladushkin," the young man introduced himself.

What a fine, young, Soviet name.

They went along together down the narrow icy path. It was getting dark, and on the sunset side (let's avoid saying the west), in the gray mash above a row of apartment buildings, several glints of light appeared, resembling pieces of orange peel.

"What do you do, Vadim, if not sports?" the captain asked gently. And got no answer, just a smile. "I mean where do you work?" Skanshchin amended.

Nothing but a smile.

Hm. Skanshchin peered into his new friend's face. Hm, this is getting interesting.

"Excuse me, Valery." And here Vadim Raskladushkin took the fictitious Valery by the arm. "We live in complex times. Right? Alas, I can't tell you where I work and I don't want to lie."

Skanshchin blushed with joy: one of us! With every cell of his hand the young KGB man felt every cell of the other's hand—one of us! Vadim was right—the times were complex, and you couldn't be too precise about where you worked.

"Not insulted?" Vadim asked gently. "Personally, I never ask new friends about where they work so as to avoid ambiguous situations. I hope this won't keep us from becoming friends."

"Then call me by my real name," the captain said. "Call me Vladimir Skanshchin."

They looked at each other and laughed with understanding. Maybe there'll be so many of us soon that we won't have to hide from each other, thought Skanshchin joyously.

The ice rang beneath the skates of the young men as they went arm in arm, skating synchronously in the direction of the dressing room.

"Somehow I don't want to say good-bye," said Skanshchin. "Would you like to drop in somewhere, Vadim?"

"Why not?" Vadim checked his illuminated watch. "I'm going off to see some people, of course, I don't know, maybe you'll be bored. Do you like art?"

"Very much!" Skanshchin burst out.

And they looked at each other again and smiled with understanding, as if they had been friends since the days of Skanshchin's rink pranks.

"There's no problem with fuel," Vadim said. "The only problem is getting a taxi now."

"And what's my Zhiguli for?" the captain responded enthusiastically.

2

AND SO IN Skanshchin's Zhiguli the two young men with indefinite places of employment came to the Zamoskvorechye district, to the air-shaft courtyard of a prerevolutionary building, faced in tiles of the pre-catastrophe era. Snow was still falling from dark-reddish skies, covering the field of foreign-made automobiles. The sole narrow space revealed a lulling view of the cupolas of All Saints Church. But you had to be alert when parking between a Mercedes and a Volvo. Captain Skansh-chin gave Vadim a meaningful look, shutting his eyes sorrowfully. What can you do? he seemed to say.

The elevator was overloaded and they had to struggle up the stairs above the eighth floor to the huge attic, which was filled with light and full of people. Why, it was all foreigners here, the captain realized. All around, literally right up close to him, people were speaking foreign languages. And the captain lost his nerve. . . .

It happened sometimes—in the course of his duties there was a lot that was foreign: a piece of a letter to Ogorodnikov from his New York agent, Bruce Pollack, a recording of a conversation between Ogorod-nikov and Hiroshi Nagoya, a photograph of the boots brought for Ogo-rodnikov by Signora Odoletti. . . . You'd think he might have got used to the West by now, but the captain lost his nerve.

Some floozie asked him quite comprehensibly, "Don't you have a lighter?"—that is, she wanted a light, and made perfectly understandable gestures, but Skanshchin, instead of whipping out his prize Ronson, turned to wood.

And where's Vadim? There he is, the cutie, actively grazing at the buffet, and the table is groa-aning! What a situation! That's how our boys must be losing ground, in situations like that! But just then Vadim turned to him with an encouraging smile—come on over, eat and drink. He felt a little better—it's always easier when your comrade is nearby!

The captain went to the table and picked up a bottle of "our native Stolichnaya." A lady looked at him: adorable!

"Ça va?" she asked in French.

"Sova," he heard in Russian—owl.

"Where?" Skanshchin gasped.

Everyone laughed marvelously. Witty! Bravo, monsieur! He slugged down a full glass, and his tongue loosened. The conversation flowed in the right direction. Now everyone was watching him, and the lady even put her bare forearm on his shoulder, thanks for the trust.

"Please, Jeanine, come visit me in the Northern Caucasus! I am the boss of the region! Do you like heights? You don't get dizzy? Welcome! Bienvenue! All the tourist bases, all the hunting lodges are ours!"

Later, in the fuzzy, fizzy wee hours, the captain asked himself miserably, Where did I get the Caucasus from, where had I heard such boasting nonsense before, whom was I imitating?

Incidentally, the guests at this attic opening—and this was an opening, only our captain had not noticed the paintings on the walls—were buzzing with the rumor that a major Party man of the "new generation" was present, a member of the Central Committee, the boss of the Northern Caucasus, and this was definite proof of the upward movement of "fresh forces" and the possible liberalization of the arts.

"They'll come to their senses, they have to," the owner of the attic was saying, one Mikhailo Kaledin, a painter, graphic artist, and metal engraver. His wrinkled face peered from behind his huge moustache, sideburns, and graying hair, glowing at his powerful guest. "Vadim, really, why don't you introduce me already!" he asked Raskladushkin.

At that moment Skanshchin was mixing Scotch scotch and English gin in a goblet. He smiled at his host. An artist? You want to create on a glacier at the Central Committee's lodge? Welcome! A monarchist? Room for everyone, come to the Northern Caucasus! And suddenly the captain almost dropped his goblet.

Over his host's shoulder he saw a maquette of *Say Cheese!* He couldn't miss the enormous slab in the colorful cover tied with shoelaces, for just last night at the operative meeting the general had showed pictures of the "object," made by "our man" inside the infamous photographers' group. The general would not name the man even to his own colleagues, saying only that the critical moment was approaching—the defector Ogorodnikov was trying to get the album from across the sea. And here it was, the album, leaning on a shelf against an ancient samovar, made in Poltava from a Swedish cuirass. Standing there in the middle of a suspicious crowd, half foreign and partially Jewish, the object of the concerns of his operative group, of the whole sector, really of the whole PhID of the Ideological Control . . .

Captain Skanshchin broke out in a sweat, and all the foreign alcoholic influences dissipated in a flash. How had he allowed himself to become so shamefully disoriented? Where am I and why aren't there some familiar faces around? They were all over the place, these Cheesers! There was Alexei Okhotniker with his red beard, and there was Probkinovich—he was putting the moves on Jeanine. At the sector they added Jewish endings to the names of undependable photographers—just fooling around, to keep from dying of boredom, nothing anti-Semitic about it. Wait, hold on, spouting off in the corner was none other than Andrei Drevesnevich, best friend of the defector Ogorod (they never gave him an "evich," since his pop was part of Party history), and there was Slava Germanovich (when did he get out of the hospital?), and there was the rogue's mug of Shuz Zherebyatnikovich himself. . . . What a mess! Captain Slyazgin, that piece of shit, had completely missed out on this get-togethernevich, very lax of our comrade Slyazgin. And what if they pass the album to a foreign agent right here? Say to this young fellow here, boy, his hand is hard, boy, he's squeezing. . . .

"Philip." The young stranger in the gray three-piece suit introduced himself to Vladimir Skanshchin.

"Nikolai," our captain said, using one of his operative names and responding with pressure to the pressure.

"Vladimir or Nikolai?" asked the above.

"It's almost the same thing," Skanshchin said. "And why are you here?"

"I'm here to visit Moscow's attractions," Philip replied clearly.

What excellent preparation in that comrade! This, without a doubt, was a dangerous Philip. Of all the Philips, he was most dangerous. Oh, he'll carry off our album to foreign shores! Here was a visual illustration—he felt a thrill—of the wise words of Leonid Ilyich Brezhnev, which had resounded at their last seminar: "There are no vacuums in ideological work, and wherever we permit ourselves goodguyism [now that was a word!] the enemy immediately sneaks [in or into] there!"

For the duration of the attic bash Captain Skanshchin did not take his eyes from the enormous album. Philip was gone, and Jeanine vanished (with that Probkinovich, of course), all the foreign filth had flown from the attic, and the domestic ideological immatures had wandered off, with the exception of the very drunk, while the captain still sat in the corner on a bearskin rug, refusing whiskey and gin, drinking only "our native stuff," growing glassier with every glass, until he passed out.

3

THE VOLVO NEXT to which knight of the ideological war Skanshchin had parked belonged not at all to a foreigner but on the contrary to Andrei Drevesny, hereditary Russian intellectual and until recently "one of the leading masters of the Fourth Generation of Soviet photography." He had got the car five years ago thanks to the efforts of Probkin, naturally. Once Drevesny had been proud of the Scandinavian machine, had liked the way people looked at him when he got out of the silvery car, how they sometimes said behind his back, "Drevesny drives a Volvo!" In

general once, that is, just five years ago, everything had been different—
brighter, livelier, more spontaneous. There had been serious talk of
nominating him for the first Nobel Prize for Photography. Women had
been five years more desirable. Even smells had been stronger and more
eloquent.

Strange thing: five years for a Volvo or something is a rather long
time, but for a man, for an artist, in principle anyway, it's a piffle, isn't
it? When I was buying this thing, it had 39,000 on the odometer. Nothing for a Volvo, Probkin told me then. It had as many thousands as I
had years behind me. Hm, I thought then. Idiotic attempts at banal
symbolism. Now I'm forty-four, and the car's got 80,000 on the odometer; that means that I'm eighty, at least. And I'm experiencing something comparable to its problems with ignition.

Andrei Drevesny was exceptionally handsome, a harmonious man
with a good-featured and clean face, large cold eyes, and thick hair. The
gray at the temples and the moustache he grew at the time of the Volvo
purchase did not detract from his looks, but brought into harmony an
auxiliary charm that his friends when drunk called "anti-Soviet."

Andrei Drevesny was one of the last to leave Mikhailo Kaledin's
opening night, and as he went down the stairs that stank of cat piss he
regretted that he had not been one of the first to leave. A pointless
evening in a dubious crowd. How many times had he sworn not to go
to gatherings like this, and if he did go, to comport himself commen-
surately with his name and position in art, to gab less, and if he did gab,
not to tell "stories" when people weren't particularly listening.

He had begun noticing society's astonishing disdain for any artist
with a name. You would think that the minute I open my mouth, the
bastards would shut up respectfully, but that doesn't happen. Am I
beginning to undergo the process that befell Ygrek, Zed, and Omega,
those stars of the first magnitude who suddenly stopped being *counted*?

I'm gradually being pushed out of official photography—not a single
album in two years—and they're spreading a rumor that I'm finished.
You'd think the unofficial world would support me, raise me as their
banner, but all I get is grimaces—Drevesny, yes, that favorite pet of the
Agitprop. . . . And the attitude toward me in the West is changing

because of this internal vileness. I'd like to say the hell with them all and go over the hill, like Alik Konsky, like ... Ogo? Has Ogo really? Yes, he has, too!

The Volvo was covered with snow. Attic guests were walking by, Germans. They smiled. Probably thinking their usual banalities—the Russian intelligentsia wants to look like us so much. Drevesny brushed off the snow. I'll go into emigration, but not like those *stilyagi,* I'll hide out in Russia, I'll go off into the mountains, the mountains conquered by Kuchelbecker and Yakubovich....* No one has ever shot better mountain slopes than I! Ogo never even dreamt of it, he's superficial, fashion-conscious, he has no sense of the cosmos....

A truly wild thought came to Andrei: I'll seduce his wife, Anastasia, and stay in the mountains with her forever. He doesn't love her anyway, and you can't find a better woman than her nowadays.

Getting on the seat that burned cold through his jeans, he began running the starter. Once upon a time it took less than a quarter-turn for everything to come alive in the car, for the dashboard to glow and the music to sing, connecting him to contemporary humanity. What was the point in the destruction of metal? There may actually be more unfairness in the aging of mechanisms than in the collapse of the flesh, eh? Man in his bustling grows more tiresome, hysterical with every year, boring nature and abhorring common sense. Time for the dustheap.

The engine turned over at last, everything that was supposed to light lit up with a hint at the past, and there was still something precious that connected him with life and even—with every push on the camera shutter—with the astral plane: photography! The car was warming up, hot air blew at the windows. Well, really, it's silly to capitulate like this. Tomorrow I'll stay in bed with the phone and call everyone....

At that moment someone peered into the car on the passenger side and vanished. Someone was coming around the back of the car. Dre-

---

*For unknown reasons the mountains evoke to Andrei the names of two exiled poets, former participants of the 1825 "Decembrist Uprising," rather than the names of true conquerors of the Caucasus Mountains, princes and generals. That's the way artists usually downplay the significance of the history makers.

esny looked into the rearview mirror. A woman in a fur coat. A second later he recognized her: it was the mother of his children, Polina, formerly Shtein, currently Mrs. Fotii Feklovich, the mighty mother-secretary. Her face was now close to his, beyond the glass with the melting drifts of snow. The eyes are still magnificent, madame! He lowered the window.

"Andrei, can you come out? I need to talk to you!"

Fantastic, those were the very two sentences, one interrogative and the other declarative, that she had said to him then from the phone booth on Peter Khalturin Street. And in the same tone.

"Why don't you get in the car," he said.

She put her goose-down knit mitten to her mouth and for some reason spoke through it. "No, you get out."

He stood in the narrow space between the Volvo and the snow-covered Zhiguli. "To what do I owe the pleasure?"

"I've been waiting a whole hour for you. Let's walk for five minutes. No, no, I don't want to get in the car. Come on, we'll walk down the street."

He saw that she was shivering, either with the cold or with excitement, and he finally realized that something was up: her fur coat was buttoned crooked and her mouth was smeary. Had something happened to the children? "No, no, the children are fine. It's not the children, it's you, Andrei." Oho, a surprise!

They were walking down a small side street, empty at that hour. It ended at a church fence with huge snowcaps on the stone gates. Not a single sign of the Soviet regime in evidence, Drevesny noted to himself. Somehow, nothing that remained in his memory connected to Polina had anything of the Soviet regime in it at all, as if their affair had been in a different era—a guards officer and a student at the Bestuzhev Courses for Women.

"You have to leave New Focus immediately and take your works out of *Say Cheese!*"

"Madame, madame," he said with a gentle smile: "What are you going on about?"

Polina grabbed his sleeve and pulled. His sheepskin jacket tore in the seam of the armhole. "Andrei, you can't even imagine how serious this is!"

"Polina," he cried almost sincerely, "I have to ask you to be careful! My things are expensive, but old! What's serious?"

"How can you not understand—it's serious business with your underground job! The thunder is going to rumble very soon! The PhIDs are focused only on you. You'll ruin yourself if you don't get out of the group immediately and go off to ... well, to the Caucasus, say."

"We're not doing anything illegal," Drevesny managed.

"Oh, stop it, stop it, stop it!" She raised her face and almost closed her eyes. Her hands—once again with excessive strength—clutched the lapels of his sheepskin jacket. "Don't you understand that our days are gone, that these days belong to others? Then again, maybe you have something ... special planned, too, like Ogo?"

"And what is that supposed to mean?" he asked, gently freeing himself.

Now she was clutching her own fur coat somewhere near her throat. Ah, what a fine woman she had been, how she had *blazed*! "Andrei, you must understand, I simply can't tell you everything I know, I can't even believe all of it, but ... but Ogo definitely, understand, definitely wants an enormous scandal, publicity, lots of money ... there, there, not here ... and he's dragging you into it, you, and Slava, all of them ... he wants to hide behind you, and that just makes the PhIDs happy ... they're going to blow this up ... I never told anyone ... and I never ... I'm just an old woman with a lot of kids ... go away, Andrei, before it's too late. ..."

Polina's fur coat flew open. A whiff of the familiar warmth came from inside. Andrei took a step back.

"Shame on you, Polina," he said quite distinctly. "You smell of Fotik."

Having stepped into a snowbank, filling his shoe with snow, he went around his former wife and headed for Mikhailo Kaledin's yards, where the Volvo waited. Twenty meters later he turned around. Polina, without moving, was watching him.

"Are the children well?" he asked.

She nodded.

"Come to the car," he said, and thought: Before she would have come right away, but now she'll vacillate for at least half a minute. Well—he thought his regular thought about this woman—it's her own fault. She's to blame for everything. She's that kind of a woman, it's her own fault.

4

CAPTAIN SKANSHCHIN WAS awakened by soft Slavic singing. Mikhailo Kaledin's female household was sitting around a communal worktable, drinking kvas and sour soup and singing the heart-rending "The Russian Brigade Took the Galician Fields." Horrifying swollen faces, like a meeting of the city Party activists, floated toward him from the walls, and it took him awhile to realize that they were surrealistic paintings that were messing up his hung-over mind.

Then the captain remembered the object, the secret treasure, for which he had sacrificed himself last night. Surely the parasites had taken it away! The muscular Philip must be near Copenhagen by now.

Turning his head with difficulty, Captain Skanshchin panned across the attic and saw the giant folio in its former place—the sun was playing on its colorful, pheasant-decorated cover.

"Lasses!" howled Mikhailo Kaledin. "Lookie, the lad has waked. Honor him, my lasses!"

Skanshchin supported himself on one elbow. "Thanks for your kindness. As we say in the Caucasus, Allah Verdy. By the way, Comrade Kaledin, what's the archcurious book over there?" The captain casually pointed in the direction of *Cheese!*, but turned his face toward the singing ladies.

"That's the photo album *Say Cheese!*," Mikhailo explained readily. "Someone brought it over last night and forgot it."

5

INCIDENTALLY, STILL SEVERAL hours before the soldier on the invisible front woke up, the phone rang in the apartment of three women on

Gagarin Square. A hoarse and pickled voice asked for Anastasia. Has to be a debaucher, her mother gasped with apprehension. But still, who's calling her at this hour?

"That shouldn't worry you, madame," the debaucher rasped. "A man is calling. A male friend."

The mother was so taken aback and so sleepy that she took the telephone without demur to her daughter's warm bed. "Nastenka, wake up, there's a man calling!" The aunt immediately stuck her head out of her small room. What had happened? Who was calling? "A man friend," the mother said in bewilderment.

It was dawn, and the pale moon was in no hurry to dissolve in the bluing skies, and it hung obliquely like a pillow feather over the former Kaluga Gates, over the monstrous rocket that was a monument to The Cosmonaut, and over the ton of Russian wisdom: "The People and the Party are Truly One!"

"A friend wouldn't call at this hour," Anastasia growled. "It's some bastard."

She had just been communicating with her legal spouse in her dream. With his idiotic, dandified walking stick, which always irritated her, the boring professor Ogo was instructing her, a lackadaisical pupil.

"What's the matter, Nastya, too much booze or too much fucking?" The glaciologist heard the familiar, horrible voice. "Come on, cover your ass with warm panties, to keep your treasures from freezing, and haul it downstairs. Don't worry, I won't molest you."

No, no, that wasn't the Academy of Sciences, she thought. Nobody has a raspy voice like that at the Academy of Sciences. It had to be one of the photographers. Probably Shuz, who else would put an invitation so politely . . . ?

Shuz Artemievich Zherebyatnikov was considered by the ideological higher-ups to be one of the main villains. "Of course, unlike Ogorodnikov, that bastard, Shuz at least has a reason to hate us," General Planshchin would sometimes say.

Shuz was no longer young. Half a century ago he was conceived in a system of Party enlightenment and after birth was saddled with the acronym of those holy words School, University, Zenith.* In 1956, when he met his father, after the latter came back from the prison camps, Shuz said, embracing the Party man lovingly, "For a name like that, Pa, if I were Uncle Joe Comrade Stalin, I would have given you a full quarter instead of just a dime." By that time Shuz had done, and not completely, only the first letter of his predetermined life path, and was driving a Moscow taxi and was known as someone who had been around, that is, had lost count of his VDs and LTs (lost teeth). His parents grieved—their little Shuz (weighing in at an eighth of a ton) had not remained faithful to the ideals of Leninism.

Shuz's photography began, actually, with pornography. Sexually active young people used to gather at a "hut" in Cherkizovo in those days. Shuz came there once with his Zenith, a flash, and a new word he had fished out of a philosophy dictionary—aesthetics. "This might just be fucking to you, boys and girls, but to me it's aesthetics of eroticism. Attention! Cheese!"

After the birdie came a criminal investigation. All the rakes and sluts got away, and only the photographer got five years. Shuz laughed—so long, parents, now it's my turn to supply the country with coal.

The camp benefited Shuz. Despite Khrushchev's thaw Shuz met quite a few anti-Soviet photographers, learned professional mastery and philosophical terminology from them. When he got back to Moscow in the early sixties, Shuz went deep into the underground, that is, into the alcoholic "men's club" of Moscow with branches in numerous bohemian attics and cellars, and into the Rosfoto Restaurant. Packets of his photographs made the rounds.

Suddenly someone (either Ogorodnikov, or Drevesny, or German, anyway, one of the biggies) said something like "Why, it's like Chekhov rewritten in the latest slang!" There he was, the new "bard of the twilight

---

*In the early twenties and late thirties devoted communist parents had been giving their newly born children the "new names" made of some ideological abbreviations: Vladlen (Vladimir Lenin), Marlen (Marxism-Leninism), Kim (Russian for Communist International of Youth), Elmira (Electrification of the World), Velira (Great Worker).

In accordance with this mode I would dare to propose a "new name" for Gorbachev's era: Gor (*Glasnost*, Openness, Restructuring).

of social consciousness"! The crooked-mouthed, drunken, and mean-ingless Soviet Union . . . the winos . . . the ruberoid beer kiosks . . . cop-ulation in filthy doorways . . . mornings in drunk tanks . . . the smirking pockmarked faces of Uncle Joe, shining everywhere through the sky of the homeland. . . .

"Well, brothers, shall we look to the West for our heroes, fight for future Russian democracy, and ignore the senile masturbator with his hand in his cavalry trousers and his medals dangling? Shuz Zhereby-atnikov is the new password of modern Soviet photography!"

Ogo and those people started talking about him and made him famous within a few weeks. Shuz's name and pictures began appearing in European and American magazines. There was even interest in Brazil! Never a member of the Union of Soviet Photographers, Shuz became their main bugbear. He was denounced at Party meetings for his "petty-bourgeois naturalism" and his intention to "blacken Soviet reality." Shuz laughed: What the fuck are those crab lice bugging me for, why don't they blame their shitty reality, I'm a simple man, what I see is what I photograph, I'm no writer, I lack imagination, motherfuckers! Shuz was thus the source of the goofy argument of his brethren photographers: "We're no writers, pick on your writers!"

Shuz strolled the empty courtyard, waiting for Anastasia, kicking a piece of ice with his marvelous Swedish boot, massive and grand in his heavy leather coat with fur collar. By Moscow standards he looked like a very rich man. He gave her a grim smack on the cheek, demonstrating by the grimness that there were no sexual overtones to the kiss.

"Well, what's happened, Shuz?"

He took out a long Western envelope from his pocket.

How many times lately had she promised herself not to get wet over this faithless gypsy driver, this lousy ambitious sensualist? An uninter-esting fellow, basically, a petty self-centered bum, with only one positive quality—loyalty to his snuffed-and-repressed Photography. That's how it happened in life sometimes—were it not for that small positive qual-ity, he wouldn't have existed at all for her and certainly, at least, her hands wouldn't have shaken as she removed from the envelope one heavy sheet of paper with watermarks.

"Dear Shuz," she read, "the person who will give you this letter has great sympathy with our art. You can trust him as you would me, kdc. Many friends here are hungry for cheese. Philip has offered to bring it. Think it over and decide, it's all up to you, kdc. Your Ogo."

Naturally, there wasn't a word about his wife, everything was an expression of his "only positive quality."

"What's 'kdc'?" she asked.

Shuz was sipping Zubrovka vodka from a flat bottle. "Aha, even you don't know. KDC is 'kosher dill cock.' About a hundred years ago your man and I improvised on that theme. It's used here, as far as I can tell, as confirmation of the identity of this Philip. Get it?"

"No, I don't," she said.

"Suck on this," he said, offering her the bottle. "You don't want it? You're turning down hard-currency Zubrovka? You're really something, girl."

He drank for them both and sighed, not without sorrow.

"So, shit, we end up with a conspiracy. We're forced into this fucking game by those shitheads. The guards are looking, the world press is rushing, the trained couriers are carrying. In short, this evening a copy of *Cheese!* has to be given to this Parisian prick and you, my illegitimate child, victim of abortion, are the one to do it!"

"Really! That's the way you joke!" Anastasia exclaimed, with a tone of academic outrage that surprised even her, as if that tone would protect her, a Soviet scholarly worker, from a suspicious enterprise. Having exclaimed, however, she felt ashamed and muttered something incomprehensible. What do I have to do with it, what's it to me. . . .

"You're shitting in the wrong outhouse there, my child," Shuz said, and gently took her by the arm.

"Listen, Shuz, really, watch your language!" She was angry. "You're talking to a woman, you know!"

"What did I say? What did I say?" he went on, hands on his chest. It was the strangest sight—a respectable-looking, large old man with a hooligan's mannerisms. "I thought I was behaving kulterny, didn't grab your tits. You're Ogo's dame, that's why I came to you."

Her tender cheeks blushed. Even though it was disgusting being "his dame," it was nice when others admitted it.

"I wouldn't ask you if they weren't following me," Shuz said seriously now. "Yesterday the agent Skanshchin even dragged himself to Misha Kaledin's opening night. It looks like the PhIDs are going to close down our chapel. Your Ogo screwed them, and they're furious, like autumn flies. Nothing good will come of it, even though it's impossible to stop it now, because, as the poet said, 'It's shameful and destructive to grow white in this slavery and sleep as an old man,' and that's for fucking sure.

"Anyway, Anastasia, here's the plan. I will give you 'something' now and you will hide it until this evening. Okay? At eight I'm taking you to a cocktail party at the house of a Senegalese diplomat. Philip will be there. He'll try to pick you up, and you'll get picked up, play the arch-whore. You'll leave the reception as if going off to bed. Don't shudder, I said 'as if.' Of course, you can have a shot for a good cause. I'm giving you an indulgence in advance, and old Ogo will understand, too. In short, during the night you must give Philip our thing. Your mission ends there. Oh, oh, those cheeks are turning red again, you frigid little.... Oh, Nastya, if only I had gotten my hands on you twenty years ago!"

A few minutes later she was dragging the huge slab, which could have been concrete, of the album *Say Cheese!* from the trunk of Shuz's car to her elevator.

6

CAPTAIN SKANSHCHIN, TREMBLING, reddening like a Komsomol fire-brand, hiding his vile hangover, came running to the apartment of the old general in the thick-walled apartment house with capitals, built for Chekists' accommodation in the forties. It was a holiday—December 5, the anniversary of the undeservedly forgotten Great Stalin Constitution.

In the general's dining room a carafe and *zakuski* were served. Planshchin, wearing a fur vest that was a gift from his Bulgarian colleagues, was celebrating with his neighbor, the retired Comrade N, whose name was connected to the strengthening of socialist legality in the western regions of the Ukraine and Belorussia.

"Sit down," the general said sternly but paternally, putting a halt to Skanshchin's youthful impetuousness. "Pour yourself some." A sharp glance with his left eye. "I see you need it." After that he continued his interrupted story, swimming with human kindness for his elder comrade.

"... And so, we were catching trout after trout in those streams. We gave the whole catch to Ibragim—the louse of course was hiding the fact that he was a member of the treacherous balkarets tribe and pretended to be a loyal kabarda, and I admit my fault, I accepted him because he was a terrific chef—and our feast began under the pines of the Baksan Crevasse. We had shashlik, and trout, and cheeses, and everything—I repeat—everything was fresh! That's the Northern Caucasus!"

That's where "Caucasian lying" came from, Skanshchin realized grimly. He wouldn't wish the way he felt even on a dissident. He went into his pocket for a handkerchief, and diplomats' calling cards fell out. That didn't escape the general's attention.

Elder Comrade N, smacking his lips, pulled out a travel chess set from his People's Commissar–issue pajamas. How about a game?

The general's wife peeked in with a wordless question—bring on the soup?

"Set up an exercise while the young man and I tell secrets for a minute," the general told his neighbor.

In his study, the general put his hands to his chest for some reason, an almost feminine gesture. Well?

"I saw the object yesterday," Skanshchin began solemnly. "It's on a shelf in the apartment of the monarchist Mikhailo Kaledin. The details are in my report, Comrade General, but now it's an emergency! They're getting ready to pass the object over the border!"

"So," the general said, hardening professionally in an instant. "And you, Comrade Captain, appeared at Mikhailo Kaledin's in what capacity?"

Does he already know? thought Skanshchin sadly. First of all, he's using my rank, things are bad. That evening couldn't have passed without a stoolie. Oh, if I could only get into a sauna now and then under my darling's blanket, with my Viktoria....

"In the capacity of a Party worker," Skanshchin admitted pathetically. "I said I was the boss of the Northern Caucasus. . . ."

The general smiled. It felt good to have an influence on the new generation. What a clever boy, pretending to be a Party worker from the Caucasus! He'll go far, very far! A soft movement of the hand across the widow's peak and into the tangles of hair, a strategic pause for thinking.

"Well, your behavior, Skanshchin, will be the subject of another discussion. For now I praise your initiative. Act, put together an operative group, take Slyazgin and his men, buy a case of cognac since you're . . . the boss of the Northern Caucasus . . . take . . . hm, for work like this, take our Ella to that attic and give her what she loves. . . . Go to Mikhailo Kaledin's and continue playing the fool. Keep in constant touch with Slyazgin. If you see the album leaving, act decisively, but try to keep the resonance down. Understand? Mute the resonance!"

"I understand, I do," Skanshchin said, nodding. "Mute the resonance, I understand that. May I go?"

Skanshchin left, while Planshchin quickly changed into his gray office suit. He went back into the dining room and playfully wagged a finger at his aged partner.

"I see you're setting up Korchnoi's trap for me? That won't work, we've figured that variation out a long time ago!"

Peeking in one more time about the soup, his wife saw the general with his coat over his arm, standing over the chessboard and making quick moves. She fell in love with him all over again during such moments of "agent's exploits," and she always had a thermos and sandwiches ready in the kitchen for these occasions.

7

THAT DAMNED OGORODNIKOV, this is just like him—he'll lead me to the convent wall, while he plays around in Paris with his bimbos, thought Anastasia, smoking a cigarette under the attentive eyes of her aunt and mother."

I'm a louse, she thought further, I should be proud to be helping him in his battle with the authorities. He didn't do all this for himself, but

in the name of the ideals of liberty and justice, and I sanction his sac-
rificial . . .

As usual, the deeper she went into "positive" thoughts, the more
banal they became.

"What's that heavy thing you've brought home, Daughter, may I
ask?" her mother asked, while her aunt's chin grew longer.

No, you can't ask! She thought that she couldn't leave the thing at
home: the horses would start sniffing around and it wasn't clear how
they'd react once they found it. One could recall, for instance, their
squealing fifteen years ago, when seventh-grader Anastasia had her girlfriends set a secret session to discuss "your sex symbol." Auntie, on
Mama's urging, ran right over to the school. Real Soviet homunculi, as
Ogo put it. That's the way we were all brought up, if you don't squeal,
you're not brave enough! Overcoming that upbringing, isn't that a moral
exploit, to which our nobility calls us . . . pfui!

Just then Anastasia thought of the dissident invalid, that is, her own
father, grabbed the thing and ran off.

She called her father from a phone booth and started with a horrible
gaffe: "Are you up and around yet?"

The old man replied with a chuckle, "Figuratively speaking, yes.
Who's this?"

"Give me your address, I'll be right there!" she cried.

"Anastasia!" He was so shocked, he could barely recall his own
address.

When she got there in a taxi, he was waiting at the gate. He lived in
a real village house in the middle of faceless, multistoried Moscow: the
tiny wooden building had miraculously survived right next to the Kolo-
mensky Monastery. Seeing the beauty in her sheepskin coat, he glowed:
What a daughter!

Anastasia looked over the home of her unfamiliar father with curiosity: pyramids of books, piles of old newspapers, several radios starting
with a war trophy Telefunken and ending with a new Sony, a lathe and
woodworking tools, pictures of Sakharov and Solzhenitsyn, and an
enormous globe.

When she told him what the plan was, he merely exclaimed, "Well,

Anastasia!" This had to be the happiest day of his life. His daughter had come to see him—the daughter he had thought was brought up to be hostile to him, and she came as a friend and not just as a friend but as a collaborator in the struggle for human rights, and what could be more wonderful than a father and daughter struggling together for human rights? He understood everything in a flash and figured it all out. Time—midnight; place—the Lenin Hills, the observation platform, a usual tourist stop, everyone goes there to admire the view of Moscow.

Finally, shyly, he asked permission to look through *Say Cheese!*—after all, it was created for none other than "thinking Russia," right?

What a sweetie Father turned out to be, thought Anastasia, counting himself part of "thinking Russia." Just a child, they're all little children, these dissidents, and they're up against grim men who outnumber them a thousand to one. . . .

All day long Anastasia was in a bad mood, growling at her aunt and mother, pretending to look through old glacier tables, tossing them aside, chasing away thoughts of Ogo, and trying to think instead about her old friend Eduardas Pyatrauskas, the lifeguard from the Mount Elbrus Refuge of Eleven.

He really was such a unique Lithuanian, living at a height of 4,000 meters, she thought. An example for some, that knight without fear or reproach, and how he skis on the saddle of Elbrus—*really*! And his looks—*really*!

As for Ogo, she could recall that he was afraid to swim out too far, that once in Leningrad he ran away from only *two* hooligans, shamefully shoving his lady, that is, Anastasia, into a taxi and kicking at them. Or just recall Ogo's looks—his build was a total wreck, his crooked shoulders, sunken chest, an unattractive portrait—eyes with yes, yes, a tin color, fetid hair. . . .

Two opposite worlds—Eduardas's of dazzling snow, bottomless sky, and young knights, who treat women in the best traditions of Frank Sinatra songs; and Ogo's world, smoky, alcoholy, sneering . . . And how could she put the vile hedonism of Comrade O (they say there is a lewd film called *The Story of O*) next to that exceptional loyalty which radiated, yes, yes, radiated from every look of the deep eyes, pfui, of Eduard, filled with spiritual content, directed at the object of his touching, hopeless love, pfui, pfui, pfui!

At six o'clock her aunt ran in with square eyes. "There's a horrible man here asking for you."

The apartment filled with aromas from the central market. It was said that Shuz sometimes glued on a false moustache and sold the spicy *adjiga* sauce there. In any case, Shuz had pals at all the food suppliers of the capital; he was one of them in that world. "And here's a present for your moms." From the pocket of his leather jacket came a wax-paper packet. "Right, moms, smoked salmon. Just like that, by the way. If you need any other eats, we take orders."

"What a nice man you turned out to be. It's nice that she has such sweet acquaintances now, so simple, without all that ..." a pause with pursed lips: Ogorodnikov was on her mind, "—without tricks. ..."

"Merci, madame." Zherebyatnikov embraced both women with his huge paws and even mauled the aunt's rear a bit, which brought the maiden lady into complete and long-lasting confusion.

"And where are you planning to go with bare shoulders?" he addressed the younger generation. "Look out, they'll get you for sure in a dress like that!"

The ladies gasped at the low-cut beauty. "Comrade is right in pointing out the excessive frivolity of your outfit, that could put you in an ambiguous position in any group."

"Perhaps I did not properly understand you about tonight?" Anastasia asked Shuz haughtily. She gave her mother and aunt a triumphant, schoolgirl-silly finger and demanded her fur coat.

On the way to the diplomats' ghetto, stopped for a red light, Shuz jerked his thumb behind them. "There they are, the curs, sniffing." Anastasia, apparently accidentally—a Mata Hari!—turned with her cigarette and saw a gray Volga right behind them and two muskrat hats in it. "Now I'll maul you a bit," Shuz warned her, "as if you were an ordinary whore." Tilting her head back, he gave her a garlic kiss. Responding, she realized that she wildly wanted a man. What a miracle—any man! She wanted to be under a man! Damn Ogo! Off in Paris! Then she remembered that today she was an agent of world imperialism and allowed herself a vulgar laugh.

"That's great," Shuz approved, "got my pecker up!" The light had changed to green awhile ago. The detectives gave a tactful beep from behind.

The group gathered *chez* Claude-Marie Blonde, the Senegalese attaché (and incidentally, a rather pale-skinned gentleman), was intrigued by the appearance of an unknown beauty. Everyone here, in principle, either knew each other or had seen each other, but this was Anastasia's first foray out of the zone of Marxism-Leninism and without a single sip she was already high and incomparably lovely.

She was astonished by Shuz's fluent, or at least shameless, French. He kept addressing her in the language of Turgenev, "Mush! Stuff your face! Senegal is a rich country! You'll meet people later!"

The guests and M. Blonde himself with his wife stood around the table with hors d'oeuvres, eating peacefully and exchanging peaceful phrases on the latest premiere at the Theater of Lenin Labor Unions, where in the second act through the use of lighting effects and trembling hands a daring hint was made about the possibility of the sex act between a woman and man. The play was banned. At the present moment the liberal public of Moscow along with the world press was fighting for its reinstatement.

Anastasia was floored when she saw who was serving drinks—*mamma mia,* a real bartender in a white jacket with gold braid on the left shoulder! A real bourgeois event! She was even more astonished when she heard herself from a distance, so to speak, and realized that she was talking and laughing in English! Really! And with whom? Also a uniform, but not a bartender. Gray temples, a scar on the cheek, eagles in his buttonholes, an American military attaché—well, well, well, quite a crowd. . . .

"I am a scientist," she said. "I study the mountains."

The colonel laughed readily.

"Excuse me, friend," Shuz said, moving the colonel a bit. "Nastya, eat! Gin and tonic is a treacherous thing! Que désirez vous manger, cutie?"

Anastasia, recalling her role, laughed cheaply. The American recoiled, for he was aware every minute of his wife's loving stare between his shoulder blades.

A lady with sharp protocol eyes, from the Ministry of Culture on ties with Francophone countries, made her way over to Shuz.

"And who's this, Shuz Artemievich, your new bride?"

"Bride!" He laughed. "I just met her toward nightfall yesterday."

"And straight to a diplomatic reception? Not bad, not bad." The lady even moaned from some unknown sensations.

"Why not? Straight ahead! Right on!"

Next to Anastasia stood a magnificent young man who looked like a mannequin for men's clothing in a good store.

"I have familiarized myself with many attractions in Moscow," he was saying, "but I haven't satisfied my curiosity and continue meeting new attractions."

"Meet this one," Shuz growled. "This is Philip."

"Ha, ha, ha! Hello, Philip!" Anastasia played it very convincingly and for greater authenticity touched him with her hip.

Now that was an evening—diplomats, spies, bartenders—even high-altitude euphoria couldn't compare!

Anastasia didn't realize, of course, that she was the cause of excitement at this routine Senegalese reception. The presence among the protocol guests of a tipsy and absolutely available beauty agitated the men and infuriated the ladies.

8

MIKHAILO KALEDIN, AS usual after a "big noise," was in a terrible state. Having chased away all his lasses, he lay alone in the attic, beard pointing at the ceiling. A huge light from the neighboring construction project inappropriately illuminated the pathetic objects of daily life. The tail of a previously unnoticed slogan hung in one of the windows, with a cudgel of an exclamation mark. The radiators were hissing madly. The despised beard was filling with despised sweat. He didn't have the strength to get up, block the streetlight with a curtain, or open the small pane in the window to let in cold air.

Well, why didn't I emigrate? thought Mikhailo Kaledin. I don't have the strength to play the Russian fool in the Soviet kingdom any longer. I don't have the strength for anything, including having no strength, save me, a fool, O Lord.... The monarchist artist had no idea that at that very moment he would become the epicenter of a real theater of military action.

A few hours earlier the PhID collegium gave General Planshchin the go-ahead for the operation and encoded it with the two letters MK, that is, the initials of the depression-tormented artist. V. K. Planshchin himself directed the operation from his office with the view of the Kremlin's ruby stars. Over the radio the general was in communication with several operative cars—including Captain Slyazgin's group, which was covering Captain Skanshchin's landing. The case used eight cars and forty men.

Mikhailo in his astral depression was awaiting something familiar, something like the effect of levitation when his heavy body seemed to lift from the cot. At that moment, sometimes, a silent chorale sounded and his spirits would lighten a bit.

Instead of chorale that night he heard the tinkle of cow bells and the trumpet of shepherd's horns, that is, the entry system worked. What bastard would be coming now? thought Mikhailo, I've trained them all not to show up the next day. That bastard, knocking, ringing, blowing—I won't open up for anything.

The floor creaked, something bumped down near the table, as if a case of cognac were being set down, a woman's heels clicked nearby, and then a man cleared his throat.

"Mikhailo, why don't you close the door when you're sleeping?"

"Go to hell," Mikhailo responded weakly.

Someone clicked a lighter. The flame traveled along the shelves, as if inspecting all the samovars, jugs, steam irons, a gramophone, the photo album *Say Cheese!* ... can't lift my hands to clean up in there, junk sucks me in....

A metallic female voice said, "Where's the warm one? I want the warm one!"

In the dining room, beyond the corner of the wall, a light went on. Now he could see the broad-shouldered figure in a sheepskin coat examining the shelves. A black marketeer, probably, estimating what he could get in hard currency for the "antiques."

"I want a warm man," the girl said, coming around the corner. She was wearing a spotted artificial fur and big boots. A girl of medium height with a round face and bulging eyes like a soldier's buttons. A bright-red splotch of a mouth.

"Watch out, Ella, you'll fall in love!" the stranger warned without turning around. "Mikhailo is quite a man. You'll fall in love till your dying day." He was entranced by something in the shelves.

"Who are you, what do you want?" the artist moaned. "Get out! Or I'll shoot!"

He had nothing to shoot with, as opposed to his uninvited guest, whose hand went straight to his pocket at the word "shoot."

"There he is!" The girl leaped like a lynx and dropped her unwashed hair over Mikhailo Kaledin. "Oh, you sweet beard, you!" Throwing off her cheap coat with spots of a filthy life and revealing a tiny mini, she grabbed Mikhailo's crotch. "Got a dick?"

To the amazement of the spread-eagled artist the demanded organ let itself be known with full conviction.

"Oh, what a good worker!" the girl exclaimed.

"I'm in the way, aren't I?" At last, the male visitor turned his smooth-shaven face with its clear Russian expression. "A third wheel, right, kids? Okay, I'll sit in the dining room for a while, leaf through this album. You take care of the sexual revolution, and then we'll have some cognac."

It was all said with naïve Russian friendliness.

"Your name, man!" howled Mikhailo Kaledin, trying to awaken his famous Siberian might. His hand, however, was reconnoitering in the slightly smelly but nevertheless wildly desirable crack of the unknown woman.

"Put an end to it, Mikhailo!" The uninvited guest shamed him. "When you come to visit me in the Northern Caucasus, I'll recognize you."

"Ah, it's you, Comrade," Mikhailo said, remembering.

"And don't worry about Ella. She's from the North Caucasus, a tested worker."

"Well, buzz off, Caucasian, buzz off." Mikhailo Kaledin took Ella's face, soft as a roll, in his hands. "Oh, my little lass, my vixen, my little witch. . . ."

"Grrrr," growled the Komsomol activist before plunging into busy silence.

9

LIKE AN ENORMOUS hockey puck, Shuz came flying out of the arch of the diplomatic house. Just as bulky, the militiaman belatedly tumbled out of his guardhouse, in which he barely fit with his sheepskin coat and felt boots and galoshes. Shit, look at him go, you'd think he swiped something from the Senegals.

Shuz ran over to his Zhiguli. Just as expected, the lock was frozen and his key wouldn't fit! He pulled from his pocket a bottle of House of Lords gin he picked up at the reception, splashed a bit on the lock, and the key fit. Straight ahead! Rip the scar! Right on!

The PhIDs, who were waiting nearby in their Volga, certainly had not expected their object to run off from a capitalist happening, and yet there he was, racing past, hot, full, non-Soviet . . . a stranger! And of course, "the bread will fall butter-side down," the Volga wouldn't start, damn it, even though it had a Finnish ignition. Flooded!

It was only at the embankment, when they really hit the gas and caught up with the fugitive, that they remembered: Where's the broad? Why did he leave the snazzy babe to the Senegalese? What an obnoxious lout we have living in our capital! That Shuz has to be a Jew, and not one of our kikes, but one of the ancient ones.

"Dove, Dove!" the PhID called over the radio. "Graybeard left unexpectedly. At this point in time we are following him over the Borodin Bridge."

"He's going to Zamoskvorechye," said Dove, aka General Planshchin. "Keep an eye on him, Swallows, don't lose him! Do you have everything?"

"The woman stayed behind, Dove," the agent said with hesitation.

"What woman, Swallows? Why didn't you report on the woman earlier?"

"He's driving us crazy with his broads, Dove. The fourth today."

"What does she look like, Swallows?" the general barked.

"Which one?" the agent asked.

"Are you asleep at the wheel?"

"We're at a red light."

"What does the woman look like whom Graybeard left at Black's?"

"A typical, typical . . ." muttered the recent graduate of the training school.

"Typical what?" roared the general. Such people he had to work with to settle important questions! "A typical whore, do you mean?"

"Right, what you said, Dove." The agent was relieved.

"Well, call a spade a spade. We're not in kindergarten here!"

10

"AMONG REPRESENTATIVES OF Western youth, I do want to assure you in the below-mentioned, highly sexual relations are established without superstitions on the agenda." So spoke the international man Philip to tipsy and laughing Anastasia, wrapped in a Canadian sheepskin coat. They were strolling along the esplanade on the Lenin, formerly Vorobyov, Hills above the lights of Moscow, formerly called the same.

"What are you trying to say?" Anastasia asked.

Philip strode next to her, hands in pockets, rosy-cheeked and serious; his gray coat had large shoulders and was tight around his narrow rear.

"I stress that among the many notable spots of Moscow, you, Anastasia, why hide it, will be the leading notable memorial gift, even if your grandmother was the cat's pajamas."

"You really can talk, Philip! Where did you learn Russian? How can I become your memorial gift, Philip?"

"A person of the female sex, Anastasia, is an equal partner in a sexual undertaking. That is how, actually, many scholars teach in the West. Is that new to you?"

At that hour there were several tour buses and quite a few people at the observation platform.

"Is that new to you?" Philip repeated his question.

"What?" asked Anastasia. The seriousness of the young ambassador from the West rather surprised her.

"The question of equal partners?"

"Where?" she asked.

"Excuse me?" Philip was confused.

"Where are you proposing equal partnership?" she asked.

At that moment her father drove up. He was piloting what he called with respectful seriousness a "passenger automobile," in other words, a bastard put together from bits and pieces of a Moskvich, a Volga, a Gazik, and a Czech Skoda. In amazement Philip even used a non-Russian phrase: *C'est une voiture.* In principle, he had been prepared for anything, but not for a vehicle like that and that's why when he found himself in the back seat next to the enormous slab of the album, he thought that it was a barrier designed by the Russians for transport of passengers of mixed sex.

"Here, take it!" Anastasia's mitten patted the barrier. "Regards to the editor in chief! Where will you see him? In Paris? Rio?"

"New York," Philip said, and hefted the object as if testing its weight, as if its weight was the main problem in transporting it to New York. Then he shifted the object to the floor at his feet and turned to Anastasia.

"I would be taken with extreme satisfaction to receive your palm, dear Anastasia."

Having received it, he began sending his bioenergy into his Russian partner. If you fill a woman to the necessary level with your bioenergy, she will be more willing to meet you halfway.

"Do you feel my vibration, madame?"

"No, not yet."

"Then I will continue. Scholars with great names teach that feeling the vibration you are partly already with your partner and no longer worry about the location of the coming intercourse, with whether it is a garden or an isolated yard. . . ."

"Now I feel your vibration," Anastasia said. "By the way, I'd like you to meet the driver, my father."

"Tell me," her father entered the conversation, "are you familiar with the new currents in European unions?"

"Yes," Philip said. "I can be the intermediary link between new independent Soviet unions and European unions."

"Aren't you spreading yourself thin, Philip?" worried Anastasia.

"No," the young man reassured her. "Everything will be done at the right time and in the right place. You can depend on me absolutely."

The unique vehicle rolled merrily down the embankment of the Moskva River. Philip, as he participated in the necessary dialogue, also observed the shimmering domes of the Novo-Devicy Convent, the attractive Moscow attraction. They approached the Borodin Bridge, over which Shuz had driven a mere hour earlier with his motorcade. The traffic cop, stopping traffic, came over to the jalopy to check on the inspection sticker and, if possible, get money for a bottle, but when he saw the war veteran's serious face and all the military awards pinned right to his coat, he merely smiled wryly and saluted.

11

"THIEF! THIEF!" THE roosters cried.

"Hold her!" wailed the weeping willows.

Mikhailo Kaledin was running barefoot through the puddles of the Jewish town of Vitebsk, begging the thief who had flown from his canvas (premonarchial period) to return and to return what she had taken, the undrawn, the natural thing without which modern art is impossible both here and abroad. Then Mikhailo Kaledin woke up when someone shook him by the shoulder and a Soviet voice said in his ear, "Get up, Comrade! Thieves got in your house!"

The studio's floor boards were bouncing under official boots. Huge shadows distorted reality. Beams of light pierced the composition. There was something revolutionary about the whole thing, the men needed bandoliers over their shoulders for the complete effect. In the center of this heavy monochromic group of figures a horrifying girl in a torn pink slip fluttered like a huge butterfly. Her breasts fluttered on their

own, and on one of them (the left) a tattooed *papillon* fluttered like
a woman.

"Fuckmyeyemyassmyarmpitfuckyou!" the girl yowled.

"Citizen Kaledin, do you recognize this citizeness?"

The girl abruptly shut up and sagged in the guards' arms. A mean-
ingless smile and convex button eyes illuminated her face.

"I do," Mikhailo Kaledin said. "That is my latest love. A young
daughter of the steppes."

"There's an all-Union warrant out on her," the cop said. "On your
daughter of steppes. Incidentally, allow me to introduce myself—Militia
Major Bushbashin. I'd like to have you up to fill out the report."

"She's innocent," said Mikhailo, and rose with amazing ease.

"Your surname is Dymshits according to your passport?" Major
Bushbashin asked. "We assume that you've lost quite a few valuable
things. Take a look, Citizen Dymshits, at the thief's accomplice. Do you
know him?"

The guards moved aside and Mikhailo Kaledin, aka Misha Dymshits,
saw his pal Shuz in a scornful pose at the table, smoking a Benson &
Hedges with his right hand.

"Where'd you put Captain Skanshchin?" Shuz demanded haughtily
of the knight of the revolution who called himself a major. "I saw him
hauling a case of cognac down the stairs. As for you, bitch—"

The girl immediately made a move toward Shuz, but was stopped by
a patrician gesture from the major.

"Easy! The subject is doing himself in!"

"Release these innocent people!" implored the owner of the scene of
action, or rather the renter of the scene of action, since it, like everything
else, belonged to the state of workers and peasants. "Release my friend,
mutilated by the cult of personality, release this maiden, victim of the
worse half of the human race!"

The girl started howling like an evil spirit.

12

THE ABOVE-MENTIONED events went unnoticed, naturally, by the bulk of
the population of Moscow, and the capital began the next cloudy day

without even suspecting that in the surrounding December air there were two people who had been feeling total satisfaction since morning with what they had done.

The first such person was without a doubt General Planshchin, sitting in the bowels of the nonexistent PhID HQ, a magnifying glass in his eye and with its help enjoying the photographic sedition captured yesterday by that brilliant maneuver.

The other such person, of course, was the foreign representative Philip, flying in the first-class cabin of a Sabena jet to his foggy home. In hand by him was champagne (that's how it sounds in literal translation), and in his suitcase next to the export samples from Sovcaviarsevrugabelugaexport was the canvas-wrapped photo album *Say Raisin!* (in the original) or *Say Cheese!* as it was known in the language of the North Atlantic Treaty Organization.

MANY HATS ON

I

ND THERE WAS CHETVERKIND! "Hi, Fima! My, you've grown since I last saw you. Let's go for a walk."

"There's a lot more dirt here than there was four years ago. Where else is it supposed to go? The roads and sidewalks are even more beaten up. A bus trip up Madison Avenue is like a trip in a garbage truck in Ryazan. However, out of those potholes and pits giants of reflecting glass on steel legs continue to grow, like that new Hyatt Hotel. Remember how we used to dream about this island when we were young, Ogo? Our youth dragged out unbecomingly, adenoidal adolescents at forty.... Remember how we used to sing? Watch out for that mess, sir. You can't wash it off, it has to be scraped, but no one does scraping anymore. The dirt on Fifth Avenue reminds me of the dirt in Kuibyshev when I was a child, during the evacuation, except it didn't have that rotten smell, because they would have gladly devoured half of New York's garbage. Remember how we sang, 'We're up on the hundred second floor, where the boogie-woogie's out the door.' New York reminds me of a man who worries about his fancy hairdo but never wipes his ass. The city is being destroyed by the scum of the Third

World. That might be new for you, Ogo, but our émigrés here are quickly turning into racists. An ocean of blacks is lashing at our city—"

"Your city, Fima?"

"Who else's? Our Jewish-Slavic-formerly-Anglo-Saxon city is being defiled. Look, look at that savage pulling out his appurtenance and pissing two feet away from Tiffany's. In Russia we always thought that Western civilization brought decadence. That's nonsense, it is really the only bastion of common sense. The communist world is surrealism in pure form, while the Third, so-called, is sending tsunamis of lascivious losers. The darker the people, the more perverted...."

But the skyscrapers still glowed, as if promising something to mankind. On Fifty-seventh Street a squad of six-foot girls, obviously models, came toward them. "Masha!" shouted Ogorodnikov.

One turned around: "I'm Olya!" The squad got on a bus with darkened windows.

From a corner coffee shop came the smell of stale hamburgers, frankfurters, bremeners. *Die Fahne hoch!** Proletarians of the world, unite! Two steps away, by the way, was the luxurious entrance of one of the best places—the Russian Vodka Room—which smelled of expensive cigars. A long cloud, just like a refreshing rag, passed along Fifty-seventh from the East River to the Hudson.

Ogo and Fima went into the Russian Vodka Room. Fima had been such a typical Muscovite, but after long wandering in America, he had become a typical New Yorker and, moreover, an inhabitant of Many Hats On, as he familiarly referred to Manhattan. "I don't think I'd be able to live anywhere else," he'd confess, "and that's why so much here outrages me. Take the rents, for instance. I'm paying eight hundred bucks for a lousy two-bedroom apartment on West Thirty-fourth Street, and the landlord, a damned Syrian, is planning to raise the rent eight percent. Isn't that robbery?"

Fima was in the traditional business of Russian émigrés in New York: he drove a taxi. "I spend two weeks behind the wheel, and two weeks jerking off in art, that is, I make the rounds of the ad agencies....

---

*"Raise high the flag!" A line from the Nazi hymn "Horst Wessel-Lied."

People here don't see photography the way they do in Russia, Ogo, where it's been ideological since the days of Catherine the Great. Here at best it's pleasure for the eye, and, at worst, chewing gum. I came to this country with my works of genius, Bravo, they said, you're a genius, that's Mother Russia for you! they said. Three shows in a row, reviews in the major magazines, and—basta, no money, no commissions. Some of our photographers and I formed a collective called 'Soviets Through a Hidden Camera,' and we thought, well, this'll be a sensation. And it was, with reviews, TV coverage, and then—no money, no commissions. That might be all right when you're twenty-five, Ogo, but I'm forty. I have to feed Rima, send the kids to school. In general, I decided to drop 'Russian creative genius' and go into advertising. I haven't gotten inside yet, but I will. I'll photograph girls with bare backsides, advertise beauty creams. . . ."

They were sitting in a semicircular red leather banquette, eating what was listed in the menu under the Russian word *zakuski*. The walls of the famous restaurant had rather nice paintings of symbols of their distant homeland—the firebird and troika birds and dragon snakes. A black waiter in a Russian shirt brought them a second round of Black Russians. Ogo looked at his watch. Konsky was already twenty minutes late. Ogo looked at Fima. The man hadn't changed at all over the years, the same bull-like slope of neck, the facial expression of a toothache, even the same old neck scarf, but it was curious that Fima hadn't asked about Moscow even once; not about any of the guys, not about anything. . . .

"Tell me, Fima, are you all right in general?" He put his hand on his old friend's shoulder. I won't develop the theme, I won't ask anything else, let him say what he wants.

"If you mean alcohol, I don't have a problem with that anymore. But you must be talking about art, right? You know, I have to tell you one unpleasant thing. In New York, it's hard to work seriously in Russian art unless you kiss Alik Konsky's ass."

"Wait a minute, what are you saying? That Alik dictates fashion?"

"And how! That's the least of it. Everything is in his hands. He's a universally recognized authority on Russian photography. Didn't you know that in Moscow? Just imagine, he's started this snob idea in New

York, that Russian photography requires translation into Western languages. Now in all the major publishing houses our negatives are treated with this idiotic translating developer, a mixture of potash and chili sauce, and the whole process is done under the supervision of the main expert, that is, Alik Konsky, or one of his groupies. And if you dare say anywhere that it's all bullshit, you immediately become an Eastern Barbarian and are sent off to the second rank. . . ."

Fima had obviously stepped on one of his favorite corns. He got excited. His face was distorted with grimaces. Just then Alik Konsky entered the restaurant.

This lunch-à-trois had been Ogo's idea. Out of the corner of his ear he had heard about the quarrel between his two old pals and thought he could smooth things over as a "representative of the center." Konsky handed his coat to the maître d', but got no farther than two steps before he was hailed, and he stopped near the bar, scratching his beard and distractedly replying to the questions of a cheery group of young Americans.

"Alik is hauling it in here," Fima went on. "You should see his studio—the twenty-first century. You won't recognize him! He's a different man. I can't stand him. The past is completely forgotten."

Ogo watched Konsky. He had moved another ten steps deeper into the room. Now he was stopped by a fat lady wearing a pince-nez. He was introduced to the lady's companions, undoubtedly "people of the arts." Meeting him, they all bulged their eyes and opened their mouths, as if to say, Really, the one and only? Konsky leaned to one side, his hand in his jacket—scratching his armpit.

Finally Fima noticed him too, stopped in midsentence, and looked at Ogo. "Well, thanks a lot, Max!"

"How was I supposed to know about your relationship?" Ogo asked with a shrug.

Fima started getting up from the table. His belly, grown bigger in New York, dragged the rooster-bedecked tablecloth partway with him. He tossed a twenty-dollar bill on the table and, huffing and puffing, went off.

Konsky, no longer answering questions from the people in the arts, watched Fima Chetverkind go with unblinking blue eyes. Then he continued his path.

"I can imagine the lies he's told you about me," he said to Ogorodnikov, and finished Fima's Heineken.

They hadn't seen each other in over five years and, you would think, they should have embraced, but somehow it just didn't seem right to Ogo, even without what Fima had told him. It didn't seem to suit Konsky, either, who sidled into the banquette, as if having an ordinary lunch with a friend from around the corner.

People in Moscow recalled Alik Konsky with a sigh even six years after his emigration—what a genius the country had lost! His photographs were compared to ancient friezes: such perfection of line, such Grecian art! Eternally without money, eternally under surveillance, under threat of exile to Kilometer 101 outside Moscow, or even farther, he valued his semiunderground, semiforbidden fame, and semifreedom. In the midsixties German, Drevesny, and Fotik Klezmetsov got a selection of his pictures cleared to run in *Photogazette*. If those shots had been published, Konsky would have immediately and noisily joined the Fourth Generation, become a member of the Soviet Renaissance, been accepted into the Union, in a word, would have become a Soviet nonconformist—but at the last moment Konsky pulled the selection out, apparently determined to maintain his image of the lone, persecuted, not Soviet, but *real* genius. In principle, it was the right and reasonable decision, his friends later thought. Too reasonable for a genius, a skeptic added.

His work began appearing abroad, and then in albums. Every pseudo-intellectual foreigner asked about Konsky in Moscow. All the Ogorodnikovs, Drevesnys, and Germans had to share their fame with the unbribable genius of pure form and sometimes accede to his priority. In general, they did it gladly, because they themselves loved Konsky's "Hellenic photography" and loved Konsky himself with his empty blue eyes—a real photographer who sees nothing but the picture! And if the PhIDs began messing with him, all the recognized geniuses rallied and raised a stink smelled round the world—We won't give up our national treasure! Of course, with the course of Brezhnevism the public recognition waned, and Konsky's supporters all ended up at the famous Canal exhibit, where they were beaten up along with Konsky by the People's Volunteer Corps.

Soon after that Alik Konsky "began leaving." First he tried the matrimonial method. There were brides galore in Europe and America. Even Brazil responded. However, Konsky's personal *kurator,* Major Krost, flatly stated, "We won't let you marry a foreigner, Konsky!" Why not? "The decision was made, that's why. Leave as a Jew." Suddenly it was learned that Alik Konsky wasn't a Jew. According to his passport and all his papers, he was a Greek! That was the source of his Grecian motifs! "For us," said Major Krost, "anyone who goes against the Party line is . . . well . . . anyway, not one of us, not an internationalist." One way or another, the exit visa was made up for Israel, and after a month's good-bye partying in Moscow, Leningrad, and Tbilisi the "photographic Mandelstam,"* as he was sometimes called, headed into the sunset.

Now, six years later, he and Ogorodnikov met as if it hadn't been a week. Interestingly, thought Ogo, Alik hasn't asked anything about Moscow either. Even a formal curiosity is lacking—well, how's old XYZ? As if there were nothing there but puffs of steam.

Just then Alik Konsky asked wanly, "Well, how are things there in general?" and waved to a young woman coming from the bathroom, leg warmers over her jeans. Ogorodnikov decided not to answer: he was insulted on behalf of Moscow. All we talk about is the ones who left and it turns out that to them their Moscow friends are like provincial relatives!

But the answer wasn't particularly needed. Excusing himself, Alik got up—"for a minute." To pee? To catch the girl? No, actually, he knew people at the next table, a collection of spectacles worth, say, a thousand dollars. Ogo listened to his pal (he assiduously chased away the word "former") gab in English. He really chatters, and he didn't know a word when he left! They were talking about somebody named Richard

---

*Osip Mandelstam, a great poet unrecognized during his lifetime who finally perished in the Gulag. We use here our "photographic M" so as to show a trite penchant of the so-called circles for labeling their pets: "Pushkin of painting," "Mozart of prose," etc.

who was supposed to come, but didn't, with some Susan. Konsky's jacket was the worst, he must have gotten it from the Salvation Army, that was his style in this city.

"Well, how do you like my angliiski?" Konsky asked when he came back.

"You get that fucking 'I can't help but' mixed up," Ogo said. Konsky turned white.

"Impossible!"

Ogo got the bill and put out his American Express card.

"Hm," said Konsky.

"And how are you in general?" Ogo asked.

"In general, fantastic!" Konsky said. The old slang woke him up. "You know, I'm taking things from holography now. Some computer innovations reveal . . ."

"That's not what I'm asking about," Ogo said. "Have you gotten married?" Ogo was responding to Konsky's indifference to Moscow with indifference to Konsky's art.

Konsky must have understood, and he smirked. "No, I haven't gotten married, what for? Have you?"

"Yes, of course I have."

"Really? I haven't yet."

"This is my seventh wife."

"You're to be envied. I never have married. Ogo, do you sense the compression of space?"

"As much as its expansion, you mean?"

"It's not too cozy in either direction, is it? How long has it been since you've experienced the feeling called joy? It's vanishing, along with certain elements of what is simply termed swinishness—isn't it? It's a good thing that we don't have to call things by their real names yet, right? I'd give my last pairs of pants for that pleasure. . . ."

This rather rapid and not fully intelligible dialogue brought them back to former times, when they used to communicate "on the intercellular level," somewhere in the Arbat with a jazz record and a good bottle. They were both pleased to have stirred up the past so easily, without pressure. "You probably got baptized," one asked the other. It happened: a cross was pulled out from beneath a shirt. "It happened to me, too, though I confess, sometimes I think I'm a ..." "Don't finish, same here. . . ."

With a sigh of relief the intercellular communication came to an end.

"Tell me, Alik," Ogo said then. "What was that nonsense Fima was giving me about translation of Russian photography into foreign languages? Is he still hitting the bottle too hard?"

"He's just an asshole and a clod, but you ... haven't you heard ... about the process?" Konsky spoke quickly, as if he had been waiting a long time for the question. "Of all people, Ogo, you must understand ... this would seem like nonsense only to a clod ... after so many years of bolshevism, an automatic transition to Western photography is impossible. That's why I got the idea for so-called translation. Not all Russian works, alas, give in to this reworking, however. . . ."

"Alik? Are you all right?" Ogo asked. "I thought Fima was joking, but you really have become a serious lad, haven't you. I see you're all very serious here. Try translating my *Splinters* into Canadian Eskimo."

"What does *Splinters* have to do with it?" Konsky asked with unexpected harshness.

"Would you care for anything else, gentlemen?" asked the black Ivan, letting them know they'd overstayed their welcome.

They went out on Fifty-seventh Street. An oblique low-altitude storm cloud traveled over the street, dragging with it the smells of New York's ethnic gastronomy. Under Konsky's frayed cuff was an excellent watch—a Rolex.

"Shit, I'm really late!" he said.

"Me, too," said Ogorodnikov. "Remind me of the fastest way to get to Pharaoh."

"Pharaoh? Why are you going there?" A strange tension appeared in Konsky's voice again. He took Ogo by the arm. "Let's walk for another five minutes? Fuck them, they'll wait. Listen, do you know what those people said about you in the restaurant? Your friend, they said, looks like a typical loser. Imagine? Physiognomists! When I told them that you are the most famous Soviet photographer, their mouths flew open. Listen, Max, to tell the truth, I'm not convinced that you made the right decision."

"What decision?" Ogo asked, and squinted down at Konsky, who was leading him through the crowd by the arm. The graying Greek hair of the master fluttered beautifully over the young face.

"Well, the decision to stay in the West."

"There was no such decision."

Konsky dropped Ogorodnikov's elbow. "Wait a minute, then how is your interview to be understood? You're not planning to go back after that?"

"What interview, Alik, I don't quite understand."

"Here, I just happen to have it in my pocket. . . ." Konsky pulled out a not-very-fresh copy of the émigré newspaper *Russian Arrow.*

" 'Rebellion of the New Wave,' " read Ogo. In smaller print it said, "Interview with the famous Soviet photographer Maxim Ogorodnikov." And in even smaller type.

QUESTION: Tell me, Max, what tendencies are prevalent in Soviet photography right now?

ANSWER: You see, Ambroise, the stifling atmosphere of socialist realism . . .

"My goodness," Konsky said. "I really am late. Where's the Pharaoh publishing house? Honestly, I don't remember, I think it's about ten blocks south . . . Pharaoh, hm, that almshouse. . . ."

He stepped back and was engulfed by the crowd. Ogorodnikov lifted his cane, hailing a cab, holding the newspaper before his eyes with his left hand.

QUESTION: Tell me, Max, is a new renaissance possible in Soviet photography?

ANSWER: You see, Ambroise, the Party bureaucrats are suppressing the slightest expression of artistic freedom. . . .

QUESTION: Tell me, Max, is creativity compatible with a communist dictatorship?

ANSWER: You see, Ambroise, it seems to me that creativity and communist dictatorship are incompatible. . . .

Alik Konsky looked back at the intersection and saw tall Ogo getting into a cab. Alik rubbed his hand in front of his face, as if erasing the image. The taxi did in fact disappear, actually poured into the yellow humped herd of other taxis. However, what made him want to howl was still there—the stench of banality. The farther away you go, Konsky thought, the more often you see the stench and filth. When you look at all these meetings, lunches, dialogues, and walks from the side, everything seems normal, but as soon as you're alone with yourself, it's all covered with that unbearable stench. All because of *words*. I hate words, Russian and English. Whatever can't be exhibited, words, the invisible smoke of banality.... Always with you....

Konsky often recalled that evening the previous spring at the Seven Samurai—or rather, what was said then by the one with the moustache and to the one with the moustache. If he were to make an exhibit of the memory, it would be quite a scene. Genre: a dim and empty Japanese café, two Europeans with cigarettes, behind them a video game.... But if he were to play back the tape—and who could swear that one didn't exist?—the burning banality would be there again. And the most disgusting part was that it all centered on Ogo, damn it—but then, of course, that wasn't the most disgusting, it was merely disgusting, no more disgusting than the rest.

Why was it that the moment the fellow with the moustache and trenchcoat, a moth-eaten version of Robert Taylor in *Waterloo Bridge,* had crossed the threshold of the Japanese restaurant where Konsky often dined, the moment their eyes met, Konsky had known he was—

"Mr. Konsky? Excuse me, I recognized you, I couldn't resist the temptation ... an old fan of yours ... of course, I'm an official representative, but I hope you have ... I'm glad you have no prejudices ... and *there,* believe me, *many* people don't have them either ... oh, much will change, and in the near future ... the power of our cultural potential ... you as a truly nonpolitical artist ... Russia, remember Mandelstam: Russian, Lethe, Lorelei ... by the way, about Maxim Ogorodnikov: things are not so simple with him ... has he never told you about me? We're half-brothers...."

Before Konsky had sat a man of charming international mien, resembling a writer of the Hemingway species, and the conversation for all its vileness had reminded Konsky of casual but masterly tinkling of the ivories, and it was only when he left that the Seven Samurai had filled with the burning stench, from which he had to run a long time, and wash long and unsuccessfully.…

2

OGORODNIKOV, WHILE HE was in the taxi and in the elevator going up to the twenty-fourth floor, was extremely upset. Of all the *not-simple* things said by Konsky, the one he remembered most was "typical look of a loser." He examined himself closely in every mirror and reflective surface that came his way. Could that gang have been right? Everybody used to think just the opposite. Maybe everything had been sagging lately? Lift that chin! He had always looked like an offensive volleyball player. They didn't play volleyball here. Hm, maybe what looks like a winner *there* is considered a loser *here?* He would have to ask Doug.

The President of Pharaoh Publishers, Douglas Semigorsky, had been known to Ogorodnikov since 1972, and on his last visit to America they had even played tennis, so that they had total justification for calling each other by abbreviated names: Doug, Ogo, Doug, Doug, Ogo, Ogo.… "Tell me, Doug, do I really look like a loser?"

"Tell me, Doug, do I really look like a loser?"

Mr. Semigorsky, dressed in a worn three-piece corduroy suit, sat cross-legged, with a soft, corduroy smile.

"We'll ask Margie," he said.

His secretary came in, the marvelous tennis American Margie Young.

"Margie really runs the shop here," Semigorsky said. "Besides which, she's a talented beginner photographer. Margie, of course, you know who Mr. Ogorodnikov is?"

"You bet!" She flashed a first-class smile.

"What do you think, Margie, does Ogo look like a loser?"

"Are you kidding, Doug? Mr. Ogorodnikov radiates fame."

"Hear that, Max? Feel a bit better?"

"Thank you, Miss Young! Thanks, if you're not kidding."

The girl moved around the office of the president with charming informality. Apparently, her relationship with the boss couldn't have been better. She put a file full of Ogorodnikov's affairs in front of Semigorsky and disappeared, with another smile, this one over her shoulder.

"I understand where you got that silly idea," Semigorsky continued softly. "However you shouldn't let the failure with *Splinters* spill over to the rest of your creativity. Just look." He opened the file. "The royalties on your first three albums are still coming in, and Brazil just made inquiries on *Drifting Dryland*. Brazil, Max!"

"You said the failure with *Splinters,* Doug?" Ogorodnikov repeated. He realized that the door was about to open, the door he tried not to notice and walk by, even though it should have been opened a long time ago.

"Alas, Max, in New York, we have to consider the opinion of a man like Alik Konsky. Max, what's the matter with you? Don't tell me, please, that you didn't know how Konsky torpedoed your *Splinters?*"

Ogorodnikov couldn't say anything at all. Apparently, he looked so different that Semigorsky called in Margie and asked her to bring some whiskey.

"Please, Doug, tell me this charming story," Ogo said at last.

The straight Chivas Regal gave this New York situation and story of betrayal a strangely natural feel.

"I got your album from Bruce Pollack about two years ago," Semigorsky began. "Our people liked it. To tell the truth, I didn't see it myself, but anyway we made Bruce a good offer, I think, twenty-five grand, if I'm not mistaken. Well, Max, nowadays all the Russian stuff published in major houses get reviewed first by Alik Konsky. And then, he has that new 'translation technique.' . . . Anyway, we sent him *Splinters,* though it was a pure formality in your case, Max. First of all, because you have a big name in the West, and secondly, everyone knew that you were friends, I remember how we met in Moscow in 1972, what a good time we had, I was amazed by how close you all were.

"So now, just imagine my astonishment, Max, when Alik calls me at the office and says that *Splinters* is shit. I said, Do you mean shit in some special meaning, sir? I thought there might be something metaphysical he was getting at, but he said, No, just shit, all-around shit, a piece of shit, and I don't want to say anything else about it. Well, you understand, Max, he didn't say it only to me, he said it to a lot of people in town, and soon, I would say in a week's time, there was a new atmosphere. Even the people in Pharaoh who had approved your album began looking at it ... hm ... skeptically would be the kind way of putting it. . . ."

"What's the problem? Can't they tell shit from candy on their own?" said Ogorodnikov with brilliant coldness. I guess this is how I'll have to talk in New York—with brilliant coldness. You can't get through this mafia with heat. Alik Konsky had taken them with this armpit scratching, a sign of independence. . . .

Semigorsky sat on the edge of his desk, handily demonstrating the "corduroy style." "There are so many good photographs now, Ogo, that society has to develop authorities to develop opinions. Come on, friend, now you have a chance to become an authority in this city."

The cold look of "future authority" Ogo moved from the speaker to the city landscape. The office opened on the classic view of downtown Manhattan: two slabs of the World Trade Center carried their hundreds of stories with vague rectangular significance above the collection of smaller slabs. The early December sunset rose above them slightly and an ancient frigate of clouds bent slightly over them. Really, it was just like his youthful dreams! Americans had no idea how many allies they had in Stalinist Russia. There were fewer now. Now there were fewer allies for anything at all. There was too much of everything. Then what was humanity's hope? Cooking. The countries with well-developed gastronomy would survive. Russia and America are doomed! How did I get plastered again? Oh, yes, Semigorsky's secretary was pouring.

"I understand that it's upsetting you, Max," the publisher said, "but it's been leading up to this for several years. I admit that from an egotistical point of view, I'm glad: it's their loss, our gain. I'm glad that you'll be among us, and believe me, you won't be lonely. It's a country of refugees."

"You've read my interview, Doug? Where?" Ogorodnikov asked with icy sharpness.

"It came on the Agence France Press teletype yesterday and was reprinted in many newspapers. Who's this Ambroise?"

"An ordinary traitor."

Incidentally, it was quite a December day, discovering two traitors. Of course, that wasn't so many for a man of his age. Chivas ages twelve years, hm.... Strange idea, to put it chronologically....

"When was it, Doug? I mean the call about the shit?"

"In the very end of May, Max, yes, yes, after Memorial Day, that's for sure.... Oh, Max, don't despair." Doug Semigorsky sympathized in the soft, corduroy style. "Besides the bad news, I've got good news. No objections?"

"Let's hear it," Ogo said.

"Let's go down to Soho together, all right? Our mutual friend Bruce Pollack is opening a new gallery. He's waiting for us and he has good news. Afterward we'll loosen up, recall Moscow 1972. All right? Splendid! Margie, please call Foxhill and leave a message for Mrs. Semigorsky, that Mr. Ogorodnikov and I are going to Pollack's gallery and would be glad if she joined us. By the way, Margie, maybe you would join us, too? Add a little beauty?"

Margie Young turned up her smile. "Wonderful, Doug! I'd love to!"

Now that's a real pal, thought Ogorodnikov. In honor of Moscow 1972. I gave him a fur hat, and he's reciprocating with his secretary.

3

NOWADAYS THERE'S NO more amusing place in New York, probably,* than Soho. And so, to Soho! The grimmest streets, façades blackened

---

*The tolerance of the Russian language! Take the word "probably" and put it as you wish in front of any word in the above-written sentence or after any word. Probably, nowadays ... nowadays, probably.... And what about the arabesques of our subjunctive mood? I doubt there's a bird anywhere in the world that could fly even halfway through it! Truly, Russian can add to its famous acronym GMTF (Great, Mighty, Truthful, and Free) another two letters in parentheses, GT, that is, Generous and Tolerant. It's incredible how that Cheerful, Casual, and Wandering (CCW) language survives under a regime that bends even photography to its will, won't allow independent publication of one tiny album of pictures, and thus transforms our narrative from a chamber novella into something resembling a spy story.

by countless fires. The iron stairs on the façades, meant to rescue the inhabitants from fire, have clearly never saved anyone, but they do create a marvelous impression of a trap. They work with the peeling columns in the style of the nouveaux riches of the 1880s. Add to this picture overflowing garbage cans, torn-up streets, and a stink.

Now let us illuminate this entire setup with the lecherous smile of Bohemia, moving here, to these very ex-warehouse lofts, let's quickly inflate the prices for yesterday's flophouses, let's open new galleries and cafés, let's scribble a half dozen articles in *The Village Voice,* and then we'll be able to see Rolls-Royces swaying in the potholes and limos with telephones and pale pre-Raphaelite girls with bright lips and tiny curls, and everybody who's somebody.

While they looked for the right place, they asked directions from passersby several times and each time got an answer in a thick Russian accent. Ogo had the impression once that a Leningrader he knew was giving them directions. He looked out of the back seat of the limousine where he was chatting in cold dignity with Miss Young—and there he was: Sasha Pankov with his big dumb dog, which it seemed it was only yesterday he was walking along Liteiny Boulevard.

At last they saw the electric sign of light bulbs in the old-fashioned manner: BRUCE POLLACK ART GALLERY NEW YORK–PARIS–SANKT PETERS-BURG. The broken glass in the front door was covered with a piece of plywood that had "Welcome" in three languages. Gooey glop fell from the end of a sewer pipe onto the so-called sidewalk, which lacked only a pair of Gogol's Mirgorod-shtetl pigs.

Inside, guests were greeted by a Puerto Rican monster in white wig, stocking, and gloves. It rasped, "Watch your step."

The house, recently purchased by Pollack's office for the realization of some Napoleonic artistic ideas and, in particular, for the monopolization of Russian art, was enormous and ugly. Not all the lofts were in use yet, but from the jangling elevator one could see at least three floors of totally uninhibited artistic life: pale faces with those bright lips and those curls, multicolored and multicalibered beards, illuminated paintings and sculptures, a gypsy woman with a guitar, a circle of dandies in white tie, and a passing naked man carrying a half gallon of cheap vodka: his weenie stuck out below his fat belly.

Meanwhile, Pollack's office was a completed masterpiece of the business style, cozy, filled with the good aromas of coffee and cigars, and decorated with an enormous pre-Columbian antique globe on which there was no America.

"Well, here's the good news." Young international Philip was waiting in Pollack's office.

"Have a successful trip?" Ogo asked.

"Exceptionally successful," Philip replied with a smile.

Something human appeared in the smile, animating the mannequin. Red-haired Bruce Pollack rubbed his hands. "Champagne, gentlemen! To our success!" In the corner round table under a bright clamp-on lamp lay the slab of the album.

"Terrific!" exclaimed Marjorie Young.

"Remarkable, remarkable!" added Douglas Semigorsky.

The three exclamations were like a scale from a jazz trio. Everyone turned to Ogorodnikov—it was time for his solo. He stretched out both hands and did what everyone expected. "Burning with desire to see my baby!" Everyone applauded. He had a sense of humor! Not all Russians did, but Ogo was the happy exception. They may be right about the humor, thought Ogorodnikov, but everything else is on low. *Cheese!* is in New York, safe, on the verge of a luxurious edition—but I'm just taking it in stride. I'm losing my natural spontaneity, I'm doomed to finishing off my days in shitty snobbery. But still we'll publish our album in Moscow, we'll demand that the PhIDs give us back the rights to our souls! We'll show you "the second most important art"! That's what you think! They've spread out the arts like fish at a market in order of importance to them.

"You've done a great thing, Philip. Thank you from all Russian photographers!" exclaimed Ogorodnikov.

"I was glad to be of service to Russian art!" exclaimed Philip. It was demonstrated that neither the West nor the East was unfamiliar with pathos. They stood with their champagne glasses.

"Pharaoh can start an advertising campaign tomorrow," Semigorsky said.

Bruce rubbed his hands again. "Gentlemen, there is no better place to present this unique album to the public than the Gallery New York-Paris-Sankt Peterburg! Let's set a date for the opening."

"I'm afraid that will have to wait," Ogo said. "Gentlemen, you'll have to wait for our signal."

"Your signal?" Pollack asked carefully. "From where?"

"From Moscow, of course. We'll try to tear through Lenin's trousers there first."

Everyone exchanged glances.

"Don't tell me, please, that you're trying to go back to Moscow," Semigorsky said.

"I'm telling you. That's just what I'm planning to do."

There was a pause. Crowd noises came from the gallery: the reception with wine and cheese, that is, on the cheap, was at full speed.

"You see," Philip said sincerely, "according to given information you can expect nothing good in Moscow."

"Where did that information come from?" Ogo wanted to know.

Everyone smiled, and Philip made his bows. With Philip's departure, an awkwardness took over, as if there were nothing further to discuss. Bruce Pollack rubbed his hands again. Ogo twitched. "Couldn't you refrain from those movements? It's beginning to smell of burnt flesh in here."

Pollack lifted his chin with an injured air. "That's tactless, sir. I'm afraid the only smell in here is Russian."

The door opened and a waiter said that reporters were waiting in the next room. All Ogo and company could do was open their hands in discouragement. And go to the reporters with discouraged hands. All right, then, we understand each other, Ogo said, not a word about the album yet.

"Do nothing till you hear from me...." He sang the line from the famous blues song with incongruous playfulness, then asked Pollack to stay a minute. "Tell me, Bruce, what are these games being played around me? I'm asking you as my lawyer now."

The red- and curly-haired man ran across his study, and of course did not refrain from rubbing his hands.

"It's not all clear to me, Max. This Ambroise Zhigalevich, as he calls himself, has nothing to do with *Photo Odyssey,* as you have surmised by now. It's clear that someone is trying to push you into making a decision. I hope you realize it's not me. I'm a professional and the interests of my clients come first. A professional lawyer never makes any decisions for his client. Besides which, in purely human terms I consider that really lousy. Any attempt to change someone else's fate is lousy. Besides, let me add, dear Ogo, that in the years of our work together, I have developed feelings of friendship for you, and that may be the most important thing.

"I realized it was a phony the minute I read the interview. It's not your vocabulary, or that precision which is so unlike you. Who was Zhigalevich working for? In our modern world the only response can be opening the hands. . . ."

Serves me right, Ogo said to himself. Look whom I'm asking. No one knows nothing for sure and can't possibly know. A chilly vacuum went streaming near his lower back again. He took a bottle of cognac from Pollack's bar and poured himself a full glass.

"By the way, Ogo, drinking cognac by the glass is really barbaric."

A wave of booze warmth cascaded down and washed Ogo's nether chakras. "Listen, Bruce. I think we'll have a noisy opening in Moscow, something like a ball for the remaining liberals . . . sounds good, huh? . . . You know, a 'champagne breakfast' or something. . . . That will be the signal for you and Doug, then you can have the opening in this bordello. Okay?"

Pollack thought for a minute, then a smile appeared on his freckled face, the red spirals of hair became electrified, and his palms were rubbing each other even harder. "A beautiful idea! Gorgeous! You sure know how to play! Risky, but beautiful!"

Thank you for that opinion. Ogo bowed and pulled on a broad-brimmed hat. The trenchcoat with upturned collar. The scarf. No one would recognize him. They would think that Dickens had come to New York again! In parting I would like to ask you, Mr. Lawyer: "Why didn't you tell me anything about Konsky's treachery?"

"You want to know why, Max? Imagine, I don't have an answer. It's hard to get involved in the relations between two friends, especially if they're both your clients."

"Thanks. That answer is simple and curious, both from a legal and a moral standpoint. You're not as simple as you are red, my friend, and please don't take that for political tactlessness. . . ."

He embraced his big friend, the big professional, the big louse. Then Mr. Ogo, the disguised maestro and daring player, went into the first room of the exhibition. Just the place! It was Alik Konsky's room. The large and awed crowd contemplated ancient motifs: from behind columns and olive trees peeked the little face of Urania or the little heel of Euterpe; alas, both resembled the features of Marina Grizodubova, a pilot of the Stalin era.

Ogo pulled out his camera and took aim a few times in parting at his beloved New York crowd with its streams of smoke above its bumpy surface. What would happen if smoking were banned completely? The first to die would be the openings, the next, tobacco companies. A drunk and angry Fima came over. "Tell me, Ogo, is it true that Fotik is living in my two-room apartment?"

"It's true, it's true, Fima. Does anything else interest you?"

"No, nothing at all."

In the hallway, moving from Konsky to Rauschenberg, Ogo literally bumped into Kasha, a girl he had slept with ten years ago in an archaeologist's tent in the Crimea. She was French-kissing a middle-aged black man. She turned a wildly dilated eye toward Ogo but did not recognize him. But he was recognized by the great patriarch Alexander Spender, who on this evening was surrounded by his happy pupils. "Come here, come here, talented Russian!" The hell with it, later, later! I'm walking through the steam of the past. Basically, no one recognizes me.

A bitter sadness overwhelmed him. He kept looking through the viewfinder, but never once pushed the shutter.

4

FROM THE WINDOW of the room at the Biltmore, Forty-second Street and Madison Avenue, the sky appeared only in the shape of an elongated geometrical figure resembling the state of Israel. This figure appeared before Ogo's eyes every time he rolled off Miss Margie Young after yet another failed attempt. He was furious: this hadn't happened to him in

a long time! At his "marvelous forty-two" he performed on demand in
any regimen, and some ladies even complained of exhaustion in his
company. Of course, he had always assumed that the complaints were
feigned. "I don't understand what's the matter with me today," he mumbled, covered with sweat, gritting his teeth in despair. He translated his
bewilderment into English, the language of his partner, and thought,
What's the matter with me?

"Oh, poor thing," whispered Margie, caressing his damp nape.
"Come on, hold on and try again. . . ."

The dark angles of skyscrapers. The figure of Israel with Sinai torn
off in an astonishing deep blue. You couldn't blame Margie. The girl
had tried every aid known to intellectual circles. Now she lay quietly,
her hands under her head, stretching out her long and smooth body,
frustrated by all the fumbling. So much for the Russians, she thought,
how strangely unexpected, so much for communism, so much for
medium-range missiles. . . .*

However, thought Miss Margie Young, I can't just leave in the middle of the night. I can't fall asleep, he keeps trying. Maybe I should ask
him to use his hand or some other part that's in working order?

Just then the telephone warbled gently near her ear. "Those bastards,
they don't leave you alone even at night," grumbled Ogo, and suddenly
found a way out. I'll blame my failure on nighttime phone calls! Just
when I get in the mood, the bastards call! They don't let me spend time
with the girl, they have nothing but politics on their minds! Bastards,
what bastards! He rolled over and reached across Margie. His chest and
belly felt the warmth of his bedmate again. He even imagined he felt
his little fool stir. He turned on the light and picked up the phone.

"Mister Ogorodnikov?"

From the way his name was pronounced, he knew it was a Russian.
"Who's calling at this hour?" Ogo roared. Something miraculous was

---

*It must be said that in our times the extremely rare occasions of sexual relations
between representatives of the two superpowers do not transpire without semicon-
scious or subconscious military and political comparisons. Ogo was also running
some drivel through the nauseous drowsiness: I'm casting a shadow on a millennium
of history . . . seven decades of slavery. . . . More blame on totally blameless communism. . . .

happening. The sleeping warrior suddenly arose, as it had in his best campaigns. Bells seemed to be swaying in Margie's astonished eyes.

"Max, is that you?" inquired a not-so-young, hoarse voice.

"Yes, it's me!" He kneeled between her raised legs and attacked with his battering ram of love, holding the receiver between cheek and shoulder.

"What are you doing there? You're not fucking, are you?" Someone laughed briefly, woodenly, and seemed to take a sip of something, most likely Scotch on the rocks, the best drink for the middle of the night. Of course, the caller could have been drinking his morning coffee. The distance must have been enormous, for the receiver was filled with the resonance typical of calls bounced off satellites. Suddenly, he figured it out! It was none other than his own half brother, October Ogorodnikov, columnist for the newspaper *Chestnoye slovo (Word of Honor)*, laureate of the Lenin Prize for Journalism, Bolshevik box office boffo of the ideological war.

"October?"

"December!"

This simple joke had been like a password for many years.

"Where are you?"

"At the zoo. Listen, Maxie, I'm calling you now, because just yesterday I was still there."

"Where?" Ogo asked with forgivable stupidity.

"Home!" barked October.

"I see," said Ogo, even though he hadn't seen right away that his brother meant the USSR when he said home. Nor did he see at that moment that October would never have called him abroad if it weren't for some extraordinary occurrence. Most disturbing to Max was the situation in which this telephone conversation was taking place: he was looking down at Margie's wandering smile and her hair spread out over the pillow. Some situation, really. Some situation, that's what this situation is like, a situation. . . . The wild English word "situation" caused an added, and in part unnecessary, movement of the troops. Miss Margie Young bit her lip.

"What are your plans?" October asked.

"Really, dear brother, what an impertinent question. Ah, you must have heard that stuff about my not coming back? Relax, as my beloved Margie would say, we have more important work." At that moment Margie did what he passionately desired—she placed her hands on his hips, on his protruding buttocks, and squeezed gently. Oh, *gracias, señorita!* "Tomorrow," he said, "I'm flying," he said, "home," he said.

"What for?" His half brother's voice sounded strange.

"What do you mean, what for? I have a lot of things to do." He gently stroked her breasts. "My exhibition is coming up...."

"You won't have anything *there* anymore," October Petrovich said. "Do you understand me? Nothing!"

"Oh, gracias, gracias, gracias, señor," muttered the golden Miss Young, who did not resemble a Spaniard in any way.

Wait a minute, where did this Spanish motif come from? After all, I had thanked her mentally, not out loud....

"Why are you silent?" October demanded.

"I'm listening to you," Ogo rasped, almost at the edge.

"I've said everything I have to say!" October barked. "Now I'm listening to you!"

"I don't know what to say." Ogo leaned away from the phone and began touching her lips with his.

"I see you are screwing after all," roared October. "Should I call you tomorrow?"

"Tomorrow's ... too late ... to Moscow ... Moscow...." Ogo dropped the receiver on the floor, put both arms around Margie's shoulders, and began rubbing himself into her. From the floor came the distant cry of his half brother:

"You can't go back to Moscow!"

5

IT TOOK AT least a half hour before Margie Young managed to free herself. She had never even dreamt of anything like this. He climaxed over and over, at least seven times, and each time the quantity, which amazed her, turned into quality. So this is Russia, she mused, so this is dialectics. She shuddered. Oh, why don't I have my camera with me to capture this? Even after releasing her Ogo, or rather his body, continued functioning; every four or five minutes he rose up and expelled what he apparently could not contain. The owner of the body, no longer trying to resist, lay on his back, hands over his eyes, so as not to see the shame around him—the drenched and drying sheets, the rug, the girl astonished and dragging away her clothes and shoes in an effort to protect them from all the trajectories. The shame of this unthinkable emptying grew until it burst, leaving room for a silly but perhaps saving irony.

"Try to call an ambulance, darling!"

"What should I tell them?"

"Well, just say that the man's cream apparatus is rebelling, or even more simply, that it's a crisis of dialectics. . . ."

THE ATLANTIC

T HE ATLANTIC OCEAN is sometimes called the Big Drink, and that might be a good excuse for us to pause in the narrative. We'll suspend one of our heroes* in his seat on a four-hundred-passenger jet. And we will place earphones on his head so that he can listen to the soundtrack of the movie *Enigma* or to one of six other channels coming from the armrest, and we will leave him microscopically creeping against the earth's rotation, that is, toward the east, while we do some thinking.

M. Daguerre, in inventing his plate, and Fox Talbot, mixing iodine and gelatin to fix the images, could hardly have suspected that some one hundred and fifty years later those strange images of life, pulled from the flow of time and which probably seemed as beautiful as they

---

*At first, according to plan, he wasn't supposed to be the main hero, for that hero was intended to be the noble and unrecognized muse of Photography itself, but he gradually pushed his way into the part by virtue of his height, or his brazenness, or perhaps his noble Bolshevist background, or perhaps simply because it was his lot.

did incomprehensible, would be so widespread that they would make civilization itself, the enlightened nineteenth century, unthinkable without their presence.

The tsar, His Imperial Majesty Alexander III, posing at the head of his own convoy, personifying the unshakability of the Russian Empire, could hardly have thought that the plate removed from the wooden box on a tripod and the image printed on that plate would be more lasting than the Empire, and more dependable than the officers of his convoy, in protecting for his descendants the image of the mighty father at the head of his loyal company.

Peter Maximilianovich Ogorodnikov, deviating from reactionism and joining, as usual, the majority, could hardly have thought, as he adjusted between his knees the saber given to him by the Eighth Party Conference in Czechoslovakia and stared at the lens of the machine that had been expropriated from the petty bourgeois of the just-won city of Rostov—he could hardly have thought that dialectical materialism was threatened and that his own, as-yet-unconceived children would reject what was being captured at that moment: the bulging eyes, the implacable curve of the mouth, the historical determinism.

The great avant-gardists of the twenties, Alexander Rodchenko, Tatlin, and El Lissitzky, rejecting "old photography" with its pictures taken at belly level, scrambling up and down, shooting from below and from above, introducing double exposures and collages for "new photography"—could they have thought that they were moving closer not to the aluminum expanses of futurism but to the mystical past in the *crème brûlée* parochialism of the Stalinist Style?

The marshals of the RKKA (Workers and Peasants' Red Army)—did they imagine that their courageous faces, some with twirled moustaches, would be washed out of the negatives by the censors of the photography section of the OGPU (KGB) to give historically valuable photographs real *authenticity*?

Honorable Dr. Kristof Adolf Baldwin, the sorcerer and alchemist, trying to capture in his crucibles the tail of the Universal Spirit and finding a glowing residue in his retorts—did he think that this might be what he had been passionately seeking, sent to him for his hard labors and sleepless nights, this man who had been called to the enor-

mous reflecting surface of humanity so that they would not lose their
memory and turn beastly but grow in nobility and reason?

Cosmonauts of the USSR linked with Nikita Khrushchev, taking off
from secret bases and giving secret speeches, reflected in a multitude of
copies on immortal emulsion—did they consider those reflections more
serious than the glory of their own beloved Communist Party?

The five-year-old kid in the orphanage jacket, who would not say
Raisin! or Cheese! but was hypnotized by the promised birdie—did he
think that many years later, on the way back from the fair he never
found, he would begin a novel about eccentrics obsessed with but one
goal—the preservation and support of the dignity of photography?

. . . Tired of rhetoric and question marks, let us now recall one of our
heroes and be surprised not to find him where we left him, that is, over
the Atlantic in a seat of a TWA jumbo jet. What did he do, step out?

Actually he did step away, but not outside, of course. Maxim Petrovich Ogorodnikov simply stepped out of our book to the place where
kings walk, if that expression is suitable for a modern airline.

O grief, O shame, thought Ogo, sitting on the can in the snug little
room and looking at his face, lengthening in surprise with every profuse
defecation. The bowl beneath him had been filled several times. Would
the plane have enough of that elegant blue rinse? Would the steward-
esses smell him out? He had another crazy thought—will I pollute the
Atlantic? No, we have no idea of the scale of the elements. The ocean
manages to take the excrement of whales and walruses, it can dissolve
the spills of huge tankers.

My excrement, no matter how monstrous and Rabelaisian (there's a
good word!), is no more significant, in terms of the ocean's size, than
the droppings of—what? who?—a stormy petrel, folks!

And once again and again his lower intestine sent signals into the
burbling labyrinths and once again and again cascades of feces and
slime landed in the bowl, filling it quickly and threatening his bent
thighs. If only the plane doesn't run out of the elegant blue rinse! This
vile, undeserved stuff has locked me into this closet, and yet I always
had a rather romantic view of these places, imagining myself locked in
one with Emmanuelle. And once again and again the silly lengthening

of the face, the grim roar below, the acrid odors of human underground, then a knock at the door. I'll probably be led through all the cabins and turned over to the sanitation authorities in Copenhagen, that is, of course, only if it ever stops coming out of me, if it doesn't . . .

It stopped, and everything calmed down in a minute's time. Hm, thought Ogo, and rose, as if nothing had happened. He combed his hair and wiped his neck and ears with Polo cologne. Have to wait a bit for the smell to go off into the dark blue expanses.

In front of him, in three-quarter height, stood his reflection. The experience had added something Gothic to his face. What's happening to me? What do all these Rabelaisian (exactly) effusions and profusions mean? Berlin, Paris, New York, the Atlantic . . . what else could come out and from where? In Moscow I'll break into a sweat, no doubt about it. Streams, rivers will pour from me as I get closer to the Kremlin. They, of course, will freeze on the spot and I will turn into an ice statue like General Karbyshev. I can imagine the exultation of the people and the PhIDs! What is the meaning of it all? Maybe the sinews connecting my body to my soul are getting weak?

He opened the door of the toilet. A small line of cosmopolites recoiled in panic. Too bad, folks, it's your own fault.

2

ALL THE CABINS of the flying movie house were plunged in darkness. On four screens KGB Major Vasilkov, pretending to do dirty Soviet deals, was actually doing noble anti-Soviet ones. The passengers of the Third World were displaying shameful indifference to the plot; that is, they were sleeping. In front of Ogo's seat snored an enormous Mexican mama in a polka-dotted dress. She overlapped her paid space quite a bit, and Ogo couldn't get his long, dried-out legs under her seat. He was about to fling them over the two empty seats next to him when he saw an unfamiliar person of youthful years in the aisle seat.

An extremely pleasant black man, whose overhead light source (sorry for the technical language) was on, sat reading a magazine, or rather a pack of solid brown paper. Shades of brown played harmonically: skin the color of good prerevolutionary chocolate, auburn suit, sienna tie . . . it was silly calling a man like that black, when there was nothing black about him. Let's call things by their right name, gentlemen, black is black and brown is brown.

"Good evening or morning, or I don't know which," the neighbor said.

What a pleasant human smile—zero bullshit!

"How do you do?" Ogo said and introduced himself for some reason. "Maxim Ogorodnikov, Russian photographer."

The shake of the long and cool brown hand excited the Russian photographer, and he was taken aback—is this a homosexual feeling?

"Chokomen," said his neighbor, and burst into a marvelous smile. "It comes from chocolate, of course, Maxim!"

"A fine name!" said Ogo with a growing sense of well being and warmth. "And you? . . . Are you also a photographer?"

"A beginner," Chokomen said. "But your name is well known to me from international sources."

"Really!"

"It's not surprising. You are a great master. I never thought I'd be talking with you like this. . . ."

"Don't be silly!" Ogo's hands flew up. "It's a great pleasure for me! . . . What are you reading, Choko?"

"Something out of the history of photography," the young artist said. "Some of it is interesting—would you like to see?" He offered Ogo one of his pages, thick and soft with ragged edges.

The contents captured our hero, and to tell the truth, he forgot all his problems and aches and never once looked out his window to see Eos' rosy fingers playing over the Atlantic, or Apollo's fiery chariot falling.

. . . At the time of the Savior's sermon, Avgar was the ruler of the Syrian city of Edessa. His body was covered with leprosy. The rumor of great miracles performed by the Lord reached Syria and Avgar. Without seeing the Savior he believed in him as the Son of God, and wrote a letter requesting that the Savior come and heal him. With this letter

Avgar sent his royal painter, Anania, asking him to paint a picture of the Heavenly Teacher.

Anania came to Jerusalem and saw the Lord surrounded by people. Because of the many people listening to the Savior, he could not get close enough for a good portrait, so he stood on a tall rock and tried to paint the image of the Lord Jesus Christ from afar. But he failed.

The Savior Himself called Anania over, called him by name, and gave him a short letter to Avgar, in which, pleasing the faith of the ruler, He promised to send His pupil to heal him from leprosy and to set him on the path to salvation. Then the Lord asked for water and a towel. He washed His face and pressed the towel against it, and the impression of His Heavenly Face was left upon it.

Anania brought the towel and the letter to Edessa. With awe, Avgar accepted the holy towel, and was healed; only a trace of the horrible ailment remained on his face when the promised pupil came.

The pupil was Holy Thaddeus, of the Seventy Apostles, who preached the Gospels and baptized the believing Avgar and all the inhabitants of Edessa. On the Image Avgar wrote: "Christ God, whosoever counts on you will not be shamed," and then he placed it in a niche above the city gate.

For many years the inhabitants kept the respectful habit of revering the Image when they passed through the gates. But one of Avgar's great-grandsons, who ruled Edessa, fell into idolatry and decided to have the Image removed from the gates. The Lord came in a vision to the Bishop of Edessa and ordered him to hide His Image. The bishop came at night with his assistant, lit a votive light, and plastered and bricked up the Image in its niche above the city gate.

Many years passed and the inhabitants forgot about the holy relic. But in the year 545, when the Persian King Khozrei I besieged Edessa and the city's position seemed hopeless, Bishop Eulalia was visited by the Virgin Mary, who told him to get the immured Image which would save the city. Taking the niche apart, the bishop found the Image: a votive light burned before it, and a similar impression was on the clay board that covered the niche. . . .

After citizens crusaded on the walls of Edessa with the Image, the Persian army retreated. The city fell into the hands of the Arabs in 630, but they did not hinder devotion to the Image, whose fame had spread throughout the East. In 944 Emperor Konstantin wished to bring the Image to the then-capital of Eastern Orthodoxy and bought it from the emir, the ruler of the city. With great honors the Image of the Savior and the letter He had written to Avgar were brought by the clergy to Konstantinople. On August 16 the Image was placed in the Church of the Holy Virgin.

There are several legends about the subsequent fate of the Image. According to one, it was stolen by the Crusaders, but the ship on which they were sailing sank in the Marble Sea. In another, the Image was passed to Genoa around 1362 and it is still in the monastery of Apostle Bartholomew.

It is known that the Image has self-replicated several times. One, the so-called ceramic image, occurred when Anania hid the image by a wall on his way to Edessa. Another, imprinted on a cloak, ended up in Georgia. Perhaps the many variations in the tradition of the first Image are based on the existence of several exact replicas. . . .

Ogorodnikov looked up—the plane was taxiing on the runway in Copenhagen. He was changing flights here to Moscow. Mr. Chokomen! His pleasant chocolate traveling companion was nowhere to be seen. Mama Mexico and the other Third World passengers were standing in the aisles with their packages and duty-free shopping bags. Ogo pushed through the crowd, sweating. It turned out there was still enough moisture in his body to soak himself and wet the people around him to general outrage and disgust. At least it happened in Denmark and not behind the Iron Curtain, where it was thirty below. He cried "Mr. Chokomen!" a few times, but the man had completely disappeared. Had he gotten out earlier? The joke wasn't funny. Dragging himself in his heavy wet clothing to the counter to check in for Moscow, Ogo looked sadly at the ephemera of the West floating past the glass wall. Will we see each other again?

He remembered that he was still carrying the brownish papyrus that had taken at least three hours to read. He wiggled his fingers and found nothing. It had been washed away.

SAMBA

I

N THE YEARS of transition from immature to overmature socialism, an addition was built onto the massive and rather ugly merchant castle on Miussy Square: a modern wing with a hint at a flight of imagination, a glass surface and a concrete visor. The result was completely vile.

Here, in the headquarters of Soviet photography, the board of the Photographers' Union of the USSR was having one of its plenary sessions. The agenda held "new tasks before Soviet photographers in light of the historic decisions of the Thirtieth Congress of the CPSU." The whole first half of the plenum was taken up with the report of the Secretary General of the PhU USSR, Hero of Socialist Labor, laureate of the Lenin Prize, four-time laureate of the State (that is, Stalin) Prize, deputy of the Supreme Soviet, member of the CC CPSU, ninety-year-old comrade Bluzhzhaezhzhin.

"Our old guard is still strong and good!" The SecGen stood on the tribune with a certain grace and read his report well, allowing himself to deviate from the text, to drop something simple and artistic, well, like, "we can, we can, friends, be proud of our young people, of our ..."

It was here, actually, that Bluzhzhaezhzhin had a small problem—he lost the end of the sentence, he simply forgot the proud word "Komsomols." The sense and the ideological content of the word, of course, were present in the old head, but the form had gotten vague, and so Bluzhzhaezhzhin, greedily desiring to get out of the prolonged pause, gummed something like "our red internationalists ..." and got deeper in the muck, the mash of incomprehensibility ... "our members of the League of Young October" ... "our Junsturmovites"—without ever losing the right declension, mind you!!—"our participants in the march of young Marxists" ... and even "our fearsome Stalinist falcons." ... Ordinarily someone would have started laughing, but this was a period when there was a very strong renaissance of "Leninist norms," so no one made a peep.

One of the members of the board was an expert on the Party's will in art—a certain Saury, a rigid fellow with the face of a village musician—and next to him was his deputy on photography, a certain Phelyaev, known in Moscow as Cobblestone, Arm of the Proletariat, or CAP, who knew all about pictures straight on and in profile. Saury and CAP did not stir while Bluzhzhaezhzhin stepped in his own shit, but merely squinted at the neighbor on the presidium, Fotii Feklovich Klezmetsov: How's the snake in the grass reacting? The comrades had an idea of the careerist's long-range plans.

Fotii Feklovich did not give himself away. He sat with a stony expression, in today's style, occasionally patting his treasure, his beard, the legacy of the revolutionary democrats. He was thinking bad things, of course: alas, there's stagnation even in the Party staff. Time to replace Comrade Saury, he's theoretically weak. And that former pickpocket Phelyaev has no place in our capital. Well, we'll see how it goes in the near future. Today's a fateful day, oh, mother of mine, the Third Dream of Vera Pavlovna!*

---

*As an intellectual descendant of Russia's nineteenth-century "revolutionary democrats" Fotii swears with the name of a character from their bible, Chernyshevsky's novel *What Should Be Done*, in which three consecutive "dreams of Vera Pavlovna" depict the future utopian society.

In the second half of the plenum the directors of the photo unions of all the fraternal republics would have to chew their cud, "Inspired by the wise ideas of the Thirtieth Congress of our own Communist Party, the photographers of Soviet Kirghizia (Yakutia, Lithuania, etc.), continuing to expand their ties with the masses, digging deeper into the heart of our people's lives, depicting more vividly the image of our heroic contemporary, the man of labor, in his creativity. . . ."

After the Estonian and before the Armenian, the proud grandson of Slavs, Fotii Feklovich, would have the floor. He would begin his speech with the regular incantations addressed to the Party and with statistical baloney—which broad masses were part of his sponsorship, how many albums were published, how many exhibits were presented at factories, how many conferences and seminars were held, how many creative discussions with colleagues from the coal basin . . . and more bullshit like that.

Then he would switch to a more serious topic, the struggle in the international arena. On the whole, he would say, the photographers of Moscow and the Moscow Region are honorably resisting the world of reaction, violence, and lawlessness . . . then, after a portentous pause and a sip from the official glass of whatever they put in it, Fotii Feklovich would pronounce a weighty "however." Another pause would follow, so that the oafs in the audience would understand that this wasn't the ordinary "however" from the editorials in .Word of Honor of the "thaw" period, that this was a different, stern, intransigent "however," related to the entire present Soviet state, led by its grim elders into a new campaign. Where to, to which beyond-Afghanistan lands?—it did not matter! We do not need a goal now, we need a tightening of the ranks!

What would follow the weighty "however"? Here's what: however, not all members of our organization clearly see their goals in the conditions of the increasing and irreconcilable struggle of two worlds. Moreover, comrades, there are among us fine-spirited, ideologically immature people who are trying to build a tower of nonexistent (sarcastic stress here) ivory, there are people victimized by their own lack of ideological discrimination, which is actively exploited by Western intelligence services. I would like to draw your attention, comrades, to the fact that a real enemy has appeared in the Moscow photographic organization!

Another pause, another sip of what served as drinking water, and then—the revelation of the enemy's name who at last had become a real agent of the CIA, burrowing into the administrative organs of the union. I mean Ogorodnikov, comrades, now a nonreturnee and traitor to the homeland.

This assertion would lead to an explosion, Fotii imagined, a huge and general gasp and then a zone of stunned silence. In that zone his voice, the confident and slightly ironic voice of a man who knows more than he says, would inform the gathering of Ogorodnikov's fall: how in the employ of the CIA he tried to undermine from within the unity of those faithful lenses of the Party, how he attempted under the guise of fighting censorship to found a pretentious album with the foolish title *Say Cheese!* . . . Alas, comrades, there are people in our milieu who nibbled at Ogorodnikov's bait of cheap Western fame and today we must with all seriousness point out to *comrades* (he would stress the dear word) Drevesny, German, Lionel, Chavchavadze, Okhotnikov, Probkin, Marxyatnikov, Fisher, Tsuker, and Shturmin, and also Rosa Alexandrovna Barcelon—we must point out to these comrades the immaturity and irresponsibility that brought them to the brink (stress that!) of a real fall into the swamp of anti-Sovietism!

Then would come the most important moment of First Secretary Fotii's speech, the moment that would determine his future position and get rid of any talk of betrayal. No, comrades, we will not give satisfaction to the ideological provocateurs of the West and to the traitor Ogorodnikov, we will not cut off our errant colleagues, we will fight for them with all the passion that Leninist humanism calls for! And that would bring on real applause.

Fotii Feklovich knew that General Planshchin was rather sour on his report: putting the question that way substantially reduced the scope of the operation planned by the Glands. No problem, let them know in the PhID that I don't work for them, they work for me, a major politician. He knew that CAP and even Comrade Saury had vacillated a long time before approving his speech. They knew what it would happen when he was done.

The break was announced. Fotii did not go to lunch right away, but allowed himself to be surrounded by the secretaries of the Union republics, on paper his equals, but in practice, as he told himself, "unsuspecting idiots." He stood in the lobby, looking at the photographers passing by, who was with them, who said hello now, and he joked with them and was looking forward to the second part of the meeting, when suddenly . . .

The "best and the most talented" (Lenin) once wrote that "the ceiling came down on us like a raven," which was approximately what happened to Fotii Feklovich, and the floor didn't behave any better—it came up at him like a gray bear. Over the heads of resting participants, through the tobacco smoke, First Secretary Fotii Feklovich saw none other than M. P. Ogorodnikov coming through the glass door.

The hardened spy came in from the cold, took off his wolf-fur hat, smacked it against his knee, opened his sheepskin jacket; the snow fell from him as he looked around cheerfully, with a brazen, clear eye. He waved to someone in the crowd and was immediately surrounded by the unvigilant and the ideologically immature, as if people didn't listen to the Voice of America, as if they didn't know what anti-Soviet stuff had been broadcast in his name!

Just at that moment Fotii was passed by a pair of *kurators,* captains Skanshchin and Slyazgin. Naturally, most of the people present recognized them, but the working assumption was that no one knew them, and therefore the captains walked by with extreme modesty, loaded with piles of books they had just purchased at the presidium kiosk, that is, short-supply books, under their arms. Of the two *kurators,* only one was actually a true bibliophile and photophile; we are speaking of Captain Skanshchin, of course. During the course of his ideological-creative work and naturally under the influence of his darling Viktoria, he had risen capitally above himself. Captain Skanshchin's "job-related" or "business-purpose" access to *special* books and albums explained his rather critical attitude toward even the best examples of domestic print. The books are marvelous, he thought, but they still lack something. Audacity, I guess. . . .

So, the officers were modestly walking along the corridors of the plenum, but without loss of dignity. As the Party favorite Zinoviev once said, "Every Soviet person is a Chekist at heart!" And suddenly right in the middle of the crowd a voluminous administrative comrade agitatedly addressed the *kurators*, a man who according to instructions was inaccessible, allegedly completely above their dirty work, allegedly on the theoretical level, allegedly not their agent Poker at all. In a burst of exceptional excitement, tugging at his beard with his left hand, making a non-Poker signal with his right: Skanshchin! A minute!

We're asked, we comply. A minute, please!

"Well, Skanshchin, take a look over there!" Fotii hissed.

Some minute, thanks a lot! A minute like that can make you shit in your pants if the commensurate musculature is not in good shape. There before Skanshchin stood the long-lost object in all his glory—Maxim Petrovich Ogorodnikov! Was it an optical illusion? He had been picturing his former client in a white blazer on board an oceangoing yacht, surrounded by a brilliant crowd of CIA agents and Hollywood stars.

"Did you know?" Fotii hissed in his ear. "Why didn't you warn me?"

Captain Skanshchin almost said, "We didn't know a thing!" but bit his tongue in time. The biggest state secret could escape like that.

"If you weren't warned, Comrade Fotii, that means you didn't need to know," he replied quite believably.

"You've ruined my speech!"

"You'll manage, Fotii Feklovich."

How unpleasant the face of the respected agent Poker could be! He began to resemble a hyena. "Yes, he was just like a hyena, Comrade General," Skanshchin would later tell his boss.

How the bell rang and how Fotii Feklovich made his way to the meeting hall, Captain Skanshchin did not notice. He was watching sweet Ogo. So he heard the call of the homeland, he's a Russian after all, he's our talent! You should watch yourself, model agent Slyazgin, that wolfish look is unbecoming when you gaze on a photographer returned from his business trip abroad. You were a jerk from a DOSAAF* shooting gallery, Slyazgin, and you still are, while Ogorod may be removed from the enemies list, moved back up to "ideologically immature". . . .

---

*DOSAAF: Volunteer Society to Support Army, Navy, Air Force.

No longer able to resist, Captain Skanshchin hurried over with out-stretched hand. Welcome back, Maxim Petrovich!

The returnee smiled broadly. "Sponsoring the plenum today?"

Skanshchin laughed. "What can you do? You see for yourself, Maxim Petrovich, all the rubes have come in for it. . . ."

2

THERE WAS A week left before New Year's, that is, it was the day after European Christmas, when a noisy party gathered at the dacha of Fritz Marxyatnikov in the Soviet Lens cooperative, thirty-eight kilometers from Moscow in the village of Developkino on the frozen river Drizina, for the occasion of the birthday of his beloved wife, Elena. It was a mixed crowd: on the one hand relatives of Fritz and members of the "technological intelligentsia," on the other hand the crooks from the Soyuzreklama advertising group, the main source of Fritz's income, and on the third hand and in overwhelming number, Cheesers and their wives, girlfriends, and foreign friends.

They had come primarily in Zhigulis, the rich giving rides to the poor. The poorest of all, Probkin, drove up in his infamous Mercedes 300 turbodiesel, which the owner, now in straitened circumstances, did not wish to discuss, simply waving his hand as if at a huge, guzzling dog.

The air was soft; it was an extraordinary evening, with the scent of the sea creeping through the pines. The men spent a lot of time outside, gabbing among their cars, discussing the problem of getting spare parts, the further decline of national morality, the vicious hemorrhoid of the head of state. Ogo showed off the air gun he had bought in an all-night Le Drugstore on the Champs-Élysées. "It fits in the palm of your hand, but shoots a mighty bullet with nerve gas. For instance, you're walking along, and the PhIDs jump you from around a corner . . ."

"*Who* jumps you?" one of the relatives asked.

"Oh, that's what we call the Glands from the state photo inspection, gentlemen. That was just an extreme example, gentlemen." The gentle-men squirmed, being true comrades. The photographers laughed. "Well, let's say, a bandit jumps you, you're not going to meekly await your fate as people did in the damned year of my birth, 1937, are you? And this little alarm gun is for situations like that."

"Do you have the bullets?" Shuz asked.

"Two hundred!" Ogo replied readily. Knee-deep in the snow, they enacted a scene from a gangster movie.

Elena, the birthday girl, tired of her kitchen work, stopped for a minute by the glass wall of the veranda and looked at the tall man in jeans and orange down parka, fooling around. Elena, old before her time, sighed deeply: just recently, ten years ago, in Koktebel . . . and then there was the time at the Riga seashore. . . .

"Look, Vera," she said to her younger sister. "Ogo doesn't age, neither does Slava German or Andrei Drevesny, what a strange generation. . . ."

"You think so?" the younger sister said haughtily. "From my point of view he's old . . . everyone around here is old . . . not a single young face in the place . . . you're all ready for the dustheap, but you keep hanging on."

But Ogo had no plans for the dustheap that evening. It was as if he had never had those scary leaks and eruptions, he was glad to be back in Moscow with his friends and the atmosphere of a brewing scandal; really, the atmosphere itself, the chemical composition of the air over the village of Developkino, warmed his blood. The chemistry of home.

"How's your ball and chain?" Shuz suddenly asked.

"Who? Anastasia? Oh, I am a bastard. She's right, I'm morally deficient. Just imagine, Shuz, I didn't give her a single thought on the whole trip. Sorry, I did have a flash in Paris, vaguely, when I was drunk. Yet I consider her the only woman I have. . . ."

"Cocksucker," Shuz gently chided.

They got out of the snow and went to the porch, where a group of Cheesers were having a bottle of vodka, with a three-liter jar of pickles in the center of the group, from which they pulled out pickles with their fingers. On the heated terrace and in the rooms, tables were set with mounds of *zakuski*, pies, and drinks, all a tremendous mix; every guest had brought whatever he could get, and so the grim drink of mature socialism called Solntsedar sat cheek to cheek with Bristol Cream. There were no chairs, first of all because you couldn't seat a huge crowd like that anyway, and secondly because cocktail parties in the American style had grown popular, though with the inevitable Russian refinements: broken dishes and noses, heated discussions, burping.

Everything was going beautifully, and there was still time for the culminating refinements. First they made a "collective," that is, a huge photo of everyone present, set up in four rows, including the ones lying on the floor. This was entrusted to Vasya Shturmin, who was working on group and wide-angle shots these days. Wearing a top hat, Shturmin raced around his camera, setting up reflecting umbrellas and screens, turning the session into a happening or a performance, and took a "kish-mish" version, a "cheese" version, and a "birdie."

After the shoot, the crowd surrounded Ogo. It's so great you came back! When the 'unimpeachable' rumor had gone around Moscow that Maxim Ogorodnikov went over the hill, the idea of an independent photo society dried up. Nothing seemed to have changed, none of the Cheesers believed it, they went on meeting at Alexei Okhotnikov's, they ate Alexei's burned blinis and flew up into the censorship-fighting and metaphysical heights, but somehow it still didn't feel right. Then a few unhelpful souls had suggested that Ogo had left just so that he could publish the album abroad in safety and grab up all the glory and millions. . . .

Another rumor had quickly joined that one—that the New Focusers were fighting among each other, and that one of the biggies, either Drevesny or German, said that he wasn't surprised at Ogo pulling a stunt like that, because he knew him well, and allegedly someone hit Drevesny or German over the head with a chair, which led to a brawl in which many valuable objects were destroyed. Then, allegedly, the geniuses met once more to disprove the filthy lie and clear up their relations and there was another fight, and Shuz—rip the scar!—was arrested in a den of drug addicts and black marketeers. Now that Ogo was back and was standing in a crowd of friends with a meat pie in one hand and vodka in the other, telling them about Paris and New York, all that nonsense began evaporating backward and the original situation was reconstructed—a merry and daring brotherhood of unofficial artists.

Ogo talked loudly, so that all could hear, about the mysterious appearance in New York of a copy of *Say Cheese!* "More miracles—I heard secondhand that the two leviathans of photography publishing, Pharaoh and Fountain, are already battling over publishing the book. I go to Fountain and they meet me with open arms! At the board of directors table, the size of a submarine, there's our modest collection, open to Shturmin's toilet series. 'Excuse me, gentlemen,' I say, 'where did you get it, I mean, how?' 'Mr. Ogorodnikov,' the capitalists reply, 'do you really think that in this day and age it's possible to contain an outstanding work of art within national borders?' And so mighty Fountain makes us an offer: a mass-market edition in ten languages, including Portuguese. Do you realize what that means, gentlemen? Brazil, gentlemen, the country of the twenty-first century!"

"Brazil!" exclaimed the Cheesers with astonishing excitement. Spontaneously and semiautomatically their extremities began twitching in samba rhythm. From the veranda it spread throughout the dacha; guests stamped their heels and wiggled their rears, and even though some dancers seemed to be doing "Hava Nagilah," in general it was arousing. Even Shuz, who was smiling condescendingly, tapped his patent-leather toe, and then, lifting his immobile face, roared with all his legendary strength: "AH, BRAZIL!"

Ogo shouted in the whirl of the samba, "Well, we'll do our first Russian edition at Belokamennaya,* right, gentlemen?"

"How? How?" the sambaists pounded.

"Easy! Any stoolies here?"

"Scar me!" spat Shuz. "How could there be any stoolies here?! You got weird in the West, Ogo!" Actually, Shuz knew that this whole samba scene was put on for the benefit of the stoolies.

"Now you, sir, aren't a stoolie, of course?" Ogorodnikov asked of a young man in a Norwegian dancing-reindeer sweater next to him.

"Why that's Vadim, our new friend, a young photographer!" cried Alexei Okhotnikov, dancing closer. He was moving his red beard, oohing, and kicking his cute knees with some embarrassment.

---

*Belokamennaya, "White Stone," is the historical nickname of a Moscow township originally built with, well, some white stones. Later on, of course, more democratic materials began to prevail—cheap concrete and red cast-iron grilles—but if you are fond of the place you use the maiden name.

The mixed group was taking on a unified inner rhythm. The mass moved rhythmically from wall to wall and back again in movements that resembled both a Greek *sirtaki* dance and Russian *cossachok*, but still retained a clear reference to the huge Portuguese-speaking tropical state.

"I'm very sorry that we haven't had a chance to meet before," Ogo said for some reason to Vadim.

"I'm very happy that it's happened at last!" the beginning photographer said with a marvelous smile.

As they danced, several people grabbed champagne from the tables and held the bottles over their heads.

"Gentlemen Cheesers, let's have a champagne breakfast for the press and announce the first homemade Russian edition! Breakfast with champagne and bagels!" Probkin was working on the hostess's sister, he already had his arm around her waist. A haughty look on her face; she wanted him. "Then we'll offer it to Sovfoto—publish it, please! Please, publish it, everything's aboveboard, no drunks here!"

"Ogo, Ogo! Bravo, bravo!"

"And a shameful end to the censors!"

"The end!"

"Shame!"

"They've tortured photographers enough! We're not *writers*!"

Several corks popped.

"Long live our frosty Brazil!"

"Long live champagne!"

"Down with the stoolies!"

"Let's make it plain!"

Suddenly the music stopped. Had there been music? In any case, the door opened. A pause.

On the doorstep, her shoulders bare, against the night sky with pines, a star, and passing plane, stood The Beauty Anastasia.

3

"SO HOW DID you manage to grow so lovely, madame?"

"Ah, I didn't come to see you at all, Ogo-rodnikov. Shuz called and said there was a party at the dacha."

"But I was waiting for you, madame, I didn't tell you I was back because I wanted to surprise you."

"Well, if I had known, I wouldn't have come. I was certain that you were abroad, Ogorodnikov. I came here looking for adventure."

"An adventure, madame?"

"Yes, Ogorodnikov, another one."

"Aren't I an adventure for you, madame?"

"Alas, Ogorodnikov, you are simply my legal husband and certainly no adventure."

"Madame!"

"I have been living in the sphere of world adventure for some time now, Ogorodnikov. A high-altitude Lithuanian is in love with me. I have friends abroad, and I've even got a vacation set up for Bulgaria in July."

"Pardon, madame, but there isn't a whiff of adventure in Bulgaria."

"You're simply not up on the latest adventure situation. After all, Bulgaria is a nonvisa resort area, and representatives of various worlds meet there."

"Does your adventure, madame, deal with the Second or the Third World?"

"The First, poor Ogorodnikov."

"I'll bet, madame, that I know his name."

"Ha, ha, ha, Ogorodnikov, name it and you'll be mistaken."

"Oh, how I've missed you, Nastya," he said, flinging his arms out along the pillows, inviting her to take her favorite position—with her head on his shoulder.

"You're lying, sire," she said, laughing happily, still crawling over him with her fingers and lips. "You probably didn't think of me even once."

"Not once, darling." He sighed.

"And you probably had quite a bit of fun abroad?" she asked hesitantly. If only he would lie!

She got the natural answer. "I have sinned."

"With bad women?"

"You're the only good one," he said.

"Why did you come back if you never thought of me?"

"Why?" He was surprised. "We have to publish the album!" Then, seeing her hurt and instant depression, he added, "Of course, not just for that. You know, I was drawn by my main model—by Russia, excuse me. Assuming that this country doesn't belong only to the PhIDs, LIDs, and other IDs, someone else has to live here, right? Besides, something else was calling me back, something forgotten. In the mornings I felt such a pull here and here ... and here, too. . . ."

"Why there?" she asked.

"I don't know, but it was a hard pull."

She freed herself, rolled to the edge of the broad bed, sat up, right in the light of the streetlamp coming into the studio from Khlebny Alley. Mmm, he thought, suddenly she has the contours of a Negro dancer.

"I think that the PhIDs are much more upset by my solo work. *Splin-ters*, I showed it to you, remember? You see, when I shot the subjects for *Splinters*, a strange thing happened—the features of this Stalinist bastard kept appearing in some of the shots. Some bigshot KGB man with a bad conscience recognized himself through all the surrealism and got pissed off. They warned me against *Splinters* back in May and they're not sparing any efforts now, either ... Maybe they're plan-ning to use our whole collective in order to push me up against the wall. . . ."

The contour of the Negro dancer extended a hand, took a cigarette, and lit a Marlboro Light. Nastya was smoking! She really had embarked on an international adventure.

"I think that you're overestimating yourself and underestimating them," she said.

"You think so? Perhaps. Or maybe vice versa? Well, I don't even want to think about it. Understand? I came back to be a free man in my own country. Understand?"

He got out of bed and went to the kitchen for a bottle of Baikal.* On the way he moved the curtain slightly and looked out on the street,

---

*A bubbling soft drink named after a Siberian lake. In the absence of other bev-erages it is not bad.

at the thaw. The alley was filled with black puddles. On the corner stood a Volga with radio-telephone antennae. Next to the car were two bruisers, smoking, looking up at his window.

4

FIRST SECRETARY FOTII Feklovich Klezmetsov was invited unexpectedly and very insistently to a meeting of General Planshchin's operative group. He kept himself aloof, as if he were an outside expert, underscoring his distance. This pose on the part of Agent Poker did not elicit delight in Captain Skanshchin. What a bastard, ready to bury all his former comrades, and he's sitting around like he's really somebody. I'll break you so hard, Poker, that your Polina won't be able to find all the pieces. I have all your anonymous letters about Comrade Saury in my safe.

In public, naturally, Captain Skanshchin maintained a meaningful silence and sipped coffee with the other comrades. Recently the general had begun serving coffee at the meetings, after the manner of their CIA colleagues. In the last few weeks, since Maxim Ogorodnikov's return, the general seemed younger. His eyes sparkled, his voice thundered, his boots creaked. He liked working Operation Cheese. For the first time in his memory these creative workers, who in general were cowards and shitheads, proved capable of serious work: Just think, they probably thought, a genuine antigovernment conspiracy! At least there was a demand for the general's forty years of experience and his tactical flair.

"Here's more news from our operative reports. Quite interesting. Ogorod is armed."

"Armed and extremely dangerous!" Captain Slyazgin repeated the popular film title and laughed.

"Laughter isn't very appropriate here," the general noted drily.

What nonsense, thought Fotii Feklovich. Ogo armed? That Planshchin is full of nonsense. Of course, theoretician Fotii merely laced his fingers on his belly without pronouncing a word.

Captain Skanshchin was less controlled. "I can't believe it," he said, squirming. "Are the reports trustworthy?"

The general handed Skanshchin a packet of photos in reply. The "intelligent and clever" foe was holding a pistol in his hand and smiling.

"Maybe it's an air pistol?" Skanshchin asked, and thought, What an infectious smile our Ogorod has!

"Combat gun," said Captain Gemberdzhi, a former Blue Beret, and all the other men confirmed it—Lyushaev, Krost, Chirdaev, Plyubyshev, Bushbashin, and Slyazgin.

"I have a question," Fotii spoke up suddenly. "Why is there one comrade, that one, on the extreme left, who has doubts about General Planshchin's information?"

"What do you mean, 'extreme left'?" exploded Skanshchin. "Don't you know my name?"

The general gave a tight smile.

"That's one of our systems, Fotii Feklovich. We play devil's advocate with one another at these meetings. It's a tried-and-true method."

"You should know all of us by name and patronymic!" Skanshchin was still hot. "We all know you as the Poker!"

"Why be so formal?" the general said, gently rebuking his favorite, but thought to himself, Good boy, show him a thing or two. "We have to feel each other's elbows in this struggle with our powerful and clever foe. Right, Fotik?"

Wise ass, thought Fotii Feklovich, he's letting me know he hasn't forgotten a thing. The foe himself used to call me Fotik, after all.... He forced a smile. Yes, yes, of course, we have to feel those elbows.

The general walked to the window. It was necessary to do that from time to time—to pause and go to the window, to take a look at what you devoted your life to defending: the bronze statue, the very existence of which proved that not all Poles were traitors and loafers; and then, to the right, the palace of children's happiness* with a huge fir tree in front. Where else do such firs grow, except in Mother Russia? The general's face cleared. Now back to work!

"Another important bit of news, comrades. Ogorodnikov, Shuz Zher-

---

*The bronze statue our general observes is the monument to Felix Dzerzhinsky (of Polish origin), the first head of the Soviet secret police, about whom it was said, "He loved kids, though he had some grudges against the grownups." And KGB headquarters is, indeed, situated next door to Children's World department store.

ebyatnikov, Slava German, Andrei Drevesny, that swindler Probkin, and Alexei Okhotnikov have decided to make the official announcement of the album's publication at a so-called champagne breakfast. Of course, the bourgeois press will be invited and in a show of mockery so will TASS, Novosti, *Photgaz*, and *Word of Honor.*"

"And where is this information from?" Skanshchin asked grimly. "I listened to the tapes and didn't find anything like that in there."

Several people exchanged glances—*Something's up with Skansh-chin*—but again the general merely gave his favorite a paternal smile. "A good question, Captain. And now, please lower the blinds while Captain Lyushaev takes care of the projector, please."

Rosfoto, the pub known to all, appeared on the screen. The operatives smiled slightly: they'd had quite a few parties there, quite a few Stolichnayas indeed, and look, there was charming Margarita with a tray and sexy Ninetochka with a "final" carafe. Though the Komsomol activists were putting on weight, they still looked good. And there was the enemy camp, meeting in their favorite corner where, since the pre-catastrophe days, as they call them—that is, since the days of capitalist slavery—the majestic Bear had been standing with a ring in his nose. As usual, pale and puffy-eyed Slava German ate little. Next to him the main contra, Ogo, was putting away a *salade provençale.* Now here came the proud and handsome Andrei (is he really not a Jew?) Drevesny, and here came Alexei Okhotnikov and Venka Probkin, one under-fucked, another overfucked, and there was Shuz the Stud, arm around Margarita's plump waist, ordering a liter of vodka. Boy, those people knew how to live.

The audio came on. The gathering, unabashed, was discussing its new project, the "champagne breakfast" at the Kontinent pelmeni house on Sokol Square. What, couldn't they find a shabbier place? They're deliberately provoking us, using the old haunt of *Kontinent* magazine. Well-known bastards from *Kontinent* magazine in Paris, too. "Captain Bushbashin, dear fellow, take on having the Kontinent pelmeni house renamed."

The bastards ate heartily, and sent for a third bottle, naturally. Shuz in the meantime told an anti-Soviet joke. "Brezhnev died, but his body lives."

"What does that mean, Comrade General?" asked Captain Gemberd-zhi. The general shrugged.

"I'll explain later," Captain Skanshchin promised.

Ogo proposed going over the guest list. They began naming people. The officers exchanged looks. The cream of Moscow's artistic and scientific world was expected at the Kontinent. Even laureates, members of our dear CP! See how much potential *revisionism* has accumulated! Suddenly the general slammed his hand on the desk.

"Attention now!"

Andrei Drevesny's lips moved, but his deep voice lagged behind. "What do you need all *this* for, Ogo?"

"We've done a little editing here," the general said. Rewind, freeze frame. Play.

Drevesny's lips, slightly curled under the White Guards moustache. "What do you need all this *for*, Ogo?"

A burst of obscenity followed. Using censorable words, and famous photographers at that. Finally Andrei Drevesny broke through again.

"You misunderstood me, guys! I'm not against the idea. I'm for it as much as the rest. It's just that we'll get our asses kicked for this. We'll wake up the fucking behemoth!" He extended his shot glass across the table toward Ogorod. "Max, you know me. . . ." Again everyone was shouting.

Shuz's words were last. "You're scarring me!"

"What does that mean?" asked the intellectually curious Captain Slyazgin.

"I'll explain that later, too." promised Captain Skanshchin.

"Lights!" ordered the general.

Fotii Feklovich tried to figure out where the camera had been hidden. Maybe in the Party committee room, through that hole in the door. Or maybe the bathroom. There had been an OUT OF ORDER sign on it lately.

"I have a question," Skanshchin said. "Why are these friends hiding nothing?"

General Planshchin squinted through his glasses. "An interesting paradox. Let's discuss it. Please speak up."

Major Krost said that in his opinion the Focusers were hiding something. "After all, it's still unclear how the album reached the West."

Captain Slyazgin harrumphed. "Ogorod brought it out himself, while our comrade Skanshchin was ... hm ... busy with theaters and weekends."

Those present laughed genially, and Captain Lyushaev slapped the theatergoer's broad shoulder. "Cut it out, guys," Skanshchin said. "I personally inquired, and Consul Zafalontsev in Berlin says that Ogorod arrived with only one leather bag, and the album wouldn't fit in there."

"Wouldn't slides fit?" asked Captain Plyubyshev.

"Let me make a correction while the meeting is in order," added Major Krost. "According to the latest information, Comrade Pollack has the original in his safe."

That Skanshchin is clearly charmed by Ogo, thought Fotii Feklovich in the meantime. I have to report it, but of course not to Planshchin. . . .

"Well, friends, we've had a fruitful discussion today," the general said, summing up. "I personally feel that under cover of openness they are planning a complex and clever action against us. Things may become clear in the next few days. Now, as they sing in the opera—'Thus, we begin.' The opening move is yours, dear Fotii Feklovich!"

"Mine?" He shuddered and overreacted. "What for? I mean, why?"

General Planshchin smiled, truly pleased with the meeting. That last slip of Fotik's tongue explained a lot.

"What do you mean, *what for?* It's not a punishment, after all! You are the leader of Moscow's photographers, my friend. It's not for the secret police to begin a campaign for the ideological purity of a creative union. Formally, these brothers haven't broken any laws."

"What do you mean, they haven't? They sent the album abroad!" Fotii Feklovich raised his voice, confused.

"Formally, that's not forbidden, either," the general said with a smile. "Freedom of creativity—remember, dear man?"

Cynical, omnipotent, they all stared at Agent Poker. Well, they had him. Fotii stood, accepting the blow.

"For me, Comrade General, the interests of the revolution are paramount. I have never refused the complex tasks of our ideological struggle." He looked at the general, to let him know that where *they* have cynicism, *we* have our sacred faith. "The Party, as always, directs all our efforts, and therefore your suggestions, Comrade Major General"—with a slight stress on the *Major*—"I consider to be a starting point for a consultation with the Party, don't you think so?"

"It's already been approved, dear man," the general said casually.

"Even at the level of Comrade Phusloff?" Fotii inquired, and knew that he had hit the mark: Planshchin had not expected him to *go over my head*! We'll see yet who's in charge of this operation, you brown-nosing PhID! I'll bet you're trying on your second star already, General? Yeah, we'll see about that!

You lousy squealer, thought the major general in reply. Everything was ruined by the mention of Phusloff, and in that lousy mood he called the meeting ended, asking Volodya to stay behind.

Captain Skanshchin suspected that his boss would want to talk about applications of the most disgusting theorem of this trigonometry. And so he did.

"How is our *Splinters* doing?" he asked. "What's happening on that front?"

"No changes on that front," Skanshchin squeezed out, "that is, in general, everything is fine."

The general peered into the captain's face. "I see that something's bothering you?"

"To tell the truth, there is a small thing," admitted Skanshchin. "After all, *Cheese!* is a collective effort, measures need to be taken against groups of these guys, that's understandable, but *Splinters*, after all, is merely individual expression. . . ."

The general put his right arm around his apprentice and mauled the muscular shoulder with pleasure. "Chase away such thoughts, Captain, be a soldier and chase them away. Freedom of creativity is not the most important thing for humanity. When you cut down trees, splinters do fall."

Young Captain Skanshchin snickered. Clever, of course. Not very witty, but at least on the funny side. . . .

5

MAXIM PETROVICH OGORODNIKOV'S apartment in the coop had been empty for over two months, but the first thing he heard as he stepped inside was water running in the kitchen. Could he have left it on two months ago? For some reason the thought had been haunting him. Two months of water smoothly running from the spout and smoothly flooding into the sewer—what a useless flow! Everything destroyed! His heart flopped. A sharp metallic taste was in his mouth. A huge pump was pumping emptiness inside him. He couldn't move his hands or his feet. I think I'm dying, Ogo thought, and the water won't stop even for a minute, what does it care? My God, am I really dying?

The mirror had a reflection, but he couldn't get a look or evaluate it because he did not recognize himself, even though he knew with his last ounce of strength that he did not recognize himself. God, whispered his poor soul in its last unknown address. God, God . . .

"What's happened?" Anastasia flew out, as if on skis, from the kitchen. "I'm doing the dishes, can't hear a thing, suddenly there's this boom. Ah, it's you, dear sire. Are you drunk?"

He sat on the floor, his back against the mirror, and stared at her. The mighty pump in his gut was now just as efficiently sucking out nothing. His body was returning. The metal was evaporating. The friendly washbasin waterfall splashed merrily.

"I would have died without you, Nastya." It was only then that her eyes widened in fear.

"What are you muttering? I can't hear you! Are you fooling around or are you really sick?"

He tried to get up but managed only a terribly amusing tremble of the muscles. Hello, pal, does your dancing partner have Parkinson's?

"Max, dear, your lips are moving, but I can't hear a word! I'm calling an ambulance! Oh, please, Max, don't die!"

"Don't need an ambulance, dear. My astral body is quickly reuniting with its physical form. We've finally switched to the informal you, you foolish Nastya. . . ."

"Oh, I can hear you now. Did you say form or was it fool?"

He got up and clutched the edge of the mirror. I said form, you fool. She put her shoulder under his arm and helped him get to the bed.

They sat on the bed all evening, holding each other, like children. They didn't turn on the light. The television screen flickered with a talented actor in a vile revolutionary role. They had tea, chewing on the hardened marmalade. They burned with tenderness for each other, but did not unbutton their pants. They fell asleep like children, holding each other.

They were awakened in the morning by a call from First Secretary Fotii Feklovich Klezmetsov.

"I'd like to speak with Maxim Petrovich," the first secretary said in Party style.

"All yours," Ogo muttered sleepily.

"What does that mean?" The leader was bewildered.

"Is that Fotik?" Ogo had recognized the voice.

"Fotik if you must, but Fotii would be better," the first secretary said drily.

"I thought it was those early birds from the Glands again." Ogo yawned.

"You keep joking, but this is serious," he said. Very serious modulations came from the phone. "We've got to have ourselves a chitchat, Maxim Petrovich." The folksy tone worked well in these conversations. "Our public is all upset and in a lather. All kinds of rumors about some hard cheese.... Are you boys planning underground stuff?"

"Some *under*ground!" Ogo smirked. "Every photographer in Moscow knows about it."

Fotii laughed in pure NKVD-37 style. "It would be good in that case for the secretariat also to know. Shall I send a car for you?"

"Oh, no, don't bother!" Ogo pretended horror. "I'll walk."

"So, two o'clock in my office."

He was still holding the phone and thinking after they hung up. It was clear—after *Splinters* and after Berlin, the games were over. Oh, if I were alone I'd give Fotik hell, really get into the dissident stuff.... But I can't make decisions for the group....

He put down the phone and turned to Anastasia. She looked at him closely.

"How do you feel, Max?"

"Like an egg!"

"Is that good?"

"No, worse than an egg!" He jumped down from the bed. Spots floated before his eyes. He pulled out an old pair of corduroy trousers: he had to look shabby for his visit to the secretariat.

When they sat down to breakfast, the anxious phone calls began. Okhotnikov, Probkin, Drevesny, German, and Georgii had also been called in.

"Well, looks like it's beginning," Drevesny said with feigned calm. "I assume they'll want to know how it went over the hill. . . ."

Ogo was astonished. "What went over the hill? None of us went, none went over the hill!"

Nastya sighed. "So much for the life of world adventure."

ROSFOTO

THAT DAY, MONDAY, was pay day at the State Photo Directorate, and the two bachelors Slyazgin and Skanshchin
treated themselves to lunch, in civilian clothes, at the buffet of the Central House of Workers in the Arts. They each had two hundred grams
of vodka, then a hundred, then they stopped—a good fighting dose.
Worker Galina Ivanovna brought the officers jellied bottom-fish with a
knowing smile—and you couldn't overlook the *zakuski*.

The captains first talked about hockey, as usual. Our icemen really
licked those Canadians last night, the superstars could only fart in
shame. Go, Russians! Getting even for Lake Placid, where the honor of
the Russian flag had been sullied.

"And it's good that none of our men defected," noted Captain
Skanshchin.

Captain Slyazgin's jaw dropped. "Do you think that's possible?"

"Why not?" Skanshchin patted his new hairstyle, lost in thought.

"I've done some figuring, just for myself. I think Zhluktov might let us down, a general's son."

Simplehearted Slyazgin had not even suspected that Skanshchin was testing him. "That's interesting, what you think about Zhluktov!"

"Well, Kolya, it's just intuition."

Slyazgin sipped his coffee and pushed the cup aside in irritation. Stupid drink, and costs almost as much as vodka. His wolfish face began to resemble something prehistoric.

What a lousy mug, Skanshchin thought, not for the first time. How can they take people who look like that into the Party Glands?

"I got an idea, Vladimir," Slyazgin said. "I want the general to have a listen. . . ."

Skanshchin winced at the poor grammar. People don't even try to improve themselves. Just awful. "Well, what's your idea, Nikolai?"

"You see, I think . . . maybe we should use physics on your Ogorod?" He was regarding Skanshchin very closely, and the latter thought that perhaps he was now being tested psychologically. Skanshchin squinted.

"Physics, you say?" Even though the very idea of material factors determining an artist was monstrous, Skanschin decided not to avoid the test. He was, indeed, of sterner stuff.

"Well, you know, squeeze him a little." Slyazgin laughed. "If the general gives the okay, I'll break him in a minute. That's the strategy in brief, Vladimir. Ogorodnikov's never seen me anywhere except in Berlin, and that was just a flick, and . . ."

"A flicker."

"Thanks for the correction. I'll remember. Well, I'll glue on a moustache, put on dark glasses. . . ."

"Take care, Nikolai," Skanshchin said gently. "Are you after a bullet?"

Slyazgin frowned. What do you mean? . . . Vova! . . . You don't think he'd lift a hand against the Glands, do you? . . . He was born in the USSR, wasn't he . . . Do you think Ogorod would do that?

"Without a doubt." Skanshchin put his hand on his comrade's shoulder. "When Ogo sees your face in dark glasses, Slyazgin, he'll do it."

The two expert photographologists finished their coffee, giving each other dirty looks.

2

IN THE LOBBY of Rosfoto Restaurant two O's bumped into each other— Ogorodnikov and Okhotnikov.

The latter had just rushed out of the secretariat, where he had been worked over by the three K's—Klezmetsov, Kunenko, and Kobyaev. They had demanded, of course, information on how *Cheese!* had reached the West. They had threatened—"Go to the opening at the Kontinent house and you'll be thrown out of the Photographers' Union!" They had wondered—"How could a son of the sea end up in a Jewish shop?" They cajoled—"Bring Kunenko your unprinted stuff, we'll print it."

Alexei had asked, "What does Comrade Kunenko have to do with photography?"

"Well, you can go now, Okhotnikov," they had said to him then. "It looks like we underestimated you."

Going up in the elevator, Ogo checked his outfit in the mirror once more. Everything was crummy, old and shabby, except for the long scarf around his unshaven neck, tricolor like the tsarist flag, falling with both ends into the area of his crotch.

All three secretaries stopped clacking away at their typewriters when he walked into the reception room. "Oh, Max, look at how you're dressed," gasped Ninochka.

"He's dressed harmonically, like in Europe," countered Simochka.

Alevtina lit up a cigarette stylishly and offered him a seat. The ladies remembered the liberal days, and sympathized with those whom they still called the "young" photographers, and naturally despised all those Kunenkos and Kobyaevs of the secretariat for being "one hundred percent uncreative."

At exactly two o'clock Kunenko flew out of First Secretary Klezmetsov's office and without a glance at Ogorodnikov, but breaking out in red patches, strode to the door of his office.

"Kunenko," Ogo said to his back. "You shouldn't confuse a vernis-
sage with vermicelli."

The executive secretary froze in the doorway. He heard it, fine. Let
the bastards know how we despise them, for devouring our homeland
and shitting up neighboring homelands, and sending their shit to distant
homelands now!

Ninochka and Simochka giggled. The door shut.

Kunenko, recently appointed to the Union, looked like a stall keeper
from the old Moscow markets: arrogant and grim, a red-faced crook.
He might be a descendant of the butcher's rows, this present-day PhD
candidate in the social sciences, who had recently defended his master's
thesis, "The Party Leadership in the Theatrical Process." Things had
been going well for Kunenko with the theaters in the Krasnopresenk
neighborhood of the capital—until the big bust. It turned out that
Kunenko had fiddled with the invoice for the lumber they needed for
the Komsomol Theater, and at the premiere of *Moscow Carillons* something had collapsed . . . something that was never supposed to collapse
. . . hush, hush. . . . That's when they had shifted him to photography.
The drama specialist had been bored at first, but once he saw the generous depths of the Photofund's coffers he had cheered up. A topic for
his doctoral dissertation was now ripening in his brain. Life, as usual,
offered the raw material, and now there was the Party's militant work
on breaking up the provocative group of *Say Cheese!*

No sooner had Kunenko vanished than the door of the main office
opened than out stepped Fotii Feklovich Klezmetsov, wearied by state
affairs of the more weighty type. His invitation was peaceful: "Come in,
Max."

There was no one else in Fotii's office, excluding the portraits of
Brezhnev and Andropov. "How're you doing, in general?" the First Secretary inquired routinely as he sat at his desk. Once he was seated, his
right shoulder slid down mysteriously, as if he were making adjustments
in his trousers. "They say you're just back from a trip? By the way, that
Abrakadin, the ambassador to the GDR, was furious, he went as high
as he could to get your soul." The first secretary's hand kept fussing
under the desk. "Those retrogrades! It's not easy for us with them. . . ."
wrong under the desk, and inexperienced Fotii let it show.

Something was wrong under the desk, and inexperienced Fotii let it show.

Kunenko came in without knocking, with even more red patches on his mug. He headed for the desk. "Sorry, Fotii Feklovich, I've been working in here all morning without you, I forgot something." Without explanation, he put his hand under the desk.

"Forgot your gun, I'll bet?" Ogo asked politely.

The bosses laughed, their faces forward, their right hands under the table. That was witty about the gun, very witty. They'd kill me without a second thought, Ogo realized. Unlimited cruelty. His former comrade's face was no different from the criminal's. Twin faces of evil.

At last the fuss ended. Kunenko left and Fotii sat back in his chair to start the conversation. His tone was quite different, for the record.

"Tell me, Maxim Petrovich, what is this underground publication you've come up with?"

"Oho!" said Ogo. "The witch-hunt begins."

"Choose your words carefully!" the leader barked.

"I do."

"How many copies of *Say Cheese!* have you prepared?"

Ogo silently showed two hands.

Fotii squinted. "Okhotnikov said it was twelve."

Ogo shrugged.

Fotii bent over and whistled strangely, like a jet. "How many?" A growing reactor jet whistle. "How many were sent abroad?" Boom, through the sound barrier.

Ogo took two fingers and made a zero.

"What is this childish game?" Fotii Feklovich laughed. "You're clever, strong. . . . Why are you fooling around? Everything, everything will be made clear, Maxim Petrovich. Everything that is hidden will be revealed."

"I'm glad you understand that," Ogo said.

Something dropped inside Fotii Feklovich. Ogo's looking at me as if he knows I'm Agent Poker. Could he?

The unpleasant thought made Fotii lose the proper tone. Something different now, collegial, yet sarcastic.

"Well, and what are the geniuses' plans?"

"The plan is fulfilled," Ogo said. "The first uncensored photo album in history has already been published."

"I see," Fotii said musingly. "So you're worried about history, are you? Well, and who's doing the mass edition—Fountain or Pharaoh?"

"The best would be Soviet Photographer," Ogo said. "Pick up the phone and call them. It can even be a small edition, and that's that. The end of the ideological diversion."

"Not a bad idea, Max," Fotii said, careful now, afraid to scare him off. "But what can I call them about? I haven't seen anything yet. Now bring the album to the secretariat, and we'll take a look and discuss it, maybe you have created a masterpiece.... Bring it in! We have no retrogrades in the secretariat now."

"Fine," Ogo said, "We'll bring it."

Fotii Feklovich was taken aback by the villain's unexpected docility. "You'll just bring it in?"

Ogo nodded peaceably. "Why not, if you haven't seen a single copy, not even the one stolen from Mikhailo Kaledin's."

The first secretary coughed and slammed his plump fist on the desk. "How dare you! What are you insinuating?"

Ogo rose. "Fotii, keep cool! We'll bring you *Cheese!*"

"Will you bring all the copies?"

Ogo shook his head.

"How many?"

Ogo silently showed one finger.

"One, you mean? Say it, one?"

Ogo nodded. "I think our authors will agree to present to the secretariat for familiarization ..." and once more he raised his index finger.

Fotii Feklovich was infuriated. "Can't you *say* it?"

Ogo sat up in his chair and brought his sinful index finger closer to the first secretary. "I'm showing it quite clearly."

Fotii banged his hand again. "You're showing one but not saying it! Is it one? Say it, yes or no?"

"Either yes or no?" Ogo asked.

"Yes!" the first secretary said.

"Meaning what?"

"What do you mean, meaning what?"

"Well, if yes, then"— he showed his index finger—"and if no, then"— he showed the circle. "Do I understand correctly?"

Fotii Feklovich got up and went to the window, crunching all ten fingers of his own. "Are you trying to play Ionesco here? You're playing with fire, Maxim Petrovich. Our conversation isn't working out."

Ogo, overcoming nausea, headed for the door. "Don't forget to turn off the tape recorder, Fotik." That was the last sentence of the audience.

Ninochka and Simochka, who had been eavesdropping of course, swayed silently, their cheeks puffed out, doing all they could to avoid bursting out laughing. Alevtina Makarovna was putting on lipstick.

3

AT THE END of the day all the evildoers plus wives and girlfriends met at Okhotnikov's. It was like rush hour on the metro. Vadim Raskladushkin dropped by, too. They squeezed him in, not without difficulty.

No fewer than ten Cheesers had been called in to the secretariat that day. Now they were all recounting how well they had handled themselves and what bastards they had to deal with. Severe agitation reigned, and it was impossible to organize the crowd. Ogo and Shuz gave up and started drinking. Only Andrei Drevesny was in top form. He climbed on top of a table to sum up.

"Before everyone gets soused, let's go over the secretariat's demands. First—give them the album to be examined by the administration and the Party committee. Will we do it? We will! How many copies?" Everyone there raised an index finger. "Second—cancel the opening in the Kontinent pelmeni house. Any proposals?" Everyone present raised another finger, the middle one. The evening ended with a cultural outing to the park at Ostankino, where feckless conceptualist friends of Vasya Shturmin, the youngest Cheeser, were having a happening at midnight with the weighty title "Hatching Eggs."

4

WHY, THEN, DID all the photographers and even the main conspirators, Ogo and Shuz, agree so easily to carrying one copy of the album into the enemy's headquarters?

Why not? would be an interrogative answer. The album was made to be looked at, to affect the souls grown harsh in the tenth five-year plan toward a greater nobility. And also . . .

After Ogo returned from the West, they had begun figuring out where the copies were. Well, the Rayevskys had one, the Panayevs another, Prince Vyazemsky had a third,* one was in Soho as sterling proof that art could not be kept within national boundaries. . . . They counted and counted and came up with eleven. . . . Where was the twelfth? Shuz finally remembered—in Misha Dymshits's attic! "Remember, we asked him to design it à la *Mir Isskustva* and then changed our minds?" He picked up the phone. "Mikhailo, it's me, yes, Shuz, motherfucker!"

A brilliant conspiratorial conversation followed. "Tell me, remember that pie I left at your place to taste and then said don't eat it, do you still have it? You don't understand? Well, our album, *Say Cheese!*, it was next to your crummy samovar. . . ." Shuz listened mouth agape to Mikhailo Kaledin, then slammed down the receiver and let loose a flood of what is known in academic circles as colloquial speech. "The comrades took it away, that night! Why didn't I figure it out! That night, shit, that fiery night! I'm scarred!"

That's why Ogo set the minitrap with Fotii Feklovich. The secretary had fallen for it, exploded it, and revealed two almost obvious truths.

Well then, under those circumstances, when one thing had already crossed the national borders, and the comrades had dragged the other thing to their lair, why play the virgin, why not give one more thing to their photographic secretaries? And then . . . what if . . . a naïve ideal still lived . . . what if up high, well, somewhere up there, someone important says something like "Well, listen, folks, what are we screwing around for, why don't we just publish this stuff in a small edition?" And

---

*Rayevsky, Panayev, and Prince Vyazemsky were noblemen and writers, liberal personalities of the nineteenth century. In expanding *Say Cheese!*'s audience to include them, Ogo certainly makes a presumptuous quest for a slice of the Great Tradition.

the impossible would come to pass: the first uncensored Soviet photo publication!

5

MEANWHILE, IN THE sections of the Photographers' Union, in the publishing houses, and among the columns of the famous restaurant, whispers flew like drafts: something serious was happening in the Moscow Union. . . .

A group of photographic artists led by the "liberal" with the round eye were strolling after lunch, rubbing elbows, down the paths of the village of Developkino. "Comrades, comrades, something is happening at the Union. . . ."

"I had calls from the Party committee. . . ."

"A blow against Ogorodnikov, right. . . ?"

"What, you haven't heard. . . ?"

"Careful, br'er rabbits, here comes Militiaman Kreshutin. . . ."

Two serious Soviet men, who regarded each other as "maestros," separated themselves from the group and stopped between the pseudoclassical columns of the House of Creativity. "Listen, old man, there's a storm coming. Drevesny, German, Ogorodnikov, that Shuz, and a whole bunch of people with them are publishing an underground journal. Imagine, Georgii Avtandilovich is among them. . . ."

"Oh, I don't think it's so serious, old man. It's a game. You can't manage in art without games, old boy. Andrei Drevesny invited me to join that journal as you call it. 'Bring your rolls, old man,' he said to me. I didn't pay too much attention to it."

"And you did the right thing, old man. It's a dirty business. The journal is going to the West. They say at the party committee that the Glands are up in arms."

"The Glands? You know, old man, these aren't Stalinist times. You've slept through history again."

"I've slept through it? It's you who's still asleep."

"All right, old man, you didn't say it and I didn't hear it, okay?"

They separated, but then turned and thought at the same time: We've been calling each other old man for twenty years, and a few more years and it won't be funny anymore.

At Rosfoto Restaurant, in the prix fixe lunchroom, the only conversation was about the mysterious campaign started by the first secretary, Fotii Feklovich Klezmetzov.

Ninochka, his secretary, rolling her eyes, quickly went through the news, and like a pebble in a pond, she gave off "well-informed circles."

"Two men came in today. Handsome young men. 'Allow us to introduce ourselves, we are from the editorial board of the album *Say Cheese!*' And they put this heavy thing, I swear it weighs eight kilos, on the desk. Kunenko jumps up, red as a beet, Simochka will tell you I'm not lying, and pulls the album to his office, not even saying hello to the guys who brought it. Then one of them, a tall guy with a pince-nez on a ribbon, I think I've seen him at the October party, says to Kunenko, 'Give me a receipt!' The man almost had a fit. 'You want a receipt, you hooligans, you provocateurs?' No manners, he ought to be a plumber. I'll tell you, girls, as a candidate for membership in the Party, people like that shame us! Then the second young man, also very handsome, stylish, says to me, 'Would you please write a receipt —"received for familiarization, one copy of the photo almanac *Say Cheese!?* ' " When we're asked, we do, I typed it on Union stationery and made a place for the signature of Executive Secretary Kunenko. Well, he signed it."

Simochka did her turn, imitating all the various people who had come running to the office that day, including, of course, the well-known personages from the Glands with smiles as if they were venereal specialists. The album was kept in Kunenko's office, and they let in one member of the Union board at a time for ten minutes and locked the door from the outside.

"Does that mean that all the decisions of the Twentieth Congress are shot to hell?" asked the deep voice of Rosa Alexandrovna Barcelon, secretary of the Bureau of Propaganda of Soviet Photography, as the long ash of her cigarette fell into a plate of jellied tongue.

Three other scenes were taking place in the same building of the generous tavern Rosfoto, but in different rooms, starting with the fireplace room, where Levitan's painting *Above Eternal Rest* hung and a mock-up of the missile carrier *M. Enthusias* stood up in the corner, ending in the bathroom next to the bar, which by strange coincidence the drinkers to photography also called the *Melancholny-Enthusias.*

Several shaggy heads gathered in the fireplace room, the so-called Russites, authors of the mediocre and influential photo magazine *Moscow Lights.* They huddled, as if discussing the next Kristallnacht instead of the latest scandal with "that dissident shit."

"Look what Zhora Sheleshov got me at the Party committee, a list, take a look at this crowd, my brothers. Fisher, Tsuker ... what does it smell like to you? And there's the ever-present German."

"Well, Slava German is Russian, it's just that last name...."

"Russian, you say? And what about his mother? And his grandmother, a Palestinian merchant wife? ..."

"He's a foreigner, he is...."

"But you can't get away from the fact that their ringleaders are impeccable: Ogorodnikov, Drevesny, Okh ..."

"They're hiding behind them. A shield."

"Too bad we're losing all these people ... it's a lesson for the future...."

"As for Ogorodnikov, my dear sirs, I'd give him a little thought. He's suspicious. The nose, the ears. His father is from that Zurich and Geneva crowd...."

"Hm, we should check him out...."

Two friends entered that fireplace room—international specialists, tireless fighters for peace, Arkasha Mekhamorchik and Gena Shukhnevich. They waved like buddies to the group but did not dare join them. They sat in a corner, casually chatting.

"I just don't understand it," Arkasha said, acting dumb. "I always thought Ogo was a Soviet guy. So he's a show-off, a modernist, but still—"

"Drop it, Arkady." Gena Shukhnevich laughed. "I ran into him in Paris once, hello-hello, take down my number, I said. Ogo opened his wallet, I took a glance, and he's got francs, pounds, greenbacks ... and can you imagine, an American Express card! Some Soviet man. I understood that he'd been pulled to the other side."

"Too bad, if it's so," Mekhamorchik said, and shook his head. "We're losing people."

There was a silence, a thoughtful shaking of heads, beringed fingers slipping over the menu. "Assorted smoked fish?"

"Well, the same as usual, the assorted fish. Alas, no comparison to an American Express card. We're losing people, we are. . . ."

"They say that Ambassador Abrakadin is demanding a criminal case."

"Well, Abrakadin should keep his mouth shut. Remember his daughter?"

"And how!"

"What, did you sleep with her?"

"Why be so crude? She defected!"

"You're kidding!"

"She defected to London with a Polack!"

"What a world!"

"How good it would be to be like that, in the Hemingway style. Run off with a Pole, shoot lions, pay for the assorted fish at the real exchange rate of four rubles to a dollar. Why don't we have Russian Express cards?"

"Abrakadin's has been burned up in a blue flame. Serves him right. An incredible bastard. Didn't spare his own people."

"Don't say he's burned yet, Arkasha, the times are different now, you don't get in trouble for your relatives. Take October Ogorod. . . ."

"What about October?"

"You know as well as I do."

Second scene: two staff provocateurs, Chushaev and Shelesin, living it up at the cocktail bar. "Pour, Stepanovna, pour, and put it on the tab! Take out your House of Lords from under the counter. What's the matter, old man, don't you know Chushaev? It just came over the TASS wire: Ogorodnikov has a million in a Swiss bank and he's buying stocks from Rothschild. Drevesny and German are faggots, they've been living with each other for the last ten years. That whole *Cheese!* was paid for by Belgian Zionists. A delayed-action mine. They're going to ruin all our friendly international ties, those damned gold diggers, they want to emigrate, they're looking fo publicity. Without publicity in the West, you'll die in the streets. Let's go, Shelesin, and take a leak. Stepanovna, we're not leaving, save our barstools, we're off to the *Melancholny-Enthusias,* be right back."

Waiting in the bathroom for the two puny shit-eaters, who always did everything together because of their bad consciences, was an enormous punishment machine—legs spread, arms akimbo, gray hair down to his shoulders. He beat them up "for slander," knocked them against the tile walls, and then shoved their two faces into adjoining urinals. "Right on!" he muttered, performing his cruel deed. "Shred the scar!" And he left, unpunished.

AH, ARBAT !

I

ONCE A WEEK Captain Vladimir Skanshchin visited his dear girl-friend Viktoria, who also happened to be one of Ogo's ex-wives. It was curious that he went only once a week, when State Health reasons called for visits to such ladies at least twice a week. This idea sometimes worried him. Of course, he got more than he gave from his older friend. In principle, he would have liked to expand the schedule, but he didn't dare raise the issue: the initiative always had to come from the more experienced comrade. It also hurt him that their dates were often of limited duration—he would have liked to master more of the complex issues that he came across in the course of his duties.

"Why does it happen so often, darling," Skanshchin said with a sigh, "that the great artists lose their delight in communism? For after all, nobody wants anything else from them anyway. Appreciate communism properly, and as for the rest—create, invent, construct, whatever you want. . . ."

"Want to know? Communism is obsolete, out of fashion," Viktoria announced didactically, getting out of her pantyhose and making abrupt warm-up stretches with her hips. "Come on, come on, Vladimir! I've got a heavy day today—a premiere at the Stanislavsky Theater. Come on, start!"

"Has it really become obsolete?" Skanshchin mumbled after the sexual act. "After all, it fascinates so many minds. . . ."

Darling was getting dressed. "As you leave, Vladimir, don't forget, there's a package for you at the buffet—a kilo of walnuts. Have a one-hundred- to hundred-and-fifty-gram day!"

"Tell me, darling." The captain suddenly remembered the general's instructions. "Tell me, to your observation, has Max any homosexual inclinations?"

"Some sleuth you are!" she scornfully pronounced from the doorway.

Skanshchin spent a long time bare-assed on the wide bed, looking at the pictures of Viktoria's relatives on the walls. What noble intellectuals. . . . He pulled out something banned from the bookshelves over his head, religious philosophy, Berdyaev or Lev Shestov, Darling had had books like that for a long time, since her divorce from Ogorodnikov. He read, cutting the pages with an ivory knife, moaning and groaning: could communism be the *enemy* of culture? It was all so strange. . . .

2

A FEW DAYS before the next meeting of the board of the Moscow Photographers' organization, the meeting at which the public gut-spilling of *Say Cheese!* was planned, Ogo was developing his foreign film rolls at his studio on Khlebny. The West appeared through the gloom of the emulsion, like an unknown country he had never seen, as if someone else had taken the pictures, as if some young man had wandered there instead of a forty-two-year-old refugee.

Suddenly the doorbell began ringing, and the Cheesers barged in. "We have to talk!" Over twenty mugs showed up in fifteen minutes. A conspiracy? He had to set aside the work, drag out all the liquor in the place. He called Anastasia.

"Bring some instant coffee, there's a whole gang here to see their leader!"

"What do they want from their leader?"

"I don't know, probably want to write a letter to Brezhnev."

"Are you kidding?"

"I'm kidding, of course."

Actually, he wasn't far off. That morning they had discussed by phone their plan to write to highly placed people, to explain the photographers' pure intentions and that they had only one aim—to develop Soviet photography, to complain about the Photo Union and its viper First Secretary Fotik, who was trying to scare them and twist their arms. Notorious Probkin, licking his bright-red lips and rubbing his frostbitten ears, was to be the spokesman.

"Really, this is a good tactic. Right, Ogo? The Party thinks we're enemies, and we turn to it for protection; give us those Leninist principles. But we just don't know how you'll react to this, Ogo."

"What do I have to do with it?" Ogorodnikov shrugged. He tried not to meet anyone's eyes, but wherever he turned he came across the tense, anticipating gazes of his friends. There seemed to be an assumption that he had his own "intentions," his own personal position. "I do what everyone does. If it's Brezhnev, then it's Brezhnev, fine." Probkin's mouth flew open and his long hair sagged. There's something cretinish in that Probkin, thought Ogo. I suppose you could say the same about me, though. There, in the far mirror, is a stoop-shouldered and grim bum. He picked up a guitar, tucked his feet under him in his favorite chair. No one said a word about the opening at the Kontinent pelmeni house. Had they all lost their marbles? A letter to Brezhnev! Could it be Probkin's idea? *Soviet Ball* magazine rearing its head?

"Max, don't be huffy," his friend Andrei said from the windowsill.

"Really, old man," added Slava, "it's just a question of tactics."

"I'm not against it, guys. On the contrary." Plucking the strings, he sang softly, "Mother dear, let's weep, let's sigh and groan, where will they send you?" The audience waited patiently in silence. Ogo raised his eyes to the ceiling. "You flow like a river, strange name, Arbat Street, ah, Arbat . . ."

"If you're planning to write to Old Bushybrows, go ahead. I'll gladly join in, along with everyone else. What, am I supposed to write it for you? Compose that crap? Why? Why not Slava, or Andrei, or Georgii, really, hero of eight republics? Who appointed me leader here, and scapegoat? Please, start, I'll be glad to support you, but I won't *start* anything for you at all!"

The whole scene began to stink of dissension and depression. The photographers meaninglessly drank vodka, cognac, vermouth, whatever they were served. They drank it all up, but hadn't started any letter. They chipped in five rubles each and sent out onto New Arbat a booze-buying expedition consisting of Shturmin, Alexei Okhotnikov, and Yuri Uri, a professor from Tartu who was supposed to pretend to be a for-eigner. And then some real foreigners appeared, the young jackals of the pen who were known as Luc and Frank.

Apparently, someone had told them that New Focus was having a meeting at the studio of its leader, Maxim Petrovich Ogorodnikov. Instead of an important event, they found a stupid party with guitar plinking and chatting in corners. The only excitement came from Mas-ter Tsuker, who arrived on the heels of the foreigners. He took off his expensive and heavy coat, "built" by his father in the first five-year plan, revealing that he had no trousers. He had a jacket and tie, there was a watch on the left hand and a ring with a massive Colombian ruby on the right, but Master Tsuker's legs were encased in woolen tights. Embarrassed at first, he explained that in his rush he forgot to change out of his "sweatpants." So that there could be no doubts left, Master Tsuker sat down right in the middle and casually crossed his legs. There, you see, his pose said, Master Tsuker isn't the least bit embarrassed, and if he's not embarrassed, then he hasn't come to a meeting without trou-sers, he's merely come in sweatpants.

The situation grew even more ridiculous. Lenses flashed. "Anyone photographing anyone else will get the scar treatment," announced Shuz. But he wasn't starting a letter to Brezhnev, either, and sometimes winked at Ogo—Right, you're doing the right thing!

And then, magically, everything changed: Anastasia showed up. She had spent an hour in line at the takeout at the Prague and with results— she bought 150! baked! liver-filled! pirozhki! Into the oven, and in ten minutes we'll have dinner! Well, why so glum, boys? "You boys! That's quite an idea you have there. . . . What do you mean, can't write it? A letter to Brezhnev! Grab a pencil, Alexei, I'll dictate one for you. 'Dear Leonid Ilyich . . .' Yes, 'dear' and not 'respected,' they don't have any

respectable people there. . . . Go on: 'We are a group of Soviet photographers concerned by the state of things in our art, and we are turning
to you . . .' By the way, Semyon called this morning."

"Which Semyon?" everyone asked at once.

"The manager of the Kontinent house. They're ready, you can bring
the show. Write the rest yourself, Alexei, we'll all go over it together."
A dash to the kitchen, to the pies, her heavy braid tossed over her shoulder, God, you really can't find a better broad. "First batch, boys!"

With their mouths full, the photographers argued whether the game
was worth playing all the way. What's the problem, wondered Anastasia.
Someone chicken out? "To carry on or not to carry on?"

Laughter—what a woman! What a casual pun! No one had chickened out, everyone wanted to carry on. "Gentlemen, gentlemen," called
Cheeser Shturmin, bustling, "let's pose for a group shot." He suggested
the classic composition of the painting *A Letter to the Sultan*; at this
even Ogo mellowed, and so the host sang a certain senseless ballad for
the group's pleasure. . . .

In Honor of a Certain Futurist Photographer
or
Ballad of the Waistband Button

He refused to shoot "from the button."
His camera wanted to fly.
He devoured this life—what a glutton!
And demanded a fresh supply.
His friend came by in top hat and felt boots,
Exuberant and insane;
Sitting for them was a pair of nudes
With flowers in their manes.

Breathing perfume and fog
Moscow squatted, shitting . . .
The dream untiring striving
Toward socialism. Sitting.

An automobile roared,
Pulled over and beckoned escape,

The bedbugs' army stomped
The divan and the drapes.
Is this life's motley crew
Or a march on parade?
Will your camera serve the era
Or the snobbery and decay?

Crystal and iron.
Blue turns into green.
Stalin smokes and frowns
At Tatlin's flying machine.

The kettle boils furiously,
Singer of the communes.
The commune raises its tiers
To one of the moons!
Where will the double exposure
Lead our working people?
And what revolutionary treasure
Will bring us to the steeple?

In Russia the swollen masses
Rejected the tsar and the priest.
His button cut from the trousers,
Sits in a jail futurist!*

3

ANDREI DREVESNY WAS mad at the snow. His date with Polina was on
the Yauza embankment, right at the spot where the Yauza sharply
turned, lost the ugly Moscow buildings, and flushed coquettishly under
a humped pseudo-Leningrad bridge. Nearby stood pretentious classi-
cism in the form of a lantern and a pharmacy. The snow, the large slow

*In this ballad Ogo refers to the Soviet twenties when many avant-garde artists
believed that the revolution was "their time." The ballad ends up in the thirties, when
many illusions were lost along with the waistband buttons cut by the prison guards
from the artists' pants.

drifting flakes, made it all seem like an opera set. But it was midnight and she was late and he was standing there like a jerk.

"Hey, pal!" said three teenagers walking past. Bastards, I'm old enough to be their father, and they say pal! My own fault, I dress like a teenager. "How about a smoke, pal? Waiting for your chick?"

At last she arrived. Running. From a distance she did look like a chick running for her date. Up close, of course, it was another story. Yes, after living with Fotik, something Soviet was imprinted on Polina's face, something that had not been there even in the most ugly situations before.

"Forgive me, I'm late! Andrei, there's no time, I'll get right to the point ... Andrei, I beg you—go away!"

"Just what I thought! Polina, don't overdramatize like this, we're not in an opera. New Focus has taken steps to present the album officially, a letter to Br or whoever they have at the top, we don't need these nocturnal anxieties." Wide-open eyes, snow. "We're middle-aged now."

"Ah, Andrei! A letter to Br! That's so naïve! Don't you understand! The machinery has been started up!"

"Did Fotik ask you to influence me? Tell me, Polina, what's making you panic like this, is it Fotik's request or someone else's?"

"No one is asking me to do this! How could you? Andrei! How could you think that? We're not strangers! You and I! Our children! And really! Believe me, I just can't sit back and watch you destroy your work! In one fell swoop! You're the most talented of them all! Believe me, I love all the guys! I'm one of you, too! But you're the most real of all of them! Forgive me, but Ogo, he's dragging you all into *his* adventure! You have to understand! I can't let it happen!"

Drevesny was affected by her feelings and the confusing flow of argument, and it seemed to him that there was something in that flow, but at this melodramatic moment it was hard to tell just what it was.

They turned the corner. The pseudo-Leningrad neighborhood disappeared into a long row of factory windows, glowing with dead light. The refuse of ugly industry was piled up behind a fence. At the end of the street appeared the green roof light of a free taxi.

"A cab!" exclaimed Polina. "What luck! I won't be late and no one will notice a thing!" Of late she had been using collective, indifferent words for the stern paterfamilias Fotii Feklovich: "everyone," "some-one," "no one"....

"I know I'm being irrational," Drevesny was saying, "but I can't spend my whole life under that damned Soviet belly. I'm not like Ogo, for me it's a personal, not an intellectual thing, you know my murdered grandfather and my father's ruined life and my mother's fear and I'm far removed from political games, but, believe me, I have to continue the Drevesny line...."

"At least don't go to the next board meeting!" she shouted, getting into the taxi. "Don't go to the plenum of the board whatever you do!"

He walked back to the embankment, where his Volvo was parked. Couldn't avoid the rhetoric after all. *Personal thing, continuing the line* ... bullshit. I have to avoid emotions now, squash all these hicks without emotion, not force my ego up against the face of technology but instead in cold courage become part of it all.... He got his camera from the car trunk and took a few shots. Foreground operatic theme with snow, in back the lifeless neon street.

When he climbed into the Swedish jalopy the damned thing wouldn't start. Wouldn't even consider it. Nothingness when he turned the key. The distributor? He got out and looked under the hood, feeling around in the cold and filthy rubber and metal, in the disgusting drear-iness of the obsolete mechanism, zero emotion unless you counted the despair and the cold courage of technology, damn it. "Lost your rotor, Andrei," said someone right over his head.

He straightened. Three men in sheepskin coats stood close. Of the three mean faces one had a drooping jaw, like a wolf's mouth.

"Where could the rotor have gone?" Andrei muttered, feeling metal-lic heat spreading throughout his body and the unprepared organs melting.

It's amazing, thought General Planshchin, staring at him, you meet someone like Drevesny on the street and you'd never think that he was so full of anti-Soviet nastiness. "We'll explain it to you," the general said. "Close the hood and come with us, your Swedish beauty won't go anywhere. Captain Slyazgin, make sure that Andrei doesn't slip."

On the road the wolfman took him by the elbow. Joyous beckoning signals from the other two toward their black Volga, parked by the pharmacy. I should ask these guys who they are, Drevesny knew, I should ask for their documents. Like Solzhenitsyn—shout, scream, scratch!

"We won't keep you long, Andrei Yevgenievich, and in the meantime, I'll bet the rotor is found."

4

DURING THOSE DAYS before the next plenum of the board of the Union of Soviet Photographers, First Secretary Fotii Feklovich Klezmetsov was right on the brink of revolt against the Glands. How could they? They were making him out to be the organizer of a major ideological campaign and yet treated him like a pawn, like a simple lousy stoolie. Well, just take today, how obnoxious. Someone comes by from Planshchin and they set up a nighttime meeting, as if Fotii were a whore, at the Hotel Belgrade. Why the stupid conspiracy? Whom were they hiding from? And what would all these hotel meetings entail? Fotii would start using simple art history arguments to prove the decadent motifs in the work of, say, Tsuker or Georgii Chavchavadze, and they would just stare at him with greasy smiles, as if they'd figured out his whole life to its end and knew all his scars and scabs, including that favorite one with the crust behind his ear. "Later with the decadent motifs. Why don't you tell us, Fotii Feklovich, whether Tsuker smokes dope or if Chavchavadze seduces little boys."

There would be someone from Phikhail Mardeyevich's secretariat at the plenum, either Tsvestov or even Glyasny. Fotii would have to raise the issue of rights gently—would have to talk in terms of "care and proper treatment of Party personnel." Planshchin and his people were cynics, they wanted Fotii's hands to do the work, to break up a creative organization and advance their own careers. Then they would start rumors about Fotii—that he was an agent who betrayed his friends, a cheap louse. . . .

"Do you, at least, understand that I am a major politician?" Fotii kept asking his wife, Polina, during the week of the plenum.

"Naturally," she would reply, passing through the living room with a cigarette, exhaling smoke and pausing in the pose he considered privately to be perfection—hand on hip, smoke over her head. "You're a politician and not only on the scale of your country, but on a European scale. Remember how you behaved with the Hungarians at that meeting the other day? Daring. Wise. Not without brilliance."

It was good to have that understanding. That was his great fortune. He revealed to her the strategy of his struggle. "Forgive me, I can't tell you everything, but it's clear with Ogorodnikov, he is a real enemy. Basically, *they* will do the talking with him, but the others ..." He stopped, waiting for her reaction. Would she give herself away, show any emotion for Andrei? Everyone knew that it wasn't over, that she still felt ...

No, she didn't show it at all, a good woman, look how naturally she puts out her cigarette, adjusts her hair, a real scene from French life. "I believe in you, Fotii! And I know that you'll find the right path."

That was it, his great fortune: a faithful and wise woman covering the rear for a great politician. No, we won't allow them to destroy Soviet photography. "We'll fight off everything provocative and extremist, and will preserve everything that is true and of the People. What time is it? Where's my scarf, Polina? Where are my smoked glasses?" Everything was prepared, of course.

"Just in case, where will you be?" she asked.

"The Belgrade."

5

OFFICIAL ANNOUNCEMENTS OF the plenum of the board were sent only to the ringleaders of the Cheesers: Slava German, Andrei Drevesny, the Probkin, Maxim Ogorodnikov, and Alexei Okhotnikov. Georgii Chavchavadze was also invited, since he had been a member of the board for many years. The conspirators arrived at Rosfoto an hour beforehand and took a table in the café, next to the stupid jukebox which responded with mincing waltzes to any five-kopek piece.

"Man, could I use a drink." Alexei sighed.

"By the way," German said quite out of the way, "Andrei called, he won't be coming. His spleen is acting up, says he'll just make things worse."

"Blessed is he who visited this world in its fateful moments," said Georgii cryptically.

"Georgii," Probkin whispered, "could you lend me twenty-five rubles?"

"Look," said Ogo, "I just got this issue of *Photo Odyssey*. New pictures by old hacks. They're outgrowing themselves."

Suddenly Andrei Drevesny came into the café. He was pale. Shoelace untied. He tripped and then made his way to his friends to the accompaniment of a sappy waltz.

What a bizarre entrance, thought Drevesny, what a role I'm playing, what shame.... "Guys," he exclaimed, "I just saw Bluzhzhaezhzhin! The old man is upset, he called me, I had to go see him, despite my spleen. Well, you do remember his *Dneproges,* all right, he was whoring, it's swinish and shit, but he's still a master, you can't take that away from him, right? Anyway, he said: can the passions. Brothers, I came to an important conclusion from my conversation with him. They're not united up there, thumb to the ceiling, on *Cheese!* Dig? Bluzhzhaezhzhin promised me that everything would be tiptop, that was his expression, if we don't push too hard at the plenum. We have to control ourselves, and that means you most of all, Ogo!"

They looked at each other. Damn it, thought Ogorodnikov, time has really damaged Andrei's looks. Ivory turning into melted wax. And those unfortunate dental bridges. If I were he, I'd watch that sagging jawline.

Georgii looked at his big gold watch. "Time, gentlemen! No need to take food and underwear along." The old man was dressed up—blue suit, polka-dotted bow tie. Everyone in the café stared at them. People peeked in from the billiard room. The counterwoman at the "lower buffet" made an alienated face. A bandy-legged stoolie hurried out of the *Melancholny-Enthusias,* pulling up his fly. "Hello, old men! Off to Golgotha? Good luck!" Both counterwomen from the "upper buffet" just waved casually: these dirty walls had seen worse. The six men were watched in every room of the restaurant; everyone knew that upstairs, in the fireplace room, the Party's lenses had gathered for an unprecedented reason: to put down a group rebellion.

The oak stairs creaked under the feet of the six photographers. Drevesny grabbed Ogorodnikov's elbow. "I'm asking you once more, Max, keep silent! Whatever they say, don't open your mouth."

"How can I, Andrei? What if they ask me to sing the Soviet anthem?" Ogo noticed that Drevesny's teeth were chattering.

Drevesny thought, He's so brazen, he really must have money in a Swiss bank.

"What's the matter with you?" Ogo whispered. "What's the matter with you? Why don't you go home, everyone knows you have a spleen condition."

"Thanks for your concern. I think this is the first time you've thought about anyone else besides yourself."

"You astonish me, Andrei."

"And you astonish me. . . ."

Red-bearded Alexei opened the door to the fireplace room and asked clearly from the doorway, "Excuse me, is this the right place?"

The board was waiting for them in full complement. About three dozen men and half a dozen women sat around a huge oval dining table, quite good for other uses such as signing an act of capitulation to a totalitarian state. At the head of the table sat First Secretary Fotii Feklovich Klezmetsov. Maintaining a mysterious smile, he was engaged in a brief back-and-forth with Comrade Glyasny of the CC.

"I like your sculpture here," muttered Comrade Glyasny, looking at the snow-white shy nymph who had stood next to the fireplace for over a hundred years.

"Ogorodnikov's the one in the green sweater," Fotii replied.

"I know him." Comrade Glyasny smiled, and chased away the silly, free thought that could have been expressed this way: I hope that beauty doesn't blush with shame today.

The six men were offered seats along the wall. Several board members were also sitting there, since there weren't enough armchairs around the oval masterpiece. Ogorodnikov looked around. Who was that next to Fotik? A PhD?

"Glyasny, from Phuslov's secretariat," Georgii whispered.

Around Glyasny, deservedly the center of the composition, was a bouquet of classics: laureates Zhuryev and Matvey Grabochey and two mediocrities from the magazine *Moscow Lights,* editor in chief Phesayev and Phalesin himself. Along the periphery were smaller fry, all familiar faces. Some of them used to stroll through the thaw's puddles in liberal galoshes. But the majority were long-lived frontliners. What greed, what shame. There was no human being among them, except maybe Julieta Frunina. She brought out eight hundred wounded from battlefields and loved screwing all her life, maybe she'd say something true.

Julieta Frunina, the "girl in the gray coat" popular now for several decades, sat with her usual expression of offended dignity. Youth in the trenches, difficult trials for girlish purity, fidelity to an ideal—whom was she supposed to hold accountable for not being loved enough? Those highly charged, emotional photos, the cranes are flying, ah, war, what have you done? Sixty years old? Never!

Fotii Feklovich opened the meeting with the traditional joke of the Photographers' Union: comrades, let's promise not to photograph each other. Everyone laughed, even though half the people had forgotten the last time they had held a camera.

Fotii put on a pair of large glasses and brought a scrap of paper close to the lenses. The pleasant smile was replaced by a nasty sneer.

"According to the latest information, comrades, Maxim Ogorodnikov is complaining about us to Leonid Ilyich Brezhnev. Says we're blackmailing his colleagues, threatening, arm twisting. Wouldn't he be better off complaining to Ronald Reagan? Closer to him, wouldn't it be, comrades!"

"Is that your opinion or is it that of the addressee?" Ogo asked.

"Max, you promised," said Andrei Drevesny under his breath.

Comrade Glyasny broke out in red splotches.

Fotii Feklovich giggled in the amazingly open manner of a true bastard. "My personal opinion, my own. Leonid Ilyich, you know, has not taken an interest yet in your fantastic person."

A slight movement in the center of the composition: laureate Matvey Grabochey scratched his bald pate. In the olden days, his militant head had reminded many people of the tip of a big penis, but alas with the years a greenish hue had appeared on top, and now people remarked that even the Party's "snipers," of whom Grabochey was one, were subject to uncharming fading.

"I'm surprised, comrades," the sniper began wearily and gently, like an adult addressing children. "I'm surprised by today's agenda." He sighed, rubbed the green spot harder, and it turned bluish. "I've been working all day, preparing for the next Pugwash Conference ... and I glanced at the map. Just picture it for a moment. All along the front there are obstacles to the march of socialism! Angola! Ethiopia! Salvador!" His voice grew still stronger. "They're fighting us, starting a crusade, and here we learn that even in the rear of a hard-fighting army there is this ... this ..."—the search for an appropriate word broke off the powerfully increasing flow of decibels—"this vileness, you see." There was a mean pause, during which the sniper's head turned slowly to face the vileness. "Seeking independence, friends? From whom? The People? The State? The Party?" And suddenly he howled at full blast, with the power that had given him the reputation as a fiery speaker. "In other words," he shouted like a criminal in hysterics, "I won't allow it! Never! Vileness! Disgusting! Right in the rear of the VACPb!??"

"Matvey! Matvey!" His old comrade-in-arms and fellow laureate Zhuryev put a hand on Grabochey's shoulder.

There was an impressive silence, ended by Probkin's polite "CPSU."

"What did you say?" Zhuryev said.

"Just a simple correction," Probkin explained. "It was the VACPb under Stalin, and after Stalin it became the CPSU."

I'd empty the whole round into him, thought Grabochey, seven bullets into the long hair.

A nice stake up Matvey's ass, thought Zhuryev, and with Grabochey's initial condescending gentleness, began talking to make clear that as far as he was concerned, as an International Specialist, and Combatant for Peace, and member of the CC, this was—a trifle.

"Matvey, as you know, gets overexcited. What can you do, it's his Komsomol and metallurgical background. But he's right, of course. Alas, comrades, we are not yet strong enough to allow ourselves the luxury of pluralism. Take the question of the space shuttle. Are we behind? Yes, we are, comrades! There will be so many more expenditures ahead, both material and spiritual! All over the world people await our help, comrades. Who knows how much more fighting there will have to be before our enemy realizes the futility of trying to stop the course of history? And then—" Here Zhuryev shut his eyes and spread

his hands, as if in anticipation of the sweet moment. His double chin
turned into a quadruple one. "And then, perhaps, we will be able to
allow ourselves the luxury of such, pardon the expression, publications."
A condescending nod in the direction of the tombstone of *Say Cheese!*
on the table. "For now there can be no question of this, and that has
to be made unambiguously clear to our comrades." A hand gesture in
the direction of the six.

Two or three of the big liberals brightened at these words. Excellent
proposal! Make clear! Not chop off their heads but simply and severely
make clear to *our comrades*, we won't call them our enemies! Zhuryev,
noticing their delight, shifted his bushy Neanderthal arches.

"And it wouldn't hurt to slap the hands of some of them! Well, we
have to decide this together, comrades! The way the Party teaches."

Covering his eyes with his hand, he peeped at Max Ogorodnikov's
equine face, his drooping moustache and the eyes that showed only
arrogance and scorn. And yet he was such a roly-poly child! Zhuryev
recalled the magnificent party at Old Man Ogorodnikov's on Granov-
sky Street: May 1939, the first steps in Party art. Ah, his mother was a
peach of a woman, slick as a lighter!

Meanwhile the object of this fleeting observation looked over the
lines of defense. Slava German held an empty pipe in his mouth and
grimaced slightly as if his shoes were tight. Georgii, as if at the theater,
listened to everything carefully, showing every reaction on his face,
shaking his head, laughing soundlessly. Alexei Okhotnikov's red beard
moved. Probkin, his hair swinging over his face, was writing down the
opening statements. Drevesny was still staring at the floor.

"I wonder," whispered Ogo loudly, "does Zhuryev believe even a
fraction of what he's saying?"

Drevesny's hand squeezed his knee. "Quiet, Max, you promised!"

"What did I promise?"

"Max, I'm begging you, everything's going all right, don't make it
worse. . . ." Ogo jerked his knee away.

The discussion continued with pretensions to spontaneity, but at the
same time following unwritten rules of rank. The third in national significance here was "poet of the camera" Phesayev. "Well, and what have
they collected in this album, anti-Sovietism, right?" He was not pleased

with the meeting—pulling him away from his art, all these upstarts keeping the People from getting the next masterpiece, and the People's patience was not bottomless!

"The problem lies elsewhere," interjected Phalesin, his colleague at *Moscow Lights*. "I'm reading their manifesto and I can't believe my eyes. 'The thing of art rarely fits into any pigeonhole.' Are they calling our work, that holy and sacred work, a 'thing'?" He spoke in the tones of an old woman upset because her dough has run off, and he resembled both the old woman and the dough. "You mean, I take pictures of our Soviet reality and my work is called a 'thing'? The creations of this great artist"—and he pointed to Phesayev—"you'd also call a 'thing'?"

"Thank you, thank you," nodded Fotii Feklovich, "for your pointed and timely comments. Attempts to photograph the past and the future definitely contain the seeds of bourgeois decadence. Soviet photography is called to deal with today, with our glistening and inspiring moment. However, allow me to digress a bit. Notice, comrades, how one of our guests is carefully recording everything. Apparently a large review is being prepared for certain organs of the press."

Everyone stared at Probkin, who kept scribbling without looking up. Apparently he was a few lines behind the orator and it was only at that sentence that the stenographer realized the first secretary was talking about him. He jumped. "What's the matter, if this isn't allowed, why didn't you warn me?"

"No, no, go on, write," said Fotii Feklovich without dropping his omnipotent scoundrel's smile. "I just wanted to remind us all of one thing. The last time one person kept writing everything down he turned out to be a master spy and a traitor!"

A whisper went through the room—Solzhenitsyn, Solzhenitsyn, the writers had a Solzhenitsyn who wrote everything down. . . .

The meeting floundered at this point and lost its smooth spontaneity. The first secretary did not want to give the floor by simply going down his list, which would reveal the plot, and so he was glad when Glyasny suggested "at least hearing out the compilers, finding out how they came to such a life," even though it spoiled Fotii's plan a bit. "Well," said the first secretary, "I suppose Comrade Ogorodnikov would like to speak?"

Drevesny's dry paw jerked like an electrocuted frog on Ogo's knee. That's what I should say to the honored board, Ogo realized: I should ask them how this normal, proud man, a master of world photography, the bard of a generation, has turned into a jerky frog. Who's frightening Andrei? Not only those whose profession it is, but all of you mindless pigs of socialist realism! You squeal on anyone who doesn't have a snout, you stink at him until he smells, too. Get up, Drevesny, come on, guys, let's get the hell out of here, why should we talk with these bastards?

In principle he could have said all that; he wouldn't have been afraid if it weren't for the album and all the photographers who didn't have to share his lot. The paradox was that without the album, there wouldn't have been this meeting. If they would just judge him alone, if they would get him only for *Splinters*!

"Comrades," Ogorodnikov said, "doesn't this seem blown out of proportion to you?" A spark flashed in Glyasny's eyes, it seemed. "It might look like there's a conspiracy," Ogo continued, "an attempt to subvert the State, but there isn't. We organized our album with a constructive rather than a destructive aim." Andrei Drevesny looked up. Ogo was saying the right thing so far. "We simply wanted to open some windows so that . . . well"—Drevesny cringed, was he going to say "it would stink less?"—"well, to let in more oxygen. . . ."

Oxygen? Fotii Feklovich jumped into the fray, glasses glinting like that Judas Trotsky. "You, Ogorodnikov, must be calling anti-Sovietism oxygen?"

Ogo said nothing, just looked at Drevesny and shrugged.

"Allow me, comrades," said Comrade Shchavski, the eternal "friend of youth," the eternal chairman of the commission on work with young photographers, through whose hands Ogo had passed, and later Alexei Okhotnikov, and more recently Shturmin. "Fotii Feklovich, we shouldn't throw out the baby with the bathwater! Anti-Sovietism? Isn't that too strong a word? Decadence, nihilism, pornography, there's plenty of that. . . ." He seemed to be pushing away *Say Cheese!*, though he couldn't have reached it on the table if he tried. "But 'anti-Sovietism'?"

"Comrade Shchavski, my dear old friend," Fotii Feklovich suddenly

mooed, "just take a look at the artistry of Shuz Zherebyatnikov! A criminal mocking the Exhibit of Economic Achievements!" Fotii waved to
Kunenko, who immediately showed two slides, taken from Shuz's work,
on a small screen.

"Here, this one's called 'Extraterrestrial Campground.'" Taken from
below: a monstrous cast-iron bull with a scrotum that seemed to be
filled with cannonballs, symbolizing the power of Soviet animal hus-
bandry. The graceful columns and gilded statues of the peoples of the
USSR were spread around the periphery; you could clearly make out
the emblem of some Union republic in the background. "If that's not
anti-Sovietism, then Ronald Reagan"—he's really full of Reagan today,
thought Glyasny, and grimaced, feeling his face turn red—"and Alexander Haig are doves of peace!"

Second slide. "And now, comrades, take a look at this, at the defile-
ment of a symbol dear to the Soviet people." On the screen were two
enormous human organisms, male and female, wildly raising or otherwise exposing their attributes, "hammer and sickle," in the famous
sculpture by Mukhina, *Laborer and Kolkhoz Girl*. Shuz had shot it quite
simply, without any tricks, and the stepladder going under the skirt of
the metallic woman looked quite simple, as did the half-drunk worker
on the stepladder with a mop. The caption modestly stated, "Monthly
Cleaning."

"Well, well," said a woman's voice.

"Hooliganism, hooliganism," the men's voices rumbled. "I'd like to
see what Shchavski has to say now!"

"Comrades," said short Shchavski leaping to his feet, "of course it's
hooliganism, vile intellectual libertinism, and subjectively it looks like
an insult to our patriotic feelings. But objectively, comrades, perhaps
I'm wrong, but there really isn't any anti-Soviet intent, is there?"

"You are wrong, dear Shchavski!" said Party photographer Kreselshchikov, as rosy and plump as a baker from a clean German town. "Hooliganism, decadence, nihilism, pornography, all this contradicts the
Leninist aesthetic, and whatever contradicts the Leninist aesthetic is pure
anti-Sovietism. Isn't that so?"

Shchavski pressed his hands to his chest and shook his head guiltily:
You got me, you got me, Kreselshchikov, can't argue with that! Well,

fine and good, Shchavski, nodded some of the other members, we can
see that you do not lack the dialectical approach to reality. Fotii Feklovich winked at Shchavski. Ogo sat down.

"Something's wrong," muttered Drevesny, "it's not right. . . ."

"What's the matter?" Ogo asked Andrei. "You didn't know how
these plenums are directed? You're not familiar with this scenario?"

Julieta Frunina raised her delicate finger majestically, and everyone
shut up: a lady! "I am a soldier," the lady said crisply. "And I am a
woman," she added more softly. "And as a soldier and as a woman I
hate pornography both of the body and the spirit! Everything in
there"—an angry gesture at the album—"is a mockery of our modest
and sweet People, but our People know how to reject corruption!" Just
like Grabochey, she grew angrier with every word and, perhaps because
of a lousy face-lift, even resembled him. They used to say that she did
a pretty good minuet, thought Slava German.

Ogo saw Fotii Feklovich looking at him and at Drevesny, studying
the situation that had arisen between the two friends. Realizing that he
had been caught staring, Fotii Feklovich did not turn away, but instead
made his meaning more clear. "I see that not all of the participants are
happy with this stinking *Cheese!*" he said, directing attention at the
stunned Drevesny. "I'm not surprised. A truly great master like Comrade
Drevesny must surely feel the falseness, the speculation, the unholy conspiracy! He can, through a misguided sense of friendship, find himself
in bad company, but his conscience as an artist will tell him where the
real fault lies. . . ."

Well, thought Ogo, this is where Drevesny will explode. All his hesitation will evaporate, and his noble blood will boil. He'll send them to
hell now, the way he did back in '68! But Andrei Drevesny was catastrophically silent.

Instead, the master from the Russian city of archangels, Alexei
Okhotnikov, blew up with a reddish flame. "Why are you blaming our
Shuz, comrades?! Do you think he sculpted that bull with its scrotum,
or he stuck that ladder up the iron lady's skirt? A discussion on this
level makes you wonder whether these comrades understand photography at all, whether they ever took any pictures themselves."

This one to the gallows, thought the Party's sniper, and gave Comrade Glyasny a meaningful look. I understand, thought the latter. Grabochey is suggesting I put him down on the list. I'm blushing again, what's the matter with me, I'm getting all splotchy again.

"... Photography, comrades, is an art that is perhaps more mysterious than painting. Have you ever thought that perhaps it holds the fire of the universe?" While they were exchanging glances, they did not notice that it was another Cheeser who was now talking—the most pedigreed, whom the motherland had most honored, the bastard. Georgii Chavchavadze stood like a rooster, fussing with his tie and with the matching handkerchief peeking out from his breast pocket like an orchid. "The moment is fleeting, the poet said," continued the Muscovite Georgian. "You open your arms, but it flies past you! Gentlemen, we capture the moment in our mysterious camera obscura. The photographer is a small soldier with a slingshot confronting Chronos. Gentlemen, forgive me, comrades, the artist is always displeased with the world contemporary to him, for he thinks of the ideal world, even if he lives at a royal court. Remember Francisco Goya! Gentlemen, comrades, Pantagruel urinated on Paris and flooded the French holy monuments, but Rabelais was not ostracized! How could we be more backward than the feudal France of five hundred years ago? I call on you to remember the flow of time and the fire of the universe!"

Laureates Zhuryev and Grabochey looked at each other in some amazement. A grenade, thought Grabochey. In Georgii's guts.

"Dear Georgii, my dear man," Fotii Feklovich mooed gently once more. "Do you really think that we do not understand you? Do you really think that eternal themes are alien to us? Your friends are here, while there"—a gesture in what was assumed to be a westerly direction—"there, there is calculation, cold treachery. And you are being dragged there by an experienced enemy!"

Ogo shuddered like a horse. In despair he thought that adrenaline was fighting with fury in his body, and whichever one won, he would be the loser. "Fotii!" he cried softly. "What are you planning for us?"

The first secretary of the Union of Soviet Photographers stared at him brazenly. "Why 'us'?" he asked. "Why are you hiding behind 'us,' Comrade Ogorodnikov? Not all of the group is experienced, like you. You would do better to answer for yourself, Ogorodnikov, and I promise"—the *s* turned into a snake hiss, even the members of the plenum were shocked, Comrade Glyasny felt for his Valium in his pocket—"that everything will be jusssst sssswell with you, Ogorodnikov."

He's giving himself away, thought laureate Grabochey, that shitty Fotik's nerves are shot. We have to finish up. I'll set him in the right direction.

"How many copies have you made?" he asked Ogo in the best tradition of an investigator of 1937: work this one over until he breaks.

In a strange way, Grabochey's voice disappeared in a morass: Ogo missed it. He was shifting his gaze from Fotik's distorted face, which at the moment was almost bursting, to the pale profile of Drevesny, which was almost an indentation. Yet when we were starting out, Ogo mused darkly, it was just the opposite: Fotik was the indentation, and Drevesny was in relief.

"Twelve copies," Okhotnikov responded for Ogo.

"And are they all here?" Grabochey continued asking Ogo, who was not paying any attention to him. Like any meeting that goes on too long, the plenum of the board of the Photographers' Union was lapsing into senility.

"Looks like only one," said Okhotnikov, making a strange loving gesture toward the imperturbable object that lay at the chairman's elbow.

"Are they all in the Soviet Union?" The Stalingrad battalion commander* was losing his patience.

"Comrade Grabochey," Fotii tried to reason with him, "there's no need to ask. One copy was smuggled to New York."

Here at last Ogo, who had been lost in space, shook himself. "And how do you know that?" he asked rudely. "Where do you get your information? Maybe you know about the robbery of Mikhailo Kaledin's studio? Maybe it was those bandits who sent the album to New York?"

"Comrades, comrades," interjected the weary laureate Zhuryev. "This is turning into a detective tale!"

---

*The rumor was that Matvey Grabochey had commanded a covering fire battalion, that is, he had simply destroyed his own people.

"This investigation is indeed in the hands of experts," Probkin giggled.

"Outrageous, outrageous," the board members buzzed, "they're behaving outrageously!"

Fotii's convexity began to deflate under Ogo's eye. Why am I afraid, he thought, why am I still afraid of being found out as Agent Poker? "Are you trying to say, Comrade Ogorodnikov, that no foreigner has seen the album?"

"Foreigners!" Ogo laughed. "Why are you all so afraid of foreigners, comrade photographers? Fotik, do you know how many foreigners there are every day in Moscow? They say up to a hundred thousand." A hundred thousand? What a number! It clearly made an impression on the plenum. So many suspects! "Lots of foreigners saw *Cheese!* We didn't count them. We're not afraid of foreigners, on the contrary, we welcome them. You gabble on about the space era, and the scientific-technological revolution, but you're afraid of everything foreign, like the suspicious priests of Old Rus."

"Your jokes aren't very funny," objected liberal Shchavski. An exchange of looks: Grabochey–Zhuryev, Glyasny–Fotii, Kreselshchikov–Frunina, Phesayev–Phalesin, and unnamed ones in chaotic gliding.

"Well, and now tell us about the opening," Fotii said simply. "Tell the comrades about the provocative gathering you are preparing in downtown Moscow." Probkin, still writing despite the dangerous comparison with Solzhenitsyn, stumbled there.

"It won't be in downtown Moscow," Ogorodnikov said, "it'll be at Sokol Square!"

Now that they'd found Fotii's Achilles' heel, Ogo jabbed it with another vengeful pin. "How do you know about the opening, Fotik? A fine creative organization, no doubt about it!"

"You've ruined everything," whispered Andrei Drevesny barely audibly.

"Comrade Ogorodnikov is denying our creative status." Fotii Feklovich chuckled. "Well, we'll have to make the corresponding conclusions. Here is a draft resolution. 'The plenum of the board of the Moscow Photographic Organization of the Union of Photographers of the USSR, having heard the report of the first secretary F. F. Klezmetsov, has denounced the photo album *Say Cheese!*, instigated by M. P. Ogorodnikov, member of the Union, as being alien to the traditions of Soviet photography, ideologically damaging, and artistically incompetent, and as holding as its main goal the breakup of Soviet photography. The plenum has expressed outrage at Ogorodnikov's provocations, and has called upon the offending members of the Union, for the reasons of the ideological immaturity of those who are part of *Say Cheese!*, to withdraw immediately from the Union.' Who's for the resolution, comrades?"

The document had such convincing shape to it that suddenly everything grew confused. Slava German stood up, hopefully silent until that point, and began waving his pipe about and trying to talk, stuttering. Oh, old comrade, have you nibbled at the dollar bait, too? Fotik feverishly pondered, forgetting that this "old comrade" had once beaten him up for being a stoolie. "Pigs" was the first word of the former genius German, who despite all his lapses, failures, drunken disorderliness, was still considered a "real photographer" by everyone in that so-called Union. "Wh-wh-why is Og-og-ogorodnikov the only one m-m-mentioned? What are we—sheep? I demand that I be included in the provocative activities! I worked as much as Ogo! I deserve your outrage, comrades! I'm immature, ideologically immature!"

In the general astonishment that followed this bitter announcement, Georgii, Probkin, and Alexei Okhotnikov joined in German's demand, and Alexei even grumbled, "No redheads excluded!"

The astonishment grew. The draft of the resolution was falling apart. The secretariat did not know how to deal with a situation in which the subject was not asking for a lighter slap, but demanding a harder one. Drevesny suggested a way out. He simply walked out, without a word.

"The secretariat is not keeping anyone," first secretarial assistant Kunenko quickly announced.

"We won't leave until you add us to your paper," Alexei announced. Georgii uttered his support.

Probkin was writing on his pad: "Pause, pause, pause."

The Party always comes to the rescue in moments of bewilderment, and thus the eyes of the secretaries and the board members involuntarily turned to Comrade Glyasny, representative of the center. His neurasthe-

nia expressed itself as spots on his forehead and nose. He had to comply
with the ritual. He had to cough. Oh, Slava, Slava, we were so young
when we partied in Georgia. . . .

"The comrades, apparently, do not realize the severity of their situation," Glyasny said. "However, we cannot disregard their words. I think
that the secretariat must rework the draft of the resolution, and the vote
will be held at our next meeting."

"Wise," squeaked Shchavski.

He's not one of us, thought Grabochey about Glyasny.

Dick-head, thought Zhuryev, Glyasny's not even pressing the point.

What dogshit, was the general hidden consensus.

I think I made the wrong suggestion, thought Glyasny, putting a
copy of the minutes into his briefcase. But I'm going home. And tomorrow, I leave on vacation, to Kislovodsk, and there—not a drop!

First Secretary Fotii Feklovich closed the meeting with a twisted face
and told the Cheesers they would get the resolution by mail. "But if the
bourgeois press learns of today's discussion or if the provocative opening takes place, you'll be sorry."

"What will happen?" asked Probkin.

"Keep your heads!"

Probkin and Okhotnikov immediately put their hands behind their
necks. "Where are the guards?"

"What guards?"

"You just said, Fotii Feklovich, that you wanted our heads to be
kept—so where are the guards?"

"You fools, your tomfoolery will bring you to a sorry end!"

The board members and the Cheesers walked along the mezzanine
and went down into the restaurant. "Fuck," said Ogo loudly.

"Whom are you addressing?" Phesayev demanded, stressing the *o*'s,
even though there was only one round letter in the whole sentence.

"You guessed it" was the reply.

6

ODDLY ENOUGH, THE viciousness of the plenum flew right out of Ogorodnikov's head. Probkin dropped him off on Smolenskaya Street, and

now he was walking alone down Arbat to his alley. It was a classic Moscow night, which in itself was worth his return from Europe. Tons of snow, a light blizzard wind, about 20 degrees Fahrenheit, charming female faces flitting by—Arbat is rich in them—and suddenly something shifted in the sky and the moonlight illuminated a stalactite hanging down from the cornice of the Vakhtangov Theater. If we had a normal life, the Arbat would be what the Village is in New York— stylish boutiques, jazz clubs, discos, all-night bookstores, galleries, and cafés. People would bustle here all night, disregarding the drop in temperature and forgetting about bolshevism.

On the corner of Starokonyushenny Alley, in the middle of the wind-swept street, there was a snowbank from which protruded a telephone booth. Ogo pushed his way in and called the studio.

"Where are you, love?" cried Anastasia. "I'm packing a parcel for you for a prison cellar, and you, sir . . ."

"And I am strolling around. There are no authorities in the city tonight, and I'm taking advantage."

"You have a guest waiting for you."

"Who? Comrade Drevesny can wait." He got out of the snowbank, all the vileness of the night returned, all the beauty evaporated. The plenum, the gathering of those monsters, wasn't enough, he still had to talk with his craven comrade.

Drevesny was waiting for him outside the studio on Khlebny Alley, strolling between snowbanks, hands behind his back, as if in a museum.

"Your guardians just drove by," he said, nodding toward the end of the street, where a lone Volga floated by, as if on waves.

"That's just a taxi, Andrei."

"If you say so. Tell me, are you repulsed talking to a traitor?"

"Come on, old man!"

"I'm sure you must consider me a traitor."

"I don't consider you anything."

"You looked at me as if I were a traitor!" shouted Drevesny, feebly waving his hand.

Now I'll have to spend half the night consoling him, thought Ogo. "Come on, Andrei, no one thinks you're a traitor, it was your spleen, your nerves.... You'd be a traitor if you were following their orders when you held us back, but you yourself wanted to go slow, it was your own idea to play at being a coward, right?"

Drevesny took off his once fluffy and now balding fur hat and put his head in the wind. "Forgive me, Max, my head is burning, my chest, my ass. I said a lot of nonsense to Anastasia up there, cross it all out, there's no one I feel closer to than you; my sister is an indifferent doll, my children are strangers, Polina is a joke! Max, Bluzhzhaezhzhin tricked me, the old bastard. He told me that there was a decision to go easy if we went slow."

Of all the people to trust—Bluzhzhaezhzhin! "He didn't offer you a glass of Stalin's wine, did he?"

"Max, I trusted him because I am a coward! Not because he promised me a trip to America! I don't need anything but peace and quiet." Drevesny suddenly fell to his knees in the snow and crossed himself. "Believe me, I can't take any more. You have stronger nerves, Ogo...."

"Ha, ha," said Ogorodnikov.

"All right, but they're not as shitty as mine. You know, I can feel old age coming on, my genes are exhausted, they killed us in the civil war and in nineteen thirty-seven half the family was shot—grandfather, Uncle Shura, all the relatives of Irkutsk, they destroyed Father's life, terrified my mother, and I had a terrible inferiority complex as a child because of them. It's easier for you, Ogo, you're ..."

"Don't talk to me about that," said Ogorodnikov. "I know." Everyone in Moscow knew that the evil of 1937 was Ogo's sore spot, even though no one in his family had been imprisoned or killed and there were no executioners—obvious ones, anyway—recruited from among his kin. Everyone knew that Ogo went nuts on the subject of the year of his birth and even tried to avoid the topic around him.

"No, forgive me, I have to say this," Drevesny insisted. "You, Ogo, come from the victors, from their camp, even though you're rebelling. You were proud of your parents as a child, but I trembled whenever anyone asked about my father. You despise the reds, but I hate and fear them. That's what your photos always lacked, Ogo—my fear, my complexes! When success came, I thought I had overcome my childhood, that I was your equal in the New Wave and we were Europe's favorites, but now I'm a wreck, all I want to do is hide, I can't take it...."

"When did they come to see you?" Ogorodnikov asked.

"Who?" Drevesny shuddered.

"The PhIDs. A bastard in his sixties and a young one, a general and a captain. They came to scare me back in May. Them?"

"They didn't come to me," barked Drevesny. He stood stunned for a bit, and then burst out angrily, "What does it matter if they came or not?"

"I'm cold," said Ogorodnikov, "let's go up to the studio. I have a bottle of Pliski in my pocket; Musya and Anya from Rosfoto gave it to me as a sign of support."

"No, I won't go up, I talked up a lot of garbage with Anastasia. Why don't you just give me a sip, Ogosha!" They opened the bottle. Disgusting. But drinking a bottle in the middle of the night under a murky streetlight, performing a "trumpet duet," brought them back to the old days and got rid of the shameful present.

"Listen, Ogoshka, let's stick together." But the present could not be banished for long. "You know, I think the authorities are planning something really evil against us."

"Stop torturing yourself, don't exaggerate, at the worst they'll take it out on me, throw me out of the Union, I can't stand it there anyway, I've decided to go the whole dissident route."

"But there are people behind you, we're behind you, we can't abandon you, that would be betrayal, we have to be clever, and you have to be clever with us. Which is what I'm doing! Let's give up the opening, Ogo! What the fuck do we need to show off like that?"

"It's a game, understand, Andrei, I'm tired of only playing their games, I'd like to play just once to my own taste, as if they didn't exist, after all it's not against them, just without them, and you don't have to go along."

"How can I not go along, I have to go along, Ogosha, that's why I'm asking you to drop it...."

"There," said Ogorodnikov. "This time they have come, the night patrol of Khlebny Alley."

A car with four men turned the corner. Usually it parked right under the streetlight where the friends were standing. Holding them in its headlights, the car seemed to stumble, then began backing up in order to park betwen snowbanks on the other side. Drevesny hurriedly finished up the Pliski.

"An interesting theme," said Ogorodnikov, "don't you think? A car in the snow, like the icebreaker in the ice.... Do you have your camera, baby?"

Drevesny showed his tiny Minolta in the palm of his hand.

"Good enough! Take a few shots from here, and I'll go closer." They began taking pictures with the two cameras of the alley covered with the snow, the streetlight, each other, the car with the antenna, and the four mugs inside. The agents, for lack of other instructions, opened four copies of *Word of Honor* in front of their noses. What am I going to do with myself? thought Andrei Drevesny in desperation.

7

HUGE SOKOL SQUARE in Moscow in the prickling thick of day: everywhere could be seen the consequences of the cult of personality, totally unshakable, mighty fourteen-story slabs, the so-called generals' houses. The signs on the first floors proclaimed "Movies," "Dining Room," "Repairs," "Gastronome," that is, left citizens no hope at all. And still, sometimes Moscow could amaze you.

You'd think the Bolsheviks would have figured out a way to keep the people from getting flashy, to build "functional" cities like the ones depicted in schoolbooks, but still they couldn't quite handle Muscovites. There was a little church ringing its bells between the generals' houses, an entrance to a theater that looked more like the entrance to a boiler room where, in the so-called theater, a daring troupe was putting on an avant-garde production of Shostakovich's opera *The Nose.* And farther along, by the way, in a Stalin-era bulging building, was the pelmeni cafeteria, the Kontinent.

So, Sokol Square had moved rather far from its original Stalinism, particularly since the role of Stalin was now being played by not-Stalin. With the dispassion of the unsuccessful but harsh father, a huge flat face from the façade of the anti-Stalinist skyscraper Hydroproject regarded the family of peoples. WHEREVER THE PARTY IS, THERE IS SUCCESS AND VICTORY, said the face in fifty-pound aluminum letters. "After the restoration of capitalism Mercedes-Benz will set up its branch there," the sly folk often said, laughing, "the letters will be used to advertise useful products, and the portraits, well, they'll go to make foot wrappings."

What are you trying to say, the reader will exclaim at this point, that the people are so unbridled on Sokol Square? Yes, they are, we will maintain, that's what the people are like exactly, or at least, this representative of the people, a big man with gray, shoulder-length curls, in a leather coat and fur boots, exhaling clouds of cigarette smoke and frosty steam.

Shuz got into Ogorodnikov's Volga and the windows fogged up. "Hi, Ogo! Hi, Anastasia! Are our tanks ready?" The first news he reported was not inspiring. "The academicians are fuck-ups!"

"Just a minute," cried an outraged representative of academic circles, Anastasia, "the two words don't go together, sir! The first precludes the second!"

"But not the other way around," countered her husband.

"Do you want details, asshole?" said Shuz. "Yesterday at the party of the singer Tarakanova, all our academicians were present, and they all chickened out. The father of the Soviet demolition bomb of the Sausenpay type, Academician Pontekorpulos, shed a tear and said that if he went to the Kontinent, he would never see his Greece again, the birthplace of modern civilization. Academician Mindal said that he was definitely coming in the sense that he would definitely come if he didn't have to be at that very hour in the city of Chelyabinsk Two, where a computer made of Japanese tape-recorder parts had broken down and which controlled Soviet earth satellites, on which depended the fate of peace in the world. Academicians Blevantovich, Rubro, and Ov slipped out while I shook the hell out of Mindal and Pontekorpulos.

"Next—"

"Huh?" asked Ogorodnikov.

"I'm speaking English, dummy. The directors aren't coming either. The chief from Solyanka was called into Demenny, he was pushed around. There's panic at the Souchastnik Theater, too. They scared off Bebka, and Bubka, and Senka, and Fenka, and Fadei-Fucker-Olegovich, warning them that they wouldn't get their Honored Artist of the Federation for May first this year.

"It's better with the writers," continued Shuz. "All the Metropolers will be here, that bunch doesn't have anything to lose."

"Well, all right," Ogo said, "will the Moscow regiment come out? Doesn't the marine unit vacillate? So we all meet near the pelmeni place, shoot into the air like Decembrists and shout: Constantine! Constantine!* And what about Semyon, the café director?"

"He's ready with his bayonet," Shuz declared. "He's just nuts about photographs. He's in seventh heaven that such famous people are gathering in his crummy joint."

"You mean he doesn't know?" asked Anastasia.

"What's there to know?"

Ogorodnikov put his hand on a boundless leather shoulder. "Listen, School-University-Zenith Artemievich, in all likelihood they're unfolding something very serious against us. Maybe we should just hightail it out of here? Why involve innocent people?"

"Are you crazy, Ogo? Cancel a great blast like that? Be cowards in public? Never! Right on! Disinfect the scar! A scandal will just help Semyon anyway: he'll get out of here to Brooklyn that much sooner, he has a brother there with a grocery store...."

They got out of the car. Ogo checked the locks and looked through the window at the yellow light of the burglar alarm. If anyone tried to break in, the car would bray like a crazed donkey. The three of them were standing on the edge of the north shore of the square.

"Well, gentlemen," said Shuz, "what do we have on the battlefield?" The battlefield was very wide and was crisscrossed by a stream of almost every form of Moscow transportation. On the opposite shore, the Kon-

---

*In mentioning the Moscow regiment and the Imperial Marines Unit, Ogo mockingly alludes to the Decembrist Uprising of 1825, when the rebellious troops shouted, "Down with Tsar Nicholas! Throne to the great Duke Constantine! Constantine! Constantine!" Extending this metaphor, we may imagine the Cheesers' demands: "Mikhail! Mikhail!"

tinent was barely visible, beyond the chaotic conglomeration of trolley lines. There were three militia vans nearby, and a Black Maria van just in case, and the Soldiers of the Invisible Front.

"Look, they're on walkie-talkies, ready for battle."

"My eyes refuse to believe this shame," muttered Ogorodnikov.

"Great," Shuz said, slapping his mittens together, "we've stirred up the hornet's nest."

Anastasia was silent, pressing her cheek against Ogo's orange jacket.

The still-cold blueness surrounded them. A white Mercedes pulled up and parked, showing foreign-correspondent plates. It was none other than Harrison Rosborn, *New York Ways* reporter.

"Max," he exclaimed joyously. "I just got back and here I am, and I bump into you first thing! Success! Where's this Kontinent and is that supposed to be an allusion to the Paris journal? Ha-ha, I see I'm not the only one from the imperialist press!"

The appearance of the excited American brought a sense of calm to the Cheesers: Well, so we'll have the event, let's go, we do our shtick as disturbers of the peace, the world press is behind us, gentlemen, it was worked out a long time ago.

The world press wasn't napping. Besides Rosborn's Mercedes the dissidents could see, on the other side of the square, the Italian's yellow VW, the Volvo of the omnipresent Danes, and even the Hispano-Suiza of the indolent and mighty Brazilians. The more experienced, though young jackals of the pen and urban partisans Frank, Luke, and David preferred to arrive at the event without cars and were cheerfully coming out of the metro to the underground passage.

"And there's NBC." Rosborn laughed. The minibus of the macro-network was casually parking between two militia cars at the parking lot right in front of the pelmeni house.

"I'd love not to go," Maxim whispered to Nastya.

"No, you have to go." She sighed.

Rosborn turned his rosy cheek over his tweed shoulder as he walked. "Lots of people in New York send their best, Max. I got mixed up, there were so many. Margie Young, you know her?"

"I'm not sure," muttered Ogo.

"She called at the request of Doug Semigorsky, and her message was mysterious. Let me look at my shorthand...."

His notebook revealed the strange phrase "Splinters are doing well." "I don't know what that means."

"Thanks, Harrison, I don't either," Ogo said. "Just what I needed," he whispered to Nastya. "*Splinters* is coming out."

There was a sign on the door of the Kontinent: CLOSED FOR SANITARY WORK. Two smirking thugs in white coats were visible through the murky glass; between them the white face of photofanatic Semyon, looking as if he had a jewel in his mouth and was afraid to swallow it. The reporters knocked politely on the glass. Just one question! Alexei Okhotnikov, Misha Shapiro, and Venechka Probkin got out of the trolleybus and headed straight for the café, each carrying a copy of the album. An invited sax player showed up. Two young beauties came over, guests of the absent Drevesny, and a few gawkers stopped. Ogo's group finished crossing the square.

"Come on, come on, citizens, clear the sidewalk," said a militia sergeant.

"What's going on here?" a gawker asked.

"We're supposed to have a special dinner here," Alexei explained, "and they've set up a sanitary day instead."

"Disgusting," the gawker said ardently.

"They took our advance and now they're tricking us!" shouted Probkin, and crouching, shouted, "Open up!"

More Cheesers, guests, and gawkers arrived. Shturmin in his top hat headed the conceptualist group. Georgii demonstrated a set of impressive medals in the opening of his shawl-collared fur coat.

"Are you having a banquet to celebrate a dissertation, guys?" asked a gawker.

"Higher than that," said Shuz, "we're celebrating a State Prize."

"They're really crazy," an old woman opined.

"Who, Auntie?"

"Everyone!"

Several burly men with "people's volunteer" armbands began scattering the crowd.

"Move along, citizens, they're going to start disinfection here. . . ."

"What disinfection?" Shuz said, shouldering his way toward the door. "I called an hour ago and there was no disinfection!"

Two volunteers began moving him aside carefully. "What, you need to go more than the rest, fellow?" One of the volunteers dealt with the gawkers. "Go home, citizens, can't you see what's happening? There are foreign journalists!" The public moved along at the sound of those unpleasant words, but new people came over. Maxim saw a volunteer observing him closely and whispering with a militiaman. A car with a blue light on its roof drove by slowly. The windows of the car were open and several mugs looked over the crowd in front of the Kontinent. One of them mumbled into a walkie-talkie. Cameras were clicking all over the place, but it was hard to tell to whom they belonged—the PhIDs, the reporters, or the photographers.

"Nice atmosphere," Harrison Rosborn said. "Reminds me of the Bulldozer Exhibition. I thought nothing like that could happen again in Moscow." Of all the foreign journalists, this Californian was the expert on the city's art underground; this was his third term in the country, and he spoke Russian almost without an accent.

There were no bulldozers, but tow vans with metal brushes appeared on the sidewalk. They had to scrape clean the concrete right in front of the Kontinent: no way out, Moscow was a model communist city.

"Hey, we have to save Shuz," said Slava German.

Two volunteers and a militiaman had him up against a lamppost: "What's the matter with you, you scoundrel, do you want to get disinfected?" Men in black coats with karakul collars came over to the TV crew. "No pictures!"

"Well, Max, you have to end this," Nastya said.

"Why me?" Ogo shrugged.

"Max, stop fooling around, everyone is waiting for you, you're in charge!"

The reporters came over. "Is the opening off?"

Ogo shrugged again. "Why don't we all go to my studio on Khlebny, we'll have the opening there, I guess—" He said it reluctantly, casually, as if the whole thing wasn't worth it. Later he berated himself: Why did I pretend, why did I try to fool myself, why can't I accept the whole responsibility? It's not simple cowardice, but if it's not cowardice, what is it?

Anyway, the episode unfolded after the invitation to Ogo's studio. The Cheesers couldn't break down the doors of the Kontinent, after all, that's just what the gorillas were waiting for, they'd put them in Butyrki Prison for fifteen days or send them out of Moscow for "malicious hooliganism." But going to Ogo's studio wasn't convenient. And it was silly to go to Alexei's coop—why let the PhIDs tape everything?—so Cheeser Tsuker invited everyone to his place.

"I won't go," Shuz announced. "I won't go until I get what we've paid for. Here's the list: six cases of Massandra champagne, two kilos of black caviar, twelve kilos of rolls, cognac ..."

"You'll get it after the disinfection, this evening," said the heretofore silent observer, the unrecognized Major Krost.

"Fuck you!" Shuz countered. "We'll have to throw out the stuff after your stink bombs. I'll go to jail if I don't get what we paid for."

"You'll have time for jail," promised the unrecognized Major Krost, and gave orders to bring the paid-for products from the café according to the list. The doors were opened, and Semyon ran out, eyes bulging, and ran his finger across his throat.

It was decided that everyone get to Tsuker's as best he could, while Alexei and Shturmin would stay outside the Kontinent, to give latecomers directions to the elegant, playful opening of the first independent Moscow photography album, *Say Cheese!*

With cases on their shoulders and packages in their arms, Ogo's group went back across the extremely wide square. The Volga and Mercedes were where they left them, but there was something strange and similar in those two not-very-similar cars—they were both sagging on their rear left wheels!

"Oh, how unpleasant," Rosborn said, slapping his sides, "the comrades are back to their old tricks!"

"What's the matter?" Nastya gasped.

"The bastards punctured the tires!" howled Ogorodnikov, as if the prospect of changing tires in the cold was the final, explosive factor. People walked past in silence. In the meantime all along the square foreign correspondents and the Cheesers were pulling out their jacks:

all the cars had flat left rear tires, as if the front right wheels had done a black deed.

8

THEY MANAGED TO change tires, got in, and arrived at Tsuker's. The apartment wasn't big enough for all the guests, but the neighbors on the landing were freethinkers, refuseniks, former mathematicians, and now floor polishers at the Zarya company. So the whole landing partied, as well as two flights of stairs. A line formed to see the album, as if in a mausoleum. Precinct Captain Prokhorchuk, sent by the PhIDs, appeared. He was given a glass of vodka and a bottle of gin for his pocket. People kept coming from Sokol Square. Everyone congratulated everyone else.

"Congratulations, congratulations!" For what? "The holiday, gentlemen, the publication of the free Russian album!"

Suddenly an upsetting phone call: Alexei and Shturmin had been arrested at the Kontinent and brought to the twelfth-precinct house. Now they were being interrogated, and the police were trying to frame them with attempted bank robbery.

Shuz called the twelfth precinct. "Hello," he said in a military-naval commander's baritone, "I'm calling from the photo group New Focus. Executive Secretary Zherebyatnikov. With whom am I speaking? . . . Please, Major. You are holding our people illegally. Come on, let's not raise our voices! Bank robbery? Fine. In that case, please speak with Mr. Rosborn, correspondent of *The New York Ways*. He's writing a story on fighting crime in Moscow. Mr. Rosborn, Militia Major Setanykh on the line!"

"Welcome," said Harrison, for he knew what to say in these situations. "In the final analysis, would you have any objections in the direction of a small interview?" The major hung up in a panic. An hour later the "bank robbers" arrived by taxi: they were released after signing a promise not to leave the city.

In the meanwhile Tsuker's neighbor Bob Wainer was terrific. He offered to vulcanize the punctured inner tubes of the victims of the ideological struggle of two worlds. The newer foreigners wondered, Why vulcanize that garbage, why not just throw it out? The more experienced ones, including Harrison Rosborn, suggested: Listen to the wise man, everything automotive is in short supply! Bob Wainer, of course, had a shed in the yard and all the tools, and the work went fast until they got to Ogorodnikov's tube. Something rattled inside. Bob went upstairs to the "betweenusnik," as he started calling the opening of the banned album.

"Hey, pal, there's something rattling inside. I can feel it. I think it's a knife." In the presence of the world press they pulled out a sharp knife-blade, 15 centimeters long, broken off at the hilt. No one but Ogorodnikov had been so honored.

9

THE NEXT MORNING Anastasia pulled out a pile of letters from the mailbox. The envelopes were festive, with drawings: Artillery Day, Tank Day, AA Forces Day, Air Force Day, Soviet Militia Day, Border Guard Day.... "Well, here you go, Ogosha, you keep complaining that our mail is intercepted. Look how many greetings we've gotten!"

They opened the first letter. On a page torn from a copybook a childish scrawl:

> To human rights activist M. P. Ogorodnikov. Three years ago I was arrested attempting to cross the USSR state border in order to pass a state secret of the unjust USSR to US intelligence services. The result was placement in a psychiatric hospital in the city of Blagoveshchensk, from which I, K. N. Vladimirov, born in 1950, escaped to Astrakhan, where I have been living without income at my wife's home at: 5, Kalinin Street, apt. 3. I know about you from foreign radio broadcasts, and I ask you to help me get in touch with centers of struggle to throw over the CPSU so that I can get financial aid.

How nice! Ogo scratched his head. They opened another envelope:

Comrade O. Urgently send us 1,500 rubles from your funds. We
the workers of Podmoskovye, inspired by foreign radio broadcasts,
have decided to lead an unending struggle against Soviet
warmongers. . . .

"This one's for you, Nastya, you see, they haven't forgotten you." It
was in the same hand:

Prostitute Anastasia: Everyone knows that you sleep with Andrei
Drevesny, and your quote unquote legal spouse is constantly at the VD
clinic. Don't shame the happy Soviet family, why don't you go to Israel
where you belong with the other traitors of the homeland. . . .

They had read three letters, and there were at least another dozen.

"Notice the postmark, madame. There's only one. It's not clear where
they're from, that's a secret of the cold war. I'm going to the post office
and demand an answer, the bastards can't think that we'll keep quiet."

"Stop it, Ogosha, don't start up!"

At the post office he spread all the letters out in a fan before the
supervisor. The poor woman looked at him in holy terror.

"This is a strange thing," Ogorodnikov said. "Above you is a quote
from Lenin: SOCIALISM WITHOUT MAIL, TELEGRAMS, AND MACHINES IS JUST
A PHONY PHRASE, but people find phony stuff in their mailboxes. This
means that the post office is not part of socialism, right? I'm asking you,
Comrade Supervisor, to make sure that this kind of dispatch isn't
repeated, otherwise I will appeal to the International Mail Union, and
they will be talking about you on the radio."

The mention of the radio this time was apropos, for when he got
home, he found his Anastasia with a transistor. She was lying on the
rug, twisting the knobs of the treacherous instrument. The phone, a
steaming mug of coffee, and a pile of magazines were next to her. A
cozy sight, he thought from the doorway. Now I pull off her jeans
and . . .

"Bruce Pollack is giving an interview!" she shouted, and frivolous
thoughts vanished from the defender of international postal regulations.
It turned out that no sooner had Ogo gone to the post office than all

the Cheesers started calling and even Alexei Okhotnikov dropped by, stuck his beard in the door, and announced:

"The Voice just said that there will be a report from Soho in New York. The opening of the independent Moscow photo album *Say Cheese!* in the Gallery New York-Paris-Sankt Peterburg. Interview with gallery owner Bruce Pollack and also with the outstanding Russian photographer Alik Konsky. Tune in, and I'll go tell the others. It looks like we're all going to get it, Nastya. So long!"

It had been a long-standing joke in Moscow that Ogo's nest was in a "bulletproof zone": There were jammers everywhere, you had to practically climb the walls to get some information, but all the radios at Ogo's came in loud and clear, as if they were broadcasting from around the corner.

"They're going to have to build a special jammer just for you, fucker," Shuz had warned.

It looked as if they had—nothing but satanic howling all along the bands. We used to listen in the kitchen, and now we're in the study, he realized. They took the transistor to the kitchen, where well-being miraculously returned, as if there had never been any jammers in the world. The Voice of America started its program from Soho. Ogo heard the hum of spectators and seemed to see what he had left just a month ago, the New York art crowd with its streams of smoke above the lumpy surface.

"We are present at a unique event in Soho," said a female voice, whose intonations revealed a recent emigration. "Photographers and lovers of photography literature gathered at the New York-Paris-Sankt Peterburg Gallery to celebrate the publication in Moscow of the photo album *Say Cheese!* by the New Focus group, independent of the official Photographers' Union. To the astonishment of everyone present—and I might say that all of photographic New York is here—the gallery owner, the famous collector and lawyer Bruce Pollack, has one of the few copies of the original edition. Mr. Pollack was also kind enough to agree to answer a few questions in this festive bustle. Tell us, Bruce, can you explain how this miracle happened—the album appearing almost simultaneously in Moscow and in New York?"

Ogo heard Bruce, in his best manner: "First of all . . . great privilege

... let me express my admiration. ..." Finally, the answer to the reporter's question crystallized: "Outstanding works of art cannot be kept
within national borders." Ogo thought that Bruce was at the moment
rubbing his hands together with furious joy.

Then the correspondent gasped with delight. "What luck! Douglas
Semigorsky, president of Pharaoh Publishers, is coming this way! Mr.
Semigorsky, the Voice of America is broadcasting on today's event for
its listeners in the Soviet Union. Would you be so kind. ..?"

"I will," said Corduroy Doug. I wonder, thought Ogo, if that secretary, the young talent ... I've forgotten her name again, that's not good
... I've told myself over and over—remember the names of secretaries.
I wonder if she's on hand with him as usual? "Deeply, deeply
impressed," Semigorsky hummed on. "No doubt, lovers of photography
in the United States will be deeply impressed by this unique collection
as a demonstration of the creative potential of Russia. Of course, our
publishing house intends to publish *Say Cheese!* in a large edition."

Once more the background noise of the opening, with a loud deep
voice proclaiming, "Why, it's you!" Then the reporter started gabbing
again.

"This just in, a teletype bulletin from UPI in Moscow. The opening
of *Say Cheese!* in Moscow was broken up by the militia and agents of
the State Photo Inspection Department in civilian dress, and the café
Kontinent shut down under the pretext of disinfection. I think this is a
repeat of the infamous Bulldozer Exhibition of 1974.... Nevertheless,
the opening in Soho continues. Discussions, meetings, interviews....
Metromedia Television comes here tonight. Right now they are inter-
viewing the famous photographer Alik Konsky, who here is called the
'greatest of the currently living ones.' I've managed to bring my tape
recorder closer. I'll try to give you Konsky's opinions. Please forgive the
sound quality and the spontaneity of translation."

"I can't help but be surprised. ..." Konsky spoke wearily, naturally
scratching his armpit. He keeps working on that difficult turn of phrase,
recalled Ogo. "I can't help be surprised, wondering what brought on
this collection," Konsky was saying. "The compilers are the spoiled darlings of photography, the official opposition at the court, hem-hem,

sorry, of Her Majesty the Party. They had everything in the USSR—
fame, money, what more could they want? ... Probably those people
were motivated by thirst for international fame, I have no other explanation for it...."

I'll punch him in the kisser, grumbled Ogorodnikov, clutching Nastya's shoulder. Next time right in the kisser!

"However," continued Konsky, "right alongside the Moscow stars in
the album, by the way, hem-hem, excuse me, why is it called *Say Raisin!*
in Russian? Why not watermelon? Anyway, there are many new names,
fresh air ... it has to be examined closely ... after the corresponding
work with the new translation techniques ... there might be some real
interest...."

"Masters," explained the reporter, somewhat chagrined, to the listeners in Moscow, "are very demanding of one another, but even more
demanding of themselves. We have been reporting from Soho in New
York at an opening connected to the appearance in Moscow of the
independent photo album *Say Cheese!* This is Semiramida Natalkina."

Almost as soon as the transoceanic noise stopped, Cheesers burst into
the apartment with mouths agape, hair disheveled, shouting in excitement. A half hour later the joint was jumping. They came one at a time,
two at a time, rushing tragically to bid their comrades a final farewell,
but once they got there they cheered up, of course, and now in various
corners of the apartment there resounded seemingly inappropriate
laughter. In the kitchen bottles opened and the refrigerator emptied.

"Things are bad," they told one another.

"Couldn't be worse. We're burning like the Swedes. Worse. ..."

"You should have thought about that before!"

"They'll shove us out of the Union, that's for sure!"

"We're being published by Pharaoh, and then we can forget the
Union...."

"Will it bring us any bread?"

"You bet! My jeans are falling apart, why don't they send us some
jeans...?"

"You see, Ogosha, they all come *here*." Anastasia sighed.

"Inexorable march of events," muttered Ogorodnikov with totally unnatural lightheartedness. He was also excited and laughing because things were bad, and he brooded: I have to expose Konsky! Tell everyone how he tried to torpedo my *Splinters*!

The phone rang again. Silence. "That must be our friend Captain Skanshchin," said Ogo, and shouted into the receiver, "What are you panting for, Captain?" Dial tone. "Well, it's starting." His face sagged and looked ten years older. "Can't get away from them now."

Anastasia hung on his shoulder. "I know a place, Ogosha." The phone rang again.

It was Andrei Drevesny.

"Well, satisfied now? You've done your thing and we have to pay for it."

"What's the matter? What do you mean?" Shocked by the uncontrollable hostility of his old friend, Ogo kept saying, "Are you nuts? What's wrong with you?" long after Andrei had hung up.

A swift blizzard swirled outside the window. The projector from the construction site lit the swaying branches. On one hung a frozen rag, stiffened in a disgusting shape.

"Look," Ogo whispered, nodding at the rag and pointing at it. "A ghost."

"It's just a sheet that fell from someone's balcony," she comforted him. "It's nothing, no symbolism, nothing."

HALF BROTHER

I

N THE MORNING the stupid rag was right before his eyes. He had collapsed into sleep right in the study, among the empty bottles and full ashtrays. Covered with fresh snow, the rag had crinkled up some more and looked like a jackal. The sun was stuck over the construction site like a yolk, and two lazy figures moved along the building. The red smear of a new slogan had been placed across it.

"Tons of butts," Anastasia said at his side in a rather hoarse voice, like a prostitute's. She had started smoking recently and had gotten quite involved in it, and she gathered butts in the mornings and evenings, "just in case," or you might get stuck without a smoke one day, and then what? Ogo was mightily irritated by that, and he shouted: Throw it all out to, to whatsit, that, you know—fuck it. The phone rang. Four legs jerked as one.

"This is impossible. Let's go to church," moaned Ogo, "I really want to go to church."

"Of course," she said, "let's go." But the phone was ringing.

"Still snoozing?" asked the lazy baritone, just right for the morning after.

"October?!"

"January?!"

It can't be long distance, thought Ogorodnikov, Moscow cut off direct dialing a long time ago; if he were calling from abroad, the operator would have come on first.

"Welcome back, October!"

"Congratulate me on leaving." His half brother laughed.

"What's that supposed to mean?"

"I'll explain when I see you."

They agreed to meet that evening at "Mommykins's." The forgotten word annoyed Ogo. Ever since he was a teenager he had called her Mama without any diminutives and sometimes simply Mother, while casual and chic October always called his stepmother Mommykins, which she definitely liked. Strangely, she always tried to maintain "proper relations," as she called them, with her own son, but was quite chummy with her stepson, who was only ten years younger than she, whom she called Ryusha, from the incredible diminutive Oktyab*ryusha*.

"So, at Mommykins's at six," October said.

"But why ... there," Ogo asked sourly, even though he had already agreed.

"I don't believe you." October chuckled. "You mean you've forgotten The Cherry Orchard?"

Back in happy Stalin times, that was their name for their home. Back then there wasn't even a whiff of dissident passion in the huge six-room apartment in the gray building on Mossovet Square, near the theoretical foundations of Moscow's All-Union Institute of Marxism-Leninism, where their mutual father aided the course of history. That historic square had many memories, including the night in 1949 when, in the height of the struggle with cosmopolitanism, the iron balls of the horse of Yuri Dolgorukii, Moscow's founder, were sawed off so that the steed would not be cheap prey thirty years later for a formalist photographer.

2

AT THE APPOINTED hour, Maxim and Anastasia arrived at the square and parked near Aragvi Restaurant. Interesting, Mother has never seen any of my wives, he thought, except for Viktoria, and I think those two are still friends to this day. Crossing the snowy square, they saw a PhID, of course. The same old game—sitting in car, hiding behind newspaper. In the entryway, Ogorodnikov felt as if he were in some old movie.

"This is like an old movie," Anastasia whispered. "Right here, between the columns, there ought to be a portrait of Stalin. Why is there a militiaman here?"

"There was always a militiaman here," Ogorodnikov explained loudly, "protecting the most equal among equals. There are no more most-equals left anymore, but there are a couple of crummy ministers."

"Whom are you visiting, comrades?" the militiaman asked.

"We're here to see the Ogorodnikovs."

"Just a minute." The militiaman picked up the phone, without taking his eyes from them, his gaze imbued with kindly KGBism. "October Petrovich, two interesting young people here for you. . . . Yessir! Please, comrades, it's the fourth floor."

October met them at the door. "I saw you from the window. Who's our boy with, I wondered? I guess you can still find women in Russia, eh?"

"This is my wife, Anastasia."

"Wonderful, that means I can kiss her?"

A pleasant elderly foreigner, thought Anastasia. He led them into the living room and immediately went over to the bar.

"What would you like to drink? There's Mexican tequila with a worm. . . ."

At first glance, October Ogorodnikov looked like an American political science professor of a liberal bent: herringbone tweed jacket, button-down shirt, British wing-tip shoes—everything worn, expensive, comfortable, and clearly beloved. Then you noticed what set him apart from the academic mold—a hint of playboy in his trimmed moustache, the neat part dividing the grayish hair, the ring with a black stone, a black metal watch. In principle, he was still the *stilyaga* of the fifties, despite his active role in the struggle for the triumph of "peace and socialism."

Maxim, looking at him, suddenly felt an emotion from the past, the powerful warm sense of safety and sturdy protection. With the arrival of his brother, all the tension and hassles vanished as if he had returned to the days accompanied by the "Gulf Stream" song. He went over to his brother and embraced the tweed shoulders. There was a large mirror in the bar and they were both reflected in it. Maxim was half a head taller than October. Deep in the living room they could see slender Anastasia, examining the photographs on the wall.

"Too bad you dragged along a chick today." October sighed.

"She's my wife," Maxim said with a smile.

"The intelligence services of both superpowers are confused by your wives," October said. "Were there seven or eight?" He looked into the mirror's depth. Not a bad little thing.

October put the bottle of exotic intoxicant on a small silver tray, its worm visible on the bottom of the bottle, and then had some Chivas Regal and Mumm champagne. Next came nuts, crackers, ice. Everything in October's inimitable Western style, "don't know any other. Too bad, we'll have to put off our serious talk." The "Gulf Stream" fox-trot evaporated. Maxim realized that his meeting with his brother belonged to "these" events and not "those." No need to put it off, no one is closer to me than my Anastasia. Man and wife as one.

In the meantime, she stood by the wall, which was covered with photographs in mahogany frames, stages in the great story of the historic father. One hypnotized her. A group of Bolsheviks, clad in good-quality European clothes, crossing trolley tracks in some German city. The photo was highly professional. You could feel the air of that day; the folds in the clothing stressed the energy of post-lunch motion. One was Lenin and the other—the other was Max, her own Ogo, the young fellow fighter of the wily Ulyanov. In the other pictures she didn't see such a resemblance of the historical father to the son, on the contrary, deepening the history, with every year she found opposite traits, but at the moment of crossing the trolley tracks with cheery émigré tread, the whole Bolshevik squad reminded her of the Cheesers—had they been drinking schnapps? Ilyich, The Great Leader, squinted like a pussycat, as if it were simply April out there and not the April Theses.

October with the tray and Max with the glasses came over. They sat down around a low table. Nastya felt a chill from her brother-in-law.

"Are you going to be in Moscow long?" she asked.

"Mmm," he said.

"What?" she asked.

"In general," he said, and began uncorking the Mumm.

"Why?" she asked.

"What do you mean?" he asked in astonishment.

"It's a rather simple question," she said.

"In general I can't take more than a month in the homeland of social-ism, that's just the way I am, I developed a strange allergy, but now, I'm afraid, I'll have to battle the allergy. It looks as if your beau here has fucked up my career, pussycat."

"What did you say?" Anastasia's eyes bulged.

"I said my career—"

"No, not about your career—"

"I said my career is fucked up—"

"No, you called me a strange name—"

"What's the matter, pussycat?"

"That's it, a strange way of addressing me."

"Strange, you say? Max, do you think 'pussycat' is a strange word?"

"Nothing strange about it," Maxim said. "I'm going to call her that myself now. Well, to our meeting! Bottoms up! And now, October, explain."

What ensued was unimaginable for Anastasia: I never thought when I looked for a gypsy cab that I'd end up in a mess like this! It turned out that October had been called back from what he called his native Washington where he had been living lo these many years—even Max didn't know this—as a representative of the Socialism Press Agency. He received a coded message to take the first plane to Moscow. Of course, he knew that it had to do with his younger half brother's artistic pranks and that his career was now fucked up. His mood was terrible. He even had the thought—we're all friends here—to take his family—turns out he has a family—his wife, Ala, a talented pianist; and his son, Andryu-sha, a little over fourteen—and head for the U.S. State Department to get exposed and ask for shelter. . . .

"I don't understand the jargon," Anastasia said.

"You don't understand it beccause you don't know that you're talk-ing to a general of the KGB, that is, you didn't know it before. But the Americans knew it very well, and worse, our people knew that the Americans knew, and therefore I— Well ... well, in general, the details are unimportant. The important thing is that I was recalled because of Maxim, there are big powers involved here that I don't know about yet, and in general, if Max doesn't drop the game, my cards are beaten, and he won't drop out and he's right, because he's tired of being ashamed all his life. Let's have a drink!"

At that moment Mommykins appeared, enveloped in dark-gray silk. What a woman!

"How am I supposed to understand this, Maxim?"

"Forgive me, Mama, what are you talking about?"

Well well, Anastasia thought, bug-eyed, the broad's covered with treasures! Three rows of pearls, rings on four fingers, priceless earrings!

"What are you doing, Maxim? Your name is constantly on the lips of those filthy anti-Soviet radio stations! You're shaming the name of your father!"

Sometimes, at certain angles, she looks like a young woman, thought Maxim. "Why do you exaggerate, Mama?"

October went over to his stepmother with a snifter. "Shut-upchik, Mommykins! Have some cognac and meet Anastasia."

"Who's this?" Kapitolina Timofeevna, sitting very straight in a straight-backed chair, seemed to just notice Anastasia, who was in a low soft armchair, that is, in a demeaned, nonaristocratic situation. Without waiting for a reply, the mother turned away her proud chin. An obvious attempt to control her sudden tears.

"Mommykins, Mommykins!"

"Ah, Ryusha!"

"Bottoms up, now I'm down!" October laughed gently as he spoke.

It must have been an old joke, thought Maxim, and sure enough, his mother responded to October with a smile. "Ah, Ryusha, it still hurts— my only son!"

Suddenly Maxim got it—they're lovers! They were lovers right under his aging father's nose! Suddenly he saw flashes from the past. You had to be a total idiot, that is, a haughty and self-absorbed youth, not to notice the relationship between your mother and half brother, that is, between stepmother and stepson. Well, of course, it began when October returned from his mysterious school. That's when the Mommykins and Ryusha began. I was eighteen, he was twenty-eight, and she was only thirty-eight and irresistible then. Photos, photos, photos, the dacha, the cutter, the car, the resort, their looks, their longing for each other. . . . Strange, I didn't seem to notice, but I remember a lot. That means—I did notice. . . .

"Oh, boys, I'm so glad that you're both here!" Mommykins said unexpectedly, and shed a tear, but without passion, easily, socially. "Well, and of course, that you are here, too, dear . . . yes, dear Nastya . . . well, come on, let's go to the table! Our Ksyusha went back to the past for us. The famous cabbage pies!"

Dinner was followed by relocation back to the living room for coffee and tea, and then to the sanctum sanctorum, Peter Sevastyanovich's study, where there were more stages of his great story, portraits of people who had made society happy by their presence and had signed pictures to their comrade-in-arms—Koba, Starik, Absolut,* even the "Party's darling," Bukharin, had been brought into the light of day. "Peter Sevastyanych, Nastya, was distinguished by the breadth of his theoretical views, he disliked only the enemies of our Party; and this, dearie, is a Packard, inside which I met the father of your husband, it's gorgeous, isn't it." And then a tête-à-tête, ladies only, the new daughter-in-law was shown a small collection of fur coats: mink, fox, red fox, silver fox, karakul, just for a change, sealskin, you'll laugh, but it's my favorite, and this fur is called kolinsky, everyone has a weakness, girl, and mine is furs, this is French, this is Canadian, and this was simply a present from the furriers of Kazan on one of Peter Sevastyanovich's birthdays, sable; Ryusha says it's the world's best. . . ."

Anastasia was stunned not so much by the furs as by the conversation

*Party noms de guerre for Stalin, Lenin, and "iron woman" Stasova.

that accompanied dinner and the subsequent relocations. "Ryusha,"
who'd had a snortful, carried on. "Do you think I'm ashamed of being
in the KGB, pussycat? Not at all! And why? Because there's the KGB
and there's the KGB! Beg your pardon, as we say in English. You run
around Moscow and think that the KGB is your PhIDs and LIDs and
so on, while, incidentally, we can't stand them, they're our scummiest
departments. . . ."

Anastasia exchanged a look with Maxim. He shrugged. This evening
was also incredibly crazy for him, not only because of October's revelations but because of the discovery of "Ryushka–Mommykins," the
new meaning of the past.

"Well, tell me, honestly, does a state need intelligence services? Intelligence and counterintelligence? Every country needs them, even ours!
No, I'm not ashamed of being in the KGB! I'm not proud of it, but
I'm not ashamed, either. I simply work in that area, understand, Mommykins, Maxie, and you, pussycat? I'm simply a highly qualified professional, got it? My American colleagues respect me, by the way. I can
do anything required of a spy. I can steal, I'm an excellent pickpocket,
at your service. Want a demonstration? Well, Nastya, do you want me
to take off your underpants so that you won't even notice?" He began
bugging Anastasia just to stroll from this wall to that, and he would try
to pick her up and manage to strip off her underpants. She sent him to
hell, laughed, it really was funny to see in the mirror an elderly man
pestering a strolling beauty. Suddenly he handed her her own watch.
"Here you are, from KGB Major General October Ogorodnikov, pickpocket first class!"

"Ryushka, you're impossible." Kapitolina Timofeevna laughed.

"Alas, all that's in the past," October went on, still playacting. "Now
I have fifty agents under me. Some big shot is actually my lackey. Of
course, that's in the past, too." He seemed to sober up and he sighed.
"Everything is collapsing. Well, at my age and in my profession I ought
to get used to it. Oh, Max, it would have been better if you had
defected for good. I swear, better for you and for me. I warned you,
remember?"

The conversation grew more serious. "You shouldn't have come back, Max. The PhIDs really want you. There's a lot of hostility against you, Brother. They won't forgive you *Cheese!* and even less so *Splinters.*"

Anastasia jumped up. "Then you're completely informed of the affair, October Petrovich?"

He smiled condescendingly. "Well, what did you think?" He was pacing the living room now, having tossed off his jacket, rolled up his sleeves, and lit up a huge cigar. "It's worth holding on to Cuba just for these!"

Kapitolina Timofeevna announced that this was her "telephone hour" and went off to her rooms.

"If you were to renounce *Splinters* now," October continued, "the situation wouldn't be hopeless anymore, but you won't renounce it and that's the right thing: enough! There's just one thing I don't understand: why the overreaction, who's running this Stalinist operation? And are they working this hard just for medals and stars?"

"It's that big?" Maxim asked. He had been trying to overcome the emptiness spreading through his bones.

"The scope of the operation, Max, is practically immeasurable. The PhIDs are pushing on the CC, and people lose their heads over any ideological deviation there. Sometimes I think that they're more afraid of some little poet with a guitar than of the American Marines. Maybe they are?"

Maxim forced himself to laugh. "Of course they are. The poets know where the Party's 'life's secret' is hidden."

"Maxim, don't say stupid things!" shouted Kapitolina Timofeevna, walking down the hall with the phone receiver at her pretty ear. An endless cord dragged behind her.

October watched it move with a murky look. A finger up at the ceiling. "They're listening to you. Literally every word is being recorded. The company doesn't mind the expense. Even the rhythm of your copulation with pussycat, if you'll allow me to say so."

"Why are you so frank, October?" Anastasia asked. "Aren't you afraid of being recorded?"

I don't think she likes him, thought Max.

October cast a narrowed eye at her. "A good question, pussycat, however, permit me not to answer it. I can just say that your *Cheese!* is done for!"

"In what sense?" Maxim was also pacing with his brother now. "What do they want from us?"

October shrugged. "Sorry, I don't know."

Repentance? Humiliation? Betrayal? Emigration? What do they want? . . . All right. . . . Maxim burst out loudly, "What do they want from me?"

At that moment they were at separate corners of the big room. They stopped and looked at each other. October did not answer Maxim's question. He shrugged.

"Will they send me up?" Maxim asked in a lower tone.

After a few seconds of silence, October, stressing each word, said, "There are people who do not want that."

3

THE EVENING CULMINATED in Kapitolina Timofeevna's very strange escapades. First she ran in like a fury, bearing in outstretched arms a large oval box of the type in which ladies used to keep hats. "In the bedroom! Accidentally! Turned on the radio! You again, Maxim! What anti-Sovietism! Anti-Sovietism!"

Maxim, trembling with anger, applied himself to the Chivas Regal. "A curious word, ladies and gentlemen, isn't it? The prefix 'anti-' makes it vile, right? However, take away the 'anti-' and instead of loveliness you end up with Sovietism. Even worse!"

October and Anastasia burst out laughing. Kapitolina Timofeevna slammed the box on the table, took off the lid, and revealed a marvelous cake with candied fruit. "Teatime, comrades! Ksyusha, bring the samovar! Tea from a samovar, in our national style!"

"I'm glad that Nastya is one hundred percent Russian," she said over tea, blinked rapidly, twisted her mouth, struggled against tears, gave in, and wept.

"Mommykins, Mommykins!"

"Oh, Ryusha, leave me alone!"

Seeing the guests off, Kapitolina Timofeevna did not look at her son, but made a point of talking with Nastya, demonstrating a newfound intimacy, and at the end astonished everyone—she gave her daughter-in-law one of her three fox coats.

"Well, well," Nastya said outside, "well, well." October came out to see them off, and under the slowly floating snow the three relatives, plus Prince Dolgorukii on his steed, were all alone on the historic square, if you don't count the delicately puffing patrol of PhIDs under the archway or the group of drunken Georgians near their Moscow embassy, the Aragvi Restaurant, or the dozen or so randomly passing pedestrians unworthy of description.

"I'm seeing the minister tomorrow," October said. "Don't expect anything good."

"What would you suggest I do?" Maxim asked.

No advice. They looked into each other's eyes one last time.

"I used to love you," Maxim said.

"Let's go," Nastya tugged at him. "Thanks for a wonderful evening, October," she babbled in a society way. "Now we'll have you to dinner."

"He can't come to us," Maxim explained drunkenly.

"Cool it, cockycock," October recommended drunkenly. "That's the most important. And watch out for stoolies."

"There are no stoolies among my friends!"

"Fifty percent!" October shouted drunkenly, then ran up to a stopped taxi, convinced the driver, and rode off in an unknown direction.

"Well, well," Nastya drawled thoughtfully, "what a coat. I never even dreamt of one like that. We have to find a taxi, too, you're drunk."

"There, Nastya, look at the Sovietism all around us," Maxim muttered, looking around in surprise at the square of his childhood, "there's Sovietism spreading all over the place. . . ."

"October was trying to scare you," she said abruptly. "Did you notice? He was doing a job. Don't you think so?"

"You're so clever, it turns out, Nastya, you're such an experienced dissident, where did you get that fox coat? Mommykins used to look irresistible in that coat, you know. . . ."

BLIZZARD

I

I N MOSCOW PEOPLE thought that Georgii Avtandilovich Chavchavadze was immeasurably rich. Actually he had eight
hundred rubles in the bank, no more. He was a man who used the word
"carouse" instead of "live." He sometimes referred to a breakfast of an
egg and yogurt as a "spree." On the other hand, dinner for thirty, on
which he blew an honorarium for many months' photographic work,
he could easily call a "snack."

In connection with these circumstances, when Georgii Avtandilovich
received his first refusal from an editor, he began thinking about what
to sell—his gold watch, his stereo, his beetle collection (how could you
sell it if it was priceless?); he also began thinking of how to get "work
on the side" and through whom; in other words, he quite calmly prepared for a siege. The rejection was unfounded and formulated with
insulting official bluntness: "Unfortunately we cannot accept your latest
series, since it suffers from obvious ideological and artistic lapses." Just
a week ago what editor would have dared address such nonsense to
Georgii Chavchavadze? No doubt about it: the Secretariat, and therefore
the CC, had sent down directives and blacklists. An honored worker in

the arts of eight autonomous socialist republics was now banned in his homeland! Well, I accept your challenge, kind sirs, and you won't see capitulation from me—enough!

Every publishing house had ladies sympathetic to Georgii Avtandilovich, secretaries and junior editors; they always got chocolate and flowers on March 8, Woman's Day, from "the most elegant photographer in Moscow." Such a lady came to him from the editor. "Everyone's in a panic, no one knows what's happened, the chief wept as he signed the letter, Georgii Avtandilovich, dear man, there are lists sent all over the place, oh, I didn't tell you that, you didn't hear it, oh, it's just terrible!"

Chavchavadze calmed down the lady, opened a bottle of cognac, put on a gypsy record performed by émigré singers, and let the lady spend the night. In the morning, over breakfast, his friend from the Caucasus, Kulan Kaimatov, telephoned. "What are you doing, dear Zhora?"

"You see, I'm carousing with beautiful Ninel." As usual in these circumstances, Chavchavadze's Georgian accent thickened.

"We're on our way, dear Zhora!"

"Who's with you, Kulan?"

"Kugul" was the reply.

Kulan Kaimatov and Kugul Chaliev were considered twins in Soviet photography, even though they were from different republics, one from the plains, the other from the peaks. The ancestors of one prayed to Allah, the other's to a salt-marsh version of Buddha. The ancestors of latter traveled nomadically with a lusty whistle of the whip, while those of the former, naturally, hung peacefully over the cliffs. They were equalized by Soviet rule. It made Kulan and Kugul brothers. Five-year plan after five-year plan passed, and everyone grew accustomed to the fact that if Kulan appeared on a rostrum, Kugul would inevitably show up. Whatever was needed—a declaration of love for our dear Communist Party, a welcome for the foreign friends of our photography, an angry voice of protest against the nuclear cowboys of Washington or Israeli warmongers—Kulan and Kugul were irreplaceable on all these occasions, eloquent as the court poets of the emir of Bukhara, unflagging drinkers, and, most important, national, a living illustration of the enormous successes of Lenin's national policies.

Sometimes, however, the tandem work broke rhythm. Drinking at banquets, one or the other, and sometimes both, began sending curses to him (or them?) who chased their small nations from their land after the war. They recalled the cattle cars in which the *aksakals** of ancient tribes gave up their soul to God; recalled Asia, which was called Central for some reason when it should be Extreme-Horrible-Last; recalled how their Party activists were beaten up by the local, that is, Central Asian, Party activists ... well, and sometimes the cognac-filled throats rang with a question alien to their national self-awareness: Who's to blame?

And here's what "Leninist norms of Party life" means: the Party did not prosecute its loyal soldier-lenses for these private lapses. Much more important for the Party was Kulan and Kugul's public position as well as their art, which never showed any suspicious shadows but always depicted the "profound and pure sources of national life" (F. F. Klez-metsov), a great love for their native land, all those charming *argamaks,†* and all those wise *aksakals* (surrounded by laughing grand-children), and their impressions of abroad, imbued with international solidarity.

Kulan and Kugul did not come empty-handed to see Georgii Avtan-dilovich. They brought as a broad hint sixteen kilos of excellent cheese. "Here, Zhora, greetings from our valleys! People love you there—simple laborers and creative intellectuals alike! And here's a collection of wines from Lake Azo, and here's a dagger and cloak from the folk storyteller Ildar. And here's a verbal invitation from Temryukov himself to visit for as long as you like. You'll be received like a king! There's a rumor, dear Zhora, that you are suffering from base material difficulties. That should not be. An artist of your scope should carouse his entire life without base material worries. Would you like us to raise a question at the Pho-tofund of a nonrefundable grant to you? The maximum—five thousand rubles! Your apartment is a bit cramped, Comrade Chavchavadze. You should get a new one at Atheist Alley. All right? You have to take care of your health, dear man, you have to apply for a dacha, the issue will get a positive response."

* *Aksakal:*   elder
† *Argamak:*   mustang
      indispensable clichés of Soviet Oriental tales.

"Who sent you, friends?" Georgii Avtandilovich inquired.

"Don't worry, pal, we're straight from the top," Kulan and Kugul boasted. "They believe in you there. We don't waste our people. People do strange things, they have very bad moods sometimes, it can happen to anyone. In general, dear Zhora, take your controversial but—we stress—talented works from that Zionist album and come back to your old friends. Let's drink to eternal friendship among all Soviet peoples! The mountains and steppes of our ancestors dictate an eternal bond. As my grandfather used to say, 'Where one nanny goat can slip, a hundred goats can pass easily!'"

"Thank you, Kulan," whispered Kugul, and recalled his grandfather's saying, "A fox laughs at one hunter, but a hundred hunters can take a bear!"

"Thank you, Kugul! Let's drink to wisdom! To the wisdom of glaciers! To space!"

"A good toast!" said Georgii Avtandilovich. "To space! Thank you, Kulan, thank you, Kugul! Let's drink to space! Forget about the rest, the proposals are unacceptable. There were no traitors in the Chavchavadze line. If I accept your gifts, if I accept your proposals, I will not only betray my young friends, I will betray my camera, and the Caucasus will not forgive me!"

Kulan and Kugul, bald heads lowered, tips of their moustaches dragging in their constant cognac, sang a sad song of their own composition, in which the steppe and mountain angsts blended and smeared in a puddle of unending hangover. "Eh," said one of them later, "your works, dear Zhora, have become classics in all the autonomous republics."

"It's a shame to throw out such classic work," said the other, "onto the garbage heap of history! Everything will be banned by the law of class struggle. And your friends won't have much to be happy about, especially, alas, Maxie Ogorodnikov. We'll expel him from the Photographers' Union."

"If you expel Maxim, I'll quit the Union. The law of the mountains!" said Chavchavadze in a very strong Georgian accent, which at the moment formed in his throat very naturally.

"We understand," said Kulan and Kugul. "The law of the mountains and of the Polish People's Republic. It's called 'solidarity.' They invented solidarity at the CIA in order to undermine proletarian solidarity. Farewell, Georgii Avtandilovich."

He watched through the window as they lumbered with their bags to a black Volga. They both had the legs of horsemen. No matter what, they still were redolent of the Caucasus, of the East. Considered a man of the Caucasus all his life, Chavchavadze wasn't one. The Caucasus for him was literary, primarily the world of Lermontov, the madness of socialism had not stuck to it, and even those pathetic alcohol-soaked propagandists did not belong with the ordinary, dreary bastards. On the one hand it's too bad that I'm not a mountain man, herding lambs, say, in the Alazan valley, sitting on a rock, my feet in warm socks and galoshes, planning to live another seventy years that way, but on the other hand, if I weren't a Muscovite, I wouldn't have such a fine appreciation of the Caucasus. Thus thought the old child. The Volga drove off. The exhaust twirled in circles. The cold twisted Moscow's face into a sneer.

2

"SO THAT'S WHAT you're like! This time Max's taste did not betray him."

"Polina Lvovna, would you like an éclair?"

"Am I so old that you must use my patronymic?"

"Not at all. You look wonderful. Tell me, did you ever sleep with Max?"

"Ah, Nastya!"

"No, no, don't misunderstand. It's just an idle question. Well?"

"Nothing special happened."

"No, I wasn't talking about that anymore. The point of your visit?"

Nastya was alone at the studio on Khlebny when the first lady of the Photographers' Union called and introduced herself: Polina Shtein-Klezmetsova. "I need to talk to you alone."

"Come over," Nastya said, "I just happen to be alone."

"What? Go there?" There was astonishment in Polina's voice, as if she had been invited to a brothel, but in less than twenty minutes she was there, "in from the cold," agitated, unkempt, fur coat unbuttoned.

What a pity that I didn't put on my fox coat, thought Nastya. I could have welcomed her, agitated, unkempt, fur coat unbuttoned. They say that in the sixties they called her the Brett Ashley of the burned generation. She was terrific in bed and slept with all and sundry. She probably wants to warn me of danger. Has she heard of some vicious plan? or is this going to be in the style of October Petrovich?

"Well, all right," said Polina, "let's get right down to it. I came here to talk about Andrei."

Nastya didn't realize at first which Andrei she meant. "Andrei Yevgenievich Drevesny," Polina explained. "The point is that because of this outrageous business he is in an ambiguous position."

The January sun beamed down onto the shaggy Macedonian rug. Separate strands of the ladies' hair, as they were sitting next to the beam, turned gold. Two cups of coffee steamed between them. They couldn't manage without cigarettes, and they were smoking, too.

"What outrageous business are you thinking about?" Nastya inquired.

"Well, that album, well, who needs it except . . ." Polina stopped.

"I see, I see." Nastya nodded.

"Damn it," Polina said, stubbing her cigarette in the ashtray, "I'm incredibly nervous, everything's trembling inside. You must understand, Andrei is an exceptional person. He's caught between a rock and a hard place. Suspicion from above and suspicion from below . . ."

"Impressive," Nastya whispered.

Polina did not detect the sarcasm in her voice and poured out what had been upsetting her in the last few days, like a skier with momentum who cannot turn or stop. "Andrei is taking such a colossal risk, and his comrades are spreading rumors behind his back that he's a coward, practically a traitor. He's a man who is . . . not capable of treachery."

"You say that everyone is taking a risk?"

"I didn't say that."

"Well, you had it in mind."

"Yes, everyone is at risk, but Andrei isn't everyone. He's so vulnerable, he torments himself, he's full of doubts, you know, everything a real artist must be. . . . Something must be done, Nastya, he has to be saved! Suspicion from his friends is horrible for him, it could force him into an irrational step, just because he isn't a coward . . . and you . . ."

"Yes, exactly, tell me what I have to do with this," said Anastasia.

The question brought Polina to a halt. She looked at Nastya, her eyes widened, fine eyes, real oceans, she picked up a new cigarette, for smoking had always meant for her not the inhalation of smoke, but a change of pose, a series of poses, which later turned into a cigarette way of life. "They say that you, Nastya, now"—stressed with a modulation of the voice—"have a great influence not only on Max but on all our"— stressed with a pause—"brethren. I know many of them, especially the 'old guard.' " She laughed and waved a beautiful hand at Nastya. "Stop, stop, you're thinking of all those rumors about it. The rumors of my dissoluteness are greatly exaggerated. But I know how a woman can change the mood of the photographic milieu. Andrei . . . must be pulled out." And her breathing was uneven again, the cigarette stubbed, strands of hair falling . . . her hair, alas, was splitting, and her skin, unfortunately, was not in the best shape. "Well, as woman to woman, I'm the mother of his children, and even now I still, you know, I have to do something. . . ."

"Forgive me, Polina, what is it that you want?" Nastya asked. "For Andrei to leave New Focus? But no one's keeping him."

"No," cried Polina. "If he leaves, Moscow will call him a coward, a traitor, and he'll never forgive himself!"

"Then, he should hold on with the rest? Forgive me, but I have to ask leading questions."

"With the rest to the end?"

"Would you like some cognac?"

"No, no, I can't have it, not for a long time now. And he can't stay with the rest. You have to understand, he'll be ground to dust, he's incapable of fighting back, he's no Max. . . ."

"Go on," said Nastya.

"I wanted to say that he doesn't have the Ogorodnikov strength, the decisiveness, the obsession, if you will. He doesn't have your husband's international ties. You, I see, are also a strong person, and you are a couple, while Drevesny is alone. You'll leave with Max, of course, you'll lead a beautiful life, go to, say, the Balearic Islands, but Russian photography will have to continue living in the same conditions, or even worse after all this. . . ."

"Go on, go on," said Nastya.

"What's to continue?" Polina abruptly pushed away the cup, ashtray, and cigarette lighter. The table shuddered under her elbow, and everything on it tinkled with growing anger. "Andrei went down into the heart of a volcano! Dove with scuba gear to the wreck of the Black Prince! Landed on the North Pole! Can't you think about Russian photography once in a while instead of your own affairs? Are we supposed to treasure our only genius, the Pushkin of Russian photography, or not?"

"I think you're in a rush, aren't you, Polina Lvovna?" said Nastya very politely. She gave her the fur coat and helped her collect the things scattered all over the table back into her purse. "Go on, go on, forgive my harshness, but you've got the wrong person."

Polina stamped to the door, where a high heel caught, and she turned to Nastya awkwardly and pathetically bent over, like a beggar. "At least don't tell the gang about our meeting."

What a woman, thought Nastya as she shut the door behind her. Total drama. Alas, I'll never be like that.

3

A HEAVY BLIZZARD began in the cozy byways of old Moscow. Vadim Raskladushkin* wore a three-quarter-length sheepskin coat, a wool cap

---

*Involved in the plot of our artistic-detective story, we are sinning against some of our characters by forgetting them. The reader has every right, say, to rebuke us: What's happened to that nice young Vadim Rask? Having appeared at Okhotnikov's with his briefcase filled with tasty things, having lightheartedly bicycled down the puddles of Atheist Alley, and then having slid down the icy paths of Izmailov Park and therein with his charming buttocks having captivated officer of the intelligence services of the East Vladimir Gavrilovich Skanshchin, having partied in a suspect foreign atmosphere at the house of the super Russian Mikhailo Kaledin, and having danced the samba at the Marxyatnikovs' dacha, that blond man, always dressed in comfortable, handsome, and soft clothing, seemed to vanish. The reader has every right to ask: What is happening to the beginning photographer in enormous Moscow, has he managed to make connections in artistic circles, has he had any success in the professional sphere? Well, basically, it's time for him to flash by again, according to the rules of plot development.

with earflaps, rosy cheeks on a face unburdened either by economic difficulties or by the ideological pressure of all-powerful Marxism. In principle, such a figure should have elicited negative feelings or at least a light gnashing of teeth in passersby, something like, Look at these speculators strolling around while we work; the very sight of Vadim, however, made people's grim eyes light up, as if he were rekindling a pleasant memory, of childhood or youth or of an unheard-of hope— why shouldn't I stroll around like that in a blizzard someday: sheepskin coat, cap, and rosy cheeks?

Vadim Raskladushkin was not alone on Herzen Street on that twilit, blizzardy day moving toward evening. Next to him stumbled a more typical Muscovite; the bottoms of his trousers were raggedy and there were buttons missing from his coat, and his glove, having lost its congenital pairness, existed in the singular. In a word, the typical Muscvoite was Nikita Burenin, former consultant on Germany, Austria, and German-speaking Switzerland, fired from a good state agency on friendship with foreign countries for "lack of vigilance and laziness."

Raskladushkin and Burenin had met for the first time in their lives just an hour earlier at the bar of the House of Journalists on Suvorov Boulevard. Vadim was having a mug of draft beer; for all his positive qualities he had a weakness for that brew, which, however, is not something negative if it stays within bounds. A tall man approached, bent under the weight of the four mugs hooked onto the fingers of his outstretched arms, a frozen smile on his exhausted face, approached. "May I?"

"Please, please, sit down, join me," said Vadim in a tone that maintained, in his opinion, a good Moscow tradition.

A few minutes later, Burenin, bringing his face, which reeked a bit of semidigested food, close to Raskladushkin's, exposed his soul to him in a whisper. "In mmmmy pppast, old mmman, there is something shameful, so vile, that sometimes I can't look at myself in the mirror."

In Vadim Raskladushkin, Nikita Burenin found a noble listener. He told him his shameful story for a whole hour, followed him out of the warm bar, and accompanied him as he walked along Suvorov Boulevard and farther along Herzen in the direction of the Conservatory, to turn onto former Brussov Alley, now Nadezhdina Street. Nikita Burenin,

who after being fired from the friendly department began falling down
in the sediment, did not believe either his ears or his eyes, he trusted
only his tongue. The pleasant young gentleman, who, if not for his nifty
modern outfit, could have been a nineteenth-century country nobleman
who had come to the capital in search of a position commensurate with
his good intentions and exceptional talents, was listening to Nikita's
every word.

The shameful story in brief. In 1957 Nikita Burenin was at the zenith
of his worldly success, a brilliant graduate student in German philology
at Moscow State U, a member of the World Peace Council of Soviet
Youth, and an active member of the International Union of Students
and of the International Festival of Youth and Students—in a word, a
rising star in the new elite of Soviet "internationalists." He had not yet
been to his beloved Germany because it was then run by the "sly fox
Adenauer," as Khrushchev called him, but Nikita was one of the very
first group of post-Stalin students sent for two months to the Sorbonne
as part of an international student exchange. And it was there, alas, in
beautiful Paris, that the shameful story began so marvelously, embody-
ing the Hemingwayesque-Remarquesque dreams of Nikita's generation.

Of course, Colette, Mme. Framboise, was ten years older, the beautiful lady of the Parisian world of journalism. Of course, they didn't
sleep together, in the sense that they preferred each other's embraces to
that of Morpheus, and of course there was onion soup at dawn at Les
Halles and night drives in a purring Ferrari to Deauville and Honfleur,
to the foamy shores of the Atlantic, and those meetings on Montparnasse, oh, those meetings on Montparnasse.... In a word, Nikita
returned to Moscow filled with love for a thirty-five-year-old Parisienne
lioness, filled with incredible energy and incredible new ideas for bringing cultures closer, a new phase of socialism within European
civilization.

Now it was Coletka's (as he called her) turn to visit Moscow, and
she did not make him wait long. At that time Western European intelligentsia was taking delight in discovering a new field of activity for
itself in the East. Yves Montand, and Jean Vilar, and Charles Aznavour
appeared on the stages of Moscow and Leningrad, and they were followed by politicians, journalists, writers, businessmen, and athletes. The

horrible red desert of Russia turned out to be a hospitable and fruitful
field. Thus, Colette arrived in a mink coat and with an amazing miniature tape recorder. Delight and joy!

The Moscow part of Nikita's fiesta began and it ended suddenly
when their taxi crashed into a live-fish delivery van one night outside
the Grand Hotel. Nothing much happened—a broken headlight, a
black eye, everyone was all right—and it wasn't clear why several patrol
cars, the militia, and people in plainclothes appeared so quickly on the
scene. It wasn't clear why they were transported in separate cars to some
crazy place with tile floors and barred windows. Later Nikita was shoved
into a cell where he was stripped, beaten long and hard on the buttocks,
his organs of love mauled; and he was photographed with a flash. On
the other side of the wall came Colette's screams: "Je suis française!
Vous n'avez pas le droit...." In response, gendarmeric laughter.

In the morning Nikita was given his clothes and led into a proper-
looking office where on the wall Lenin read the morning *Pravda,* elic-
iting a burning desire for a cup of good French coffee in the viewer.
The brilliant graduate student was met in the office by two comrades,
whose expression (a smile) let him know immediately who they were.
"How could you, Comrade Burenin, and your girlfriend, French citizen
Colette Framboise, have sunk to such a life? Maybe you learned in the
Sorbonne to abuse alcohol? Easy, easy, we talk now and you listen. You
must know, Burenin, that your mistress Framboise is an agent of Western intelligence services? Now we listen to you and you respond!" As
soon as he began talking, defending his love, a comrade banged his fist
on the table: "You louse! The State spent so much money on you! And
you betray your homeland! With the first whore they managed to hook
you to! An alcoholic! A spy!"

The chat in the office under the morning portrait ended with the
signature of a certain text and the next day the evening paper ran an
article called "The Curiosity of Mme. Framboise." It said that Soviet
people had been and were now interested in the development of friendly
ties with people of goodwill of all foreign countries. "The doors of our
country are flung wide open to those who come to us with open heart
and clean hands. The journalist Colette Framboise was also received in
our country according to the laws of Russian hospitality, but she

responded with black ingratitude. It could not have been otherwise. The progressive public of France has long known Mme. Framboise as a mature agent of the intelligence services of the West, a frenzied anti-Soviet, libertine, and alcoholic." The article had a photograph. Colette with bulging eyes covered an exposed breast in one of the "capital's specialized medical institutions." There was also a photo of "material evidence," which the newspaper reader desperately wanted: it showed Colette's purse, watch, pen, miniature tape recorder, and a page from her notebook, "filled with evil slander against Soviet people and the Soviet way of life": from the smeared script only one word could be made out—"legume." The article was signed "Graduate student of MSU N. Burenin."

"You have to bear the legacy of the times in mind, Vadim. It was only four years after the death of the Great Cockroach Stalin, fear was in everyone's bones, and I was no exception."

"I understand." Vadim Raskladushkin nodded. "I'm far from the legacy of those times, but I understand you perfectly, Nikita."

"It was all forgotten, dear Vadim, quite quickly. No one ever reminded me of that article, if was as if it had never happened, and I've never heard anything about Colette since then. They threw her out, I think the same day, and I'm not even sure if she learned about the article and my shame. Whoever sees that shitty paper in France? But it broke me, Vadim. From that night I was a different man, I understood that the 'marvelous and furious world,' in Platonov's words, that I wanted to enter was unreal, at least for me. I did not defend my dissertation, I dropped out of graduate school, and took up my humiliating assignment at the House of Friendship (they were behind it, of course) without a murmur. They've thrown me out of there now, but that's another story. . . ."

That is the brief version of what Nikita Burenin told Vadim Raskladushkin; actually it wasn't all that brief, it was very messy and bumpy, with hiccups and pauses related to glassy staring at, say, half-eaten salted fish, with subsequent shaking up of the whole unwashed organism, with a hand run through the floppy hair, with stinky crumbs flying off to the side.

Even after they left the House of Journalists, that is, during the walk along twilit, blizzardy Moscow, Burenin's monologue continued, and Raskladushkin merely inserted his tactful replies in the inevitable pauses. For instance, once he said, "You, Nikita, are one of those people who should not drink. Forgive me, but it seems to me that alcohol kills your willpower."

"You're so right," muttered Nikita, grabbing hold of a drainpipe. A boy, a child, but he talks like an older brother with me, just what I always wanted. Of all the people I drank with, did even one ever hear out my story? Even Max Ogorodnikov, because of whom I suffer, always said, All right, old man, how about next time, okay?

At the intersection of three streets, the blizzard had whipped up a carousel. The absence of Soviet rule was astonishing. There wasn't a single slogan in sight, not a single political mug, but on the contrary, at the end of the block a light glowed under an icon, it was the entrance to a small church, old women slipped through the door, behind which clearly functioned normal church life.

Vadim Raskladushkin stopped. "Here, forgive me, we must part, I have to go that way," he said, and waved his hand in a vague direction.

Nikita Burenin looked glum. "I hope our paths cross again, old man," he muttered.

"Of course they will," Raskladushkin promised. "Here's my telephone and give me yours. Among other things I'm quite concerned by the state of your footwear. It's going to be cold. I think I'll be able to share some certificates for the Beriozka store so that you can buy yourself some fur-lined boots. All right, old man?" he asked in Nikita's style, smiled an astonishingly refreshing smile, shook hands encouragingly, and crossed the street. At the corner he slowed down near a gray Volga, inside which sat some reading folk, gave them a humorous quarter-bow, congratulating them on being able to read the paper in the dark, and disappeared.

Nikita Burenin headed for the church to warm up. That's a life-giving idea—warm up in a church, I'll go, they won't throw me out, really. I can even make the sign of the cross, if necessary, even though I was brought up on Marxist vileness, but I love God, and I wouldn't surprise myself if I fell into Christianity. Besides which, it's warm in here. It smells of old ladies' rags, but deeper inside, it smells more of candles, wood, and warmed icons.

It was a long time before the evening service, but the church was not empty. The steady parishioners were on either side of the entrance, the little old ladies chewing and drinking tea from a thermos, doves cooing. Near the icons were concentrated figures of people praying alone. To the left was the figure of a tall man on his knees. A fashionable orange jacket. The drooping moustache of Max Ogorodnikov. Nikita Burenin got on his knees next to Max. He asked a stupid question: "What are you doing here, Ogo, old man?"

"Revering Saint Nicholas the miracle worker," replied Maxim. "Praying to our Lord Jesus Christ. Asking forgiveness for my sins, conscious and unconscious."

"I heard at the bar that they're going to throw you out of the Union," Nikita murmured in embarrassment.

Ogorodnikov put his hand on his shoulder. "I want you to finally tell me your shameful story."

"First teach me how to pray, Max, if you don't mind."

"I only know one prayer," Ogo said. "You can repeat it after me if you want. Our Father, Who art in heaven. . . ."

4

MOSCOW NARROWED CONSIDERABLY that winter, at least, that's how it seemed to the Cheesers and to Max Ogorodnikov in particular. All official appearances were closed to him. He got tired of going to restaurants: he hated dragging the PhIDs behind him and scaring decent folk. That left the houses of friends and the foreign embassies. As for the latter, it was as if they had conspired together (and maybe they had?) and issued invitation after invitation. Not trusting the Moscow mails for some reason, the diplomats dropped off invitations to Ogorodnikov and "Mrs." at the apartment or the studio. Nastya quickly picked up on international life, she seemed to take to it, and often would remind Max, "Ogosha, we're off to cocktails at the Canadians today, and the day after tomorrow there's a movie and buffet at Spasso House, and don't forget

Saturday, there's a reception for the Colombier Theater Group at the French ambassador's." This was all related in an insouciant, merry patter as if she were talking about a tourist field trip with shish kebabs and guitars.

And he replied with equally false lightness, "Fine," "Gotcha," "No problem." They had an unspoken agreement not to notice the falseness, not to notice the leaden gloom that was gathering over the roofs of Moscow confidently and slowly, coming for them. That slowness— they won't go anywhere anyway—carried a burning horror.

At the embassies another blessed falseness arose—the sensation of safety. Say what you will, but the PhIDs couldn't stick their faces in there, and the snitches were pretending to be Soviet public figures and remained aloof because everyone knew them and you were applauded here as a famous photographer with your beautiful wife, and nothing more. Allow me to introduce you . . . yes, yes, that one . . . you don't know . . . editor of an independent journal . . . ah, of course . . . what a pleasure . . . to meet you . . . you must come to visit us in Switzerland . . . and Belgium . . . and Norway . . . I trust you do not overlook small countries, sir . . . I am the prince of Liechtenstein.

Saturday, at the French ambassador's several hundred guests gathered in honor of the Colombier Theater Group. The crowd first moved through the gingerbread rooms of the old building, which during Moscow's glory days had housed a merchant prince, and then ended up in the new glass pavilion, where Champagne and cheeses and pâtés awaited them.

Almost all the Cheesers were there. What fine fellows the French are, they invited all our gang! Olekha Okhotnikov, a rhapsody, was wearing a shiny foreign tuxedo, bugging his eyes, and fanning a cute blonde in glasses with his red beard. Where'd he get the blonde, pal? "From Copenhagen, they say. Olekha stole her from his friend Venka Probkin, famous in the capital. Now Ophelia comes here from Copenhagen to study Northern Russian photography, and Olekha is bringing the foreigner to the heights of mastery." Venechka Probkin had brought his poor Masha, playing at model husband, but not forgetting to send signals with his eyebrows, eyes, and twitching nose in all female directions.

Majestic Chavchavadze appeared now and then in the crowd, wearing in addition to his excellent navy-blue suit a full set of his medals, which made foreigners think that he was from the Central Committee.

Shuz Zherebyatnikov, in his leather jacket and with a scarf casually tossed over one shoulder, was propping up an ornate column with his broad shoulders and directed the flow of champagne like a general, snapping his fingers.

Master Tsuker was here, too, this time remembering not only his trousers but even his grandfather's watch, chain, and charms, saved by his granny from the KGB, which he put across his belly in the conviction that everyone understood European chic.

A chevalier of the Légion d'honneur headed for Maxim with arms outspread; it was none other than the French ambassador. "Mr. Ogorodnikov, how happy to see you here! Madame Ogorodnikov, I swear by the Republic that you look marvelous tonight!"

Maxim, though not very sure that they had ever met before, responded in the right tone. "I swear by the Union of Republics that tennis suits you, Mr. Ambassador." He hit the mark. The word 'tennis' made the ambassador melt.

"We have to have another match, dear Ogorodnikov!"

"Another?"

"Yes, another! Of course, we must play again." The conversation then slid along quite lightly, and when it got stuck, Ambassador Murand-Aussi with professional flair pulled out another rail to keep things gliding—the latest film, the cold winter, a comparison of the Crimea and the Côte d'Azur. . . .

The interesting thing was that he would not let the Ogorodnikovs go. He introduced them to the honored guests, the actors of the Colombier, and at the last moment, when Maxim intended to slip away, grabbed him by the elbow. "Mr. Ogorodnikov, what do you think of the modern theater?"

Maxim and Nastya exchanged looks; the situation seemed very bizarre. Of course they couldn't get away, for the ambassador represented a sovereign state that was as enlightened as it was powerful, a nation that had given our Great-Mighty-Truthful-Free language so many wonderful words, including *buffet, douche,* and *dirigible,* and which had invented photography. Looking around, the Ogorodnikovs saw the bewildered stares of diplomats from the First, Second, and Third worlds. In the eyes of the Soviet diplomats they could discern, besides bewilderment, an unreadable savagery.

Subsequently they learned that Ambassador Murand-Aussi had violated protocol and disregarded the deputy minister of culture of the USSR for a half hour, engrossed in bizarre conversation with a notorious person. Some of the Soviet guests could have been observed whispering among themselves as they regarded the ambassador, but he laughed insouciantly and applauded, for now he was telling anti-Soviet jokes. The situation was even more piquant because just a few heads away from Murand-Aussi's group were the piebald tresses of the leader of Soviet photography, Fotii Feklovich Klezmetsov, to whom, alas, none of the diplomats paid any attention.

This lasted about thirty minutes, after which the ambassador of Gaul bade a hearty farewell to the photographer of Muscovy, extracting a promise from him to come again, to call whenever he needed anything from France, and also to bear in mind that ambassadors were also humans, who are sometimes lonely far from home and who would be quite interested in getting to know the interesting world of Moscow's artists better.

Getting away from the ambassador, Ogorodnikov made a sharp turn for the buffet: he had to get drunk before it was too late, because the reception was drawing to a close.

"Max, what does it mean?" asked Nastya, dragged along violently. He shrugged. Their liberal neighbor, tasty sandwich in mouth, flashed by and winked his round eye meaningfully, whispered a "Bravo," as silent as a soap bubble, and vanished.

"Bravo," said Harrison Rosborn, as red-cheeked and sturdy as a decathlon champ. "I timed it: thirty-two minutes with the ambassador! That's very good, Max, very, very good!"

Ogorodnikov was loading up quickly at the buffet. "What's so good about it, Harrison, what's so amazing? Enlighten me!"

"Don't playact with me, Max, that's all everyone's talking about, that demonstrative audience."

"Demonstrative, you said?" Nastya was angry.

"Stop kidding around, Ogo, you didn't come here to stuff your face,

did you?" Rosborn led them away from the buffet to a corner, where
thanks to a porcelain statue they could be a bit secluded from the
crowd. "Thanks to your conversation with the ambassador, I came to
two curious conclusions," said Rosborn. "First of all, the French seem
to have pretty good information on affairs in Moscow. Secondly, that
Murand-Aussi is clearly a nice guy, simply a nice and not cowardly guy."

"Damn it, Harrison, enlighten me, tell me what all this is called in
the political world," Ogorodnikov mumbled, mouth full, blowing his
nose into an enormous salad-green handkerchief. Nastya stood by
sternly and silently looked from one to the other.

"You see, Max, I have my sources in Moscow. For many years now,
I have known perfectly well from which bottom those sources are coming—alas, the pun doesn't work as well in English, let's say I know the
source of my sources—but, you know, besides this stupid game, we
have human relationships . . . in general, I've learned to talk with the
source and tell which is falsehood and which smells right. Yesterday I
was dining with one of my sources and we talked mostly about you,
which is natural—all of political Moscow is talking about *Say Cheese!*"

"Bullshit." The object of the conversation of all political (apparently
there was such a thing) Moscow made a brief commentary.

"I have trouble with that word," Rosborn said with a smile. "I try not
to swear in general. I once used the word among people who were all
swearing, but somehow it came out all wrong, neither bird nor fish."

"Neither fish nor fowl," corrected Nastya grimly. She kept her eyes
on Ogo and realized that despite the pâté and the Beaujolais, Max was
beginning to empty, that is, the wild sensation of expanding emptiness
was overtaking him again; she had to find a good tranquilizer for him.

Harrison Rosborn blushed: he was very serious about his Russian.
"Sorry," he said, "forgive my stupid mistake, I'm just nervous. If I could
speak Russian the way you speak English . . ."

Max hurried. "Let me tell you what happened to me in Australia. . . ."
He seemed eager to end the discussion of sources, but Nastya ended
the flow of words.

"Please, Harrison. Why are you nervous?"

"You see," Rosborn said, looking over his shoulder, "I realized that
something serious was threatening Max."

"We figured that," Nastya said, "but do you have anything concrete?"

"Yes." The journalist nodded. "They have a lampoon ready at *Photogazette*. Called 'Ogorodnikov's Hidden Camera.' My sources said they can't remember anything like this since Solzhenitsyn."

"Terrific," Maxim said. "You can be proud. A half hour with the French ambassador. An article in a leading newspaper. A comparison with Solzhenitsyn. Be proud, Nastya! Personally I will be proud all evening, and tomorrow I'll barf, shit, piss, drain off, and evaporate!"

"In his element," Nastya said. "Don't listen to him, Harrison."

"Why not? I like his plan," Rosborn said, and laughed. Then he added in a lower voice, "Please, keep me informed on how things are going, call me right at the bureau and at home. I don't think it'll do you any harm now."

Ogorodnikov partied the rest of the evening, as in the olden days. He got drunk on champagne, danced with the wife of the Brazilian ambassador and then with the ambassador himself. He bargained over the price of his wife Nastya with a representative of the United Arab Emirates. The crowd was delighted.

Gradually the guests left, and the empty and very disorderly rooms contained no one but the Cheesers and a few stoolies. An extraordinary figure appeared at the end of the suite of rooms: Vasya Shturmin in top hat and fluttering cape. The stunned servants observed his approach, which sounded as if there were jangling spurs. It seemed that he had left his mount at the door. Actually, there were no spurs and no horse. "Just flew in from Sverdlovsk, from the thick of national life. Heard you were fucking around at the Franks', and here I am."

"How did you get in without an invitation?"

"No problem, I came in the trunk of a Citroën."

"And how will you get out?"

"No problem, I'll come out drunk!"

A Song from the Depths

The communists caught a young man,
They dragged him to the KGB;

Confess, where did you get this book,
These plans for a riot-to-be?

Why did you disobey us?
Why did you slander the State?
"I shit on your Leninism,"
Said the heroic inmate.

"We'll restore the fallen republic,
In spite of the Cheka's great might,
And weary Russia will establish
The Eden for human rights!"

That's what he said to his captors;
Those were Lev Sokolkin's words.
Though young, he was brave as a king—
And his words were heard!

And then in the KGB prison
There turned up a girl of high rate,
A blue-eyed Ninochka on a mission,
One Miss Shchors, Party school graduate.

Among the tattooed criminals
In the prison nicknamed Tehran,
Ninochka saw Sokolkin
And their two hearts beat as one!

"*Influence* the young cynic"—
So advised an aging Chekist.
But in her eyes, blue and scenic,
Lived a poet, not a Marxist.

And so on for another forty-four stanzas.

5

SKANSHCHIN AND PLANSHCHIN were at headquarters of the operative
group past midnight. They had to finish going through the huge flow

of information and then definitively formulate the actions of the coming week.

The general was enjoying it: what surroundings! The large office was darkened, the two desks illuminated by table lamps, his own and the desk of his favorite student, the talented and handsome Volodya. There was good strong tea, so strong it was pitch. And there was a bottle of cognac. We'll drink when we're done. He didn't feel like going home. He was really sick of home and his wife.

The captain was in a funk. First of all, because he had to break a date with darling Viktoria Guryevna. Secondly, he hated the mountain of papers, reports, information, and denunciations. This place smelled like the sewer, it stank of shit, no other way to put it. He'd rather be reading belles-lettres. A colleague from the LIDs promised him a con-fiscated copy of *Lolita* for a few days. Thirdly, he was just sick of working. He'd like to go south! Fourth, he was afraid that the general would remember his idiotic idea of a "warning signal," which he was supposed to carry out, to keep Kolya Slyazgin from doing it. And fifth, he had the most unpleasant residual effect from the meeting with a high-placed person, he simply felt scorn for humankind. In his third year of working for the Glands, Vova Skanshchin was still astonished by the many levels of authority, or, as he had learned from the foreign-word dictionary, the "hierarchy." So this high-placed person, the one even the general feared, who was he? "Volodya, you and I are going up to such heights right now, you'll get dizzy!" They walked along various floors, rode various elevators, went up and down, you could get heights and depths mixed up. Finally they were before a person-you-wouldn't-wish-on-your-worst-enemy. This person sat in silence while Valeryan Kuz-mich Planshchin reported, no emotion showed on the listener's clay face, but the left eyebrow did creep up at the part about the 32½-minute conversation between M. P. Ogorodnikov and the French ambassador. In connection with that he said, "Hm." The general picked up on that: "In that regard we will come down on our journalists." The person made a note.

The general seemed to have orders to report only on Ogorodnikov, all his movements, words, and contacts, not a single word about the

album. That high-placed person left a strange impression: he seemed to
have approved of Captain Skanshchin's work—an abrupt upward surge,
heels together, chin up, face showing loyalty, I serve the Soviet
Union!—and there seemed to be quiet, peace, unmatched strength in
him, but still there was this strange sensation, as they write in fiction, a
strange sensation of some familiar, nauseating shame. One of Papa's pals
from the warehouse? Boy, what a bizarre idea. Suddenly in the dark
office, in the silence, Skanshchin knew: he's from *Splinters*! It was that
image that appeared in Ogorodnikov's photos of Kolyma, Taymyr, and
Pechora! Could that mug have recognized itself, could it have started
this whole machine?

"Volodya, toss over the latest information on Drevesny," Planshchin
asked gently.

"I don't have it, Valeryan Kuzmich."

"Where'd you stick it?"

"I have the report, all right, motherfucker. . . ."

"Volodya, Volodya, it's time you dropped your Komsomol slang!"

"Well, I mean, here's the report, but there's no information on Drevesny. That's what it says in Slyazgin's report—'the trail of A. Y. Drevesny is lost.' "

"What nonsense is this?" The general was perturbed. "Where could
he have got to?"

"No information, General. He's gone."

"Well, that's ridiculous! He couldn't just disappear! Remind me to
call Polina tomorrow when the Poker is out. I'll bet the genius of Russian photography is sitting it out at some dacha."

Volodya shrugged: He's the boss. The general looked at him closely.
Something odd was happening lately with his young specialist. Could
the stoolies Slyazgin and Plyubyshev have been partly right? Could such
a brilliant fellow, a real find for the Glands today, really be floating off?
"Incidentally, Volodya . . ."

Skanshchin jumped. He had been expecting that "incidentally." "Yes,
incidentally, Comrade General," he said with businesslike speed, "in all
these reports on Ogorodnikov, the 'Georgian,' and 'Moishe,' here and
there the name of this curious young man, Vadim Raskladushkin, keeps

coming up. Incidentally, about him. . . ." He shut up, as if he had forgotten—why bother with incidentallies, he'd have to listen to the general's "incidentally."

The general pushed away a pile of papers, never taking his eyes from him. "Incidentally, Volodya, what about the 'warning signal'?"

Volodya moaned, as if with a toothache. The idiotic idea belonged to the general, he couldn't argue with it. Sovfoto Publishers had just put out a book by the German peace-lover Knut Gutentag called *Warning Signal,* in the sense that humanity was in danger.

"Well, Volodya, call up Ogorodnikov and tell him you want to send him a book."

"What for?"

"He'll get it in the mail, pull it out of the wrapping, and see *Warning Signal* on the jacket. . . ."

"And so, Comrade General?"

"You don't get it?"

"Not really."

"You don't see what a blow it will be to his nervous system? You have to understand things like that."

"Uh-huh, Comrade General. . . . May I speak frankly, Comrade General?" Captain Skanshchin asked in the stillness of the night office.

"You must," said General Planshchin.

"What do you think, Valeryan Kuzmich, do they despise us a lot?"

"Who?"

"Why, all those photographers, artists . . . the ones we watch . . ."

Planshchin took the barely started bottle of Three Star cognac and filled two glasses. "Eh, Volodya," he sighed, "you really have to work on yourself, get over your wimpiness. You have to get tough, dear man, we're defending the most sacred of all things. What do you care about their emotions? Our emotions are in the foreground, and we hate those bastards, even though we remain polite. That's the basis of our work, and no wigawags!"

"Zigzags," Skanshchin corrected glumly.

"Get up!" barked the general. "Report tomorrow on mission completed. You may go!"

CHINGHIZ

I

HE BUS WAS brought to the back of the hotel after 2 A.M., and the "missing" Andrei Yevgenievich Drevesny managed to exhaust himself by then. They had told him at the information center earlier in the day to be ready by midnight and suggested he get some sleep. At midnight he was ready, really ready. His equipment packed, he was clean and pale. He overcame his trembling with long paces in his hotel room. Hunger helped him combat his fear. Good thing they warned him not to eat too much. He wouldn't mind even the fried *prostimpoma** right now, he chuckled to himself, he wouldn't even refuse an "anniversary salad. . . ."

At midnight, however, no one called. Another ten minutes passed, and he was overwhelmed with a mixture of wild anxiety and joy: What if they forgot me, left without me? Grabbing his jacket and camera bag, he hurried downstairs. The lobby was empty. The information center was closed, the administrator was absent, of course, there were only

*For "a certain period of time" a fish popularly known as the *prostimpoma* (from "prostitute" and "pomace"), taken up from the Atlantic, was the only kind of fish available in the Soviet Union. Eat at your own risk!

two Kazakhs, old and young, that is, the militiaman and the doorman, both in warm felt boots, playing chess near the radiator. Bus? The doorman shook his big head. Don't know anything about it.

A throbbing drum still came from the restaurant along with the wild song, "Yellow leaves swirl above the city." A strange bluish light illuminated a door at the end of the lobby, a place that struck fear in the hearts of the local populace—a hard-currency bar.

Drevesny sat for a while in a raggedy chair. It was Thursday, fish day, and the smell of the above-mentioned *prostimpoma* came from the restaurant. A drunken officer walked by. "Yellow faces swirl above the city...." He caught Drevesny's eye, and winked, half-dead. Faces instead of leaves, get it, pal? It's the song of Chinese paratroopers. Drevesny went outside and stood at the front entrance. Darkness, silence, a taxi with the engine running. Where could you go here in a taxi? What if they called his room? The elevator was turned off for the night. He raced up the stairs to the seventh floor. He sat on the bed, not thinking and not feeling, and then remembered Moscow, the Photographers' Union and all that, and his body itched mercilessly. What if they're gathering downstairs right now? They'll leave without me! I'll blow it!

He raced downstairs, where there wasn't even a hint of departure, of a bus, of anything. It was cold. Why was it so cold in an Intourist hotel? Two hours passed this way. Andrei Yevgenievich's left cheek began twitching, the whole undertaking seemed vile, a stupid trick.... Polina's ideas, her slyness, her cosmonautical "connections," and I'm just a spineless jellyfish.... I ran off when things got hot, abandoned my comrades....

A female administrator appeared, swinging her hips, a babe in a pink down-and-wool-knit hat. "Comrade Drevesny, what's the matter? They're looking for you, and you've disappeared...."

A huge Ikarus bus stood in the courtyard. Drevesny leaped inside. "Hello, comrades!" No one responded. It didn't look as if anyone here had been looking for him. About twenty people were scattered in various corners of the cabin, whose enormous windows were covered with a glaze of ice. Some of the people were smoking, some were napping, you could see their upturned faces. Drevesny took a seat in the middle.

All his anxieties were gone. The incredible significance of the moment.
He had to remember everything! It happens this mundanely? Would it
be all right to take a picture?

They waited at least another half hour. The windows began defrost-
ing. The radio station Mayak was broadcasting a concert of national
German music in honor of the anniversary of the GDR. At last, two
fat ladies got on the bus, followed by several cardboard boxes and metal
tubs. Someone shouted out in the darkness, "Klava, what are you going
to feed us today?"

"Watch you don't choke on it," one of the ladies replied courteously.

The bus set off and soon pulled out onto a highway surrounded by
snowdrifts as tall as a man. A few turns in the empty darkness of the
steppe. The lights of Baikonur appeared, and then from beyond a hill
loomed an enormous glowing spot. That was the launching pad. In a
strange way it did not get closer, but, on the contrary, began floating
off to the side.

All the lights vanished. Just the asphalt strip under the headlights,
snow all around. A checkpoint, three soldiers in quilted overalls. One
got into the bus, talked to the driver, shouted "Good luck!" to everyone,
and jumped down. After that the bus accelerated quickly, and the
steppe wind howled ever harder.

What if I'm on the wrong bus? Drevesny turned with a delicate question across the aisle to the massive figure covered with a sheepskin coat.
"Where are we headed now?"

"What do you mean, where?" his neighbor grumbled. "To Chinghiz."
It grew unbearably cold in the bus. The neighbor cursed. "Heater's off
again!"

"You said, to Chinghiz," Drevesny repeated.

"Well, yes, the Chinghiz Space Center. Didn't you know? The launch
is there today."

"What? We're not going to Baikonur?"

The neighbor laughed. "Baikonur is for publicity. Hard currency,
brother! We fly from Chinghiz. No more questions, I'm off into the
underground." He made a tent from his jacket and disappeared inside.

They stopped suddenly in the middle of blackness. "We've got our gals coming from the Five Year," said the driver. "Shall we pick them up?" Three absolutely frozen girls jumped in. They had been at the movies, at a theater called the Five Year.

One of the cooks bawled them out. "Hussies, you'll freeze your attributes off!"

Someone in the back laughed. "Come here, Irka, we'll warm up your attributes!"

"Ooh," moaned the girls. "Who's flying today, boys?"

"Belyaletdinov's group," came the answer.

"Oh, Maratik! Giving in to him isn't enough!" The girls flopped down somewhere. Someone in the back began warming them up quite actively.

It took two more hours before the bus stopped at the checkpoint of the working space station Chinghiz. Two projector beams scanned the sky, crisscrossing up high and then separating and lying down on the snow, the wire barriers and the guard towers. Several long dark barracks, one taller than the next, stretched along the slope of the hill. Army trucks were parked outside them. But where was She? The beam touched an ugly plaster statue of a cosmonaut, a copy of the Moscow monstrosity of stainless steel, the human rocket, outspread arms, a substitute for the Crucifixion. And there She was! A gigantic booster rocket behind the hill.

A young officer and two machine gunners got on the bus. "Greetings," said the officer, "everybody belong?"

The driver pointed out Drevesny. "There's someone from Moscow here."

"Aha, I know about him."

The officer came over. "You're a photographer? Your documents, please." He looked over the passport and then saluted silently, which offended Andrei Drevesny. Ten years ago a little officer like this with a semi-intellectual face would have been stunned: "I can't believe my eyes—you're really Andrei Drevesny?" A catastrophic decade. Not mentioning us, hushing us up, pushing forward all those blown-up village snappers—it was a carefully thought-out policy. And now what? The only names broadcast in the West are Ogorodnikov, Shuz, sometimes Slava German, they talk about those boys and almost never mention me. . . . Well, soon the name Andrei Drevesny will be on lots of lips! Really, Polina is terrific, to get me an assignment like this! There hasn't been a single photographer who's done it. . . .

A treacherous thought came to him: Don't pretend that you're after the glory, at least be honest with yourself. He cast the thought aside.

His neighbor under the huge sheepskin coat turned out to be wearing a silver space suit. This was, as he later discovered, Major Belyaletdinov himself, commander of the *Kremlin-1* crew, a Bashkir, that is, aimed to capture public opinion in the Third World. Hey, photographer, let's get a bite.

2

DREVESNY NERVOUSLY TRIED to notice all the details of the mundane and even somehow pathetic, amazingly middle-Soviet atmosphere at Chinghiz Space Center. He dined-breakfasted with the crew in a small room with lousy plush drapes, cheap hotel furniture, a portrait of Andropov, a poster that said "In the Avant-garde of Humanity," a worn copy of *Moscow Lights* magazine, a rather old TV, in a word, a typical Soviet recreation room. Grim Russian mamas served a high-calorie meal: a large jar of black caviar, Yugoslav ham, briquettes of Finnish butter, even bananas, slightly frostbitten. The bread, however, was moist and heavy, probably local, and the coffee was milky glop—it was ladled from a tub.

"May I take pictures?" Drevesny asked the commander.

He shrugged. Two other cosmonauts looked at the photographer as if they were seeing him for the first time. The older had a gold tooth that flashed interestingly during his infrequent smiles. "When did you leave Moscow?"

"Yesterday."

An unexpected question followed: "Well, what's going on at the Solyanka Theater?"

Drevesny was surprised. "Why do you ask?"

"Well, the radio said that the artistic director ran off to the West."

Drevesny jumped up. "I don't know anything about it!"

"You're behind the times, pal! You should listen to the radio!" All three laughed noisily but briefly. Then they talked about the director.

"What did he need? Just figure," said Major Belyaletdinov, "what he had here and what he'll have there." Drevesny thought of the director of the Solyanka. They drove even him off the deep end, the bastards! Now the theater, the last bastion of the sixties, will collapse, of course. . . .

Suddenly a colonel wearing a fur hat came in. "Why are you taking pictures? Who gave you permission?" Drevesny nooded at Belyaletdinov—this comrade did. The colonel turned his heavy face at the cosmonaut. "Don't you know the rules of internal order?" He beckoned to Drevesny. "Follow me."

The colonel walked ahead down the narrow corridor of the barracks. If he's in front then he's not convoying me, Andrei Yevgenievich consoled himself, but his guts stuck together with fear. I haven't done anything so terrible, they can just take away the film, I'm not subject to arrest and certainly not to execution. . . . Don't goof off, he berated himself, don't pretend you're afraid of that idiotic karakul top hat, admit that you're afraid of the consequences. . . .

The colonel stopped at a door marked INVENTORY, took a key ring from his ass pocket, and picked one for the padlock. There was no inventory room on the other side. Concrete steps led to a cellar. In the cellar they went down another corridor, but this time past heavy steel doors. A red light burned above one of them. Interrogation room? Brothel? They came in and interrupted a yawn by the only person present, a middle-aged female doctor. "Strip to the waist," she said wearily, and set aside her *Moscow Lights*. Andrei Yevgenievich obeyed and froze, covered with goose bumps. "You're kind of, hm . . . cute . . ." muttered the doctor, feeling his sides. "You wouldn't ever think you were this age. . . ."

The cuff inflated on his upper arm. The inevitable rise in mercury. "How come you have such high blood pressure, Andrei, what's it, Yevgenievich?"

They'll flunk me—the joyful thought flashed like a meteor. "Doctor, please, it's not hypertension, I have this reaction to having my blood pressure taken, the so-called cuff syndrome . . . it only goes up when the cuff is on . . . I'm begging you, doctor!"

"Something wrong?" asked the colonel from his corner, deep in the *Moscow Lights*.

"Everything's fine," said the doctor, running her finger along Andrei Yevgenievich's backbone. "The comrade is a bit excited, but that's perfectly understandable. This comrade is suitable."

"Let's go," said the colonel. "Time is short." They went down another level. It was freezing down there. Soldiers rushed back and forth, pulling something elongated and rusty, aerial bombs, maybe, no, oxygen tanks. "Well, what are you gaping at," the colonel said. "In here!" In the dimly lit dressing room silvery space suits hung on the walls, and shelves were filled with helmets marked USSR. "You have ten minutes," the colonel said. "The sergeant major will help you pick out your suit."

A wise guy in a soft jacket came over, with the puffy face of a drunkard and rogue. He pulled a suit down from its hook. "This one will fit you, get in!"

"Is this so simple: just get in?" Drevesny gasped in what he thought was charming humor, his guts boiling now.

"Crawl in first, if you please," offered the depot man.

"But the zipper doesn't open, Comrade Sergeant Major."

"Fikki-dikki," said the depot man, "the zippers are stuck! Have anything worthwhile to smoke?"

"Here's some Winstons." Drevesny gave him an almost full pack.

"That'll do." The man cheered up. "I'll find you a terrific suit, you could land on Venus in it."

Ten minutes later Drevesny came out into the corridor in a space suit with the helmet in the crook of his arm. The colonel was shouting at the soldiers, who, pieces of shit that they were, never shut the doors when they loaded, shaming the homeland and the armed forces with their disgusting appearance, "and you, Pshontso, have breath like a garbage chute, tell your commander you have three over-duty assignments!" The colonel led Drevesny to a large freight elevator. In it was a group of workers in helmets and with chains. No one spoke while the elevator was going up. The blue paint above Drevesny's shoulder had been scratched: eff, you, see, kay.... The elevator door opened, and everyone went out onto an open metal platform, cut by the icy wind of Kazakhstan.

Mighty, almost demonic music thundered. "Under the homeland's sun we grow stronger every year. We are faithful to the work of Lenin and the Party! The Communist Party of the land calls the Soviet peoples to perform exploits...!" When a yellow thread of the coming dawn appeared on the horizon, Drevesny realized that they were standing high above the earth. He took a step forward and saw below an illuminated square of trampled snow and a crowd of people on it wearing padded jackets and overalls. They all had their heads back and were looking up. A metal wall. "This way, please!" It was the booster rocket. A narrow ladder, like a fire escape, went up the side. "You're on your own from here, Andrei Yevgenievich. Well, let's have the traditional handshakes. Good luck! I hope you'll invite us to the party?"

Drevesny clambered up to one more platform, this one deserted. In the curving steel wall an oval hatch opened slowly. "Come into the *Kremlin-One,*" said a loudspeaker. For the last time he was buffeted by a stream of Kazakhstan wind, the howl of Chinghiz Khan. A step on a shaky step, then another. The hatch closed behind him. Darkness. Something of his own throbbed. His heart? Too powerful for a heart. A minute later another hatch opened, and he saw the control room of the *Kremlin-1.* Three cosmonauts were sitting back in their seats. One seat was empty. Is that for me? The heroic music played softly: "I, the earth, am seeing off my children...."

When they saw Drevesny, one cosmonaut frowned, another laughed, and the third said, in English for some reason, "Welcome aboard!"

3

NO, THIS WAS incredible! Taking off from earth? Out into the implacable, black, inexplicable? Who gave permission for this anyway? I'm completely unprepared! I'll die from gravity! These stallions are trained for years, and me they just shoved in like that dog Laika. The minute Polina whispered some nonsense like "We must protect the position of Andrei

Drevesny, we have to send him somewhere," into the ear of some big shot. I'm off into space through someone's pull! Lousy, vile, shitty irresponsibility! The photographer's body collapsed. And where would his soul be? A burst bubble, a burst bubble, a burst bubble. . . .

"Try not to crap during takeoff," Major Belyaletdinov said.

"What do you mean?" Drevesny asked with a start.

"Don't mess your pants. Bad smells in space are really bad. . . ."

Drevesny swallowed mixed feelings. "Are we really flying?"

"Not a fact," said the commander, "the chances are half a hundred out of a hundred."

"Fifty–fifty," said the English specialist.

"The booster is a piece of shit," the commander continued. "Premature ignition, and it's all over. But more likely, we'll just sit here tanning for an hour or two and then go home."

Number-two Anatolii Kimovich Pavlenko laughed. "Like we did last time, guys!"

Number-three Dedyurkin spoke with unexpected anger. "Last time we had at least a Komsomol slut from the GDR, today's goat is nothing but trouble."

Andrei Drevesny forgot all about space, he was so stunned by the look of disgust meant for him. He didn't have time fully to digest these negative emotions when the music abruptly stopped, little eyes blinked on the endless dashboard, and a voice that seemed to fill the entire cabin said, "Put on helmets! Countdown begins in three minutes!"

The rest penetrated only in tiny bursts through Drevesny's almost total absence of existence. He didn't hear the countdown, but the sound "Blast off" reached him. Suddenly came a wild, tormenting, intolerably wild compression, compression, compression, and giving up all resistance, the photographer Andrei Yevgenievich Drevesny, born in 1936, died.

But he did leak a bit, peed a drop. So I did shame myself a bit, he thought with a mischievous chuckle, when death passed. "Ah, fuck it, Andryukha, forget it," said a voice. He opened his eyes and saw next to his face the rather large backside of Major Belyaletdinov, no longer in the space suit but in sweatpants. All three cosmonauts had taken off their space suits. Dressed in soft jogging suits, they hung in the cabin's air. Pavlenko was on his side, Dedyurkin upside down.

The latter had turned from a creep into a charming fellow and helped Drevesny unbuckle and get out of his suit. "We all pee a bit at blast-off," he told the photographer, and nudged him with his elbow. "Let's get acquainted. Edik Dedyurkin. I've known you since childhood, I grew up on your pictures, so to speak." With a cheery wink and in a dissident whisper, he added, "The burned generation."

Drevesny, laughing, swam in the cabin, bumping into his merry companions. It felt like when he learned to float as a kid. Better than when he was a kid. "Ha-ha-ha"—he pointed out the porthole—"the blue planet called earth."

"That's what I love about space," said Tolya Pavlenko, "this euphoria. It's like finishing your first bottle and it lasts a long time."

Marat rubbed his hands. "Wait till we reach Station *Ermak-Eight* and put the ace in the hole."

"Edik, toss me the camera from under the seat," Drevesny asked in a rollicking voice. The camera floated over. He started taking pictures. What tumbling, what joy, the childhood of man. The first cosmic (?!!) series by Andrei Drevesny, "Childhood of Man."

"Well, enough, boys," said the all-encompassing voice. "Take your seats! *Ermak-Eight* is in view!"

The euphoria continued for quite a while as they got closer to the space lab, which looked like a Primus stove. The commander extended the docking section, quite an impressive steel phallus with carvings. "I'm inserting," he transmitted the old space joke to earth, and despite the fact that the joke had grown motheaten over the last fifteen years, the crew of *Kremlin-1* roared with laughter.

But by the time they moved to the *Ermak-8*, the euphoria had evaporated. The crossing was extremely unpleasant for Drevesny. The docking sluice was like a claustrophobic trap. For an instance he lost his orientation and began battering the sides, forgetting that infinity lay beyond the walls. But that was only for an instant. In the next instant he had pushed his face into the dusty, blurry light of *Ermak-8*. Edik Dedyurkin, who had gotten there first, grabbed him by the nose.

"Howdy, ballast! Get ready to be tossed overboard!"

HIGHWAY

I

F THE RESIDENTS of the Soviet Cadre Coop used to give Maxim Ogorodnikov sly smiling looks because he was a fashion plate, now they froze! The respectable venerable Party's lenses, and the householders, and even the nannies (especially those who spoke foreign languages) regarded him with horror: There he is, the evil Ogorodnikov, how can he walk down the street, he'd better stay home. He left Okhotnikov's and looked around—where were the "comrades"? What miracle was this? Not a single car in the alley except his own and a dark-green taxi van. Even the ambulance with the PhIDs ears, which seemed to have grown into the earth, wasn't around that day. And the day was gentle and sunny.

Do such days have an effect on the PhIDs? Do the sparks on the glazed snowcaps of the drifts elicit any sparks in Skanshchin and Planshchin? Does the trembling of these hoar-rimmed branches bring on any trembling in them? He laughed. How little a man needs—they take away the surveillance and he gets all soft—sparks and branches. . . .

What miracle was this? In the middle of winter stood a woman dressed for summer—a sheer loose blouse, tight jeans, shoes on bare feet. She was beckoning with a bare arm. Who, me? He looked around. No one behind him, that meant she wanted him. "Ogorodnikov!" the girl with white eyes called.

"What would you like, miss?"

"Get in the car," she said in a tone that brooked no argument. Bah, she got out of that green taxi, and inside are two broad-shouldered men, so much for sparks and branches. . . .

I think something terrible is about to happen. He turned and quickly headed for his car. The girl's heels struck the asphalt behind him, she was running. The damned key, as always in these situations, wouldn't get in the lock. Sorry, he'd never had these situations before. He did it, got in the seat, but the girl did, too—she was pushing in through the door, he was pushing her out, she was pushing and suddenly howled like a witch, "Let me in, motherfucker, don't you want a blow job?"

A shameful struggle, the girl stank of sweat, in the rearview mirror he saw the green van slowly approaching, two heads in muskrat hats and dark glasses. Then something happened. The girl flew across the entire alleyway into a snowbank. Bah, it was Shuz who tossed her aside, his mighty friend Zherebyatnikov. The green van stopped. No one got out to help the fallen girl. Get in, Shuz! Let's split!

Pulling out of the alley, they saw the van making a U-turn and the girl running toward it. At the first light they realized the pseudotaxi was right behind them. The driver's face was impassive. His teammate, face hidden in his collar, was talking on the radio. The girl was in the back seat with a cigarette. "At the next light, Ogo, try to run the red," said Shuz. Hanging over the back of the seat, he stared at their pursuers, but they pretended not to notice his gaze.

It was Moscow's rush hour. A solid flow of cars, four lanes on either side of Leningrad Highway. It was difficult to maneuver to get through at the last second on a red light. He managed at the fourth intersection, but there was little point: a red light didn't mean much to the comrades.

They went in the tunnel under Sokol, passed the Aerodynamics metro stop. . . . Near the Zhukovsky Academy, which spread out like an incongruous Russian pie in the middle of Soviet order, another curious car appeared in the lane to Ogorodnikov's left, black with a violet light on the roof, and two guys inside who looked like trained Dobermans.

"Everything's clear," said Zherebyatnikov. "One pushes from behind, the other from the left."

"What do they want, Shuz?" Ogorodnikov's empty vessels filled with fury. "You think it'll be as easy as it was in 'thirty-seven? You're wrong, bitches!"

The flow of cars had reached the Belorussian railroad station. "They were using the girl to get you on rape charges—an old trick. But what do they want now?" Shuz took off his leather jacket and demonstratively flexed his biceps. The Dobermans on the left regarded them without emotion, businesslike and professional.

The road narrowed, now it was Gorky Street, filled with stuffed trolleybuses and crowds of people at store entrances. A light bump from behind. The driver of the green van smiled embarrassedly: sorry, a miscalculation. The Dobermans suddenly swerved right, presenting their flank. Ogorodnikov, to avoid being hit, automatically moved right, too. In a few seconds the Dobermans had Ogorodnikov up against the curb and had managed to get in front, blocking him in.

The green taxi was behind them. One muskrat hat was on the radio, the other hidden by a newspaper. The girl was out of sight—probably lying down in the back seat. The Dobermans sat without turning around, their ears sticking out. People went by, paying no attention to the situation, not even aware of any situation.

The sky was turning green in preparation for the sunset. "The bastards cut us off from Europe and think it's forever," said Maxim.

"They can't understand that slavery is over," replied Shuz. "They think they'll show us their shitty little I.D. and we'll give in like whores. Let's scar 'em hit at the scar on Gorky Street!"

"Did you hear that, Eagle?" Skanshchin asked in the radio, and sighed. Some people . . .

Ogorodnikov pulled out his gun, unembarrassed. He put it right on the dashboard.

"Do you hear their conversation, Eagle?"

"Waiting for orders," said Slyazgin.

"Continue observation," barked Eagle, and the officers realized that the head bird was confused. You'd get confused with people like that— in cars and with gas pistols.

"How many rounds in your toy, Bim?" asked Zherebyatnikov.

"Twelve, Bom," replied Ogorodnikov. "A wonderful thing to have when attacked by bandits. Shells of powerful nerve-paralyzing action. We're also lucky to have a sturdy Volga, that light Soviet tank. We'll start banging bumpers in front and in back. And if a bandit tries to break into our car, he'll get a nerve-paralyzing shell right between the eyes. Lucky that there are so many of our noble citizens around, isn't it? If the bandits attack we shout, 'Bandits are kidnapping the photographers Ogorodnikov and Zherebyatnikov! Tell foreign correspondents—famous photographers kidnapped!' "

"Is the horn loud in your car, Bim?"

"Very loud, Bom!"

They spoke in hopes of instant relay, even though they didn't believe in such exceptional abilities among their dreary PhIDs. Suddenly the Dobermans in front pulled away from the curb, abruptly entered the traffic flow, and disappeared from view in a minute's time. Ogorodnikov immediately drove straight and soon crossed Mayakovsky Square, where a powerful spring wind passed between the statue's wide trouser legs. Did we win? No, the green van was still on their tail. Ogorodnikov put his finger to his lips—Shuz, keep quiet!

They passed the Central Post Office. Gorky Street's last block ended in a three-lane turn around the corner of the National Hotel. About a hundred meters before the turn Maxim suddenly crossed from the far right lane to the far left and made the turn on the outside. The huge expanse of Manege Square opened before them. In the middle of the square was a U-turn sign. A new wave of traffic was hurtling at them from the left, but they had a few seconds and without hesitation he crossed the entire square toward the sign. The PhIDs didn't have those seconds, because they had made the turn on the inner lane. Now the photographers and the PhIDs were separated by a flow of cars rushing down Marx Prospect.

Laughing, Max and Shuz turned around on Manege, zipped past the History Museum and the Lenin Museum, the former City Duma, dove under the arch of the Kitai-Gorod Wall, surfaced on former Bolshaya Nikoloskaya, along Bumazhny to former Ilinka, kitty-corner across Red

Square and down to the Moskva River, along the Kremlin Embankment to former Ostozhenka, and they were still laughing.

They laughed for another hour at the studio on Khlebny in the company of Nastya, and then Maxim hurled the unfinished bottle of cognac against the wall and howled, "What do they want from us?!" Shuz sat motionless at the table, in stony silence, reminiscent of the Karl Marx monument near the Metropol Hotel.

In Khlebny Alley, outside the studio, Captain Slyazgin was furious. The bosses are shackling the initiative of the operatives, and here's the result—the photographers slip out from under the Glands' noses! He approached Ogorodnikov's car, resting in the prerevolutionary twilight, pulled a knife from his briefcase, held the briefcase between his knees, and jabbed the knife into the left rear tire. Up to the hilt for that bastard Ogorod, that kikes' employee!

"Listen, what are you doing, Nikolai!" Captain Skanshchin was outraged. "It's not very Cheka-like style, you know! So banal!"

"Get away from me, Vova, you bastard, I can't stand the sight of you!" Slyazgin broke off the knife inside the inner tube and tossed the handle into the snow. "A present for you, you fascists!"

2

THE VILLAGE OF Developkino held quite a few wonderful memories for Major General October Ogorodnikov. Actually, all those privileged villages near Moscow—Barvikha, Nikolina Gora, Zhukovka, and in part Developkino, the photographers' town—in those young fifties were the land of his adventures. Auto and motoive, sweetness and light, "keys to the dacha. . . ."

Wasn't it a nice time? thought October in English, slowly driving a KGB car down the empty roads, past dachas hiding behind pine trees. A gentle spring-winter evening, mid-March. Stalin was a bastard, but who cared? I wouldn't give a damn, if I . . . He drove onto the territory of the House of Creativity of the photographers, left the car near the impressive portico with the bas-relief sentiment "THE PARTY GAVE PHOTOGRAPHERS EVERY RIGHT EXCEPT ONE, THE RIGHT TO PHOTOGRAPH

BADLY. KIM VESELY." He walked down the Allée of Classics, early stars shimmering through its trees, airplanes floating in the sky on their way to the nearby airport, Dedkovo.

That was really a terrific time. He continued recalling his youth in English. The "Gulf Stream" tune, stream to the Gulf.... As he walked down the path a solitary figure appeared, a not young lady in a marvelous sheepskin coat. Her face turned to him with some attention. A diamond earring flashed at her ear. My goodness, thought October, she resembles a girl I fucked.... It's impossible.... She resembles a daughter of a classic Soviet photographer. I fucked her right there in a standing position ... She used to be a chick!

He came to the Marxyatnikovs' dacha, but he was in no hurry to open the gate. It's hard to stand it any longer. He thought his English thoughts. I am sick of socialism, of these stupid slogans, of these miserable deceitful people, of the ghosts of my youth. It's time to ... gosh ... go back home ... to Washington.

Max and Nastya had been living at the Marxyatnikovs' dacha for a week, and October had come to see them. "Crazy," he muttered, seeing the large picture window in which, like store mannequins, stood his tall half brother and pretty half sister-in-law. I swear he doesn't understand how serious things are....

Max and Nastya were drinking coffee and talking, standing up. Both were wearing sweaters with reindeer. Hearing steps on the porch, they didn't even think of the Glands. On the contrary, they smiled, apparently expecting friends.

"You guys are something," said October, "all alone in the woods, without even a dog for protection—and you're not afraid!"

"We're protected here, " Nastya said quickly. "Who?" October asked quickly.

"Our friends," she quickly replied. "Ha-ha-ha," he laughed. "By the way, I had some not-bad news."

"Is there any good news left?" asked Maxim.

"I didn't say good, I said not bad."

"And how did you find us here, October Petrovich?"

"Brrrr, Nastya, don't ask a man of my profession that question."

"Let's have dinner! We're having dalma tonight, did you ever have it?"

"Yes, many times. The Serbian Crown Restaurant is near our house and I get Mediterranean dishes there."

"Near your house?"

Maxim laughed. "That's in Washington, Nastya!"

"Right." October nodded. "Wisconsin Avenue."

"So, what's the not-bad news?"

"There is now an opinion on your leaving for abroad."

"Hm, that's news. . . ."

"Max, two days ago that opinion did not exist."

Nastya's fingers clutched the table edge. "What was the opinion two days ago, October Petrovich?"

Maxim thought, I have to tell her to take it easier with him, he is my brother, after all.

"I don't know"—October shrugged—"maybe there wasn't one at all. It's bad when there is no clear opinion up there." His thumb pointed at the ceiling, beyond which, that is, in the attic, he figured, a bug had been placed by "repairmen." "It's in situations like those that these problems arise. . . ." He waved his hand.

"What is it already!" Nastya was really upset.

October poured out half a glass of vodka and sprinkled it with black pepper. The drink of tough guys from intelligence. As usual, there was bad news with the not-bad news. The bad news was that the case of *Say Cheese!* and the New Focusers was being turned over to the investigator of top-importance state crimes. A pause. The vodka downed in one gulp.

Strange: no reaction to the bad news, and very weak to the not bad news. Nastya went to the Marxyatnikovs' study to make a phone call. Max began putting on his orange jacket. "I want to photograph the street at night," he explained. "There ought to be a gap between the trees that is almost light blue, something cosmic. In the child's sense. Fairy tale," he explained.

They went out together.

"Boy, you have nerves of steel, Brother! You could be an agent!"

"Lucky for you that I'm not," muttered Max. He was looking through the viewfinder and taking pictures of the gap, which from the point of view of October was nothing special, just pretension. "I'd spy for you," muttered Max, "I'd ..." But he realized that only his camera could save him from attacks of emptiness and from adrenaline squalls.

October stood smoking a cigar. "While we're away from Nastya, I have to tell you the most upsetting thing. Since you have such good nerves, you must know. The Secretariat of the Central Committee has met on your case. The details are not known yet, but Zherilenko reported. Can you imagine?"

Max spat in the snow. The third man in the government. He has nothing else to do, no other problems. . . .

The door slammed. Nastya shouted into the darkness from the door-way, "Boys, hurry, a special announcement!" October, pleased by the "boys," took all four steps in one bound. Maxim scrambled up, too.

The Rubin brand TV was on full blast. For the first time in history, a Soviet man, Cosmonaut of the USSR, Major Belyaletdinov, Marat Narimanovich, had landed on the plant Venus! Despite the unfavorable atmosphere, Major Belyaletdinov was performing research on the sur-face! The hearts of Soviet people were filled with pride for the child of the Communist Party! "Thank you, homeland and party," Major Bel-yaletdinov said, "for the opportunity to make this astral exploit!" Anchorman Kirillov looked ready to shit in his pants with solemnity.

Luckily, he turned to Anchorwoman Zhiltsova, who had more con-crete information. "Cosmonaut Belyaletdinov took off for Venus from the Soviet space lab *Ermak-8*. Before that he spent days on board that famous station. Here are some photographs."

"What's this," said Max excitedly. A familiar style! "Just look, no one has ever taken pictures like that for them before. This is top class!"

"You see the crew of *Ermak-8*, preparing for the daring flight of their commander. The photographs were taken by the famous Soviet photographer Andrei Yevgenievich Drevesny, who's aboard."

Maxim flopped down on the floor right where he had been standing by the TV. Nastya, on the contrary, jumped up, and when she landed, remained on tiptoe. October, naturally, did not flinch, as if he had known all about it, as if a trick as marvelous as taking off into space from the heat of a ideological struggle could not have happened without him.

In the meantime, Kirillov, choking on patriotism, reappeared on the screen. "Our space hero is successfully growing acclimatized to Venus. He is walking, eating, and even reading. What had you taken with you, Marat Narimanovich, to read?"

The muffled voice from Venus spoke. "Well, of course, Nikolai Ostrovsky's novel *How the Steel Is Tempered*: it always helps me as a communist and as a cosmonaut. Well, a cassette with the Appassionata Sonata, the favorite work of the founder of our state. Well, and of course, I took the latest in photography, a collection of the work of our Soviet classic, Kasyan Bluzhzhaezhzhin, with a profound introduction by the combat leader of Soviet photographers, Fotii Klezmetsov. In the conditions of heightened struggle with the dark forces of imperialism," Major Belyaletdinov rasped through the Venerean steam, "it is particularly important to strengthen the principles of socialist realism. That's what we cosmonauts feel. I'm convinced that the workers in the arts will repel . . ."

Then Anchorwoman Zhiltsova explained that direct television contact with the surface of Venus was made difficult at the moment "because of interference occurring outside the borders of the Soviet Union," but the cameras would be turned on on board the *Ermak-8*. Three characters appeared floating in weightlessness. All three were wearing what looked like underpants. The presence of Andrei Yevgenievich's decadent face lent the scene a bordellolike and even surreal air, like Rousseau's *Ballplayers*.

Drevesny floated closer to the camera, his face distorted both by the wide-angle lens and by his sense of triumph. "What happiness," he said, "to be the first! Our commander is the first cosmonaut to step on Venus. I was the first Soviet photographer in space! Friendship is the first thing that comes to mind, indestructible bonds! Our friends on earth can count on us, we won't let you down!"

One of the crew members floated up behind the space photographer. Andrei Yevgenievich gave him a strange sidelong glance and twisted his hip, as if afraid of a pinch on the buttock. "I want to thank our Party for its paternal concern for Soviet photography," he said with dignity, and semi-embraced his colleague's shoulder, thereby moving him away from his rear end. The frozen smile on the face of the space professional left no doubt that he was about to repeat his attempt.

The broadcast from orbit ended on that. An enormous choir sang, "Under the homeland's sun we grow stronger with every year. . . ."

Nastya could barely control herself. "Well, what do you have to say?!"

"I think he was hinting at the indestructible bond in the *Say Cheese!* album," said Maxim.

"What a fantastic expedition," said October, "but why did he mention paternal concern? That was a mistake. Our Party is a lady. The concern should be . . . what, Nastya? Maternal, you mean?"

Nastya was furious. "I've never heard anyone say maternal, they always say paternal." Headlights shone beyond the fence. She jumped up. "They're coming here."

I need another shot of vodka . . . to brush aside all that junk, thought October.

Nastya returned with the American correspondent Rosborn and his wife, Beverly. Soon after, the other "corrs" began appearing at the dacha—the Italian, a couple of Frenchmen, a Dane, Germans, the Japanese Yasha Kimura, and even the correspondent for the Brazilian journal *Jornal*.

October told himself, I've got to keep a low profile! and pretended to be the older brother, a man of technical education. Stopping Nastya in the kitchen, he asked, "Did you invite them on purpose to impress me?"

The glaciologist laughed. "Don't be silly, they came on their own, it's like this every night."

A multilingual noise reigned at the table, but Russian gabble predominated. The reporters were excited by the space news, even though with the nasty habit of casting a shadow on all our achievements, they couldn't help gossiping. According to one of them, the trick with Venus was pure trumpery before the conference of unaligned countries.

At the height of the evening Chavchavadze called and announced that *Photogazette* had galleys of the squib "Your Negatives Have Been Exposed, Gentlemen!" and that the secretariat was meeting to expel

Maxim Ogorodnikov from the Photographers' Union. "Don't worry, *batono!**" the old man shouted in a strong Georgian accent. "I'll follow you!"

Even though he had been upset by the day's news, Maxim was really stunned by this: he somehow couldn't picture himself outside the Union, where he had been accepted triumphantly only twenty years earlier. He went outside to see his half brother off. The fairy-tale gap now had a loaf of moon in the middle of it. The weather was changing, promising a blizzard for tomorrow.

"What are you driving now?" October asked.

"Here are my wheels." They had stopped near Max's Volga. "Does it go?"

"Not bad at all. This is the export version, a V-six."

"Remember our old tank?"

"Of course? We were in the back ... with Eskimo...." Eskimo, Eskimo, you are dancing in the alley.... "I haven't seen her since. You know, she's an émigré...."

October patted his cheek. "Be careful at the wheel, kiddo."

"What do you mean?"

"Just that. Be careful, be attentive, be accurate behind the wheel. So long!"

3

THEY HAD TO move from the dacha the next day. Events were overwhelming. According to the squib "Your Negatives Have Been Exposed, Gentlemen!" the whole affair with the independent album was set up by the intelligence services of the subversive part of the world, that is, the West. Ideologically unstable, undiscriminating, susceptible like M. P. Ogorodnikov to cheap Western fame, they become playthings in the hands of reactionary ... sworn ... dyed-in-the-wool ... There they are—the fruits of uncritical praise, the inaccurate work of our photographic criticism, which did not realize in time ... The Photographers' Union must come to conclusions....

---

*A Georgian word showing "the highest respect," "most refined politeness," "supreme cordiality."

Ogorodnikov sent his membership card in the mail, without a note. Suddenly there was dissension among the Cheesers. Some said that he did not have the right to quit by himself. They should have all quit, and now he'd be the sole martyr. Others said, It's not too late now, let's call a press conference and announce a mass exit. The corrs were in an uproar. *Evening Moscow* printed a selection of workers' letters under the rubric "Pornography of the Spirit," wrathfully exposing the mysterious album, never seen by any of the workers. Suddenly Master Tsuker's studio caught fire in the middle of the day. After the fire the committee of Veterans of the Housing Administration demanded that the victim as a social parasite be moved outside the one-hundred-kilometer line of Moscow's city limits.

On one day of the many filled with such garbage came a call from the half-forgotten man Slava German. He laughed grimly, in his style. "What's the matter, brothers, have you forgotten me, do you think I'm also out in space?"

German had been paired with Drevesny ever since their youth and their first exhibit in the Transportation Museum. German and Drevesny—all of Moscow poured into that exhibit and was stunned. Not even coals were left from their once fiery friendship. However, the name Drevesny inevitably suggested the name German, and vice versa.

"Just imagine, Ogo, ha-ha-ha, I'm sick, ho-ho-ho and a bottle of rum, maybe you'll drop by. I feel shitty and I need to talk."

He lived, of course, in a communal flat, it couldn't have been otherwise. It was an enormous apartment near Chistye Prudy, rebuilt and redivided hundreds of times, but it still retained something of its aristocratic past. A half-dozen bells on the door. Maxim thought that he hadn't been there in years, and since all his other visits had taken place in a drunken swirl, he simply didn't remember which was Slava's.

The door was opened by a neighbor, with an elaborate hairdo and wearing an incredible Egyptian robe. She breathed a heavy dose of cognac on him. "Maximka, it's you?" So I'm Maximka here! "So glad you've come!" Pressing her soft hip against Ogorodnikov's protruding bones, the lady led him down the typical, almost cinematographic— Gorky Studios—hallway with the obligatory ancient bicycle hanging on the wall, the basins filled with soaking laundry, reproductions from *Mos-*

cow Lights, including sappy and nauseating the first five-year plan shots. "He needs this very much now," the neighbor whispered hotly, and shouted into the depths, "It's Maxim, Maxim!" Apparently, the apartment remembered him.

German was reclining on the couch. Scattered around him were magazines, photographs, and albums with notes. "Flu or hangover?" asked Ogorodnikov.

"Simply not moving," replied his old friend.

He used to be so chic, Ogorodnikov thought for some reason. So old-fashioned. Women fell for him like mad. The guitar? Of course, it's in its old place. His repertoire drove the snobbish Petersburg girls wild. It always had smelled of cognac in here, but never before of urine. Through the window, trees and the statue of Griboyedov, his powerful back—I remember some of this. Next to the window a photograph of the window, German's famous masterpiece. And here's something new, rather, something that floated up from the past—a girl on the beach, holding her heavy hair in a slender hand, Polina Shtein in the old days. . . .

"Read this!" Slava handed him a crisp sheet of fine paper.

" 'To the Photographers' Union USSR. In connection with the filthy slander of the photo album *Say Cheese!* and of M. P. Ogorodnikov I am quitting the Union and returning my membership card. Svyatoslav German.' "

"Really, Slavka!"

"It's nothing, no problem."

"What do you mean! You have to live!"

"That's the point, old man, I don't have to anymore. . . ."

What's this gloom? Suddenly Ogorodnikov understood that something horrible had happened, as German rose up on his elbow with a crooked smile on his full, almost Negro lips, and pushed aside the papers on his desk to get something in a brown wrapper. An X ray.

"That's my chest, old man. There, that dark spot—that's the end and very soon. They used a bronchoscope and took a biopsy. So you see, Ogosha, why that piece of paper isn't costing me anything?

" . . . Come on, stop it, Max, come on. . . ."

Something had happened between ellipses. After that, Ogorodnikov understood that he had lost consciousness for an instant. Slava German was smiling shyly. "I never thought that you . . . so strongly . . . too much . . . what's the matter with you?" Maxim realized that he was opening and shutting his mouth as if trying to say something. "I didn't want to shock you like that," Slava said.

"Slava-Slavka," Maxim muttered at last. He couldn't get anything else out.

"I'm glad you came," German said. "I can strike poses—don't be upset, Max, it's nothing, it happens. Without that it's unbearable. You know, I'm trying to think about my life now, but I can't do it. No fundamental conclusions, not even any worthwhile memories, they've all turned into a pile of photographs. Just one thing comes to mind and shames me immeasurably. All my life I tried to impress people and actually, old man, I never worried about anything else. Every chunk of life plays like cheap theater. I'm always posing. . . . Or, like good theater. What's the difference? Always posing. Even now, Ogosha . . . I asked you come, and I was picturing the 'At the Friend's Deathbed' scene. Handing you the X ray is a dramatic effect . . . along with my announcement of quitting the Union, that's really . . . brrrrr. . . . Telling you in the twilight about this crap becomes another scene. Alas, that's the only thing left connecting me to life. Without that I howl, Max. With that I howl, too, but not so loud, more of a whine, but without it, everything is over and only the howling is left. . . . In general, why don't you go now, Max? Do me a favor, let's do the departure scene. . . ."

In the dark Ogorodnikov thought he saw something the size of a toad hopping on the couch near the pillow. The lights of a passing trolleybus slid along the ceiling, and he saw that it was German's hand reaching toward the bed table. He leaned over and kissed Slava's prickly cheek. "Do you want a priest, Slava?"

German shuddered. "Yes, yes. You know, Max, I was reaching for religion even without my illness, but I was afraid of overplaying it. . . . This is horrible, and I'm even glad that the theater is closing. Go, Ogosha, go! Find me a priest before the curtain comes down."

Ogorodnikov went toward the door. German's voice caught him there. "Max, remember?"

"What?"

" 'I'll light up with streetlights.' ... No, it's all right, go ... 'the thin ribs of walls ...' "

Outside perhaps the last snow of the year was falling beautifully. There was no sign of Soviet authority in sight. He cleared the snow from the car windows and suddenly experienced the forgotten and strange sensation of normality. A normal Moscow evening, a normal man clearing snow from his car, who had just visited a normally dying friend. He got in, the car started up normally, skidded a bit normally at the light, the traffic cop pulled him over normally, normally checked his license, examined the car from all sides, returned his license, saluted— be careful, it's icy. . . .

While he was driving down Myasnitskaya, enveloped in normal ennui and sorrow, he kept remembering things from the past. Something very early, very young, forbidden, and colorful—dances in the late fifties, girls in platform shoes, punched noses, the inseparable trio—Slava, Andrei, Maxim. . . .

The traffic cop went over to the gray Volga parked under the Gastronom archway. "Mission accomplished," he said, saluting ironically to the two mugs from the Glands.

"And so, he just drove off?" One of them squinted at him.

The cop shrugged. "Why shouldn't he drive off? Everything was in order."

"Well, Sergeant, thanks for that." The Volga slid out of its cave. The traffic cop gave it a dirty look. Drones, he thought, real drones.

4

THE TWO HALF BROTHERS Ogorodnikov came to the Crystal Restaurant alone. The huge room with four-faceted columns had a glass wall down which melting sheets of ice slid during the day and which now, at evening, was getting frosty again. Nevertheless, the glass still gave a good view of the Moscow Hero City obelisk, a masterpiece of the Brezhnev behemoth period.

"It doesn't look like anything," October said. "Everything that is around me now doesn't look like anything. At first glance you might recall Las Vegas, but you forget it at second glance." He peered at the waiter who approached them. "No, everything's completely different, doesn't look like anything."

They managed to get a table far from the band, so that they could talk. The waiter wanted to seat a "nice couple" with them, but Maxim shoved some money in his pocket, "Forget it," and they were alone. "Well,"—chuckled Maxim—"some more horrible news?"

"That too," said October, removed his marvelous glasses, rubbed his tired temples with thumbs and forefingers. "Congratulations, you're a CIA agent!"

A soundless clap of emptiness quickly spread through all his cells and continued to expand. It took some time before October's words started penetrating into Ogo's empty spots.

". . . I felt that that's what they were headed for . . . it was terrible to admit to myself what I was feeling. Yesterday at a closed Party session at the Photographers' Union Vanka Fadnuk declared you were a 'major resident of the American spies,' and then that shithead, that former SMERSH agent Farpov demanded that they apply wartime laws to you. . . . You, of course, know who those bastards were speaking for. . . ." October's hands were shaking. He was looking to the side where through the restaurant's murk two officers of his institution, male and female, were watching him do his assignment.

Something tore through the restaurant's front door. Anastasia running. "Thank God, you're here! I found out by accident. Kapitolina Timofeevna let it out! Why are you trying to scare Max, October? Were you asked to scare him?"

"Wait, Nastya, listen!" Her arrival at the Crystal brought everything back to order. The emptiness evaporated through Ogo's skin. "Listen, Nastya, you don't know—I'm a spy! They're planning to shoot me!"

"Of course I know, I know all that," she muttered, picking up objects from the table, as if testing their reality. The waiter, watching her carefully, placed bottles and *zakuski* on the table. "Everyone knows," she went on, "and they're all laughing. I just had a call from Simka, she heard it from Volodka. They're all laughing. . . ." Her muttering trailed off and in a strange way that he had never noticed before her lower lip protruded. Silence reigned.*

October rose. He put one hand on the shoulder of his half brother, the other on the shoulder of his half sister-in-law. He squeezed lightly— farewell. He turned and began crossing the restaurant toward the stage. Unbearable, he thought as he walked, and his back expressed that feeling. Ogo watched him and besides the thought "unbearable," perceived alas, a large bald spot. Of course, as October moved away, the thought became less obvious and the bald spot blended into the parameters of his head. Without thought or bald spot October approached the orchestra, gave the leader a twenty-five-ruble note, gave them a request, and went off, downstairs, where he got his hat and coat. The bald spot was completely hidden by an Irish tweed hat, the thought was expressed by the movement of his arm getting into the sleeve. Unbearable. October went out on Kutuzovsky Prospect. A few minutes later the band played his request—the fox-trot "Gulf Stream."

<h2 style="text-align:center">5</h2>

MAXIM AND NASTYA, leaving the Crystal, immediately decided to run away. Not at all with the aim of saving Ogorodnikov's skin, which was unsalvageable, but simply to run off from Moscow for a while, from the collection of PhIDs, and hack snappers.

Their car, naturally, had two punctured tires, and that gave them a chance to escape. It was possible that the PhIDs, having taken care of two tires at once, would take off the tail today—how far could the Ogorodnikovs go? But go they would. To the Caucasus! "Really, I can allow myself a vacation before being executed," joked Ogo in fine style.

They hailed a cab. "Want to make a hundred?"

*A marvelous expression, isn't it? The kingdom of silence is the pride of the Russian. It implies something like the obelisk with four granite idols around it. Less commensurate with this pearl of native speech was the atmosphere of the Crystal with its wailing and squealing electric guitars and a good hundred citizens of all weights and sizes, working out in modern dance their striving for happiness. But you can't take your words back, and so it is in the kingdom of silence that we offer our reader the opportunity to witness the last action in this novel of the international observer for the Socialism Press Agency, Soviet spy October Petrovich Ogorodnikov.

The driver, talking to Ogorodnikov, stared at Nastya. "Can do it cheaper." He grinned crookedly.

Ogorodnikov pulled out a hundred-ruble note. "Quick, pal, fix our two tires!" The driver checked to see if they were kidding and leaped out with alacrity.

He was a young Moscow wolf with a neat rear end. They took guys like him into the Glands'. He had everything necessary in the trunk, including spare inner tubes. He worked fast behind the Moscow Hero City obelisk. The blackened snowbanks along the curbs still stood in their pockmarked majesty, but the street was clean and seemed to ring somehow beneath the passing cars, calling them to drive off.

A traffic cop came over interrogatively. "I'm helping out this unprofessional comrade," explained the driver. The cop said nothing but looked the pretty sheepskin coat, that is, Nastya, up and down. "How did it happen," asked the driver, "that you got two flats at once?"

"Her husband must have done it," Ogorodnikov said unexpectedly. "We're getting away from her jealous husband."

"Her husband," the young man gasped joyously.

"My husband," confirmed the pretty coat, "Comrade Old and Mean!"

This information inspired the driver. As he worked, he recounted his own astonishing sexual escapades. Nastya's presence did not inhibit him. He was one of those cabdrivers who assumes every female passenger is a prostitute. "She tells me 'a fiver to Zatsepa,' and I say, 'and a blow job.' ... I'm driving a lady from the airport, a chemist, and I pull into the woods, and what she starts with me ..."

"Max, Max—" Nastya laughed into the ear of Old and Mean, "what is he talking about? He's making my ears wilt. . . ."

"You, friend, seem to enjoy the French version of the sport," said Ogorodnikov.

Of course, what else? the driver seemed to imply.

When he finished, he gave Max the two punctured tubes. "Get them welded somewhere. The husband left you a present in one of them. You're lucky he didn't castrate you." They got in and drove off.

On the fourth day of their journey they arrived at the foothills of a gigantic Caucasian mountain. There Ogorodnikov suddenly, blissfully felt himself take a second billing. Everyone knew Nastya, they all cried, "Nastya's here," and he was for the time being only "Nastya's husband."

They spent several days in the resort area, among the tourists and skiers who crowded around the only ski lift in the region, bearing the daring slogan on its engine hut, "OUR GOAL IS COMMUNISM!" They also frequented the so-called cafés, which offered sandwiches with dried, buckled cheese. Grim men of the local ethnic minority sat in the cafés. Torn from the Koran, they adhered to alcohol. Squeezing the shot glasses in their hands, they clinked fists to commemorate the fortieth anniversary of their expulsion from their native crevasses in the steppes of Kazakhstan; that's how long they held a grudge.

After a few days, Nastya's colleagues came for the couple in a jeep. They went a thousand meters higher up the mighty mountain, to the barracks of the permanent glaciological expedition Four Troikas. The colleagues, who had partially lost contact with the Soviet Union because of their long stay in the wild heights, gave Nastya and Max a down parkas, skis, and other gear.

Days of Nastya's total triumph followed. Ogorodnikov was an absurd sight on the slopes, rolling down with the grace of a telephone pole and turning into a snowman when he fell. Nastya glided around in airy christies.

Once the very special person Eduardas Pyatrauskas came down to the Four Troikas. A whole kilometer higher he had a hut with some scientific equipment. He called the hut the "refuge of the pathetic Balt," which the other mountaineers picked up. Constant ultraviolet burning turned Eduardas into a mythical creature who always looked like he was about to say something in Sanskrit. "It's kind of strange drinking cognac with you," Max admitted, "it's like drinking with a ... a saga, I guess."

"Please?" Eduardas asked in the Baltic manner. He cast glances at Nastya and shone. The bastard's in love, Ogorodnikov guessed, and began asking for an invitation to the "refuge." He wanted to photo-graph the enamored manly face amid white and blue valleys. A day later they went up.

Max instigated walks à trois, and then slipped away, leaving Eduardas alone with Nastya, photographing the simplehearted Nibelung with a

zoom lens. "For you, my dear," Nastya said, "I'd even get into Edik's
bed."

"Don't have to do that yet," the photographer replied, "I'd rather get
into his inner world," and he treacherously started up conversations with
him.

Eduardas admitted that it was hard for him to come down from the
mountain. Even the Four Troikas seemed like a noisy resort, and farther
down, in the ski center, he simply fell into a trance. As for his green
and flat homeland, he recalled it without any reference to reality, almost
like a former incarnation. It turned out that he also frequently and seriously thought about nuclear holocaust. In case of that catastrophe the
only undamaged areas would be mountain peaks. Nuclear winter would
envelop the land below, and the remains of humanity would fall into
degeneration and savagery. Many autonomous hearths of civilization
had to be created as high as possible. It would take several generations
for the earth to cleared of the fallout, and then the mountain tribes
would come down from the islands in the clouds and continue the
human race.

"You made that up yourself, Edik?" Maxim asked politely.

"Please?" asked Pyatrauskas.

Colossal sunrises graced the slope; there were no sunsets, the sun
simply fell beyond the teeth of a nearby peak. "Listen," Eduardas said
to Maxim one day, just after sunset, "there's lousy news, really shitty
news." Ogorodnikov thought that today the mountain man was talking
to him for the first time as an individual person and not as an annoying
annex to the object of his devotion. But a pal below, at the ski base,
told him via the radio that the local Glands were in a uproar. A group
had arrived from Moscow. They were questioning everyone about Ogorodnikov. "They haven't learned yet where you are or where your car is
parked, our guys are playing dumb, but still . . . you understand. . . ."

Maxim replied that he understood and that he was leaving immediately. He couldn't resist a final provocation. "Should I leave Nastya
here?"

"Listen," the Lithuanian said, placing his hand on Ogorodnikov's
shoulder, "if you ever want to slip over to Turkey, I can help you. I
know places on the border where there is hope of success."

"Well, Eduardas," muttered Ogorodnikov, "well, Edik, damn it. . . ."

That night he took them down, bypassing Four Troikas. In the boundless, moonlit expanses, the thought of Glands and PhIDs seemed ridiculous. By morning they reached the highway. Ogorodnikov's Volga was waiting patiently where they had left it, in the village of Karabakh-chi, in the yard of meteorologist Ravil Gazdanov. They said good-bye to Ravil and Eduardas and set off.

Below, spring was in full bloom. They were selling lilacs along the Stavropol road. In Rostov the trees were green. Huge masses of feathered violators of the sacred Soviet borders were flying north. There was still snow around Oriol, but the road was dry and the car sped along. On the last day of the trip, around eight in the evening, they drove up to the roadside diner with the playful name Mother-in-law's Blini, known to all Soviet drivers.

Several local muzhiks sat on the sagging porch. They were a horrible sight: their skin blackened by the chemicals in the rotgut they drank, they sat almost motionless, calling, calling out weakly, "Hey, pal, I need a drink"; and not getting change or a response, smiled meaninglessly. Healthy people stood around the porch—long-haul truckers. They smoked and told dirty stories. A lopsided lamp illuminated the filthy lawn, where several people were squatting.

"They haven't fixed the toilet in the last three years, then," Ogorodnikov noted bitterly.

"Well, that's not so awful," Nastya said gaily, "the girls from that bus have gone off behind the bushes, I'll join them."

"Three years ago they had some food at least," Max said, when she returned. "I remember blini made with cornmeal."

They went inside and almost fell out again from the horrible smell: this was the time at Mother-in-law's Blini when they cleaned the pots and pans. "Look, people are eating even now—look, they're chewing!"

"I can't handle this, Max, let's go," begged Nastya.

"But look, Nastya, they're chewing something that's meat!"

"Max, it's something pimply! It's udder! Here's the menu: 'LHC udder with mashed potatoes, sixty-seven kopeks.'"

Without eating they raced along the highway of roaring engines and spewing exhausts, past Spassky-Lutovinov, through Turgenev's Russia.

It was only a half hour later, when they had gotten their breath back, that they pondered the abbreviation LHC. Suddenly Nastya slapped her forehead: "How could I not have known—teats of long-horned cattle!"

"You know," Ogorodnikov said, "I can't joke on this topic anymore."

With all these adventures, they naturally had not noticed that they had been expected and were watched at Mother-in-law's Blini. The wandering hidalgo from the KGB department rushed to his motorcycle the second they left and hurried to headquarters to let them know farther up the highway—the fascists were on the road!

At night, there was less traffic. Nastya made the last of the instant coffee in the thermos bottle and unwrapped some leftover processed cheese. Still driving, they had dinner.

"Maybe you don't know this, but I have a shortwave radio in the car," Max said with a look at his wife. They hadn't listened to the "enemy stations" for the last two weeks, that had been their agreement.

"Well," Nastya said with a shrug, "it doesn't matter now, tomorrow we're back in Moscow."

The Turgenevian fields were not yet covered by jammers and the reception was excellent. They listened to the whole evening program of the Voice of America: ... *Panorama* ... *Book World* ... *Events and Comment* ... the familiar voices of the Washington superstars Victor Frantsuzev, Ludmila Foster, Ilya Levin. ... Under the title *American Press on the Soviet Union*, there was a mention of *Cheese!*, and the personal name of the owner of the successful radiocar was not forgotten either. Harrison Rosborn, correspondent of *The New York Ways*, reported that the photographers' resistance was continuing. After the attacks in the press on Maxim Ogorodnikov three more photographers had quit the state-controlled Photographers' Union. ...

In Tula Oblast, during the *Collectors' Jazz* program, a highway patrolman pulled them over. He came up, checked their documents, asked, "You're not sleepy?" and looked inside. From the open window of his checkpoint the same jazz filled the air.

Program for Night Owls began near the Oka River. Nastya slept in the back seat. White birch trunks flashed in the dark. The mysterious disappearance of the major Soviet journalist October Ogorodnikov got a lot of play in the world press, said the familiar Voicer's voice, who seemed to be running alongside the birches next to the motionless highway. Runs away and doesn't disappear, can that be possible? Maxim shook his head and rubbed his face. Another moment like that and I'll end up in the ditch. The news was developing. The Soviet embassy in Paris has protested to the Ministry of Foreign Affairs of France in connection with the disappearance of October Ogorodnikov. In an article published in *Izvestia,* columnist Mekhamorchik maintained that October Ogorodnikov was kidnapped by American intelligence agents. The article, however, did not report that the missing man was the brother of the famous Soviet photographer Maxim Ogorodnikov, who recently with other members of the official Photographers' Union issued a challenge to Soviet censorship. . . .

Instead of birches, the farms of Serpukhovsky were now running past the windows of the still car.

6

GENERAL PLANSHCHIN AND Major Krost went home in total silence. Their car was significantly over the speed limit; however, the traffic cops could tell at a glance which type of car the seemingly indistinguishable Volgas were, and so they merely watched it go past. Some even saluted. That's too much, the general thought—there's no need to show that you know who we are.

General Planschin had become quite irritated in the last few days by the Ogorodnikov situation. The fellow was being sly, hiding again, losing his tails. That forced Planshchin's group to be sly, too, and trick the higher-ups, pretending to be fully informed—how many cigarettes he smokes a day, how many times he screws his live-in, what his stool and urine are like. But that wasn't the main problem. The main irritation came from the absence of the presence of certainty. The higher-ups never once had given a definitive statement on Ogorodnikov. He had to keep guessing. Funny as it was, all of the group's options were in suspension—neither accepted nor rejected. The last one, which began being developed at the closed Party meeting of photographers, seemed to have approval; however, after October's treachery it had to be dropped for obvious reasons. The present option was not bad in concept, though rather direct and instructive, that was its main distinction; however, there was no certainty that subsequently there would be no trouble afterward: there was no way he could refer to higher-ups.

And that Klezmetsov ... that damned Poker was making trouble, stubbornly pushing his not-quite-clear line, flitting around the floors of the building on Staraya Square,* he weaseled into Phikhail Mardeyevich's office again yesterday. . . .

The radio rumbled. Swallows calling Dove. "Pick up the phone, Krost!"

"They probably want to talk to you," muttered Major Krost.

"Do it," the general barked. The apparatus was getting flabby, he had to repeat orders every time. He lowered the window slightly. A stream of night spring air, almost warm, came in. Retirement! dreamed the general. Divorce from his wife and escape to his brother's place in Dagomys! His brother was rich, raising nutrias illegally, we'll get richer in the hat business together. . . .

On the right side of the highway, the slope was free of snow, and only the birches showed white.

7

AT 4 A.M. ON THE long platform at Chekhov Station two young men walked—Vladimir Skanshchin and Vadim Raskladushkin. They had met just fifteen minutes ago and, of course, totally by accident. First Vladimir had come up, melancholy, on the moonlit, concrete strip. Through the fog, Mother dear, the rocky road shines, he thought. The night is quiet, and the desert hearkens to God. . . . Strange, Lermontov was a progressive for his times, and he wrote like that. . . .

Then at the far end of the platform a slender figure appeared. As he

---

*Where the CPSU Central Committee's compound is situated. There is a popular song about a late Politburo member, Voroshilov:

> Oh, poor Marshal Voroshilov,
> He visited Staraya Square,
> He joined a faction!
> He'd have done better to join something simpler,
> Oh, poor man, he joined the faction!

came closer, Skanschin saw he was carrying a basket. Even closer—
Vadim! "What brings you here?"

"I've been picking mushrooms."

"Mushrooms? Now?"

"Thanks for the joke, I've been in a lousy mood." Vadim lifted the
cloth and in the basket lay row upon row of mushrooms, glowing like
Saint John's ferns. . . . "Some other time, Volodya, I'll show you the
local mushroom spots."

"All right!"

Both looked at their watches, both had illuminated dials. Four oh
one. "Want to walk a bit? I'm worried they're going to fire me soon
from the Glands, Vadim." Skanshchin sighed. "I've gotten too smart.
Lots of problems."

Four oh seven. "Is your watch right?" Raskladushkin asked.

"I set it by the Kremlin chimes every night," Skanshchin assured him.
They walked on. Skanshchin felt the stupid nighttime loneliness.

"What does yours say?" Raskladushkin asked.

"Four twelve and a fraction," Skanshchin said. And to himself he
said, Oh god. And then he thought, hmm, in Tamizdat,* they always
capitalize God. Is that an overabundance of respect, or what? Just about
the same thing is happening in photography. . . .

They stopped and both looked at their glowing watches at the same
time. It was four nineteen and eight seconds. Raskladushkin put his
basket down on the platform, took Skanshchin by both hands, and
wrapped him in an enormous embrace with his hands behind his
shoulderblades. Both young men's heads were thrown back, and they
saw the unbound starry and unfamiliar sky. Several seconds passed this
way. Then the embrace fell apart.

"You don't have fits, do you, Vadim . . . ?"

8

LESS THAN NINETY kilometers from Moscow, Ogorodnikov saw the distant headlights of an oncoming truck. Those lights were very bright.

*Along with Samizdat (self-publishing), Tamizdat (publishing *over there*, i.e.,
abroad) is an alternative to the official Soviet publishing industry.

Ogorodnikov turned off his brights, waiting for the truck to do the same in accordance with the rules of night driving. The truck paid no attention. What a boor, thought Ogorodnikov: He's big metal and doesn't give a shit. At the turn in the highway, two other distant and single lights showed behind the dark mass of the truck. Looks like two motorcycles. Ogorodnikov began slowing down—the four headlights were blinding him. He signaled twice more. No reaction. When you're blinded by oncoming lights you slow down to the minimum, keep the wheel steady, no maneuvers, that's the easiest way to manage on a narrow road.

And then the incredible happened. A hundred meters before they would meet, the truck switched lanes and headed straight for him. The motorcycles stayed in their lane. That blocked the entire highway. It seemed as if some additional headlights were activated the truck. Everything blurred before his eyes and then took on volume. The huge sparkling sphere was hurtling right at him, two smaller spheres were flying to the left. He heard the cry "The end!" Either he was shouting or Nastya had awakened. Understanding nothing, Maxim Petrovich Ogorodnikov turned the wheel as far right as it would go and then hard to the left, flooring the gas pedal, slipping along the edge of the deep ditch and past the truck.

For a minute they drove in silence, then looked back. The red lights of the truck and the two motorcycles were receding, vanishing at a turn.

Four twenty A.M., Kilometer 86 of Simferopol Highway. Husband and wife began shivering: too much adrenaline.

THE HAPPENING

I

BY MID-APRIL THE fields around Moscow dried up, and the time came for romantic conceptualism. It was decided to have a basic action-performance beyond Staraya Ruza called "Pulling a Seven-Kilometer Reel of Clothesline from the Grove." The leader was the Cheeser Vasya Shturmin—soldier's greatcoat over his shoulders, top hat on his head.

Thirty viewers stood or sat on the hillside. The seven conceptualists laughed were at first hidden in the grove, which stood about three hundred meters from the hill. A cold wind. There was a absence of symbolism, if you didn't count the donkey ears of the jamming tower in the southeastern sector of their space, and indeed no one paid them any attention.

Shturmin came out of the grove, where the reel of clothesline was hidden, and set up an ancient camera on a tripod. Covering himself with the coat, he lit the magnesium. After the explosion and puff of steam from the grove, two girls appeared. They were dragging the clothesline and approaching the hill with it. The viewers greeted them with applause.

The action developed, rather unreeled, successfully in the course of an hour and a half. The photographers had joined forces with the conceptualists. Olekha Okhotnikov and his Danish girlfriend worked well. The couple had been waiting a month for permission from the Soviet Union to get married. If the giant was benevolent, another conceptual action was planned in one of the appropriate wedding palaces in the capital. "Many find my marrying Nellie to be strange," Olekha said, "but historically Arkhangelsk is much closer to Copenhagen than, say, to Rostov-on-Don. The Hanseatic League, gentlemen, northern seafaring. . . ."

"I gave Nellie to my friend Olekha," Venechka Probkin bragged. "I'm very glad they're happy. What could be better than a happy friend? What could be more important than the ability to share with a friend? It's no trick to give the shirt off your back, it's much harder to give a blond foreigner or a turbodiesel Mercedes!" Incredible moral changes had taken place in the Muscovite semicrook since he had joined *Say Cheese!* It was no secret that some photographers looked askance at him, and some even asked, Is he a PhID decoy? Even those skeptics gasped when Probkin went to Georgia in his priceless Mercedes and returned in a rattly Zaporozhets. He had sold the limo and helped out his needy friends with the proceeds—some got a thousand, some five hundred.

There were more and more of the needy. Klezmetsov demanded betrayal in exchange for bribes. Amazingly, the Cheesers found that rate of exchange unprofitable. An unprecedented event in the history of USSR creative unions; the campaign was on for several months, and no one had made a shit of himself yet. Andrei Drevesny had done a dubious exploit in space, but at least he hadn't turned anyone in.

The line was still unreeling. Two flutists played among the viewers on the hill. Shuz Zherebyatnikov warmed himself with a hip flask. The performance was not his thing. "I'd understand if the whole thing ended with a group roll in the hay, but since that's not in the works, I condemn this as decadence. Want a slug, Max?"

The Ogorodnikovs were there, too. The happening in Staraya Ruza was the perfect excuse for Nastya to get Max outside to see people and breathe some air. Ogorodnikov just couldn't get over the adrenaline squall on Kilometer 86 of the Simferopol Highway. He had several attacks a day of what he came to call "elementary agony," that is, the "empties," dizziness, and nausea. In between attacks he preferred to sit in an armchair and watch whatever was on TV. He was stunned by the thought that an attempt had been made on his life ... or the imitation of an attempt? ... Maybe it was a real attempt? ... Maybe the driver was just half-asleep? ... And still it was mind-boggling that there was a section of the mighty power that was concerned specifically with Max Ogorodnikov, and specifically with the idea of exterminating him. What the fuck was upsetting them? Why be so furious with artistic folly? And really, where did they come off pretending to have total power in Russia! Didn't Russia once tolerate her *skomorokhi*, buffoons?

The other day Harrison Rosborn added food for such thought. His sources were whispering that Zherilenko, secretary of the CC, was proposing some specific actions in re *Cheese!* and New Focus. The sources were whispering in the night, murmuring like fountains, dictators, salt of the Russian earth, masters of the largest warehouse of explosives in history, they meet in secret session to settle the fate of a bohemian group. Tell me, Harrison, do you despise Russia?

Rosborn and his pipe. Stronghold of humanity—the Anglo-Scots enlightenment. Before, yes, he used to despise Russia, but now he's learned not to blame the people for bolshevism. That's not easy, my friends. Oh, yes, it's not. The revolution makes a colossal selection, in general, of the less-than-best part of humanity. Let's put it this way, of human trash. It floats to the surface. Every nation has a lot of trash, but the theoretical revolution has not befallen every nation. I say "theoretical," because it has no bearing on real life and experience. How can you not become a metaphysician?

"The hell with all this," Nastya said that morning. "Look, Ogo, it's another day and you still are not executed. Let's go to Staraya Ruza, let's breathe some Russian conceptualism." They went. Max even took his camera and, sitting on the hill, on that spot of Russian land where they never hunted down the *skomorokhi*, took a few pictures.

After an hour and half's efforts, the clothesline was fully hauled out of the grove and lay in an impressive heap at the foot of the hill, begging to be a monument to a major event in Soviet culture. They were about to open the champagne when two jeeps pulled up at the edge of the field and a second, unplanned part of the happening extended from the grove—a group of people's volunteers. "Too bad we don't have a machine gun," said Shuz, "the bottles aren't enough to fight them off." The jeeps were approaching from the rear. The operation had been tactically thought out.

Militiamen and several bosses in mufti came out of the cars. "Everyone, show your papers!" The volunteers were coming closer, glowing with idiotic smiles.

"What right have you!" barked Shuz. The young people were docilely pulling out their worn papers. For some reason the best-quality Soviet work got messed up quickly with people like that. "What right have you?" Shuz went on.

The militia captain smiled and promised, "We'll find one."

"What's the matter, Shuz, you're so upset," said Vasya Shturmin—monocle in his right eye. "Nothing much going on, it's the usual stuff."

"Citizens," the captain announced loudly, "you are all detained until further notice. Please follow me."

A large group of people, who from a bird's-eye view resembled a demonstration for land reform, moved through the ugly field of winter wheat. On the way to the village club, the place of detention, the volunteers were intermixed with the artists, exchanging cigarettes. They asked curious questions. What were you trying to say with the rope? That the whole kolkhoz system should be hanged? Or was it about Soviet slavery?

As soon as they got to the club, "further notice" arrived in the person of PhID Captain Vladimir Gavrilovich Skanshchin. He ran around with a worried look, from the authorities to the detainees, fussily clarifying minor inaccuracies on residency permits, in ultimate surprise making square eyes at the artists, and just spreading his hands—what can you do with the village dolts!

Ogorodnikov observed his *kurator* from afar and suddenly thought that this whole affair was affecting him, too. The recent Komsomol roundness was gone. If he weren't a Chekist, you'd think you caught glimmers of despair in his eyes. . . .

Soon everyone was released and headed for the train, tired but pleased: the happening was a success! They were satisfied with the explanation given by the representatives of the local authorities, too: We have a resort for people with stomach complaints nearby, the volunteers said, and we have to be extremely vigilant.

2

THE BUCOLIC MOOD, alas, did not last long. Before dawn, a telephone sandstorm shook them. Shuz had been arrested in the night; Probkin, Chavchavadze, Shturmin, Tsuker, Marxyatnikov, and even dying German had been searched. . . . Copies of the album were confiscated, both the originals and the contraband deluxe editions from Pharaoh. Also confiscated was all exposed film, correspondence, books, typewriters, and even the means of production, their cameras. . . .

All those whose apartments were searched were summoned for interrogation at the procurator's office. Okhotnikov's place was destroyed, they even stripped the wallpaper. Olekha and his Danish girl were taken away by the PhIDs, interrogated for three hours, and then released after they signed a document promising not leaving town.

No one came to Ogorodnikov's, even though two cars were parked under the window all night and the powerful projector beam shone from the construction site into the window.

3

"BUT YOU PROMISED there would be no victims! You called yourself a politician of major significance!"

"You still have doubts about that?"

"Now, after the arrests and searches, I do!"

"You shouldn't. Look at it calmly. That Shuz Zherebyatnikov is a real enemy, almost of the same caliber as Ogorodnikov. After his arrest, Max has nowhere to go, any step will lead to a cliff! It's the end for Ogorodnikov and at the same time for the filthiest blotch in Soviet photography. As for the rest . . . well, I'll tell you a secret . . . the rest will survive! This was arranged by me, I stress, by me at a level . . . well, you can guess. The ones who want to make their careers in Soviet photography will have to go elsewhere! This doesn't mean that the *Cheese!*

gang will get off scot-free. They'll have to answer to their colleagues, the Party, and the People!!!! No, no, I don't need water, I'm fine! They think they're pure, free artists, masturbating on their solidarity, on their false concept of comradeship! There is no freedom now! Nowhere! There's only struggle!!!!"

"You can't go on like this! You're killing yourself! Think of the children! Here, take this, and drink it down! And this pill, too, no, take two!"

"Is everything clear to you now?"

"Yes, there's only one thing unclear."

"I can guess."

"Well then?"

"Say it!"

"All right. His trip to Brazil is off."

"Do you think we'd send such a dubious hero to Brazil?"

"Do you want him to wallow in shit?"

"Yes!!!"

"I ... beg you ..."

"Beg? That's good. Then it has to be that way."

"Which way?"

"The way you don't like."

"No! I've warned you: never again that way!"

"Exactly...."

4

SVYATOSLAV GERMAN BURNED like a dry leaf. He almost never recovered consciousness the last few days of his life, drugged in the Herzen Institute. Once his right hand fell from the bed into a tub of water. The people sitting around his bed saw a blissful smile on his face. His hand played with the water. He had been a good swimmer, and maybe he was visualizing (remembering? imagining?) the hours of youthful happiness at the beach.

Slava's elderly wife and grown daughter came from Baku. It turned out that the first-class Moscow bachelor had had a family in Baku all his life, and he used to rest in its bosom from time to time, and then, returning to "his circle," would respond to questions as to where he had been with a mysterious smile. His wife insisted that Slava's body be sent to Baku to be buried next to the graves of his great-grandfather, grandfather, and father, Russian Caucasians, an engineer, a lawyer, and a doctor.

About a hundred of the "remaining" Muscovites, as they used to say then, came to the Herzen Institute morgue to pay their respects. Several weeping women were in the crowd. Slavka's eternal love Polina Shtein-Klezmetsov did not show up. Andrei Drevesny, the "cosmic hero," stood pale and as straight as a guards officer. All the Cheesers came. Georgii Avtandilovich gave a three-minute speech ... genius ... knight ... ungrateful homeland.... Through the tiny window in the zinc coffin Slava really looked like a knight—a stone face filled with gloom and peace.

They wandered away from the hospital courtyard, no one could speak. Only beyond the gates on Begovaya Street, someone hailed Max. Drevesny came over. "Max, where are you going?"

"We're off to Developkino, to the Marxyatnikovs'."

Drevesny seemed not to notice "that alpinist," as he called Nastya. "What a coincidence, I'm off to Developkino, too."

Ogorodnikov was mildly surprised. "To the Marxyatnikovs'?" Everyone had gotten used to the fact that after his flight Drevesny no longer participated in the gatherings of New Focus.

"No, no," Drevesny said hurriedly, "I'm renting a room there."

"He's lying," Nastya said under her breath. Ogorodnikov remembered that the cosmic photographer had recently been given two rooms with a terrace at Developkino. His photos were printed in *Word of Honor* and in the Komsomol *Word of Honor* and the Moscow *Word of Honor*. He ought to have a dacha at Developkino by now.

"Taxi!" Andrei rushed forward.

"Why get a taxi?" Maxim Petrovich nodded with his long nose. "There's my car."

Andrei recoiled visibly. "What, you're still driving?"

Nastya laughed crudely. Drevesny squinted at her haughtily. "What's the matter with you?" Ogorodnikov opened both doors. Everyone got

in. Drevesny had started grinning strangely of late, showing all his teeth
for no reason. "You should be very careful at the wheel, Ogosha," he
muttered. "You know how many hooligans there are, what the mores
are, how much cruelty. . . ."

"You weren't this scared up in space, Andrei Yevgenievich?" Nastya
asked in honeyed tones.

Drevesny smashed two fists together angrily. "Tell your alpinist to
stop provoking me."

They drove off and everyone calmed down. In the evening rush hour
no one paid any attention to Ogorodnikov's car. The flow moved past
the Vagankov cemetery, down 1905 Street and along Bolshaya Pres-
naypa, on the barricades of which Moscow once fought against St.
Petersburg, and then farther along the embankment, to take a direct run
in the direction of the sinful village of Developkino.

Should I tell Andrei why we're going to the Marxyatnikovs'? thought
Ogorodnikov. No, I won't tell him about the press conference, he'll
think I'm trying to drag him into this again. The gathering for the free
press was New Focus's last card. After the searches and arrests, the
board of the Union had another round of summonses, urging rejection
and repentance on everyone, young and old, except Ogorodnikov. They
left him alone, if you didn't count the telephone calls like "Bastard, go
down to Kolpachny tomorrow and ask for a visa to Israel," or "Don't
go out of your house, asshole, we kill betrayers of the homeland," or—
in an agitated female voice—"Excuse me, we the teachers of Zhitomir
and Zhmerinka are worried—is it true that Comrade Ogorodnikov has
been arrested for being an American spy?" All that became part of the
daily routine. Well, the wall socket in the front of the apartment burned
out recently, but that could have been just an accident, faulty wiring.

So, the press conference was the last attempt to get their friends out,
save the confiscated film and copies of the album. Hit for hit. "They"
would either get meaner or cut it out. The world press, really, was the
only thing "they" took into consideration at all.

A wondrous golden sky spread over the western suburbs of Moscow.
Drevesny and Ogorodnikov simultaneously recalled the distant spring
when on just such a golden evening they went to Lithuania with Slava
German.

"Are you going to Baku for the funeral?" Andrei asked.

Maxim scratched his head, which resembled an abandoned stack of low-quality hay. "How about you?"

Andrei rested his hand on his friend's bony shoulder, as if not seeing the alpinist's nasty look, and sighed. "I'm ashamed to admit it, but I can't. Slavka will forgive me. I'm going abroad tomorrow."

"Where to?"

"Bulgaria."

"He's lying," Nastya whispered, "he's off to Brazil. . . ."

A huge airliner flew above them. Hmm, planes nowadays have miraculously learned how to brake before landing. That huge thing is simply hanging over the highway in the golden sky.

"I hope, Max, that we'll see each other there, too, sometimes, if, of course, they let me go," Drevesny suddenly said.

Ogorodnikov suddenly shuddered. "Where?"

"In the West," Drevesny suddenly explained. "Where will you live? Probably in New York, right?"

"Why?" Ogorodnikov suddenly demanded in astonishment.

"It's the best way for you!" Drevesny suddenly began explaining passionately. "Go, and go quickly! I'm telling you this as a friend!"

"Don't you dare! Don't interfere in this!" Nastya suddenly screamed.

"Don't listen to the vain fool!" Drevesny's eyes suddenly began bulging, revealing a lot of yellow in the whites. From the back seat he pushed against the driver's seat and with his extended face climbed into the rearview mirror. "Don't drag the boys into this! It's not their fault! You started the whole thing, you take the fire! Remember 1968, I acted alone then, I didn't take anyone with me! You're taking everyone with you! Do you think I don't know where you're going now?! You're forcing everyone to take extreme actions, and if anyone doesn't follow you, he'll be called a traitor in the West!"

The golden light instantly dimmed. In the dark a huge swirling, iridescent electrical ball hurtled toward Ogorodnikov. Two smaller balls flew from the left. "The end," one of them or all three of them shouted. There was no sound. In the silence after the collision the car fell apart and all the bodies flew out.

EPITAPH

THE RAIN WAKES him up. And right after awakening, he feels a chill in his bones. *I'm lying in muddy clay, in a soaked pit. The least little move makes everything slurp around me and in inside my clothes. A fine thing—thrown in a ditch!* His cheek lies on the slope of a ditch. A rivulet flows past his eyes down to the puddle in which his feet repose. Red spots show in the rivulet. *His smashed mug is still bleeding, but, it looks like he can . . . he can manage it. . . .*

Slipping, he makes his way out of the ditch. As he rises, the world appears less and less attractive. Innumerable dump trucks drive past, spraying mud. Clouds drag their sagging bellies over the tops of lampposts and the clumsy contours of the roofs of the condom factory of Fakovka Village. "A BROADER SCOPE FOR SOCIALIST COMPETITIONS"—one of the holiday slogans on the gates. An aluminum idol of Lenin stands like an up ended plane. Had there been a factory like that in his birthplace of Simbirsk, millions of copies of that statue would have never been spawned. Fakovka Village's modest rubber hackwork corrects history.

The factory helps him orient himself in space. Not far from the highway a side road leads to the valleys and peaks of Developkino. It is harder to orient himself in time, but he heads down the side road, where, through the fog, show clumps of Mother Nature—bushes and rocks.

It is deserted: no people, no cars, forget about dogs—the fine creatures must have grown extinct in this zone. He finishes an asphalt descent and begins an asphalt ascent. Now he is surrounded by firs. Twice the headlights of a sleuth's car show in the avenues of the dacha settlement, but they evaporate in the fog. It's hard for them to find me, he thinks, and gloats. But they do. A clear figure is coming down toward him. As it gets closer it becomes blurrier, but it is coming closer. Why are they pursuing me inexorably? Really, there's no cause for them to be so inexorable.

Ogorodnikov bursts into tears. Trying to cover his face, he picks up a handful of tears. He takes his gas pistol from his pocket.

"Don't, Max, don't," a young voice says. "Drop your toy, it's useless!" Vadim Raskladushkin stands right next to him. One of his distinguishing traits is the clever ability to dress appropriately for the weather conditions; now he is wearing a British raincoat, with a plaid scarf around his neck, and rubbers on his feet. "This way." He indicates a narrow passage between two plank fences.

They set off. It is slippery, dizzying, clayey, slimy. "May I have your hand?" A hand, imbued with dependability and strength, is immediately offered.

Soon the fences end, and the path heads upward, toward a stand of pines. A breeze moves through the crowns of the trees, the fog lifts a bit, and between the trunks they can see a cozy cemetery.

Right after the cemetery begin the ugly buildings of the Frezerov-shchiki Station. Real slums. Semidilapidated garages, forgotten warehouses, crooked fences. At one turn they see a graffito in pitch on a concrete pipe, "DOWN WITH COMMUNISTS!" They turn a few times in those jungles, until they reach a brick building resembling an ancient Volga storehouse. A rusty metal door, a big padlock. Painted on the wall is a crumbling star of the Army, Aviation & Chemistry Volunteer Society (AACVS), a rifle, and a gas mask. Raskladushkin has a key, he takes off the padlock and removes the latch.

"Follow me, Max, don't worry. This is the Chapel of Saint Nicholas."

A dusty votive candle is lit under the high vaulted ceiling. The icons, strangely enough, are still visible through the plaster of Soviet eras. In one spot it has fallen off, and Ogorodnikov can see Christ on a donkey. The room is filled with broken office furniture and all kinds of things, including a training aid—a Maxim machine gun sawed in half lengthwise. He is worried by the huge bottles sealed by the filth of five-year plans. Ogorodnikov asks if he can smoke here, whether there are flammable materials here—benzene, kerosene, motor oil, napalm.

In response Vadim Raskladushkin blows the dust from a night table and pulls out a pack of Northern Palmyras. "They don't smoke these anymore, but the tobacco's not bad."

Ogorodnikov inhales. "In general, everything here has something to do with the thirties, right?"

"Thirties and forties, as far as I can tell," Vadim Raskladushkin replies thoughtfully. "There, take that gramophone. The record is from that period so awkwardly called World War Two."

It hisses and rasps. *"I'll remember the infantry and the second platoon and you because you gave me smoke...."*

Vadim leads Maxim deeper into the chapel-warehouse. In the corner they come upon a sagging but comfortable leather couch. Things like this are priceless now. It's useful for everything, including love games. "Oh, yes," confirms Raskladushkin. "Actually, it's the back seat of a 1936 Packard limo."

He puffs up his cheeks a few more times, blows the dust from objects around the couch. Several faces appear in various angles and dimensions, including the passionless features of the patron of seamen, Saint Nicholas. Beneath him Vadim Raskladushkin places an undying battery-powered flashlight. Then he seats Ogorodnikov on the leather couch.

"This is where you must rest, Max."

"What am I supposed to do here," wailed Ogorodnikov, "pray, or what ... ?" He takes Raskladushkin's strong white hand. "Vadim, don't leave right away!"

"Pray, if you want," Raskladushkin says, and places his hand on Ogorodnikov's head. "And if you don't want to, don't pray. Sorry, I must go...."

Ogorodnikov is racked with sobs again. "Wait, friend, don't leave me! Don't you see the enormous flow of moisture from my eyes? Unceasing tears."

"That's probably a good thing," says Vadim. "They say that of all the human moistures, tears are closest to the roots of the soul. Others feel that the tear is part of the world ocean. Referring, as certain circles maintain, not to the ocean of storms and struggle, but the ocean of sin and sorrow."

With those words he takes his hand from Ogorodnikov's head and goes away. Ogorodnikov can hear him latching and locking the door outside. He covers his wet face with his hands and allows the tears to flow violently between his fingers, along with bubbles created by the simultaneous flow of saliva and snot. He prays with the wildness typical of every person with a Soviet education.

Lord God, Creator,
And you, blessed Nicholas,
I foresee the grass rising
Over our ashes and cinders.

I captured the fleeting image
And in that, sinner, I was zealous
And did not notice that I was limited
By the sweep of arms, the roar of mouths,
The flight of legs, the movement of hips.
Seeing everything, I flew off the handle,
Like a red rebel knocked off
The barrels of 1905.

Lord, is it true that hidden in the movement of the stars is the path leading
    beyond the stars?
Merciful one, share the secret of black spaces!
Is the place we call Russia here
Something more significant than geological slag?

Children's parties,
The babble of lilac souls,

But it's time to accept
The shower of fierce rites.

The quiet honey of youth,
The fragrance of Crimean plums ...
It's time to step forward
Into the hogwash of awesome theories.

Eternal chirp of fledglings,
Brief trumpet of elephants.
Time.... The monk Francis
Hobbles through the ravine.

Lord, enlighten, where will I be with my friends accommodated in the
    multitude of distant souls?
All those combinations called generations, is it true they are not random?
Merciful Lord, One in the trinity of Father, Son, and Holy Spirit,
Remember your children in the midst of materialism!
Do not allow me to stand before Your absence!
Lord, perform a miracle and shame atheism!

2

BY THE TIME Vadim Raskladushkin leaves the Chapel of Saint Nicholas,
it is dark. Not far away, the search car's headlight combs the walls and
roof of the barracks. Raskladushkin goes out on the highway and raises
his hand. The search car stops. "Give me a lift to the station, Volodya?"

"Of course, get in, Vadim!"

Skanshchin is alone in the car. He drives slowly and shakes his head
bitterly, clearly wanting to share something important with his companion. "It's terrible, Vadim, I've lost hope of ever finding Ogo, but I have
to find him, dead or alive."

"What do you need him for, Volodya?" Raskladushkin asks. A
healthy curiosity always shines in the eyes of that gifted youth.

"I have to give him a summons, Vadim, in the case of Shuz Zherebyatnikov. We recently arrested the hardened enemy."

What a strange gesture. A pianist's fingers take his ear and slightly rub it as if it were a cabbage leaf. A refreshing fever courses through his body.

"There is a vicious affair under preparation in your office, Volodya."

"Really? What a strange and unscientific formulation, Vadim. We are performing an operation approved by the high Glands." The pianist's finger—it's fingers like that that participate in banging out the Apassionata Sonata, that "inhuman music," in the words of the great Lenin— gets deep into the ear and pulls out a clump of wax on the tip of the nail. And Darling has just said last night, You need to clean out your private parts, Captain! I agree, who can question the benefits of such an action? The eardrum vibrates in a new way; oxygenation of the hemoglobin cells, about which much good had been said in high school, increases sharply.

"It would be better not to look for Ogorodnikov, Volodya," Raskladushkin suggests. "Don't take part in evil."

The wax plug in the left ear pops out under pressure of fresh air without the intervention of the musical finger. "But it's an enormous risk, Vadim! I'll be fired from the Glands! And worse, I'll be thrown out of the Party!"

"But you won't be a villain, Volodya!"

Those words make his eardrums ring the way they did in his Pioneer childhood. "Do you guarantee that, Vadim? Promise?"

"We're here, Vova! So long!"

3

THE NEXT MORNING is crystal clear and fresh. The atmospheric pressure somehow has balanced overnight, so that a great number of negative blood-vessel reactions, which sometimes lead, according to Raskladushkin, to stupid Party and government decisions, do not occur.

Vadim is riding his bicycle toward Miussy Square, and in order to make the time go faster, is declaiming a few lines from Pasternak's early poems. "I drink the bitterness of tuberoses, the bitterness of the autumn skies . . . beneath it melted spots blacken, and the wind is potholed with cries, and the more random the more dependable ... I grew, and like Ganymede, I was borne by bad weather, by dreams." It's not bad, thinks Raskladushkin, it's not so far from what is called the truth.

At that hour at the Photographers' Union the closed session of the secretariat is beginning, the one that is supposed to sum up the struggle of the fighting division of the Party's lenses to solidify their ranks in the face of yet another provocation from the Western intelligence agencies. The *Cheese!* campaign has tired all of them. The creative indices for this period have dropped. Well, we'll sum up today and then—on to our deserved, even very deserved business trips abroad!

They have to pass a resolution approving the arrest of the pseudophotographer Zherebyatnikov by the PhIDs. Then they have to approve the text of the article "Alien," on Ogorodnikov's treachery. The text expresses the wishes of the Photographers' Union USSR to bring the traitor to criminal justice. Further comes the suspension of all the Cheesers, including those who have announced they are quitting and those who are still vacillating. You cannot leave the Union, or the Party, on your own, just as a single individual cannot rise above the People! The suspension is for one year. In that time the healthy elements will come to their senses and the rotten ones will be cut out!

The great elder Bluzh himself comes to the session. In the last few months Klezmetsov and Bluzhzhaezhzhin have grown close. It is said that the old man is grooming Klezmetsov.

As soon as they sit down around the table, "spreading human kindness to one another,"* the door opens and Ninochka the secretary comes in, eyes popping with significance, and says that "a comrade" is asking for Fotii Feklovich. Klezmetsov gasps, coughs, bangs his hand. "Don't you understand what is happening here, Nina Sergeyevna? Tell him I'm not here!"

Ninochka wrings her thin fingers. "No, I can't lie!" She is delicately moved aside, by the waist, and a light-eyed young man comes into the room.

---

*From Vladimir Mayakovsky's poem on Bolsheviks: Though made of steel they "spread human kindness *to each other.*"

"Lying is bad!" he says with a friendly smile, and bows. "I am Vadim Raskladushkin. May I join you?"

The members of the secretariat, stunned, stare at the uninvited guest. All the mugs spread, as if pulled by a single magnetic motion of the facial muscles, into a single collective smiling face. How nifty and unexpected in its simplicity! Well said, Comrade Raskladushkin! Lying is . . . how did you put it?

"Bad," Raskladushkin prompts, already sitting between Klezmetsov and Bluzhzhaezhzhin and patting the elderly shaking knee in the First Cavalry wool pants. "Besides which, lying is useless, because everything is known."

"Bravo!" says Bluzhzhaezhzhin. "I had always suspected that, kind sirs, that is, comrades!"

Just then the factotum Kunenko blushes. "Why not kind sirs, gentlemen! Why should we deny our cultural heritage?" Everyone agrees, even such comrades as Pharkov and Phanduk, the Stalinist falcons who have been around. Bluzhzhaezhzhin raises a contemporary of the First Congress of the RSDRP, that is, his index finger, and begins teaching those present, saying that even such Kremlin secrets as chocolate bonbons and semisweet Kindzmareuli wine are known where they need to be and thus His Excellency Mr. Raskladushkin is quite right to say that lying is useless!

"About that later," Vadim says. "For now you must liquidate all the filth that you comrades—no, no, comrades, that's easier—have prepared against honest photographers."

Everyone buzzes in agitation. Of course, and the sooner the better! Dump the vileness! Into a basket! And put the basket in the oven! And the ashes in a box! And the box either into the Kremlin wall or the deep blue ocean! Ninochka, Simochka, and Alevtina Makarovna do not need to be asked twice, they quickly gather up the prepared materials, including the "spontaneous responses from the audience." Soon the table is cleared, and all the participants of the secretariat session are leaning on it toward Vadim Raskladushkin. What other proposals?

"Order lunch," the young man says.

Everyone is completely delighted. If all problems were solved this way!

Vadim waits until the *zakuski* and the bottles have been brought, clinks glasses with the disheveled, sweaty, and slightly rakish Fotik, makes himself a sandwich, hooks a cucumber, and makes his bows: "I have more work in town."

4

AT THE PHID offices, meanwhile, arrested citizen School-University-Zenith Artemievich Zherebyatnikov is being interrogated. The interrogation is being performed in accordance with modern practice, that is, without "undue" humiliation. In past times, the villain would have had needles under each nail!

There is a chair. On it sits mighty Shuz. Around him pace Major General Planshchin, Majors Plyubyshev and Krost. Captain Slyazgin is taking notes, replacing Captain Skanshchin, who will probably have to take a treatment to get back to creative work.

Plyubyshev and Krost peer into the elderly hooligan's haughty face. "Confess, Zherebyatnikov, did you take money from a foreigner named Leroy?"

Zherebyatnikov blinks from the pressure, as if there is something in his eye. "I admit it," he confesses.

"How much?" the general presses from behind his back.

"I got a hundred thousand, but I could have gotten more."

"In what currency?"

"In Mongolian turgriks, Citizen General."

The investigators switch places, the general takes the frontline position, and burns Shuz with his glance. We will not allow you to mock us! "Oh"—the writing Slyazgin shakes his head—"if you'd let me have a private chat with him!"

"Forget it, Kolya," his suspect says, "look at me and look at you. Nothing good will come out of our tête-à-tête for you."

"Silence, Citizen Zherebyatnikov!"

Vadim Raskladushkin comes in with two bottles of Massandra champagne. There is something comical in his movements. Everyone gasps, of course. The Chekists gasp to themselves; their training keeps them from gasping audibly, from showing emotion. Their victim, a male human being, Zherebyatnikov, gasps loudly. "Vadka, how'd you get in here!"

"Entrance seven," the guest explains thoroughly.

The general grabs the phone. Oh, I'll be furious now! He feels that official fury is the only thing that can save him from the charm of this person, and even that is questionable. Letting strangers into the interrogation block! Heads will roll! Two days ago some woman wandered in, looking for Children's World department store, and last year fur hats were swiped from the Chairman's reception room. ... It's all right if it's our own boys, but what if it was agents from NTS?* "You so-and-so's at the door, whom did you let in?"

"Vadim Raskladushkin" was the answer.

"Do you want to be shot? Who signed his pass?"

"Don't fool around, Comrade General," the guard replied. "What pass? We let Blue Eyes through without a pass. The comrade came, after all, to ... wait, I wrote it down, here it is ... to 'dissipate errors and prejudices interfering with society's normal life.' "

The general, stunned, hangs up. "What's the champagne for?" he asks gently.

"To celebrate Shuz's release," Vadim explains and asks for the glasses. Vova Skanshchin comes with glasses for everyone. He has checked out of the hospital on his own. "Clear the table, you ass," he says to Kolya Slyazgin. They sweep all the investigation crap into a basket and set up the glasses. Raskladushkin struggles comically with the cork. At last—*boom*. Hurrah!

The glasses of bubbly beverage fly up in a joyous wordless toast. This is good, the general thinks or says. Vadim Raskladushkin came just in time. What a vile deed we were preparing, I can't even believe it! I have enough in my past; enough is enough. Just remembering the

---

*NTS (Russian abbreviation for the National Labor Union), a leading anti-Soviet émigré group based in Western Europe. Considering the mild European climate, why do they need fur hats from the Chairman's reception room? Duh.

Northern Caucasus I can't pee. I never thought champagne was good for that.

5

RASKLADUSHKIN WANTS TO slip right under the arch of Spassky Tower on his bike, but no. A couple of gorillas grab him and work him over. "The Kremlin is closed today to Muscovites and tourists, and you'll really get it for trying it on a bike. Who are you?"

"Drop it, boys, really." Vadim laughs, as if being tickled by the militiamen. "I'm here on serious business, I'm going to a Politburo meeting, and my name is Vadim Raskladushkin."

They let go and salute. "Welcome, Vadim, to the historic fortress of Marxism-Leninism!"

In the closed sector of the Kremlin, from the terrace, where no human foot has trod—and where stand the real Tsar's Cannon and Tsar's Bell, and not the plaster ones for tourists—four soldiers watch in astonishment as Vadim Raskladushkin walks his bicycle across the court. Their instructions are to shoot anyone appearing here without warning. The instruction, of course, is meaningless, because even a bird can't pass the electronic alarm system without many layers of permissions; however, it seems that there was a reason for that regulation: there is a guy with a bike heading straight for the sanctum sanctorum, where at the given moment our wise men are meeting. What to do? They can't kill such a nice guy.

"Hi, guys," Raskladushkin says. "Sunbathing? Move your guns, I'm coming to the Politburo meeting. The fate of my comrades is being decided there."

The next regulation concerns the guards of the Politburo sessions. The soldiers of that unit are supposed to immediately destroy the building guards at the slightest violation of the rules. They in turn are subject to destruction by the forces of the General Secretary's personal guards, made up of three independent groups that watch one another. Every single one of them is subject to destruction by the other two in case of any problems. This system, naturally, also has several electronic systems which preclude the necessity for these rules.

Vadim Raskladushkin explains his goals at every checkpoint and

moves on until he finds himself in the last wide and airy corridor, leading straight to the holy doors. The last four supersoldiers come out of
the walls with snub-nosed armor-piercing semiautomatic Uzi rifles made
in Israel, preparing to squash him like a fly. But he explains his aim to
them, too.

Then comes the very last hope, the head of the personal bodyguards
of the General Secretary, General Stepanov, limping, panting, and with
an unclean pistol in his jacket. "What's going on here? Why has the
alarm system failed? The CIA must have sent their invisible plane. I
won't live to get my pension. "

But his men are smiling: no basis for panic, Comrade General, it's
just Vadim Raskladushkin going to the Politburo, he has a good reason.

That door has never creaked, and now it does. The Politburo members, candidate members, secretaries, and assistants, about fifty guys in
all, turn toward the door. In comes a modest and sweet young man
dressed in retro style—an Oxford check cardigan and plus fours. He
sits in the corner and waves his hand—continue, go on, comrades!

Brezhnev looks at him warily. Even though this uninvited guest is
better than a Tatar,* he still looks like a foreigner, and the General
Secretary has never understood those people. "The comrade is here to
discuss what?" asks Brezhnev, squinting at his assistants. Stunned, they
say nothing. Brezhnev grows cold. Can he be here for the whole
agenda?

"Don't worry, Leonid Ilyich, I'm here only for *Say Cheese!*" Vadim
Raskladushkin says.

The General Secretary majestically smacks his lips. Cheese? What do
we have with cheese? The whole Politburo is amazed at how well the
leader pretends at this moment. If the comrades only knew how hard it
is for him! Inside he is flailing, drowning, surfacing, and drowning again.
Will he be able to fool Vadim? He has fooled Khrushchev, he has
fooled Dubček, he soporifies Carter with a kiss, he has even confused

---

*"An uninvited guest is worse than a Tatar," says a Russian proverb which cer-
tainly goes back to the times of the Tatar Yoke. This proverb and the like contradict
the principles of Lenin's internationalism. That's the Rus where so many contradictions live side by side.

"Scratch any Russian and you find a Tatar!" said Napoleon, Bismarck, and Jean-
Paul Sartre.

Andropov in the final analysis.... "What cheese? I don't seem to remember ..."

"Don't lie, Leonid Ilyich," Raskladushkin says, and comes right up to the head desk of the Empire. The composition is reminiscent of the takeover of the ministers' cabinet in October 1917, but the present visitor is armed not with a Mauser but with a smile.

Brezhnev groans. Inner struggle contorts the features of his face. The sight is one you wouldn't wish on an enemy! "It's a question of ideology, Comrade Raskladushkin," moans the General Secretary. "The Party can't compromise on an ideological question. Put yourself in our shoes. We want humanity to be happy...."

"You must refrain from cruelty." Vadim Raskladushkin begins walking around the big table. He stops by the secretary of the Central Committee, Comrade Tyazhelykh, looks into his eyes, and adds "This means everyone."

Sobbing waves the Bolsheviks' rows.* The deepest secret of the Party has been revealed—the real power. For it is Comrade Tyazhelykh with his old-lady's little face—and not the General Secretaries Malenkov, Khrushchev, Brezhnev, and Andropov—who pronounce the magic phrase "there is an opinion" in the post-Stalin Central Committee.

"There is an opinion," says Comrade Tyazhelykh under Vadim Raskladushkin's eye. "To close the case of the photo album *Say Cheese!* To raise the issue at the next session of the Supreme Soviet of separating art from the government. That's all for now."

Brezhnev, as usual, beats Andropov by a half second. "I'm for it!" General Stepanov rolls in a cart with fruit ice cream. As usual, the sight of raised arms brings tears to the old man's eyes.

6

SLAVIC SENSITIVITY IS incorrigible, said someone prone to generalizations. And he was right, thinks Ogorodnikov, standing in the doorway of the Chapel of Saint Nicholas, the former warehouse of the AACVS, at the

---

*Another line from Vladimir Mayakovsky's poem on Bolsheviks. Their rows waved when V. Lenin died.

Frezerovshchiki Station on the Kiev line. Slavic sensitivity is permanent, especially if you add the Northern European influence or something else, actually, anything else. . . .

The lock has fallen off on its own, and the rusty door opens without waiting to be asked. Now the Russian Vale of Tears lies before Ogorodnikov in the bright sunlight. Miracle of miracles—at the end of the alley a frail fence is bent under the weight of lilacs, blooming in this damp weather. The Russian, and as usual, negative sentiment overwhelms the cried-out Ogorodnikov, but at the same time somewhere nearby Stan Getz's sax is playing "Old Stockholm," which for all its nonobligatoriness somehow unites the Russian negative with the Western positive.

At the end of the alley, between the spool of cable and the support for the high-voltage line, a tiny figure appears. It stops for a moment, sways, losing its balance, and grabs the support. She needs help, thinks Ogo, but he can't move. Nastya moves on with difficulty. She clearly has not learned to use crutches yet. Wrapped in a royal-blue pants leg, the stump of her amputated left leg dangles, trying to participate in the process of walking. He stands without moving and she comes closer. Her face looks down in search of safe ground, contorting with suffering, and then looks up toward her husband and fills with joy. At last, their hands touch. Ah, Ogosha!

They go into the desecrated chapel and with childish glee and greed make love on the back seat of the 1936 Packard. "Of course, I'm sorry about your left leg, Nastya," he says, "I really liked putting it on my right shoulder."

"You're such a lecher and such a sinner, my darling," she says.

"Aren't you a sinner?" he asks. "Confess now, how many times have you deceived me?"

She adds it up. "No more than five."

"In the last year?"

She nods. "And never before."

They have forgotten to shut the door, and animals keep peering into the chapel: a wolf, a fox, a deer. . . . "Do you know what happened to Drevesny?" she asks, and immediately tells him. "He's crippled, but went to Brazil."

"You can't pass up an opportunity like that," he says.

He looks at his watch. "We have to get to Red Square. No hope of a taxi now. I'll carry you in my arms, beloved."

7

THE GATHERING OF the population of the Soviet Union on Red Square begins exactly at noon. Spring is at its height. Blue firs fill the air with their fragrance along the Kremlin wall. The wreaths placed in memory of heroes smell even better. You can barely smell the bad odor on the square.

People come by the millions and they come alone. The skeptics, of course, doubt that there will be enough room. But there is more than enough. At the steps of the Mausoleum, for instance, the populace of the Soviet Baltic is accommodated without crowding. Moldavia and Kara-Kalpakia fill the flowerbed around the monument to Minin and Pozharsky.

So they spread out, flowing into the square. The mood is, if not festive, then at least not lousy. No one is rude to anyone else. There are no cries of joy or howls of repentance. They haven't gathered for that, after all.

Of course, as they say, there are no rules without exceptions. At Execution Block the solitary figure of the fighter pilot who brought down an international passenger jet is cramping in a frenzy of pangs of conscience. Naturally, no one is planning to execute him, but no one is in a hurry to help him, either. Actually, no one pays much attention, because the comrade isn't addressing the issue.

They continue coming. The KGB isn't watching anyone today. All its millions are also at the square among the rest and take their places simply. This does not mean that life in the Land of the Soviets has stopped. The populace does not notice the interruption in the work of its beloved organs and glands, for this entire gathering is simply an instant's holding of the breath. The same holds for the other important state and ideo-institutions of the country.

The above-mentioned Politburo, of course, is just a drop in the human sea here. The second most populous structure after the KGB, the Army, appears in campaign configuration, but spread out humanly on the square. The ministries, departments, the crummy Komsomol, all the children of factories and plowlands, prisoners of camps and jails, parasites of propaganda and agitation, figures of science, literature, and the arts—everyone flashes before us, everyone is here; however, the country, we repeat, does not suffer, because the gathering is just an instant's held breath in the scale of history. Similar inhalations, by the way, are often found in yoga; they are beneficial and promote better use of oxygen to the weakened and coarsened alveoli.

With a complete and total gathering of two hundred seventy million, it's somehow not polite to speak of insignificant groups; however, the character of this gathering is such that people do not blend into a face-less mass, but on the contrary, each one stands out clearly, and therefore it will not be out of place to point out here that the entire Soviet dip-lomatic corps is present, having come from abroad, all those working abroad, including the conquerors of Afghanistan, and the crews of float-ing territories, that is, of ships. The nationally active émigrés are also present. At the curtain the country's main exile, Sakharov [Sugar], comes from his bitter [Gorky] city.

It goes without saying that the rather strange heroes of this novel also find a spot among the people of the Soviet Union on Red Square of the hero city. Miraculously avoiding their unattractive fates, by the last page they have forgotten all the preceding ones. Forgotten are the fears and ambitions, the pangs of conscience and the surges of the spirit. With everyone else they are preparing for a brief and serious act. The reader can at will subtract them or add them to the statistics on the last national census.

At the appointed hour the signal comes, similar to a single peal of a bell. On the roof of the Historical Museum, between two towers, Vadim Raskladushkin appears. Everyone can see him. Merrily waving to the people, he sets up his camera on a tripod and addresses the square:

"Say cheese!"

The population of the Soviet Union readily and simply obeys. The magnesium explodes. A puff of smoke. That is it.

Pulling his sweater over his head, the photographer feels a blissful release and, behind his shoulders, a blissful, rustling, silky unfolding spread.

November '80–December '83
Ann Arbor, Santa Monica, Sugarbush Valley, Washington, D.C.

CAST OF CHARACTERS

ABRAKADIN: Stalin-loving Soviet Ambassador to East Germany

ANASTASIA (NASTYA, NASTENKA): incorrigibly romantic glaciologist, Ogo's current wife

BARCELON, ROSA ALEXANDROVNA: a dissident

BELYALETDINOV, MAJOR MARAT NARIMANOVICH (MARATIK): Tatar cosmonaut

BRANDT, PASTOR WILHELM ("WILLIE"): spokesperson of European common sense

BREZHNEV, LEONID ILYICH: shaggy citizen of the USSR

BURENIN, NIKA: a loser

BUSHBASIN, MAJOR: secret photopoliceman (PhID)

CHACHAVADZE, GEORGII AVTANDILOVICH (ZHORA): Moscow's most eligible bachelor

CHEVRETKIND, FIMA: former Russian genius, currently New York City cab driver

DEMENNY, PHAL: Politburo secretary "in charge of photography"

DERETZKI, JOACHIM VON: West German millionaire-revolutionary

DREVESENY, ANDREI YEVGENIEVICH (ANDRYUSHKA): genius Cheeser

FISHER, MOISEY: alleged Zionist photographer and sometime Cheeser

FRAMBOISE, COLETTE (COLEKTA): Parisian lioness

GEORGII MAXIMILIANOVICH: General Planschin's wife

GERMAN, SVYATOSLAV (SLAVA, SLAVKA): another Cheeser genius

GRABOCHEY, MATVEY: vicious watchdog of Socialist Realism

GRETZKE, TOM: representative of Berlin's "working masses"

KALEDIN, MIKHAILO (MISHA DYMSHITS): Russian monarchist Jew

KAZACHNEKOVA, VIKTORIA GAVRILOVICH: Ogo's second ex-wife

KLEZMETZOV, FOTII FEKLOVICH (FOTIK, AGENT POKER): secretary of the Union of Soviet Photographers; a dishonest wretch

KONSKY, ALIK: emigré Russian critic and, according to his own résumé, "the greatest of living photographers"

KROST, MAJOR: another secret photopoliceman (PhID)

KUNENKO, CAPTAIN: PhID

LYUSHEV, CAPTAIN: yet another PhID

MARXYATNIKOV, FRITZ: major genius, minor Cheeser, married to a woman named Elena

OGORODNIKOV, MAXIM PETROVICH (OGO, OGOSHA, OGOSHKA): a photographer

OGORODNIKOV, OCTOBER: Maxim's half-brother

OKHOTNIKOV, ALEXEI (OLEKHA): young Cheeser

PHUSLOV: top-floor person of consequence

PLANSCHIN, GENERAL VALERYAN KUZMICH: director of KGB-PhID operations

PLYUBYSHEV, CAPTAIN: yes, a PhID

POLLACK, NYC art collector: Ogo's agent

PROBKIN, VENIAMIN (VENCHEKA, VENKA): a young Cheeser

PYATRAUSKAS, EDUARDAS (EDIK): a Caucasian snowman

RASKLADUSHKIN, VADIM: an angel

ROSBORN, HARRISON: *New York Ways* correspondent

SEMIGORSKY, DOUGLAS: president of Ogo's New York publishing house

SHTEIN, POLINA: a muse

SHTURMIN, VASYA: up-and-coming Cheeser

SKANSCHIN, CAPTAIN VLADIMIR GAVRILOVICH (VOLDOYA, VOL, VOVA; alias VALERY TIMO-
FEYEV): Ogo's PhID "curator"

SLIPPENBACH, WOLF: Berlin photographer

SLIPPENBACH, LINDA: Wolf's sister and a vixen of the Western press

SLYAZGIN, CAPTAIN KOLYA: a PhID

SPENDER, ALEXANDR: a living classic of the avant-garde

TIMOFEEVNA, KAPITOLINA (MOMMYKINS): Ogo's mother and October's stepmother; a baby

TSUKER, MASTER: another genius Cheeser

YOUNG, MARGIE: secretary to Douglas Semigorsky (coffee, tennis, and other services)

ZHERYABTNIKOV, SHUZ ARTEMIEVICH: hooligan-Cheeser

ABOUT THE AUTHOR

VASSILY PAVLOVICH AKSYONOV was born in Kazan in 1932. His first novel, *The Colleagues,* published in 1960, was followed by *Half-way to the Moon,* which attracted the attention of the world press and established his reputation as the representative of a new, Western-oriented, questioning generation of Soviet youth.

In 1979 Aksyonov spearheaded the efforts of a group of "intellectual gangsters" to create the first uncensored anthology of Soviet literature, *Metropol.* He resigned from the Writer's Union after two of his fellow editors were expelled from it and was forced to emigrate from the Soviet Union in 1980 when his scathing satire of the Moscow intelligentsia, *The Burn,* was smuggled to the West and published there.

Currently Aksyonov is Clarence J. Robinson Professor of Russian Literature and Writing at George Mason University in Fairfax County, Virginia. He lives in Washington, D.C., with his wife, Maya, and their spaniel, Ushik.